"Remarkable. . . . Louise Erdrich rediscovers her genius."
—Ron Charles, *Washington Post*

"One of our era's most powerful literary voices."
—*Christian Science Monitor*

"Thrills with luminous empathy."
—*Boston Globe*

"Spellbinding, reverent, and resplendent."
—*Booklist* (starred review)

"Erdrich remains an essential voice."
—*Publishers Weekly*

# Praise for *The Night Watchman*

"Louise Erdrich is one of our era's most powerful literary voices. . . . In *The Night Watchman*, Erdrich's blend of spirituality, gallows humor, and political resistance is at play. . . . It may be set in the 1950s, but the history it unearths and its themes of taking a stand against injustice are every bit as timely today."

—*Christian Science Monitor*

"A spellbinding, reverent, and resplendent drama. . . . A work of distinct luminosity. . . . Through the personalities and predicaments of her many charismatic characters, and through rapturous descriptions of winter landscapes and steaming meals, sustaining humor, and spiritual visitations, Erdrich traces the indelible traumas of racism and sexual violence and celebrates the vitality and depth of Chippewa life. . . . Erdrich at her radiant best."

—*Booklist* (starred review)

"Erdrich delivers a magisterial epic that brings her power of witness to every page. . . . I walked away from the Turtle Mountain clan feeling deeply moved, missing these characters as if they were real people known to me. In this era of modern termination assailing us, the book feels like a call to arms. A call to humanity. A banquet prepared for us by hungry people."

—Luis Alberto Urrea, *New York Times Book Review*

"Louise Erdrich rediscovers her genius. . . . This narrator's vision is more capacious, reaching out across a whole community in tender conversation with itself. Expecting to follow the linear trajectory of a mystery, we discover in Erdrich's fiction something more organic, more humane. Like her characters, we find ourselves laughing in that desperate high-pitched way people laugh when their hearts are broken."

—Ron Charles, *Washington Post*

"*The Night Watchman* is a singular achievement even for this accomplished writer. . . . Erdrich, like her grandfather, is a defender and raconteur of the lives of her people. Her intimate knowledge of the Native American world in collision with the white world has allowed her, over more than a dozen books, to create a brilliantly realized alternate history as rich as Faulkner's Yoknapatawpha County, Mississippi." —*O, The Oprah Magazine*

"In powerfully spare and elegant prose, Erdrich depicts deeply relatable characters who may be poor but are richly connected to family, community, and the earth." —*USA Today*

"Erdrich's newest novel thrills with luminous empathy." —*Boston Globe*

"No one can break your heart and fill it with light all in the same book—sometimes in the same paragraph—quite like Louise Erdrich. . . . She does it again, and beautifully . . . in her gorgeously written, deeply humane new book. . . . Erdrich's writing about the bonds of marriage and family is one of the greatest strengths of her fiction. She captures all the affection, teasing, pain, and forgiveness it takes to hold a family together." —*Tampa Bay Times*

"What is most beautiful about the book is how this family feeling manifests itself in the way the people of *The Night Watchman* see the world, their fierce attachment to each other, however close or distant, living or dead." —*Minneapolis Star Tribune*

"National Book Award–winner Erdrich once again calls upon her considerable storytelling skills to elucidate the struggles of generations of Native people to retain their cultural identity and their connection to the land." —*Library Journal* (starred review)

"*The Night Watchman* is above all a story of resilience. . . . It is a story in which magic and harsh realities collide in a breathtaking but ultimately satisfying way. Like those ancestors who linger in the shadows of the pages, the characters Erdrich has created will remain with the reader long after the book is closed."

—*New York Journal of Books*

"A stunning novel. . . . Erdrich has chosen a story that is near to her heart, and it shines through on every page."

—*Philadelphia Inquirer*/Associated Press

"In this kaleidoscopic story, the efforts of Native Americans to save their lands from being taken away by the US government in the early 1950s come intimately, vividly to life. . . . A knowing, loving evocation of people trying to survive with their personalities and traditions intact."

—*Kirkus Reviews* (starred review)

"This clever, artful, and compelling novel tells an important story, one to open our hearts and minds. If you're looking for a book that is smart and discussable, tender and painful, riveting and elegant, you'll find it in *The Night Watchman*."

—BookReporter.com

"An extraordinary novel . . . with a cast of distinct and lively characters. . . . A story of power and prejudice, tradition and self-discovery, and the Native fight against oppression that is as relevant now as it was in the 1950s."

—*BuzzFeed*

"Erdrich's inspired portrait of her own tribe's resilient heritage masterfully encompasses an array of characters and historical events. Erdrich remains an essential voice."

—*Publishers Weekly*

*Also by Louise Erdrich*

NOVELS

*Love Medicine*

*The Beet Queen*

*Tracks*

*The Bingo Palace*

*Tales of Burning Love*

*The Antelope Wife* (1997; revised editions, 2012, 2014)

*Antelope Woman* (2016)

*The Last Report on the Miracles at Little No Horse*

*The Master Butchers Singing Club*

*Four Souls*

*The Painted Drum*

*The Plague of Doves*

*Shadow Tag*

*The Round House*

*LaRose*

*Future Home of the Living God*

STORIES

*The Red Convertible: Selected and New Stories, 1978–2008*

POETRY

*Jacklight*

*Baptism of Desire*

*Original Fire*

FOR CHILDREN

*Grandmother's Pigeon*

*The Birchbark House*

*The Range Eternal*

*The Game of Silence*

*The Porcupine Year*

*Chickadee*

*Makoons*

NONFICTION

*The Blue Jay's Dance*

*Books and Islands in Ojibwe Country*

# THE
# NIGHT
# WATCHMAN

A NOVEL

LOUISE
ERDRICH

HARPER PERENNIAL

NEW YORK • LONDON • TORONTO • SYDNEY • NEW DELHI • AUCKLAND

HARPER ● PERENNIAL

FIRST HARPER PERENNIAL EDITION PUBLISHED 2021.

*Designed by Fritz Metsch*
*Title page illustration © 2020 Laura Hartman Maestro*

Library of Congress Cataloging-in-Publication Data has been applied for.

ISBN 978-0-06-267119-6 (pbk.)

21 22 23 24 25   LSC   10 9 8 7 6 5 4

*To Aunishenaubay, Patrick Gourneau;*
*to his daughter Rita, my mother;*
*and to all of the American Indian leaders*
*who fought against termination.*

On August 1, 1953, the United States Congress announced House Concurrent Resolution 108, a bill to abrogate nation-to-nation treaties, which had been made with American Indian Nations for "as long as the grass grows and the rivers flow." The announcement called for the eventual termination of all tribes, and the immediate termination of five tribes, including the Turtle Mountain Band of Chippewa.

My grandfather Patrick Gourneau fought against termination as tribal chairman while working as a night watchman. He hardly slept, like my character Thomas Wazhashk. This book is fiction. But all the same, I have tried to be faithful to my grandfather's extraordinary life. Any failures are my own. Other than Thomas, and the Turtle Mountain Jewel Bearing Plant, the only other major character who resembles anyone alive or dead is Senator Arthur V. Watkins, relentless pursuer of Native dispossession and the man who interrogated my grandfather.

Pixie, or—excuse me—Patrice, is completely fictional.

*September 1953*

## Turtle Mountain Jewel Bearing Plant

THOMAS WAZHASHK removed his thermos from his armpit and set it on the steel desk alongside his scuffed briefcase. His work jacket went on the chair, his lunch box on the cold windowsill. When he took off his padded tractor hat, a crab apple fell from the earflap. A gift from his daughter Fee. He caught the apple and put it out on the desktop to admire. Then punched his time card. Midnight. He picked up the key ring, a company flashlight, and walked the perimeter of the main floor.

In this quiet, always quiet expanse, Turtle Mountain women spent their days leaning into the hard light of their task lamps. The women pasted micro-thin slices of ruby, sapphire, or the lesser jewel, garnet, onto thin upright spindles in preparation for drilling. The jewel bearings would be used in Defense Department ordnance and in Bulova watches. This was the first time there had ever been manufacturing jobs near the reservation, and women filled most of these coveted positions. They had scored much higher on tests for manual dexterity.

The government attributed their focus to Indian blood and training in Indian beadwork. Thomas thought it was their sharp eyes—the women of his tribe could spear you with a glance. He'd been lucky to get his own job. He was smart and honest, but he wasn't young and skinny anymore. He got the job because he was reliable and he knocked himself out to do all that he did as perfectly as he could do it. He made his inspections with a rigid thoroughness.

As he moved along, he checked the drilling room, tested every lock, flipped the lights on and off. At one point, to keep his blood flowing, he did a short fancy dance, then threw in a Red River jig. Refreshed, he stepped through the reinforced doors of the acid washing room, with its rows of numbered beakers, pressure dial, hose, sink, and washing stations. He checked the offices, the green-and-white-tiled bathrooms, and ended up back at the machine shop. His desk pooled with light from the defective lamp that he had rescued and repaired for himself, so that he could read, write, cogitate, and from time to time slap himself awake.

THOMAS WAS named for the muskrat, wazhashk, the lowly, hardworking, water-loving rodent. Muskrats were everywhere on the slough-dotted reservation. Their small supple forms slipped busily through water at dusk, continually perfecting their burrows, and eating (how they loved to eat) practically anything growing or moving in a slough. Although the wazhashkag were numerous and ordinary, they were also crucial. In the beginning, after the great flood, it was a muskrat who had helped remake the earth.

In that way, as it turned out, Thomas was perfectly named.

# Lard on Bread

※—|—※

PIXIE PARANTEAU dabbed cement onto a jewel blank and fixed it to the block for drilling. She plucked up the prepared jewel and placed it in its tiny slot on the drilling card. She did things perfectly when enraged. Her eyes focused, her thoughts narrowed, breathing slowed. The nickname Pixie had stuck to her since childhood, because of her upturned eyes. Since graduating high school, she was trying to train everyone to call her Patrice. Not Patsy, not Patty, not Pat. But even her best friend refused to call her Patrice. And her best friend was sitting right next to her, also placing jewel blanks in endless tiny rows. Not as fast as Patrice, but second fastest of all the girls and women. The big room was quiet except for the buzzing light fixtures. Patrice's heartbeat slowed. No, she was not a Pixie, though her figure was small and people said wawiyazhinaagozi, which was hatefully translated to mean that she looked *cute*. Patrice was not cute. Patrice had a job. Patrice was above petty incidents like Bucky Duvalle and his friends giving her that ride to nowhere, telling people how she'd been willing to do something she had not done. Nor would she ever. And just look at Bucky now. Not that she was to blame for what happened to his face. Patrice didn't do those kinds of things. Patrice would also be above finding the brown bile of her father's long binge on the blouse she'd left drying in the kitchen. He was home, snarling, spitting, badgering, weeping, threatening her little brother,

Pokey, and begging Pixie for a dollar, no, a quarter, no, a dime. Even a tiny dime? Trying to pinch his fingers and his fingers not meeting together. No, she was not that Pixie who had hidden the knife and helped her mother haul him to a cot in the shed, where he would sleep until the poison drained out.

That morning, Patrice had put on an old blouse, walked out to the big road, and for the first time caught a ride with Doris Lauder and Valentine Blue. Her best friend had the most poetical name and wouldn't even call her Patrice. In the car Valentine had sat in front. Said, "Pixie, how's the backseat? I hope you're comfortable."

"Patrice," said Patrice.

Nothing from Valentine.

Valentine! Chatting away with Doris Lauder about how to make a cake with coconut on top. Coconut. Was there a coconut patch somewhere in a thousand square miles? Valentine. Wearing a burnt orange–gold circle skirt. Pretty as a sunset. Never even turning around. Flexing her hands in new gloves so that Patrice could see and admire, though from the backseat. And then with Doris exchanging tips on getting a stain of red wine from a napkin. As if Valentine had ever owned a napkin? And drank red wine except out in the bush? And now treating Patrice like she didn't even know her because Doris Lauder was a white girl new to the jewel plant, a secretary, and using her family car to get to work. And Doris had offered to pick up Valentine and Valentine had said, "My friend Pixie is on the way too, if you . . ."

And included her, which was what a best friend should do, but then ignored her and refused to use her real name, her confirmation name, the name by which she would—maybe embarrassing to say but she thought it anyway—the name by which she would rise in the world.

Mr. Walter Vold stepped down the line of women, hands behind his back, lurkishly observing their work. He left his office every few hours to inspect each station. He wasn't old, but his legs were thin and creaky. His knees jerked up each time he took a step. There was an uneven scratching sound today. Probably his pants, which were black and of a shiny stiff material. There was the squeak of shoe edge against the floor. He paused behind her. In his hand, a magnifying glass. He leaned his sweaty shoebox jaw over her shoulder and breathed stale coffee. She kept working, and her fingers didn't shake.

"Excellent work, Patrice."

See? Ha!

He went on. Scratch. Squeak. But Patrice didn't turn and wink at Valentine. Patrice didn't gloat. She could feel her period starting, but she'd pinned a clean folded rag to her underwear. Even that. Yes, even that.

AT NOON, the women and the few men who also worked in the plant went into a small room where there was supposed to be a cafeteria. It contained a full kitchen, but cooks had not yet been hired to prepare lunch, so the women sat down to eat the food they had brought. Some had lunch boxes, some had lard buckets. Some just brought dishes covered with a flour sack. But usually those were to share. Patrice had a syrup bucket, yellow, scraped to the metal, and full of raw dough. That's right. She had grabbed it going out, so rattled by her father's raving that she'd run out the door, forgetting that before breakfast she had meant to cook the dough into gullet bread using her mother's frypan. And she hadn't even eaten breakfast. For the past two hours she'd been sucking in her stomach, trying to quell the growls. Valentine had of course noticed. But now she was of course talking to Doris.

Patrice ate a pinch of dough. It wasn't bad. Valentine looked into Patrice's bucket, saw the dough, and laughed.

"I forgot to cook it," said Patrice.

Valentine looked pityingly at her, but another woman, a married woman named Saint Anne, laughed when she heard what Patrice said. Word went out that dough was in Patrice's bucket. That she'd forgotten to cook it, bake it, fry it. Patrice and Valentine were the youngest girls working on the floor, hired just out of high school. Nineteen years old. Saint Anne pushed a buttered bun across the table to Patrice. Someone handed an oatmeal cookie down the line. Doris gave her half a bacon sandwich. Patrice had made a joke. Patrice was about to laugh and make another joke.

"All you ever have is lard on bread," said Valentine.

Patrice shut her mouth. Nobody said anything. Valentine was trying to say that was poor people food. But everybody ate lard on bread with salt and pepper.

"That sounds good. Anybody have a piece?" said Doris. "Break me off some."

"Here," said Curly Jay, who got her name for her hair when she was little. The name stuck even though her hair was now stick-straight.

Everybody looked at Doris as she tried the lard on bread.

"Not half bad," she pronounced.

Patrice looked pityingly at Valentine. Or was it Pixie who did that? Anyway, lunchtime was over and now her stomach wouldn't growl all afternoon. She said thank you, loudly, to the whole table, and went into the bathroom. There were two stalls. Valentine was the only other woman in the bathroom. Patrice recognized her brown shoes with the scuffs painted over. They were both on their times.

"Oh no," said Valentine through the partition. "Oh, it's bad."

Patrice opened her purse, struggled with her thoughts, then handed one of her folded rags beneath the wooden divider. It was clean, white, bleached. Valentine took it out of her hand.

"Thanks."

"Thanks who?"

A pause.

"Thank you damn well much. Patrice." Then a laugh. "You saved my ass."

"Saved your flat ass."

Another laugh. "Your ass is flatter."

Crouched on the toilet, Patrice pinned on her new pad. She wrapped the used one in toilet paper and then in a piece of newspaper that she'd kept for this purpose. She slipped out of the stall, after Valentine, and thrust the rag pad down deep into the trash bin. She washed her hands with powdered soap, adjusted the dress shields in her armpits, smoothed her hair, and reapplied her lipstick. When she walked out, most of the others were already at work. She flew into her smock and switched on her lamp.

BY THE middle of the afternoon, her shoulders began to blaze. Her fingers cramped and her flat ass was numb. The line leaders reminded the women to stand, stretch, and focus their eyes on the distant wall. Then roll their eyes. Focus again on the wall. Once their eyes were refreshed they worked their hands, flexing their fingers, kneading their swollen knuckles. Then back to the slow, calm, mesmeric toil. Relentlessly, the ache returned. But it was almost time for break, fifteen minutes, taken row by row, so that everyone could use the bathroom. A few women went to the lunchroom to smoke. Doris had prepared a precious pot of coffee. Patrice drank hers standing, holding her saucer in the air. When she sat down again she felt better and went into a trance of concentration. As long as her shoulders or back didn't hurt, this hypnotic state of mind could carry her along for an hour and maybe two. It reminded Patrice of the way she felt when beading with her mother. Beading put them both into a realm of calm concentration. They murmured to each other lazily while they plucked up and matched the beads with the tips of their needles. In the jewel plant, women also spoke in dreamy murmurs.

"Please, ladies."

Mr. Vold forbade speech. Still, they did speak. They hardly remembered what they said, later, but they talked to one another all day. Near the end of the afternoon, Joyce Asiginak carried the new boules out for slicing and the process kept going and kept going.

DORIS LAUDER also took them home. And this time Valentine turned around to involve Patrice in their conversation, which was good because Pixie needed to take her mind off her father. Would he still be there? Doris's parents had a farm on the reservation. They had bought the land from the bank back in 1910 when Indian land was all people had to sell. Sell or die. The land was advertised everywhere, for sale, cheap. There were only a few good pieces of farmland on the reservation, and the Lauders had a tall silver silo you could see all the way from town. She dropped Patrice off first, offered to drive her down the iffy path to the house, but Patrice said no thanks. She didn't want Doris to see their crumpled doorway, the scrim of junk. And her father would hear the car, stumble out, and try pestering Doris into giving him a ride to town.

Patrice walked down the grass road, stood in the trees to

watch for her father's presence. The lean-to was open. She walked quietly past and stooped to enter the doorway of the house. It was a simple pole and mud rectangle, unimproved, low and lean-ing. Somehow her family never got on the tribal housing list. The stove was lighted and Patrice's mother had water boiling for tea. Besides her parents there was her skinny brother, Pokey. Her sister, Vera, had applied to the Placement and Relocation Office and gone to Minneapolis with her new husband. They got some money to set up a place to live, and training for a job. Many people came back within a year. Some, you never heard from again.

Vera's laugh was loud and bright. Patrice missed how she changed everything—bursting through the tension in the house, lighting up the gloom. Vera made fun of everything, down to the slop pail where they pissed on winter nights and the way their mother scolded them for stepping over their brother's or father's things, or trying to cook when they had their periods. She even laughed at their father, when he came home shkwebii. Raving like a damn boiled rooster, said Vera.

He was home now and no Vera to point out his sagging belt-less pants or the shaggy mess of his hair. No Vera to hold her nose and twinkle her eyes. No way to pretend away the relent-less shame of him. Or fend him off. And all the rest. The dirt floor buckling underneath a thin layer of linoleum. Patrice took a cup of tea behind the blanket, to the bed she had grown up sharing with her sister. They had a window back there, which was good in spring and fall when they liked looking into the woods, and terrible in winter and summer when they either froze or went crazy because of the flies and mosquitoes. She could hear her father and mother. He was pleading hard, but still too sick to get mean.

"Just a penny or two. A dollar, sweet face, and I will go. I will not be here. I will leave you alone. You will have your time to yourself without me the way you told me you want. I will stay away. You will never have to set your eyes on me."

On and on he went in this way as Patrice sipped her tea and watched the leaves turning yellow on the birch. When she had drunk the faintly sugared last sip, she put down her cup and changed into jeans, busted-out shoes, and a checkered blouse. She pinned up her hair and went around the blanket. She ignored her father—lanky shins, flapping shoes—and showed her mother the raw dough in her lunch bucket.

"It's still good," said her mother, mouth twisting up in a tiny smile. She gathered the dough from the bucket and laid it out in her frying pan, using one smooth motion. Sometimes the things her mother did from lifelong repetition looked like magic tricks.

"Pixie, oh Pixie, my little dolly girl?" Her father gave a loud wail. Patrice went outside, walked over to the woodpile, pulled the ax from the stump, and split a piece of log. Then she chopped stove lengths for a while. She even carried the wood over and stacked it beside the door. This part was Pokey's job, but he was learning how to box after school. So she went on chopping. With her father home, she needed something big to do. Yes, she was small, but she was naturally strong. She liked the reverberation of metal on wood on wood along her arms. And thoughts came to her while she swung the ax. What she would do. How she would act. How she would make people into her friends. She didn't just stack the wood, she stacked the wood in a pattern. Pokey teased her about her fussy woodpiles. But he looked up to her. She was the first person in the family to have a job. Not a trapping, hunting, or berry-gathering job, but a white-people job. In the next town. Her mother said nothing but implied that she was grateful. Pokey had this year's school shoes. Vera had had a plaid dress, a Toni home permanent, white anklets, for her trip to Minneapolis. And Patrice was putting a bit of every paycheck away in order to follow Vera, who had maybe disappeared.

# The Watcher

※—┼—※

TIME TO write. Thomas positioned himself, did the Palmer Method breathing exercises he had learned in boarding school, and uncapped his pen. He had a new pad of paper from the mercantile, tinted an eye-soothing pale green. His hand was steady. He would start with official correspondence and treat himself, at the end, with letters to his son Archie and daughter Ray. He'd have liked to write to his oldest, Lawrence, but had no address for him yet. Thomas wrote first to Senator Milton R. Young, congratulating him on his work to provide electricity to rural North Dakota, and requesting a meeting. Next he wrote to the county commissioner, congratulating him on the repair of a tarred road, and requesting a meeting. He wrote to his friend the newspaper columnist Bob Cory and suggested a date for him to tour the reservation. He replied at length to several people who had written to the tribe out of curiosity.

After his official letters were finished, Thomas turned to Ray's birthday card and letter. *Can it really be another year? Seems like no time at all since I was admiring a tiny face and tuft of brown hair. I do believe the first moment you spied me, you gave me a wink that said, "Don't worry, Daddy, I am 100% worth all the trouble I just caused Mama." You kept your promise, in fact your mama and I would say you kept it 200%. . . .* His flowing script rapidly filled six pages of thoughts and news. But when he paused to read over what he had written, he could not remember having written it, though the penmanship was perfect. Doggone. He tapped his head with his pen. He had written in his sleep. Tonight was worse than most nights. Because then he could not remember what he had read. It went back and forth, him writing, then reading, forgetting what he wrote, then forgetting what he read, then writing all over again. He refused to stop himself, but gradually he began to feel uneasy. He had the sense that someone was in the darkened corners of the room. Someone watching. He put his pen down slowly and then turned in his chair, peered over his shoulder at the stilled machines.

A frowsty-headed little boy crouched on top of the band saw. Thomas shook his head, blinked, but the boy was still there, dark hair sticking up in a spiky crest. He was wearing the same yellow-brown canvas vest and pants that Thomas had worn as a third-grade student at the government boarding school in Fort Totten. The boy looked like somebody. Thomas stared at the spike-haired boy until he turned back into a motor. "I need to soak my head," said Thomas. He slipped into the bathroom. Ducked his head under the cold water tap and washed his face. Then punched his time card for his second round.

This time, he moved slowly, shifting forward, as if against a heavy wind. His feet dragged, but his mind cleared once he finished.

Thomas hitched his pants to keep the ironing crisp, and sat. Rose put creases in his shirtsleeves, too. Used starch. Even in dull clay-green work clothes, he looked respectable. His collar never flopped. But he wanted to flop. The chair was padded, comfortable. Too comfortable. Thomas opened his thermos. It was a top-of-the-line Stanley, a gift from his oldest daughters. They had given him this thermos to celebrate his salaried position. He poured a measure of black coffee into the steel cover that was also a cup. The warm metal, the gentle ridges, the rounded feminine base of the cap, were pleasant to hold. He allowed his eyelids a long and luxurious blink each time he drank. Nearly slipped over the edge. Jerked awake. Fiercely commanded the dregs in the cup to do their work.

He often talked to things on this job.

Thomas opened his lunch box. He always promised himself to eat lightly, so as not to make himself sleepier, but the effort to stay awake made him hungry. Chewing momentarily perked him up. He ate cold venison between two slabs of Rose's champion yeast bread. A gigantic carrot he had grown. The sour little apple cheered him. He saved a small chunk of commodity cheese and a jelly-soaked bun for breakfast.

The lavishness of the venison sandwich reminded him of the poor threads of meat between the thin rounds of gullet that he and his father had eaten, that hard year, on the way to Fort Totten. There were moments in the hunger he would never forget. How those tough threads of meat salvaged from the deer's bones were delectable. How he'd torn into that food, tearful with hunger. Even better than the sandwich he ate now. He finished it, swept the crumbs into his palm, and threw them into his mouth, a habit from the lean days.

One of his teachers down in Fort Totten was fanatical about the Palmer Method of penmanship. Thomas had spent hour after hour making perfect circles, writing left to right, then the opposite, developing the correct hand muscles and proper body position. And of course, the breathing exercises. All that was now second nature. The capital letters were especially satisfying. He often devised sentences that began with his favorite capitals. Rs and Qs were his art. He wrote on and on, hypnotizing himself, until at last he passed out and came awake, drooling on his clenched fist. Just in time to punch the clock and make his final round. Before picking up the flashlight, he put on his jacket and removed a cigar from his briefcase. He unwrapped the cigar, inhaled its aroma, tucked it into his shirt pocket. At the end of this round he would smoke it outside.

This was the blackest hour. Night a stark weight outside the beam of his flashlight. He switched it off, once, to listen for the patterns of creaks and booms peculiar to the building. There was an unusual stillness. The night was windless, rare on the plains. Just inside the big service doors, he lighted his cigar. He sometimes smoked at his desk, but liked the fresh air to clear his head. Checking first to make sure he had his keys, Thomas stepped outside. He walked a few steps. A few crickets were still singing in the grass, a sound that stirred his heart. This was the time of year he and Rose had first met. Now Thomas stood on the slab of concrete beyond the circle of the outdoor flood lamp. Looked up into the cloudless sky and cold overlay of stars.

Watching the night sky, he was Thomas who had learned about the stars in boarding school. He was also Wazhashk who had learned about the stars from his grandfather, the original Wazhashk. Therefore the autumn stars of Pegasus were part of his grandfather's Mooz. Thomas drew slowly on the cigar. Blew the smoke upward, like a prayer. Buganogiizhik, the hole in the sky through which the Creator had hurtled, glowed and winked. He longed for Ikwe Anang, the woman star. She was beginning to rise over the horizon as a breath of radiance. Ikwe Anang always signaled the end of his ordeal. Over the months he'd spent his nights as a watchman, Thomas had grown to love her like a person.

Once he let himself back into the building and sat down, his grogginess fell away entirely and he read the newspapers and other tribes' newsletters he had saved. Subdued jitters at the passage of a bill that indicated Congress was fed up with Indians. Again. No hint of strategy. Or panic, but that would come. More coffee, his small breakfast, and he punched out. To his relief, the morning was warm enough for him to catch a few winks in his car's front seat before his first meeting of the day. His beloved car was a putty-gray Nash, used, but still Rose grumbled that he'd spent too much money on it. She wouldn't admit how much she loved riding in the plush passenger seat and listening to the car's radio. Now with this regular job he could make regular payments. No need to worry how weather would treat his crops, like before. Most important, this was not a car that would break down and make him late for work. This was a job he wanted very much to keep. Besides, someday he planned a trip, he joked, a second honeymoon with Rose, using the backseats that folded into a bed.

Now Thomas slid inside the car. He kept a heavy wool muffler in the glove box to wind around his neck so his head wouldn't fall to his chest, waking him. He leaned back into the brushed mohair upholstery and dropped into sleep. He woke, fully alert, when LaBatte rapped on his window to make sure he was all right.

LaBatte was a short man with the rounded build of a small bear. He peered in at Thomas. His pug nose pressed to the glass. His breath made a circle of fog. LaBatte was the evening janitor, but often he came in on a day shift to do small repairs. Thomas had watched LaBatte's pudgy, tough, clever hands fix every sort of mechanism. They'd gone to school together. Thomas rolled down the window.

"Sleeping off the job again?"

"It was an exciting night."

"Is that so?"

"I thought I saw a little boy sitting on the band saw."

Too late, Thomas remembered that LaBatte was intensely superstitious.

"Was it Roderick?"

"Who?"

"He's been following me around, Roderick."

"No, it was just the motor."

LaBatte frowned, unconvinced, and Thomas knew he'd hear more about Roderick if he hesitated. So he started the car and shouted over the engine's roar that he had a meeting.

# The Skin Tent

SOMEDAY, A WATCH. Patrice longed for an accurate way to keep time. Because time did not exist at her house. Or rather, it was the keeping of time as in school or work time that did not exist. There was a small brown alarm clock on the stool beside her bed, but it lost five minutes on the hour. She had to compensate when setting it and if she once forgot to wind it, all was lost. Her job was also dependent on getting a ride to work. Meeting Doris and Valentine. Her family did not have an old car to try fixing. Or even a shaggy horse to ride. It was miles down to the highway where the bus passed twice a day. If she didn't get a ride, it was thirteen miles of gravel road. She couldn't get sick. If she got sick, there was no telephone to let anybody know. She would be fired. Life would go back to zero.

There were times when Patrice felt like she was stretched across a frame, like a skin tent. She tried to forget that she could easily blow away. Or how easily her father could wreck them all. This feeling of being the only barrier between her family and disaster wasn't new, but they had come so far since she started work.

Knowing how much they needed Patrice's job, it was her mother's, Zhaanat's, task during the week to sit up behind the door with the ax. Until they had word where their father had landed next, they all had to be on guard. On the weekend, Zhaanat took turns with Patrice. With the ax on the table and the kerosene lamp, Patrice read her poems and magazines. When it was Zhaanat's turn, she went through an endless array of songs, all used for different purposes, humming low beneath her breath, tapping the table with one finger.

Zhaanat was capable and shrewd. She was a woman of presence, strong and square, jutting features. She was traditional, an old-time Indian raised by her grandparents only speaking Chippewa, schooled from childhood in ceremonies and the teaching stories. Zhaanat's knowledge was considered so important that she had been fiercely hidden away, guarded from going to boarding school. She had barely learned to read and write on the intermittent days she had attended reservation day school. She made baskets and beadwork to sell. But Zhaanat's real job was passing on what she knew. People came from distances, often camped around their house, in order to learn. Once, that deep knowledge had been part of a web of strategies that included plenty of animals to hunt, wild foods to gather, gardens of beans and squash, and land, lots of land to roam. Now the family had only Patrice, who had been raised speaking Chippewa but had no trouble learning English, who had followed most of her mother's teachings but also become a Catholic. Patrice knew her mother's songs, but she had also been class valedictorian and the English teacher had given her a book of poems by Emily Dickinson. There was one about success, from failure's point of view. She had seen how quickly girls who got married and had children were worn down before the age of twenty. Nothing happened to them but toil. Great things happened to other people. The married girls were lost. *Distant strains of triumph*. That wasn't going to be her life.

# Three Men

MOSES MONTROSE sat calmly behind a cup of bitter tea. The tribal judge was a small, spare, carefully groomed man who wore his sixty-five years lightly. He and Thomas were at their meeting hall, Henry's Cafe—a few booths and a hole-in-the-wall kitchen. Order of business: the one part-time tribal police officer was up north at a funeral. The jail was under repair. It was a small sturdy shack, painted white. The door had been kicked out by Eddy Mink, who usually spent the night singing out there in his fits of drunken joy. He needed more wine, he said, so he'd decided to leave. They talked about a new door. But as usual, the tribe was broke.

"The other night I made an arrest," said Moses. "I locked Jim Duvalle in my outhouse."

"Was he fighting again?"

"Real bad. We picked him up. Had to get my boy to help shove him inside."

"A cold night for Duvalle."

"He didn't notice. He slept on the shitter."

"Got to find another way," said Thomas.

"Next day, I put on my judge shirt, brought him to my kitchen court. I gave him a fine and let him go. He only had one dollar of the fine, so I took his dollar and called it square. Then I spent the day feeling so bad. Taking food from his family's mouth. Finally, I go over there and give the dollar to Leola. I need to get paid. But some other way."

"We need our jail back."

"Mary was mad I put him in our outhouse. Said she almost burst during the night!"

"Oh. We can't let Mary burst. I talked to the superintendent, but he says the money is extremely tight."

"You mean he's extremely tight. In the butt."

Moses said this in Chippewa—most everything was funnier in Chippewa. A laugh cleared out the cobwebs for Thomas and he felt like the coffee was also doing him some good.

"We have to put Jim in the newsletter. So write down the details."

"He's in the newsletter already this month."

"Public shame isn't working," said Thomas.

"Not on him. But poor Leola walks around with her head hanging."

Thomas shook his head, but the majority of the council had voted to include the month's arrests and fines in the community newsletter. Moses had a good friend in the Bureau of Indian Affairs Area Office in Aberdeen, South Dakota, who had sent him a copy of the proposed bill that was supposed to emancipate Indians. That was the word used in newspaper articles. Emancipate. Thomas hadn't seen the bill yet. Moses gave him the envelope and said, "They mean to drop us." The envelope wasn't very heavy.

"Drop us? I thought it was emancipate."

"Same thing," said Moses. "I read it all, every word. They mean to drop us."

. . .

AT THE gas pump outside the big store, Eddy Mink stopped Thomas. The matted blocks of his long gray hair were tucked into the collar of a sagging army coat. His face was starred with burst veins. His nose was lumpy, purple. He had once been handsome, and still wore a yellowed silk scarf tied like a movie-star ascot. He asked Thomas if he would stand him a drink.

"No," said Thomas.

"Thought you was starting up again."

"Changed my mind. And you owe the tribe a new jail door."

Eddy changed the subject by asking if Thomas knew about the emancipation. Thomas said yes, but it wasn't emancipation. It was interesting that Eddy had heard about the bill before anybody else—but he was that way. Brilliant, once, and still scavenging news.

"I heard about it, sure. This thing sounds good," Eddy said. "Hear I could sell my land. All I got is twenty acres."

"But then you wouldn't have any hospital. No clinic, no school, no farm agent, no nothing. No place to even rest your head."

"I don't need nothing."

"No government commodities."

"I could buy my own food with that land money."

"By law, you wouldn't be an Indian."

"Law can't take my Indian out of me."

"Maybe. What about when your land money runs out. What then?"

"I live for the day."

"You're the kind of Indian they're looking for," said Thomas.

"I'm a drunk."

"That's what we'll all be if this goes through."

"Let it go through then!"

"Money would kill you, Eddy."

"Death by whiskey? Eh, niiji?"

Thomas laughed. "An uglier way to go than you think. What about how it will affect all the old people, people who want to keep their land. Think about it, niiji."

"I know you got a point," said Eddy. "I just don't want to take your point right now."

Eddy went off, still talking. He lived alone on his father's allotment in a little shack. Even the tar paper on it was flapping loose. The reservation was dry so he'd gone half blind from a bad batch of bootleg. When Juggie Blue made chokecherry wine, she always gave a jar to Eddy to keep him from the bootlegger. In winter, Thomas sent Wade over on their remaining horse to see if Eddy was alive, to chop wood for him if he was. In the old days, Thomas and his friend Archille had gone to bush dances along with Eddy, who could fiddle like an angel or a devil no matter how much he drank.

---

MOST PEOPLE built close to the main road, but the Wazhashk farm was set at the end of a long curved drive, just over a grassy rise. The old house was two stories high and made of hand-adzed oak timbers, weathered gray. The new house was a snug government cottage. Wazhashk had bought the old house along with the allotment back in 1880, before the reservation was pared down. He'd been able to buy it because the land needed a well. Another story, that well. Ten years ago, the family had qualified for the government house, which had thrilled them when it appeared, pulled on a heavy-duty trailer. In winter, Thomas, Rose, her mother, Noko, and a changing array of children besides their own who were still at home slept in the snug new house. Today was warm enough for Thomas to take his rest in the old house. He parked the Nash and emerged, craving the moment he would lie down beneath the heavy wool quilt.

"Don't you go sneaking out on me again!"

Rose and her mother were arguing, and he considered slipping into the old house right then. But Rose leaned out the door and said, "You're home, old man!" She had a delicate smile. She slammed her way back into the house, but even so, Thomas knew her weather was good. He always checked the weather of Rose before he made a move. Today was blustery but cheerful, so he came in the door. The toddlers Rose was taking care of were babbling in the big crib. There were two iced cinnamon rolls for him on the table. A bowl of oatmeal. Someone's chickens were still laying and there was an egg. Rose was toasting two slices of bread in lard and as he sat down she dropped them on his plate. He dipped water from the last full can.

"I'll fetch water when I wake up," he said.

"We need it right now."

"I am beat. Right down to the ground."

"Then I'll wait the washing."

This was a big concession. Rose used a tub with a crank paddle, and liked to do her washing early so that she could take full advantage of the sun's drying power. Thomas squeezed love for himself out of her sacrifice, and ate with emotion.

"My sweetheart," he said.

"Sweetheart this, sweetheart that," she grumbled.

He got himself out the door before she reconsidered the washing.

SUN FLOODED the sleeping floor of the old house. A few late flies banged against the window glass, or died buzzing around in circles on the floor. The top of the quilt was warm. Thomas removed his trousers and folded them along the creases to renew their sharpness. He kept a pair of long underwear pants under the pillow. He slipped them on, hung his shirt over a chair, and rolled under the heavy blanket. It was a quilt of patches left over from the woolen coats that had passed through the family. Here was his mother's navy blue. It had been made from a trade wool blanket and to a blanket it had returned. Here were the boys' padded plaid wool jackets, ripped and worn. These jackets had surged through fields, down icy hills, wrestled with dogs, and been left behind when they took city work. Here was Rose's coat from the early days of their marriage, blue-gray and thin now, but still bearing the fateful shape of her as she walked away from him, then stopped, turned, and smiled, looking at him from under the brim of a midnight-blue cloche hat, daring him to love her. They'd been so young. Sixteen. Now married thirty-three years. Rose got most of the coats from the Benedictine Sisters for working in their charity garage. But his own double-breasted camel coat was bought with money he'd earned on the harvest crews. The older boys had worn it out, but he still had the matching fedora. Where was that hat? Last seen in its box atop the highboy dresser. His review of the coats with their yarn ties, all pressing down on him in a comforting way, always put him to sleep as long as he rushed past Falon's army greatcoat. That coat would keep him awake if he thought too long about it.

Thomas left his last conscious thoughts on his father's old coat, brown and quiet. Down the hill, across the slough, over the picked-bare furrows of the fields, through the birch and

oak woods, there was the narrow grass road that passed between their lands and led to the door of his father's house. His
father was so very old now that he slept most of the day. He was
ninety-four. When Thomas thought of his father, peace stole
across his chest and covered him like sunlight.

# The Boxing Coach

LLOYD BARNES'S brightest math student fought under the name Wood Mountain. He had graduated last year, but still trained at the gym Barnes had set up in the community center garage. It was said the young man would be famous if he could keep away from spirits. Barnes himself, a big man with thick, strawlike blond hair, trained alongside his boxing club of students. They went three and three—skipping rope for three minutes, rest, three minutes, rest, three more. That's how Barnes had set up all of the exercises. Intervals, like the rounds they would fight. He sparred with the boys himself, so he could coach them on skills. Barnes had learned to box in Iowa from his uncle, Gene "the Music" Barnes, an unusual presence in the ring. Barnes had never been sure whether his uncle, a bandleader, got the nickname because of his day job, from his habit of humming while he danced at his opponents, or because he was an excellent boxer and the sports pages invariably declared that so-and-so was slated to "face the Music." Barnes had never gone as far as his uncle, and after a serious knockout had decided teachers' training school in Moorhead was his destiny. He'd gone to school on the G.I. Bill and what loans he'd had to take out were forgiven once he signed up to work on the reservation. He'd transferred three times, from Grand Portage to Red Lake, from Red Lake to Rocky Boy, and had been in the Turtle Mountains now for two years. He liked the place. Plus he had

an eye on a Turtle Mountain woman and was hoping she would
notice him.

LAST WEEKEND, Barnes had been in Grand Forks watching
Kid Rappatoe fight Severine Boyd in a Golden Gloves match.
Skipping rope with his students now, he mulled over how
Boyd and Rappatoe came out of their corners popping swipes
at each other like cats. They were both so fast that neither
could connect more than a grazing punch. For five rounds it
was like that—dazzling motions, clinch, step apart, then they
started dabbing the air again. Rappatoe was famous for wearing down his opponent, but Boyd usually went the distance
and hardly broke a sweat. During round six Boyd did something that Barnes thought was questionable, but admired
just the same. Boyd stepped back, dropped his guard, hitched
his trunks, gave Rappatoe a blank look just as he slid off an
untelegraphed long-range left jab that snapped back Rappatoe's
head. All along, Boyd had been leading up to this with fakes.
Dropping his guard at odd times. Pretending there was a problem with his trunks. And those blank looks. Every so often,
like he was maybe having a spell. They seemed like harmless
tics until Boyd came under Rappatoe's guard with another left,
this one to the body, and then a right to the head that dropped
Rappatoe momentarily, stopped his momentum permanently,
and won Boyd the match.

Sitting ringside, Barnes had turned to Reynold Jarvis, the
English teacher, who was also in charge of putting on school
dramas.

"We need a drama coach," said Barnes.

"You need more equipment," said Jarvis.

"We're raising money for gloves now."

"And a speed bag? A heavy bag?"

"Burlap, sawdust. And a couple old tires."

"Okay. I see. Drama could be helpful."

Many things, including strength and even stamina, could be faked. Or even more important, many things could be hidden. For instance, one of Barnes's most promising kid boxers, Ajijaak, looked like his namesake heron. He was like Barnes himself, lean and tall, so nervous he seemed to tremble. Ajijaak held himself with an air of meek apology. But the boy had a startling left jab and shorebird reach. Then there was Pokey Paranteau, who was all raw talent with no focus. Revard Stone Boy, Calbert St. Pierre, Dicey Asiginak, Garnet Fox, and Case Allery, all coming along very well. Wade Wazhashk was working on his mother to let him box in a match. He, too, was promising, although he had no instinct. Thinking was good, but Wade thought twice before he punched. Barnes spent a lot of time driving the boys to matches with other towns—off-reservation towns where the crowds broke out fake war whoops and jeers when their hometown favorite lost. He drove the boys home after matches, and after practice, which lasted long after the school bus had gone out.

Right now, the boys were lifting weights all wrong. Barnes straightened them out. He didn't like to put too much weight on the left because his goal was to develop in each boy a left jab as fast as the opening to the Music's fabled "surprise symphony," a powerful, unpredictable flurry of strikes that had once forced Ezzard Charles onto the ropes. Well, of course, that was before Charles went big-time, then to the top. The Music had been a subtle fighter who eventually connected with a brawler who burst his spleen.

Wood Mountain had taken a welding class, and had made

weights for the club by filling cans of all sizes with sand and welding them back together. The weights had come out unevenly so the boys lifted 1½-, 3-, 7¼-, 12-, 18-, and 23-pound cans of sand for strength. But for speed Barnes did things differently.

"Now watch," he said.

He made a fist of his right hand and pressed his knuckles to the wall.

"Do like me."

All the boys made fists and did the same.

"Pressure, pressure," said Barnes. Again he pressed his fist against the wall, thatch of hair flopping down his forehead, until the muscles along his forearm began to burn. "Harder. . . . Okay, let up."

The boys stepped back, wringing their hands.

"Now the left."

The trick was to develop only the proper muscles to fill out the punch. The Music had been obsessed with speed and stealth. He had also taught Barnes mental tricks. Barnes signaled for break time. The boys lined up at the porcelain water fountain, then stood around him.

"Speed drills," said Barnes. "Now I want each of you to name the fastest thing you can think of."

"Lightning," said Dicey.

"Snapping turtle," said Wade, who had been bitten by one.

"Rattlesnake," said Revard, whose family went back and forth to Montana.

"A sneeze," said Pokey, which made everyone laugh.

"A big sneeze," said Barnes, "an explosion! That's how you want your punch. No warning. Now picture it, each of you, fastest thing you never saw. Shadowbox. Three minutes on. Three off. Like always."

Barnes took out his stopwatch and prowled behind them as they feinted, punched combinations, feinted, punched again. He stopped Case, tapped his arm.

"Don't flare that elbow! See your jab a mile off!"

He nodded at their progress.

"Do *not* draw your arm back! Do *not*!"

He himself threw punches toward Pokey, teaching him not to flinch. Barnes knew where that came from. And who.

He had them run interval sprints, then a few slow laps to cool down. Calbert and Dicey lived close enough to walk. The rest piled into Barnes's car. On the way to their houses, he talked about how Boyd had beaten Rappatoe. He couldn't make it sound right. He couldn't give the picture.

"We need Mr. Jarvis to show you," he finally said.

Pokey was always the last to be dropped off. His house was farthest, and off the road, but Barnes insisted on driving down the path even though he'd have to back out. At first it was because he knew about Paranteau, wanted to make sure Pokey was okay. Then he saw Pixie. Now Barnes drove down the road because there was always a chance he'd see Pixie chopping wood. Pixie. Those eyes!

BARNES MADE it back to the teachers' dining hall just after the food was cleared away. He lived in "bachelor's quarters," a small white bungalow beneath a cottonwood tree. The female teachers, and other government employees, lived in a two-story brick building with four generously proportioned rooms on the second floor, two on the first floor, plus a communal kitchen, and a recreation area in the substantial basement with a small room for the caretaker/cook, Juggie Blue. She was washing dishes and getting ready to mop her way out of the kitchen, which she always did at 7 p.m. Juggie was a stocky, well-muscled, shrewd-looking woman in her forties. She was on the tribal advisory council with Thomas. Like Barnes, she was always trying to give up cigarettes, which meant that when they slipped, they slipped together. But not tonight. Or probably not. He was working with Wood Mountain later.

Juggie always kept a heaped plate of dinner warm for him. Now she slid a pie plate out of the warming oven in her beloved six-burner cooking range. The range had not one, not two, but three ovens with black speckled enamel interiors and stainless-steel racks. It had been hauled up from Devils Lake at Juggie's insistence. She had clout with Superintendent Tosk. The expensive range allowed her to bake several items at the same time, and even slow-cook one of her famous beef stews. She made the stew in an ancient Dutch oven, brought overland by an ox team in the last century, using an entire bottle of her own chokecherry wine, and carrots bought from Thomas, who buried them for the winter in his cellar, deep in a bin of sand. She coaxed things from everyone on the reservation. Which was odd, because she was entirely lacking in charm.

"Potpie," she said, and went back to fill her mop bucket.

Oh god. Barnes was hungry. He was always hungry. And potpie was his favorite, or second or third favorite, of her reliables. She used lard from St. John in the rich crust, and got her chickens over the border from a Hutterite colony. The Pembina potatoes, which she picked every year herself, and hoarded, were small and new because it was September. The carrots were perfectly cooked through but not mushy. The lightly salted golden gravy. The soft tiles of onions, browned first. She had sprinkled in a liberal amount of Zanzibar pepper. When he finished, he bowed his head. Juggie was the reason that some of the teachers renewed their contracts, and it wasn't hard to see the source of her power over Superintendent Tosk.

Barnes sighed and brought the pie plate over to the counter. "You outdid yourself."

"Huh. Got a smoke?"

"No. I really quit this time."

"Me too."

They both paused, in case . . .

"Let me finish my floor," said Juggie. Then she stood straight up, narrowed her eyes, glanced around, and plucked a wrapped parcel from under the counter. Supper, for her son. She shoved it toward Barnes.

WOOD MOUNTAIN was already at the gym. Barnes found him at the sawdust bag. Little puffs of dust popped from the burlap when Wood Mountain struck with his left. He had more power in his left, though he was right-handed. Barnes put the package down by the neat roll of clothing that Wood Mountain had brought with him. He was Juggie's son with Archille Iron Bear, a Sioux man whose grandfather had traveled north with Sitting Bull, on the run after Little Big Horn. A few families had stayed in Canada, some at a sheltered spot on the plains called Wood Mountain. Most people had forgotten the actual name of Juggie's son and called him by the place his father had come from.

"Looking good," said Barnes, shedding his jacket.

Barnes picked up a pad he'd sewed together from old horse blankets, more sawdust inside. He held it up and danced it around for Wood Mountain to hit. There was a ragged circle of red cloth stitched onto it. Barnes changed the location of the circle every few days.

"You're clenching up before the strike. Relax," he said.

Wood Mountain stopped and bounced, his arms dangling loose. Then he started again. Barnes's forearms began to ache, absorbing shock after shock behind the pad. It was good he'd stepped out of the ring before Wood Mountain got there. Barnes was taller, but the two of them fought the same weight class. Both middleweights, topping out at 170, usually, though now Barnes weighed more. He blamed Juggie.

# Noko

THOMAS DRIFTED to the surface of his sleep. He heard the mice, skittering pleasantly behind the plaster and reed insulation against the roof. He heard a car drive up, then the buggy his father still kept. Rose and the girls were hooting and laughing. The babies shrieking. He was too buoyant. He tried to weight himself, to sink back under the surface of the noises. He pulled the pillow over his head, and was gone. The next time he came to, the sun was paler, the light half spent, and his body had relaxed into such a pleasant torpor that he was pinned to the thin mattress. He finally loosened himself and left the old house, walked to the little house, into the kitchen.

Sharlo, his daughter, was a sharp, lively senior in high school, dark hair pin-curled every night, jeans rolled up her ankles, checkered blouse, sweater, saddle shoes. Fee was quieter, just eleven, dreaming as she worked the pedal on the butter churn. Rose was frying onions and potatoes. Wade was in and out, popping air punches, supposedly filling the woodbox.

And the babies, oh the babies were always up to something. One was blubbering lightly in sleep and one was trying to get his chubby foot into his mouth.

Rose had a kettle of hot water ready on the stove. She gestured at the basin. He poured a measure into the bowl, and she added a dipperful of cold from the water can. After Thomas washed, he whisked up lather in his copper shaving mug, dabbed the foam on his upper lip. The small square mirror in its carved wooden frame belonged to Rose. It was made of good thick glass, well silvered. She had brought it with her when they married. Thomas had about forty whiskers on his face. He stropped his razor, elaborately shaved them off. Then he stripped to his waist and used a cloth to wipe himself clean. He took the cloth and bowl into the bedroom to complete the job.

Rose's mother was dozing on a chair beside the washing table. Noko snored lightly, head bowed. Her fragile old skull was bound in a brown head scarf, tiny shell disks hung from the drooping petals of her earlobes. Her gnarled hands rested in her lap. She twitched, dreaming. Then her head jerked up, her lips pulled back, and she hissed like a cat.

"What is it, Momma?"

"Gardipee! He's at it again!"

"Gawiin, it's okay, that was a long time ago," said Rose.

"He's right there," she said. "He busted in again!"

"No, Momma. That's Thomas."

The old woman glared suspiciously.

"That man's old. Thomas is a young man," she said.

Rose put her hand over her mouth to hide her laugh.

"What, Noko, don't you think I'm young anymore?" Thomas grinned.

"I'm not a fool, akiwenzi. You're not Thomas."

The old woman said this with firm indignation, and slowly folded her skinny arms. She remained like that, watching every move Thomas made. He sat down at the table.

"What are you here for?" She narrowed her eyes as he ate the plate of fried mush Rose put in front of him. "Are you after my daughter?"

"No!"

"Why not?"

"Noko, I'm Thomas. I got old. I couldn't help it."

"Rose is old too." Noko widened her eyes and looked help-lessly at her daughter, whose hair was nearly all gray.

"Rose *is* old. Rose *is* old," said Noko, in a wondering voice.

"You're old too," said Rose, irritated.

"Maybe," said Noko, sneaking a crafty look at Thomas. "You gonna take me back home? I'm damn sick of this place."

"Stop talking like that to him," Rose cried out.

It was difficult for her when Noko became too estranged from this life. She yelled, as if that would jolt Noko back into the reality they'd once shared. Now, overcome, Rose picked up an armload of laundry and rushed out to the shed, where her wringer washer was set up. Thomas heard the gurgle of the last of the water and remembered how she held the washing back so he could sleep. The rain barrel was empty. He'd better hop to and fill the cans at the well by the lake. He touched Noko's hand and said, "You're tired. Can I walk you over to your bed, so you can sleep?"

"I can't get out of my chair."

"I'll help you up," said Thomas.

"I'm stuck."

Thomas looked down and saw that Noko's long thick white hair had wrapped around the doorknob. Sharlo loved to comb her grandmother's hair and had left it loose.

"Come here, Sharlo," he called, and together they unwrapped the hair.

"Oh, Noko," said Sharlo. "I tangled up your hair!"

"Don't you worry, my girl," said the old woman, stroking Sharlo's face. "Nothing you can do could hurt me."

But when Sharlo went outside to get her mother, Noko

despaired again and tried to surge out of the chair. Thomas caught her and held her hand.

"Stay still, you could fall and hurt yourself."

"I wish I would," said Noko. "I want to die."

"No you don't," said Thomas.

She glowered at him.

"You raised my sweetheart," said Thomas. "You did a good job."

"Tell that to Thomas," Noko said. "He don't believe it."

Thomas reached around the chair and helped Noko to her feet. She collapsed. He pulled her up and they tottered stiffly to the bed. Rose had the sheets off. She was washing them today. Noko fell onto the bare mattress face-first. Thomas rolled her over and lifted her legs onto the bed. He arranged her there, stocking feet sticking straight up.

"You can't put her on our mattress like that," said Rose, standing in the door. Her voice sounded almost tearful. "She needs a soft pad underneath. The mattress buttons will give her bruises. Her skin takes bruises so easy now. We should buy her a fancy mattress pad for her little cot."

"With what money?"

"Your car money."

Thomas stood quietly under the raking heat of anger. It was coming off her in jagged waves. But then, as he stood there, he could feel it ease and the Rose with the funny little smile came back. She caught her breath and laughed.

"Oh, Momma, look at you. Little feet sticking straight up."

Rose and Thomas eased a folded blanket underneath the old woman. It was the only thing they could think of to do and now Noko was slowly crossing the river of sleep, floating away from them on her sinking raft.

*═*

THOMAS LAID down an old canvas in the trunk of his car. On weekends, he used the team and wagon to haul water for drinking. For bathing and cleaning they had the rain barrels. In winter they melted snow. He didn't have time to hitch up now. He was very careful. A spill in the trunk could freeze all winter and then, in summer, mildew. Although his caution meant an extra trip, he never hauled cans in the backseat. Of course Wade rode along with him. Smart, like all of his children, he had skipped grades. He was now in classes with boys who had got their growth.

"I went up against that ol' Albert, Daddy, gave him the one-two."

"No fighting."

"Then I gave him the ol' three-four."

"Wade?"

"Four words where three will do."

"That's my boy. Always better to talk your way out of a fight."

"Running, too, you said running."

"Honorable running."

"I don't wanta run, though. Get them callin' me yellow-baby."

"You don't have to prove yourself. I don't want you to fight, but if you did, you'd be Golden Gloves material, like Wood Mountain."

"He has a fight on the Bottineau card next Saturday. Fighting Joe Wobble."

"Joe Wobleszynski! That's my night off. I'll take you kids. Take Mama too, if she'll go."

Wade nodded in delight and put his dukes up. They filled the water cans. Bought the baking powder, sugar, oats, and tea on Rose's list. Then they went home and Thomas lifted potatoes. He was fast and Wade scrambled to bag them. They raced each other until dark.

# Water Earth

＊—|—＊

RUBBING THE back of her aching neck, Patrice walked slowly down the grass road. She knew her mother's people would be there, camped outside. There they were. A couple of frayed canvas tents, lean-to shelters streaked with dried mud. A cooking fire. Lake stones held up an ironwood branch from which a kettle was suspended just over tiny flames. The stumps that people would use to sit on were pulled away from the woodpile and arranged around the fire. At the edge of the clearing around the house, by the sweat-lodge frame, there was another tent with the open shape that signified that a jiisikid was among the visitors. Zhaanat had sent word to her cousin Gerald to come down across the border, and help her locate her daughter. That was one of the things the jiisikid did. Find people. Gerald, or the spirit who entered Gerald, would fly down to the Cities in a trance and see what was going on. He would find out why for the last five months Vera had not written, not reported in to the relocation program, not talked to anyone from the tribe who lived down there now.

Zhaanat kept a fresh bough of pine over the door. This morning, she had burned pine needles with cedar and bear root. The dim house was fragrant with the smoke. Gerald was sitting at the table with a few other people. They were drinking tea and laughing. In between jokes, they were discussing the ceremony with Zhaanat—how it would be run and who might show up with other questions, how long they should wait, if they should set up the sweat lodge too, what colors of cloth to tie in the branches and in what order. Who would lead on each song. They teased one another. Details. Patrice never talked about this part of her family's life with those who would not understand. For one thing, they wouldn't get how everything was funny. But the colors and the details reminded her of how the Catholics chose their colors and fixated on their sacraments. As if these things mattered to spirits or to the Holy Ghost.

Patrice had come to think that humans treated the concept of God, or Gizhe Manidoo, or the Holy Ghost, in a childish way. She was pretty sure that the rules and trappings of ritual had nothing to do with God, that they were ways for people to imagine they were doing things right in order to escape from punishment, or harm, like children. She had felt the movement of something vaster, impersonal yet personal, in her life. She thought that maybe people in contact with that nameless greatness had a way of catching at the edges, a way of being pulled along or even entering this thing beyond experience.

"Uncle!" She hugged Gerald, and shook hands all around. Then, with a cup of tea, she slipped behind her curtain, only to find her mother lying in her bed, fast asleep.

Patrice put her cup on the stool beside the bed, and lowered herself to sit on the edge of the mattress. She thought by sitting down she'd wake her mother, but Zhaanat slept heavily on her back, worn out by the long struggle with Patrice's father, who had at last hopped a train or so they'd heard. Patrice glanced at the pepper can she kept on her windowsill. She had filled it with decoy money, and it looked like he'd found and taken it. A relief. Her real stash was buried underneath the linoleum floor. Her magazines and newspapers were neatly piled next to the bed.

*Look. Ladies' Home Journal. Time.* Juggie Blue saved whatever the teachers discarded for her niece Valentine, and when Valentine was done with them she gave the magazines to Patrice.

The window faced west and the last of the sunlight, shifting through the golden leaves of birch trees, flickered across her mother's finely made face. Pleasant lines starred out from the corners of her eyes. Arched lines set off her slight smile. Her hair was long and the smooth braids had accidentally, comically, swept upward over her head, so that it seemed she was falling. Her arms were bent at the elbows and her powerful small hands lay still across her chest. Her unusual hands that frightened some people. Patrice shared her mother's tilting eyes, strength, and willful energy. But not her hands. They were Zhaanat's alone.

Zhaanat's dress was made of midnight-green calico dotted with tiny golden leaves. The style was from the last century, but Patrice knew it was only a few months old. Her mother had sewed the old-time dress from over four yards of cloth. The sleeves were slim and ran down to her wrists. There were shell buttons in the front, and the dress had a sweeping gathered skirt. Beneath it, Zhaanat wore woolen men's underwear, a dull red-orange color. Her moccasins were deerhide with rawhide soles, decorated with colored thread, blue and green. She often wore a brown plaid shawl. She had pulled the edges of it around her shoulders before she slept, as if for protection. Patrice smoothed her hand along the shawl's fringes and her mother opened her eyes.

Patrice could tell from her mother's frown of confusion that she'd slept so heavily she didn't know where she was. Then Zhaanat's face sharpened and her lips curved away from her teeth. She pulled the shawl closer.

"Damn if I know how I got here," she murmured.

"Gerald's out there."

"Good. He'll find her."

Patrice nodded. Gerald had found people now and then through the years, but sometimes he flew in circles. Sometimes their place was hidden.

THAT NIGHT, he flew for a long time, inhabited by a particular spirit. After a while he did find Vera. She was lying on her back, wearing a greasy dress, a cloth across her throat. She was motionless, but she wasn't dead. Perhaps she was asleep. Patrice would have thought that her uncle had found an image of her mother from that afternoon, except that Gerald said he had found her in the city, and there was a form beside her. A small form. A child.

THE NEXT day, Patrice put aside the troubling, and yet reassuring, information from the jiisikid, and jumped into the backseat of Doris Lauder's car. It was a rainy fall morning and Patrice was extremely grateful to be picked up and brought to work. She offered, as she had before, to contribute money for gasoline. Doris refused with a vague wave, saying that she'd be driving anyway.

"Maybe next month." She smiled into the mirror.

"Maybe I'll be driving next month," said Valentine. "Daddy is fixing up a car for me."

"What kind?" asked Doris.

"Probably an all kinds of car," said Valentine. "You know. A car made of other cars."

The rain streamed in silvery bolts across the back window. Nobody spoke for a while.

"I hear Betty Pye's coming back to work today," said Valentine.

"Oh goodness," said Doris, with an abrupt laugh.

Betty had taken her year's week of paid sick leave to get her tonsils removed. At her age! Thirty years. She'd gone to Grand Forks for the operation because it was apparently more serious to have them removed as an adult. But she'd been adamant about doing it. She'd insisted that her neck swelled up every November and stayed thick all through the winter and she was through with that. The doctors had examined her throat and told her that her tonsils were unusually large, "real germ collectors." Everybody knew the details.

"I can't wait to hear how it went," said Patrice.

The two in the front seat laughed, but she hadn't said it to be mean. Betty would certainly make her operation into a drama. Patrice didn't know Betty very well, but work went so much faster when she was there. And Betty was, indeed, very much present when the women arrived at the jewel bearing plant. Betty's round face was a bit ashen, and her voice box hadn't healed yet. She spoke in a thready croak. But as always she was round and rolling, wearing green checks. A focused worker, she did her job. She had brought a large covered bowl of rice pudding for lunch, and when she swallowed her eyes watered. She was quiet all through work, whispering that it hurt like hell to talk. As they left for the day, Betty slipped a folded piece of paper to Patrice, and walked off. As Doris and Valentine spoke in the front seat, now pitying Betty for the pain she obviously suffered, Patrice took out the paper and read, *I heard your looking for your sis. My cousin lives in the Cities. She saw her and wrote to you—with her L hand because she broke her R finger pointing out my faults. That's Genevieve for you. Watch the mail.*

Patrice folded up the paper and smiled. She was drawn to Betty because she was so much like her sister in her ability to make life's bitterness into comedy. *Broke her right finger pointing out my faults.* What did that even mean? She tipped her head back, closing her eyes.

ON SATURDAY morning, Patrice put on the swing coat she'd pulled from the piles of mission-store clothing. What a find. It was a lovely shade of blue, lined with flannel wool under top-quality rayon. The coat was tailored, and had a fine shape. She tied on a red and blue plaid scarf, and shoved her hands in the coat pockets. There was a path through the woods that would take her four miles, straight into town and the post office. Or she could walk the road and likely get picked up. Although the sky had cleared, the ground was still wet. She did not have overboots, and didn't want to soak her shoes. Patrice took the road. It wasn't long before she was picked up. And by Thomas Wazhashk. He pulled his car over slightly ahead of her and waited. A rope tied down the trunk lid, and she could see the dull galvanized tin of their water cans. One lucky thing about living so far back in the bush, their spring still ran. And it ran clear. Most people closer in, near town, or out in prairie land, had lost their water or cattle had ruined their springs. Even the dug wells were drying out.

Thomas and Zhaanat were cousins—Patrice was unclear on exactly how they were related and "cousins" was considered a general word that covered a host of relationships. Thomas was an uncle to her and so his sons were also cousins. She sped forward and took the front seat when Wade got out and gave her the honor.

"Thank you for stopping, uncle."

"At least this time you're hitching on dry land."

Last summer, she had swum out to his fishing boat, surprised Thomas. She'd hitched a ride out of the lake. It tickled him to talk about it. He didn't know exactly why she'd been swimming out there so far.

Patrice was one of the only young people who addressed him in Chippewa, or Cree, or in a combination of the two. They didn't speak exactly alike but understood each other. If Wade was puzzled, let him absorb the language out of curiosity, thought Thomas. They chatted for a while and Thomas learned that Zhaanat had set up the special tent. Gerald had seen that Vera was alive and that she had a child beside her. Patrice got out at the mercantile, which also held the post office. He would return to pick her up. While he and Wade filled the water cans, Thomas thought about how his grandfather had consulted with someone like Gerald, long ago, when they needed to find out about Falon. So it happened they knew Falon had died well before the official message arrived.

ON THE way back, Patrice decided to read the letter from Betty Pye's cousin again, out loud, to her uncle.

> I saw your sister down in the Cities, and something was wrong
> with her. Last I knew, she was at Stevens Avenue Apartments,
> number 206. I know because a number of Indians live there and
> I was staying on that floor too. Saw her in the hallway with
> her baby and she wouldn't talk to me.

PATRICE TOLD her uncle she wanted to walk back from his house. She needed to think. The road to her house ran alongside water, and the cool air smelled of rain drying off the yellow leaves. The cattails on the sloughs were soft brown clubs, the reeds still sharp and green. On the lake, wind was ruffling up blue-black waves so lacy that foam rimmed the beach. The sun beamed from between dark scudding clouds. Vera had always wanted to stay where she could see the birches and sloughs. She had worked on an old cabin up the hill from their mother's house. Vera had camped there, trying to reclaim it. She had cleared away some trees that were trying to grow up through the floor, and she had drawn out her plans to make the cabin into her ideal house. Patrice had helped her work out a large room with a kitchen and a dining table, even two private bedrooms. Every detail of the drawing was labeled. Vera's penmanship was squared off and even, like on a real blueprint. There was a special close-up of a mullioned window with striped curtains. Patrice still had that picture. Vera, who dressed distinctively and was elegant rather than Pixie-cute, loved home economics class and had copied that window from a book called *Ideal Home*. She hadn't wanted to leave, but she'd fallen in love. It was sudden, and Zhaanat hadn't been in favor. Zhaanat had turned away rather than say goodbye to her daughter when she left for the Cities. Patrice knew this haunted her mother.

"Stay where you are. I'll find you," said Patrice, out loud. She snatched a stick from the path and struck at the grasses, sending out puffs of golden seed.

PATRICE WAS nearly home when the clouds thickened to a dark sheet. She started running. Then quit. Her shoes. She couldn't ruin them. She bent over, took them off, bundled them beneath her coat, and kept walking in the rain. Took the grassy turnoff that led through the woods. Going barefoot was not a problem. She had done that all her life, and her feet were tough. Cold now, half numb, but tough. Her hair, shoulders, and back grew damp. But moving kept her warm. She slowed to pick her way through places where water was seeping up through the mats of dying grass. Rain tapping through the brilliant leaves the only sound. She stopped. The sense of something there, with her, all around her, swirling and seething with energy. How intimately the trees seized the earth. How exquisitely she was included. Patrice closed her eyes and felt a tug. Her spirit poured into the air like song. Wait! She opened her eyes and threw her weight into her cold feet. This must be how Gerald felt when he flew across the earth. Sometimes she frightened herself.

BEFORE THE trail gave into the clearing around her house, Patrice heard the yowl of spinning tires. She thought of Gerald's people, although he'd left before dawn. When she reached her mother's house and stepped around the far wall, she realized that the stuck whine was coming from the narrow, boggy grass path that led to the house. The other cars would have weakened the wet ground that morning, when Gerald and the rest of them left. Another car might have broken through. From outside the cabin, she raised the window near her bed, tossed her shoes in. She considered climbing in herself, but instead stepped around the house, across the smooth mud. She passed the wet black ashes of the cooking fire. Continued out onto the brushy track. At the entrance of the path she saw the turquoise and cream Buick that belonged to Pokey's teacher. Mr. Barnes was heaving at the front of the car, trying to push the left tire out of a watery hole. His large head of yellow hair was like a stack of straw. Hay Stack, they called him. Pokey was behind the wheel. She stopped. Tried to ease back into the leaves.

# Juggie's Boy

*+==+*

ON THE way to Minot they decided this would be the night that Wood Mountain would beat Joe Wobleszynski. They argued how.

"Decision," said Thomas.

"KO," said Rose. She was happy to get out for an evening. And she loved the fights.

"You're a bloodthirsty woman," said Thomas.

"Pokey's fighting. Exhibition," said Wade. "He's wearing fat gloves and a rubber helmet."

"His head is still growing," said Rose, glaring back at Wade.

"C'mon. Why can't I fight?"

"When your head is finished, you can fight."

Sharlo laughed.

"Your heads aren't finished yet either, Sharlo, Fee."

Wade swiped at his sisters in the backseat. They gripped paws and sawed their arms back and forth, growling. Rose swatted at them from the front seat, laughing along. Then she fell silent and stared peacefully out the streaked window. Thomas sensed her pleasure, and didn't speak. They were driving through rain. They passed the extraordinary round barn of Telesphore Renault. The yard where he kept his gigantic prize pigs. The road to Dunseith. Farther along, a coyote crossed the road and evaporated into a ditch. Snow geese were massing in a field, plumping themselves up on waste and weeds.

. . .

THE RING was set up in the state teachers' college gymnasium, with maroon-and-gold banners across the walls, and a few rows of folding chairs. Most of the crowd was in the bleachers or standing. The crowd cleared a path for the fighters to pass through, then closed again. By the time the Wazhashks arrived, the exhibition fights were over. They went to the bleachers. Pokey, Case, and Revard looked glum sitting next to Mr. Barnes. They had all lost their fights. Now the main card was about to begin. Tek Tolverson vs. Robert Valle. Sam Bell vs. Howard Old Man. Joe Wobleszynski vs. Wood Mountain.

Tek won the first fight with perhaps an underhanded low punch the crowd saw but not the referee. Half the crowd became indignant, the other half booed the first half, and nobody was happy with the outcome.

Howard Old Man won on decision. The Fort Berthold Indians quietly cheered and the Turtle Mountain Indians pitched in. Old Man had picked up their hopes.

Then Joe Wobble and Wood Mountain came through the crowd. Many years back, the first Wobleszynski had encroached on the land owned by Wood Mountain's grandmother. Since then, the Wobleszynskis sent their cattle to graze on Juggie's land so often that her family had finally shanghaied a cow. This happened during berry-picking time, when there were extra people camped out everywhere, so if the cow was stolen it was quickly absorbed into boiling pots. Nothing was ever traced or proved but nothing was ever forgotten, either. Over the years, resentment between the families had become entrenched. Then it so happened that a boy from each family began to box in the same weight category and provided the perfect focus.

Joe entered the ring first, head lowered, shy. He had thick

milky skin, sandy eyes, and sandy hair. He was wearing a dark brown robe and when he shed it his body had a bull-like heavy pride. He weighed four pounds more than Wood Mountain, and was an inch shorter. He was a power fighter, but in tight control. He beat his fists together rhythmically, gathering energy, while Wood Mountain, Juggie's boy, sauntered in wearing a blue robe he'd borrowed from Barnes. He shuffled to hide his nerves, danced a little as he shed the robe. Hopped up and down. His hair was thick and the waves were oiled back. He had brilliant, watchful, close-set dark eyes. A thin long nose. Cheekbones. Generous curved lips. His body was ropey and lean, all grace and force. But Joe Wobble was a year older, a more seasoned fighter, and had already beaten him once.

At the bell they moved on each other to jeers and cheers, both cautious and confident, pawing the air and dancing back, neither connecting. Then Joe slipped in a right and tapped Wood Mountain's jaw. Wood used Joe's momentum to slide around his body and land a solid blow to his midsection, which did no harm. Joe tiptoed back and feinted the same right, came around with a left, glancingly kissed at Wood Mountain's cheek. Wood again used Joe's momentum to thump his midsection, softening him up perhaps, or maybe Joe's guard was too strict for Wood. He seemed to leave no other openings. But as the heavier fighter, he was also a fraction slower and in the second round Wood Mountain danced aside and deftly brought his left under Joe's leading arm. He connected a surprise hook and followed with a strong right. Joe staggered back but the round ended before Wood Mountain could enlarge on the blow. In the third round they kept getting into clinches and practically nothing happened. Which brought the crowd to a certain tension.

Patrice and Valentine were standing up in the back row.

They could barely see the action. Valentine liked the fights and Patrice didn't, much. But they were stirred by the crowd's excitement and were making themselves heard. There were Indians who had come from all around—Fort Berthold and Fort Totten, from Dunseith and Minot, even Fort Peck in Montana. Juggie was up front, and loudest of them all. Still, they were much outnumbered by the crowd who supported Joe Wobleszynski. So perhaps the tribal supporters cheered a little harder than seemed right to the farming communities, who were used to deferential Indians. To most of their neighbors, Indians were people who suffered and hid away in shabby dwellings or roamed the streets in flagrant drunkenness and shame. Except the good ones. There was always a "good Indian" that someone knew. But they were not a people who had champion fighters. Anyway, it didn't look like this Wood Mountain had the stuff. He became tentative, almost squeamish, guarding his head, opening up his stomach to punishment, then lowering his guard and barely missing the increasingly confident haymakers Joe began swinging his way.

Someone gave an incoherent shriek.

Valentine yelled, "Hit 'im hard!"

Patrice, using Chippewa in her excitement, screamed, "Bakite'o!"

She could see Thomas and Rose and their children a few rows in front of her, Thomas quiet, watching intently, holding Fee in his arms, Wade and Sharlo hopping around throwing rabbit punches. For a moment, she wondered about Thomas. There was something about his stillness within the motion of the rest of the crowd. As if he were watching something other than the fight. And it was true. There was a visceral quality to his watching.

Thomas was flinching mentally at the blows, but he was seeing something different than the rest of the crowd. The Wobble fans had begun to cluck and laugh. The Indians called desperately, hope sinking. Thomas saw that the blows that Joe Wobble landed slid away, harmless. He saw that Wood was accepting but deflecting the punishment. Then he saw three other people in the crowd were tense and quiet as he was— up front ringside, Barnes and his sidekick, the English teacher who directed all of the school plays. And Juggie Blue. They were anticipating something. There was one minute left to the round when Wood found the opening he'd been studying. He stepped away as if in fear, drawing a greedy swing. It would have been a knockout blow had it landed. All Joe's strength was behind it, which put him off balance and open to Wood's full-on left hook to the jaw. Followed swiftly by a right blow to the side of the head. Then a musical combination. Joe's guard went to pieces and he stumbled. Wood moved in and the bell rang, too soon.

Barnes jumped into the ring shouting, "Foul! Foul! Fifteen seconds left!"

The referee fended him off, checked the clock, admonished the timekeeper, and restarted the round. Which went on points to Joe Wobble although anyone could see that the timekeeper had cheated for Wobble and interrupted the momentum, rattling Wood Mountain, who surged back twice in the next round but ultimately lost the fight.

Everyone filed out quietly, Indians shaking hands with Indians, farm people now satisfied. The fight had turned out as it was supposed to turn out and they, too, were muttering peaceably. The excitement had fallen out of everyone and nothing new had happened. There was a stiff black wind and people hurried to cars or pulled their coats close and hunched along quickly through the streets.

On the way home, the girls mourned. But Thomas had seen that Wood Mountain had improved to such a degree that he was becoming the faster, cannier, even better fighter. He'd come close on points. Thomas wondered if Barnes could fix whatever was holding back Juggie's boy. Even with the cheating timekeeper, Wood Mountain could have triumphed.

WITHIN THE first five miles everyone but Thomas fell asleep. As usual, he was left to think. Wood Mountain's father, Archille, had been well over six feet tall, powerful, with a beak of a nose and a broad smile. He and Thomas had train-hopped together, following the winter-wheat harvest through July, hiring on to threshing crews until finally the last crop, corn. In those days, corn had to dry on the stalk late into the season so the workers could pick by hand. One year, they started south and just kept going all the way down to where the desert began. Somewhere in Texas, in 1931, they were passing by a church on Sunday morning when the sheriff appeared. Squads of just deputized police agents pushed them toward the church, then surrounded the people who poured out of the church, all Mexicans.

"Damnitall," said Archille, "they think we're Mexicans."

They were swept up in one of the hundreds of Depression-era raids in which over a million Mexican workers, many of them citizens, were rounded up and shipped across the border. Texas didn't like Indians any better than Mexicans, so their papers didn't help. Working on the harvest crews, both Thomas and Archille had learned to be elaborately polite to white people. The surprise worked better up north. Sometimes it set them off down here.

"Excuse me, sir. May I have a word?"

"You'll go back where you came from," said the sheriff.

"We're from North Dakota," said Archille. His easy smile didn't work on the sheriff. "We're not Mexicans. We're American Indians."

"Oh really? Well, consider this Custer's payback."

"Since my grandfather killed him," said Archille, "there is a certain justice to the idea. Still, Thomas here is a bona fide American citizen. I'm Canadian. My brother fought in the trenches. My uncle was at the Somme."

The sheriff's neck enlarged and he bawled out an incomprehensible epithet. Then he gestured at a couple of the officers. Thomas and Archille were thrown in a truck with the others, trundled down to the border. Along the way, they learned some Spanish and Archille became infatuated with a girl who pinned up her elaborate braids and dressed in only white. This was the first time they had ever met a woman with a certain "look" and they talked about it after. How she, Adolfa, possessed this distinction. Maybe it was a discipline. She was doubtless poor, but the white dress and the hair gave her an air of wealth. Her father wore a straw fedora hat, suspenders, and a white shirt. The two of them, in the same truck but looking like they carried first-class tickets, were an inspiration to Thomas. When they were finally able to sneak back over the border, he bought a wide-brimmed fedora made of soft brown felt. They headed back up north on the freights. The people at the stations were whiter and blonder with every stop. And at each stop the hoboes in the yards were colder, wearier, sicker. They paid for the last tickets, on the Galloping Goose. The two got off at St. John. There was Juggie waiting at the station with her hands on her hips. How she knew they were coming in on that train was a complete mystery.

"Hi, Archie. Supper's ready," she said.

A month later they were living together. They never married. Juggie was too independent and wanted things her way. When the coughing started, Juggie brought Archie to San Haven, north of Dunseith, where he died within the year. It was still common, then, to die of tuberculosis. Lots of children at Fort Totten had been sent to the children's sanatorium at Sac and Fox.

Roderick.

Thomas had friends on the other side. More and more friends. Too many. Sometimes he talked to them. Archille. Talked to them. Why shouldn't he? It helped to think they had moved to another country. That they lived on the far side of a river you could only cross once. In the dark night, in the dashboard light, he spoke to Archille, but only in his thoughts.

"Your namesake's got a job."

"Howah, brother."

"And you'd be proud of your own son. He never stops punching."

"Of course not. As the great-grandson of—"

"That talk about killing Custer always got you in trouble."

"True. How's Juggie?"

"Still cooking pies for the chimookomaanag. This Barnes, a teacher, brings your son his dinner every night."

"He always could eat."

"So could you."

Thomas stopped. The unlikeness of Archille at the end, wasted and beyond wanting. In the white bed. In the dry hills.

"I'm fighting something out of Washington," he said. "I don't know what, Archie. But it's bad."

# Valentine's Days

*⊷—⊷*

"YOU HAVE three days total," said Mr. Vold. He tapped his feet together underneath the desk. His shoes made an insect-like rasp. Betty Pye had started calling him Grasshopper. The nickname fit him distractingly well. Patrice watched his square mouth and jaw move like a grasshopper's mandibles. He shifted papers, his long fingers grasping and plucking. His breath swam across the desk, strong and swampy, like he'd been eating wet hay. He pushed a sheet of paper toward Patrice. She picked up the paper and read it. She would have to work six months to accumulate three more sick leave days.

"It's about my sister," she said, "sir."

Patrice explained the situation with Vera as best she could. She was the only person in her family who could possibly travel to Minneapolis. She showed her boss the letter from Betty Pye's cousin. He pored over it, reading it several times, and Patrice understood that by pretending to read the letter many times he was sorting out the possibilities.

"Okay, Miss Paranteau," he said finally, putting down the letter, "this situation you couldn't call illness. I could give you a leave of absence, without any pay, see, no guarantee that you would keep your job if you had to stay on, say, over the allotted time."

"How much time would that be?"

"One week is the most time allowed."

"May I think about it overnight?"

"Go right ahead," said Mr. Vold. "By all means go right ahead."

He seemed excited at the false generosity of his phrase and kept chewing on the words even after they were uttered.

FOR THE rest of the morning, Patrice worked silently, trying to decide whether she should risk her job. At lunch break she took out her battered syrup pail and removed a boiled potato, a chunk of bannock, and a small handful of raisins. Sometimes people traded their government commodities for Zhaanat's baskets. Raisins were prized. She ate them slowly, for dessert, letting each one soften and melt against the back of her teeth.

"Raisins!"

Patrice handed her friend the bucket and Valentine scooped the remaining raisins greedily into her mouth. She glanced at Patrice and caught sight of her dismay before Patrice could hide it.

"I'm sorry."

"It's all right."

"But you're upset."

"Over Vera. I'm scared to take a leave because if it's complicated, and I have to stay longer, then I lose my job. I just have three days."

"Of what?"

"Three days of sick time."

"Huh?"

"Three days of sick time."

"Sick time?"

"With half pay."

"Oh. I didn't even know we had that."

Their break was over. Patrice drank the stale coffee at the

bottom of her cup. The boiled potato anchored her and she went at her work with the sudden focus that had become habit. She lowered the wand to spread a drop of cement. Her hand was steady.

Later, on the way to the car, Valentine said, "You can have my days."

"What do you mean?"

"My sick days. Mr. Vold told me that I could give my days to you. Under the circumstances."

Patrice was so ablaze with relief that she reached her arms out, embraced Valentine, and then stepped back.

"I'm so thankful. What a surprise."

"I know," said Valentine. "I'm all contradictions."

For Valentine to name this quality about herself startled the two of them to silence.

"Contradictions!"

"Is that some kind of a game?" said Doris, stepping up behind them.

"No," said Valentine, "it's me. Blowing hot and cold. Naughty and nice."

"My goodness."

"But never stingy. Always generous," said Patrice.

On the way home she told the two of them about the trip to Minneapolis. She had never taken a trip before, so she was making it up as she went along.

*—|—*

HER FAMILY did not own a traveling bag. There was a handsome plaid suitcase for sale at the mercantile. Expensive. Patrice bought a yard and a half of canvas. She cut short lengths of popple, stripped off the bark. She hemmed the canvas, sewed the sides together, sewed the ends around the short poles, then used sinew and brass tacks to fasten two pieces of leather onto the poles to act as handles. The canvas suitcase looked like a workman's bag but so what? She didn't need to be fashionable, just get herself to Minneapolis. At the Relocation Office there was a train timetable. Once she found a ride to Rugby, she could purchase her ticket down at the station.

Curly Jay's sister, Deanna, worked in the small room that served as an office. Patrice sat at a table covered with papers, flipping through a stack, looking for any new information on Vera. Behind her a poster was taped to the wall. **Come to Minneapolis**. The Chance of Your Lifetime. **Good Jobs** in Retail Trade, Manufacturing, Government Federal, State, Local, Exciting Community Life, Convenient Stores. **Beautiful Minnesota**. 10,000 Lakes. Zoo, Museum, Drives, Picnic Areas, Parks, Amusement, Movie Theaters. **Happy Homes**, Beautiful Homes, Many Churches, Exciting Community Life, Convenient Stores.

Besides love, Patrice thought that Vera had probably gone to Minneapolis for Exciting Community Life and Beautiful Homes. Those drawings of the windows with the ruler-straight muntins.

"Do you want to put in an application?"

"To move to Beautiful Minnesota?"

"You get help with a job, the training, help finding a place to live and all that."

"Did Vera get all that?"

"Oh, well, yeah."

"You should really pay me to do your job for you. Going down to find her. Don't you keep track of where people go?"

"Not after a while."

"A short while."

"We have last known address on Bloomington Avenue."

"I have it too. I'm going to start there."

"Where you staying?"

"I don't have a place."

"Look up my friend."

Deanna wrote the name Bernadette Blue on a card along with her address and a phone number.

"I don't know if she's still at this number. It was for work."

"What kind of work?"

"Secretarial."

"Juggie Blue's daughter."

"The bad one," said Deanna.

Patrice lifted her eyebrows. Deanna said, "Kidding." But she wasn't. She kept flipping through the stack of papers. "And here's another name. Father Hartigan."

"I'm not going all the way there to see a priest."

"For an emergency."

"I'm not going to have an emergency."

"Vera said something like that."

"I still think you should pay me."

THAT SATURDAY, Patrice waited until Pokey was gone and Zhaanat out in the woods. Although she trusted them not to take her money, she didn't quite trust them not to suddenly need to get rid of her father. Her money was buried underneath the eighth green square from the right in the linoleum's design. That part of the pattern was underneath her bed. She pulled the flimsy bed frame aside. Careful not to crack the linoleum, she pulled it up slowly. She had buried her money box, a dented pink cookie tin painted with dancing cookies, and made certain it was smoothly covered. Now she pushed the dirt away and tugged off the cover. It was all there. One hundred and six dollars. She removed the money, reburied the box, and left eight of the dollars underneath her mother's sugar can. Doris was driving down to Rugby and would pick her up in half an hour. Patrice had kept the clock wound and figured out how many minutes it had lost overnight. The time displayed was fairly accurate. All she had to do was get on the train. What she had to go on was the unreliable address, and Juggie Blue's daughter, Bernadette, the bad one.

ZHAANAT CAME back with a basket of pine tips. They stood together, arms around each other, just outside the door.

"He's down in Fargo, right?" Patrice said of her father.

"He won't come here now, not for a while."

Patrice could feel, in her mother's grip, that her father would not return. Her fear was of letting her go. "Don't you go disappear on me too," Zhaanat whispered and clutched her harder. Fear for Pixie. Fear of what she might find. Fear for Vera. But when she stood back, Zhaanat smiled as she took in her daughter's shined shoes, her bright coat, pin-curl-waved hair, red lipstick. Valentine had even lent her gloves.

"You look like a white woman," said Zhaanat, in Chippewa.

Patrice laughed. They were both pleased at her disguise.

# Pukkons

THOMAS CARRIED his rifle on the trail to his father's house. Maybe he would flush up a partridge. Or surprise a deer. But there was only sere grass, rose hips, seed heads of black-eyed Susans, red willow. Under the stands of oak, heaps of acorns lay in the grass. With a lot of boiling, you could eat them. He thought of picking them up. But along the edges of the grass road there were bushes loaded with pukkons. He filled his hat, then his jacket, with the prickly green nuts. His father saw him coming along the edge of the field and stepped out of his doorway, stooped, leaning on his stick. Biboon, Winter, bone thin. With age, his skin had lightened in patches. Laughing, he sometimes called himself an old pinto. He wore a creamy long-john shirt, brown work pants, moccasins so worn they looked like part of his feet. He could still keep the fire going, and insisted on living alone. Biboon trembled and smiled when he saw the pukkons. They were a favorite food of his, reminding him of early days.

"Oh boy, you got some. Let's smash off the shells."

There were flat slates at the edge of the yard. Thomas put the prickly green nuts in a bag and struck the bag with a rock, just hard enough to loosen the shells. The late afternoon light slanted low from the west, and he brought out the kitchen chairs and a dishpan. It seemed to Thomas, as they sat in the sinking radiance, shucking bits of shell from the meat, dropping the nuts into a dishpan, that he should hold on to this. Whatever was said, he should hold on to. Whatever gestures his father made, hold on to. The peculiar aliveness of things struck by late afternoon sunlight—hold on to it. And the trees behind them, their shadows, wavering.

Biboon said, "Oh the devil, look here."

Inside one of the shells there was a golden beetle, like something in a teaching or a fairy tale. Its bifurcated shell was shimmering, metallic. For a moment it rested on Biboon's hand, then its golden armor parted and it flexed tough black wings. Whirred off into the loom of shadows.

"It looked like a chunk of gold," said Thomas.

"Good thing we didn't crush that son of a gun between the rocks," said Biboon.

Thomas's dog, Smoker, came out of the woods carrying a deer's leg bone. He was a mix of dogs looking like the old-time kind of dogs people had—working dogs with soft gray fur and curled tails. Smoker's fur was spotted with black slash marks, and his face was half white and half gray.

"Good boy," said Thomas to the dog.

Smoker crouched down nearby with the bone between his paws, guarding the bone even though it was white and weathered. Soon Thomas began to speak with his father in Chippewa— which signaled that their conversation was heading in a more complex direction, a matter of the mind and heart. Biboon thought more fluently in Chippewa. Although his English was very good, he also was more expressive and comical in his original language.

"Something is coming in the government. They have a new plan."

"They always have a new plan."

"This one takes away the treaties."

"For all the Indians? Or just us?"

"All."

"At least they're not just picking on us alone," said Biboon. "Maybe we can get together with the other tribes on this thing."

AS A boy, Biboon had traveled along the medicine line into Assiniboine, Gros Ventre, and Blackfeet territory. Then his family swung down along the Milk River, hunting buffalo. He had come back to the Turtle Mountains when there was no other choice. They were confined on the reservation, and had to get permission from the farmer in charge to pass its boundaries. For a while they were not allowed to go off to search for food, and one terrible winter the old people starved themselves so that the young people could continue. Biboon had tried farming with the seed wheat, iron plow, and ox that the farmer in charge had issued to him on strict condition that the family not kill and eat the ox. The first year, nothing. They had to take turns sneaking past the boundaries, picking up buffalo bones to sell to the bone dealers. The next year they did not plant the white man's grain, but corn, squash, and beans. The family dried the crops and cached the food. They didn't quite starve, but by spring they could barely walk, they were so skinny and weak. It took many years of finding what plants grew best in which soil, liked a wet or dry spot, sun in morning or afternoon. Thomas had learned from his father's experiments.

Now they had enough, plus the government surplus food, which always showed up unexpectedly. Biboon was happiest about the government's corn syrup, so sweet it made his tooth stubs ache. He cut it with cold water and added a few drops of Mapleine to make it taste like the old-time maple syrup. He remembered the taste from his very youngest days as a child in the great sugar stands of maple trees in Minnesota. And he loved pukkons roasted in a cast-iron skillet, tossed up and down as the smell of old times filled the cabin.

# Perfume

*※==┼==※*

ON THE way down to Rugby, sitting in the passenger seat that Valentine always occupied, Patrice wondered if Doris Lauder always smelled so good. She wanted to ask whether it was perfume, but wasn't sure if it was rude to ask. Patrice wondered about the medicines on her skin. She lived with bear root, wiikenh, prairie sage, sweetgrass, kinnikinnick, and all sorts of teas and medicines that Zhaanat burned or boiled every day. The scent of the medicines surely clung to her. Zhaanat had pushed a cloth bag of rose hip tea into Patrice's hands before she left, a strengthening tonic for Vera. And also cedar. Used to bathe infants. They were in her satchel, which was in the backseat. Slowly the scent of cedar was permeating the car's interior. But it couldn't yet compete with Doris.

"I like your perfume," Patrice said. "What is it called?" She had not been meaning to speak. But the steady background noise of the motor encouraged conversation.

"Eau de Better Than Manure," said Doris. "The farm girl's friend."

Patrice laughed so hard she snorted. Which would have been embarrassing but Doris snorted too. The snorting set them laughing until tears sprang from the corners of their eyes. Doris gasped that she had to calm down for fear of driving off the road.

"Do you have a boyfriend?" she asked Patrice. "Valentine says you do."

"What? I'd like to know who!"

"People say the boxing coach likes you."

"That's news to me," said Patrice, though it wasn't. Even Pokey had mentioned that Barnes was always asking questions about her.

"What about you?" Patrice added.

"I don't have anybody."

"You are wasting your perfume?"

"No, I'm just making the air around me bearable."

They laughed again, but didn't go out of control.

"I have never bought perfume," said Patrice. "If I have any money left over on my trip, I might use it on perfume."

"I bought myself a little birthday present this year. It's called Liquid Petals. I use it when I go to town, but not at work."

"I suppose it was expensive."

"Yes, but that's not why. I don't wear it because Grasshopper likes it."

Patrice absorbed the meaning of that. "You don't want to encourage him."

"Of course not. Who would?"

"Mrs. Grasshopper?"

"There isn't one. For obvious reasons."

"Isn't there somebody you do want to use Liquid Petals on?"

"Maybe, to tell you the truth, but he hasn't noticed me yet."

"That's impossible."

"Have you looked at me? I'm dumpy, sweaty, awkward, and my skin is pasty pale. I am not the blooming farm girl. No roses in these cheeks."

Patrice was silent in surprise. With her snub features and fluffy red-brown hair, her large bosom and short curvy legs, Doris was pretty. She could be saying these things to get compliments, thought Patrice, so she began giving her compliments. Doris seemed exasperated by everything she said. It seemed that Doris did not want to hear good things about herself. Patrice stopped and they rode in silence. After a while Doris said, "I don't know what's wrong with me. You're just trying to make me feel better. But I can see right through that. What do you think about Bucky Duvalle?"

It was like she'd poked an electric wire into Patrice's brain.

"What do I think? You don't want to hear. You know what he said about me, right?"

"No?"

Doris glanced at her, goggle-eyed, and Patrice gave her the lowdown on how Bucky and his friends had picked her up hitchhiking last summer. How they first promised then refused to take her where she asked to go. How they trapped her, how Bucky threw himself on her, how they took her down the road to Fish Lake and tried to make her get out and have a "picnic" and how she pretended to go along with them. But when they got down to the lake she jumped in and begun swimming toward her uncle's fishing boat. And they hadn't dared follow her.

She didn't tell Doris about how they tried to pile on her in the car, or about Bucky's face mashed up against hers, his hands on her, everywhere. She said nothing about Bucky's condition now.

"Did you swim all the way to your uncle's boat?"

"Did I ever! He was so surprised. Said he was fishing for bass, not young ladies. Anyway, he put down his fishing rod and helped me get into his boat."

"Lucky he was out there."

"I could have outswum those boys. They were drunk."

"Could you tell when you got into the car?"

"Yes, but I needed that ride so bad."

"Of course."

They rode in silence for a while, then Doris asked if Patrice knew the other boys in the car.

"I knew a couple. There were four."

"My brother's a friend of Bucky's."

Doris glanced over at Patrice and from her look Patrice knew that her brother had been one of those boys. She knew that was why Doris had asked her about Bucky. It hadn't been a real question. She could not trust Doris now. She knew all about Bucky. And her brother must have said something about her.

"What did he say?" said Patrice.

"He said Bucky was a jackass. He said he didn't know why you went off in the bushes with him."

"I didn't! What did you say?"

"I said I didn't think you'd do that."

Had Doris really defended her? Patrice was skeptical.

"And what did he say?"

"He looked at me funny. Then he said that Bucky made him swear to say that."

"Why would Bucky want that? What's in it for him?"

"Don't you know? He thinks if he ruins your reputation for nice guys you'll be softened up so he can get you. Bucky likes you, just like Barnes."

Patrice said nothing. This sounded completely true. Yet also completely false. Didn't Bucky think what other people thought? That his disfigurement had something to do with Zhaanat and with her? That somehow they'd frozen half his face and sucked the strength from his arm? That they'd cursed him?

Suddenly Doris pressed her foot on the gas and glared at the road. They were flying along, too fast.

"Slow down!"

"At least somebody likes you! You and your pixie eyes and cute figure," cried Doris. "Can't you enjoy that?"

Patrice welled up with misery.

"Why should I?" she said.

"You'd know why if the only one who liked you was Grasshopper."

*—⫞—*

PATRICE RESTED her head on the starched napkin that was already faintly stained with hair oil. She had chosen a seat by the window even though when she entered the train car, a couple of people had given her that look. But there were enough seats so she could have one by the window. Nobody would tell her she did not belong there. She hoped. Patrice fussed with her homemade suitcase and hung up her coat, smoothed its gleaming folds. She put her gloved hands in her lap. Her heart was still pounding. The train groaned, hissed, let out a giant sigh. Then the doors were closed and the floor beneath her feet gathered energy. The wheels began to clunk along the tracks and soon the train was moving at a smooth, delicious, rocking speed. Patrice smiled, looking at the houses, streets, people, whisking away behind her as the train rolled along at a magnificent gait. Nobody had ever, ever, described to her how freeing it felt to be riding on a train. The conductor took her ticket, gave half back to her. He stuck the tab into a little aperture at the top of her seat. So now she owned this seat. The other half of the ticket she put carefully into her purse. Then she removed it from her purse and surreptitiously tucked it into the little pocket she had sewed into the inside of her brassiere, where most of her cash was hidden. Her eyes grew heavy. The scent of the hair-oil spot was surprisingly pleasant, low and spicy. The swaying of the train was voluptuous, hypnotic, and she drifted to sleep on a sea of motion.

# The Iron

✴━┃━✴

THEY CONTINUED lifting potatoes in the afternoons. Wade
had his friend Martin staying over to work. He'd get paid in
potatoes sometimes. Martin lived with them these days while
Rose and Thomas did the paperwork to keep him as a foster
child. The sun was low in the sky by the time Thomas sent the
boys to wash up. As he crossed the field, he could hear Noko
scolding. Thomas stepped inside. Rose was in the other room
with the ironing. There was the scent of pressed cloth above
the meat in the pan. The glass kerosene lantern glowed on the
table. Thomas went into the next room and kissed Rose on her
neck. She smelled like the ironing, like the clean wash. Rose
liked to iron right after she took the clothes off the line, when
they were still slightly damp. For times when they got too dry,
she had a sprinkler on the windowsill, a canning jar with holes
punched in the lid. When she sprinkled, and then pressed with
the iron, there was a slow hiss of fragrant steam. When other
places began to get electricity, she had asked for a plug-in ironing machine. They didn't have electricity yet. So getting the iron
didn't make sense. Still, Thomas bought her the plug-in iron.
She guarded the iron jealously, shined it like a trophy. She kept
it on top of the dark bedroom dresser where they all stored their
clothes. She still used the old sadiron, a heavy pointed oval that
fit into an iron frame. The iron also made a good bed warmer in
the winter. But the bright wedge of the new steel iron, upright

like a little god, reflected light from the southwest window and flashed in his eyes when he rested there.

The house was neat. Everything had its place. Nothing was torn or hanging loose. Everything was mended. Rose had fierce standards.

"Daddy, come on and eat!"

Fee and Sharlo had come home from a movie at the school gym. They still had their five-cent bags of sunflower seeds. The boys begged them away. Rose had made Thomas a plate with fried rabbit and two ash-baked potatoes. There were bits of wild onion sprinkled on the food. After supper, he and the boys listened to a ball game on the radio. Then there was coming and going, in and out, as everybody used the outhouse. Thomas pulled the two roll-aways from behind the bedroom door. The cot from beside the woodbox. He unlatched the roll-away mattresses and folded them down. The beds were already made up from the morning with sheets and blankets. There were small flat pillows on top of the wardrobe in the bedroom. Fee handed down the pillows and everybody took their own pillow. The girls liked the privacy of the kitchen. Noko slept behind the door on her canvas cot. The big boys slept head to toe on one roll-away. When everyone was settled, muttering, sighing, in the dark, Rose went into their room. He followed her and shut the door. Thomas set his alarm clock for 11:05, turned the lights out. Rose got into her worn flannel nightgown.

"Soft as silk," he said, touching her sleeve.

"Paah."

Thomas took off his shirt and trousers, hung them with the creases pinched, beside his bed next to his briefcase, jacket, hat.

"Is my lunch box in the car?"

"You always ask that."

"If I didn't have your lunch to eat, I'd never make it."

"It's there."

"Then I don't have to get you up."

"That alarm will get me up."

"You'll go back to sleep, won't you?"

"Yes," she said grudgingly.

Rose turned away. In seconds, she was asleep. Thomas lay awake. He put his hand out, whispered, "My old girl." The heat from her body radiated gently toward him under the blanket and warmed his right side. His left side was cool. The warmth from the stove didn't reach into the bedroom. On very cold nights, Rose put an extra quilt on the bed and let him curl around her back. She slept hot just the way her words sometimes blew hot. She could warm him right up. He drifted a little as the dark sifted down. Smoker barked, twice, to let him know that he had returned from eating his evening mush at Biboon's house. He came home for his second supper left outside in a dented pan. If anyone came up the steps in the night, Smoker would merely growl from under foot if he knew the person, a way of saying, *Hello, I'm here.* He would leap out in a protective frenzy if a stranger approached. Smoker had a very strong feeling about the front steps.

THOMAS WOKE, at 11:04, and shut off the alarm before it sounded. Before this job he'd sing out the old hobo wake-up call, "Roll out, snakes, it's daylight in the swamp." He thought it now, anyway. He stepped into his pants, tied on his work boots, and grabbed his briefcase. He threaded his way in the dark through the sleeping children and opened the front door slowly. Before he stepped out, he said, "Ooh yay! Bizaan! Mii eta go niin omaa ayaayaan. Ninga-maajiibiz endazhi-anokiiyaan."

The dog understood Chippewa, and his tail beat on the dirt as Thomas trod down the steps. In the beginning, Thomas had set out a circular driveway so he didn't have to back the car out. He didn't use headlamps until he was well on his way. The Indian Service road was pitch-black. The moon behind clouds. The only yard lamp was in the big farm and the light gleamed off the silver silo. He passed through town and then left the reservation. On this stretch of highway he was afflicted. It felt as if his heart was being pierced by long sharp needles. He flashed on his father, the two of them sitting in late sunshine, gathering its fugitive warmth.

You can never get enough of the ones you love, thought Thomas, rubbing his chest slowly, to vanquish the pains. "Here I have Biboon with me to this great old age, but I am greedy. I want him longer."

His chest relaxed as he drove along. But an even sharper sensation dogged him. It made him want to stop the car, get out, and then what? He glanced over at his briefcase, which held the papers Moses had given him. For days, he'd tried to make sense of the papers, to absorb their meaning. To define their unbelievable intent. Unbelievable because the unthinkable was couched in such innocuous dry language. Unbelievable because the intent was, finally, to unmake, to unrecognize. To erase as Indians him, Biboon, Rose, his children, his people, *all of us invisible and as if we never were here, from the beginning, here.*

The case sat heavy on the passenger seat. The itch of dread intensified. Thomas pulled into the parking lot. The solid slam of the car door never ceased to satisfy. He walked a few steps without the briefcase, then turned back, leaned into the car, yanked it out, and hauled it along. But he didn't open it until well into the night, when he cracked his lunch box and unwrapped his sandwich from a clean old red bandanna. He poured black medicine water into the cap of the thermos. He needed to sip at coffee, to nibble at a browned and salty crust of bannock, as he read the papers again. These little comforts gave him strength.

He had been night watchman for seven months. In the beginning, his post as chairman of the Turtle Mountain Advisory Committee could be dealt with in the late afternoons and evenings. He'd been able to sleep most mornings after his shift. When lucky, like tonight, he even grabbed an additional catnap before driving to work. But every so often the government remembered about Indians. And when they did, they always tried to *solve* Indians, thought Thomas. They solve us by getting rid of us. And do they tell us when they plan to get rid of us? Ha and ha. He had received no word from the government. By reading the *Minot Daily News*, he'd found out something was up. Then Moses had to pry the papers out of his contact down in Aberdeen. It had taken precious time to even get confirmation, or see the actual House Resolution stating, as its author said, that the Turtle Mountain Band of Chippewa was targeted by the United States Congress for emancipation. *E-man-ci-pation*. *Eman-cipation*. This word would not stop banging around in his head. *Emancipated*. But they were not enslaved. Freed from being Indians was the idea. Emancipated from their land. Freed from the treaties that Thomas's father and grandfather had signed and that were promised to last forever. So as usual, by getting rid of us, the Indian problem would be *solved*.

Overnight the tribal chairman job had turned into a struggle to remain a problem. To not be solved.

# The Fruit Crate

BARNES HAD seen her fade back into the leaves. She was bare-foot. He found that charming. And so appropriate for a darling Indian girl. Ever since he was a child, there had been pictures. Advertisements. Luscious illustrations on fruit crates and dairy cartons. A lovely Indian maiden in flowing buckskin. She would be holding squash, apples, peaches, cucumbers. She would be offering a little box of butter. Perhaps the memory of these pictures swirled vaguely around his decision to come to the reservation, leaving his parents' print shop in Des Moines. Also, after high school, it had entered his head that he would not really like to continue on with the print shop. He liked math. Long division had won his heart from early on. Barnes had craved each new level of knowledge. Even now, if he wasn't boxing, he puttered around with polynomials. Numbers befriended him throughout the day. He noticed connections, repetitions. Out of license plates and telephone numbers he made equations. Even boxing was based on numbers of minutes, rounds, penalties, points. Numbers also attached to people. He saw Pixie as a 26, though she was just 19 years old. But he loved the swoop of the 2 and the snail of the 6. It went with her. He had a feeling for 2 to the 6th power. It didn't go further than that. He had only spoken to her in passing, and was waiting for the right moment to present himself.

He thought that he might go to her house. Would that be

strange? Possibly. Probably. But he'd waited to run into her, even to the point of placing himself in spots she might linger on the way home from work. The dime store. The mercantile. Henry's Cafe. But no luck. One evening when the wind had dried the roads, hopefully the path to their house, he brought Pokey home. When Pokey got out, Barnes did too.

"I'm going to say hello to your parents. Haven't met them yet."

Pokey turned, gaped at Barnes. He shut his mouth, started forward, but said nothing.

Pokey hoped that his father wasn't passed out in the yard. He knew that Patrice was on the train.

"That's just fine." Barnes hid his disappointment. "I can tell her about the progress you're making."

Pokey was silent, but his thought was "You mean the progress *you're* making. Or trying to make."

Pokey pushed the door open. When Barnes ducked through, he was shocked. He hadn't understood that he was entering a house. The outside of the place looked to Barnes like a rude shelter for animals, the stacked poles plastered with pale yellow mud. But then, even in the dim light, he saw that there were signs of care taken. The table was scrubbed clean. Upon it, a lighted glass lantern glowed. Behind the lantern, a woman sat before what he thought at first was a heavy roll of paper, then realized was birchbark. Behind the table there was a small wood-burning range and an iron stew pot, steaming. Barnes recognized a peppery venison stew cooked with cedar berries and wild turnips. Because it was a specialty of Juggie's, his mouth watered. Without a word, the woman rose and dished out two tin bowls of stew. Beside them she placed a hunk of light bannock and between the bowls a small pan of grease. She laid two spoons beside the bowls.

Barnes sat down to eat beside Pokey. The woman didn't smile. She began to speak to Pokey in her language, and then to move her hands in a slow articulate way. Barnes was fascinated by her hands—maybe it was numbers. She was missing the pinkie finger on one hand. On the other hand there was a small extra finger, a perfect thumb. Her fingers were wrong, but still added up to ten. This unnerved Barnes to the point of extreme discomfort, and after the stew, he asked Pokey to thank his mother. He wanted her to understand he thought the stew delicious and almost rubbed his stomach—but caught himself.

"My mother wants to know why you've come," said Pokey.

"Just to visit. To tell her that you are doing B+ work in math. That is very good."

Barnes nodded and smiled as he spoke, trying to catch the mother's eye. Frustratingly, she shifted her gaze or looked past him, down at the floor. She seemed to be listening, but he couldn't tell how much she understood. After he'd said all that he could think of, he waited. Nothing. She sipped her tea. After a while, she nodded at Pokey and said something. Pokey refilled Barnes's tin bowl. Barnes ate the stew. Then they sat together in the flicker of lamp. At last she spoke again to her son. Pokey frowned at the table.

"What is it?" said Barnes.

"She says thank you. But she knows that's not why you came."

Barnes was having trouble not staring at the mother's hands, and having trouble not making conversation. This situation was very different from the pictures on the fruit crates, and he hoped he was doing all right. It was as though he had entered another time, a time he hadn't known existed, an uncomfortable time where Indians were not at all like white people.

"Maybe I should go," he said.

"Okay," said Pokey.

The mother spoke.

"Pokey? What did she say?"

"Nothing."

"Please. What?"

"Well, okay then. She said that Pixie don't like you."

"What? How does she know? How come? Ask her."

Pokey spoke to his mother. Again, he seemed reluctant to translate, but finally relented.

"She says Pixie don't like you because you smell bad."

Barnes was utterly shocked. He stood, reeling beneath the low roof.

"Tell your mother thanks for the stew," he said.

"Okay," said Pokey.

Barnes left the house and walked the dark trail to his car.

"Gee, Mama," Pokey said when the door shut. "You insulted a teacher."

"I had to," said Zhaanat, in English. "She told me she doesn't like him. Not really because he smells. She wants him to leave her alone."

"Why didn't you tell him that? Now he'll just wash and think the problem is solved."

"Even if he washes, he'll still smell like they do. He can never wash that off. Their sweat is sharp."

"Oh, so you think he'll understand he has no chance to smell good? So then he'll give up?"

Zhaanat nodded as though it was obvious.

"Ma. Jeez! He don't think that way. He thinks *we* smell bad."

"Gawiin geget! Surely not!" said Zhaanat in a scandalized voice.

# A Seat on the Train

*⊰—⊱*

OTHER PEOPLE entered the car at every stop. Nobody sat next to Patrice, but soon nearly every seat was taken. A blond-haired blond-eyelashed man who reminded her of Barnes (a lot of men on the train or in the station reminded her of Barnes) walked down the aisle. He glanced at the seat beside her and Patrice shut her eyes. She was leaning against the window. The glass was cool on her temple. She felt the man's weight settle into the seat and heard him talking to a woman, who moved off. The man beside Patrice was still for a few moments, then he swatted lightly at her arm. Startled to stillness, she did not react.

"Hey, my wife's on board. She'll change seats with you."

Patrice did not open her eyes. Maybe if he'd not swiped at her arm, if he'd asked in a polite way, or apologized for supposedly waking her, she would have changed seats. But instead she decided to sink herself into a cold and closed state from which she would not be roused. He jostled her arm again.

"Hey," he said more loudly. "I said my wife will change seats."

Patrice frowned as if a dream was being fractured, then turned her shoulder on him and ground her hips more deeply into the padding. The conductor came down the aisle. He had already punched her ticket so he didn't wake her. As the conductor took the straw-haired man's ticket, the arm jostler said, "I would like my wife to sit with me. She'll change seats with this woman."

"Miss," said the conductor. "Oh, miss."

"I'll trade," said a man somewhere, quietly.

Patrice had willed herself into a stubborn torpor.

The first man rose.

"Yeah. You two belong together," he said.

Another man took his place in the seat. Patrice was drifting strangely down some cold walls. Exhausted, she dropped into a short fit of sleep. Before she opened her eyes, she felt someone watching her. When she sat up and looked around, she saw it was Wood Mountain.

"Hi, Pixie."

She forgot to tell him to call her Patrice because she was so glad to see someone from home. The train ride had only lasted an hour so far, but already she was homesick. She was ready for the adventure to be over.

"Where are you going?" she asked him.

"Fargo. I've got a fight. Maybe."

His hair was newly cut, oiled, and swirled down over his forehead.

"You were good the other night. You should have won."

"Oh, you were there?"

He knew very well that she had been there with his cousin. He had wanted to win even more on their account. He'd felt their eyes on him.

"Yes, that timekeeper cheated. And you were good," she said again.

"That's what Barnes says."

Patrice nodded. Barnes.

"He's always talking you up. You like him?"

"No."

"How come? What's wrong with him?"

"There's nothing wrong with him."

"So . . ."

"Should I like him just because there's nothing wrong with him?"

"I guess no."

They sat there, awkward. The conductor announced the next stop, not long enough to get a real lunch. Patrice had packed some food, to save money. She brought out her yellow pail and removed the lid. It was packed with Zhaanat's pemmican—deer meat, sweet juneberries, musky Pembina berries, sugared tallow, all these ingredients dried and pounded to a fluff. Wood Mountain took a small handful. Patrice took a pinch.

"Fills you up good," said Wood Mountain.

"I'm counting on that," said Patrice. "I'm going to the Cities to find my sister."

"I heard. What about your job?"

"Valentine gave me her days."

"That was decent."

His remark didn't seem to lead anywhere, only requiring agreement, and they sat again in silence until the train stopped.

"Let's get out and stretch our legs," said Wood Mountain.

"I don't want to lose my seat," said Patrice.

"If that guy tries to take it again, I'll fight him."

"Then I'm staying. No fights on my account."

Wood Mountain got out at the stop and jogged up and down the station platform. Patrice put her coat on his seat so that nobody would sit down, but still, when the train was boarding again a wiry little woman stopped by the seat, nodded, and asked, "Whose coat?"

"His," said Patrice, nodding at Wood Mountain, who stood in the aisle. The woman frowned at the incongruity of the blue swing coat, and the sturdy Indian, but moved on. Wood Mountain sat down. He was still catching his breath. His hair had flopped down on one side. He combed and pressed it back into place.

"Wind sprints," he said.

"What are those?"

"Short bursts of speed."

"That makes sense. You have to fight in short bursts."

He was surprised that she understood right away. She asked him about his training regimen. He told her that he had a hill he sprinted up about a hundred times every day. He told her about the cans he'd filled with sand and welded shut. About the rope skipping and the speed bag he'd hung on a branch. He tried not to mention Barnes because there was something about her not liking him. A feeling. He wasn't one for giving names to things. Or finding their basis. His feelings were like weather. He just suffered or enjoyed them. And now she was taking a little jackknife from her pocketbook and cutting a tiny shred from a thumb-shaped piece of bark. She folded up the pocketknife and popped the shred in her mouth. She opened her hand: there was another shaving, fragrant.

"Have some."

He held the piece of bark on one side of his jaw, then the other, letting the mellow tang of spice fill his mouth.

"What is this stuff?"

She shook her head. "It's, I don't know, miswanagek."

"What's it good for?"

"Cramps."

"What kind of cramps?"

He looked at her and she bent her face away, flinching at herself, and mumbled, "Muscle cramps!"

"I get those." He hid a smile, as if he hadn't noticed.

"You can make a tea. The tea is better."

"So where are you going when you get to the Cities?"

"I have a couple addresses."

"Where your sister lives?"

"No."

"So the plan is you walk the streets until you run into her?"

"Maybe."

"That's not a plan."

"Maybe not. But what would you do? Go to the police?"

"Not exactly."

"What?"

"Go to the not-police. Sorry to put it this way. She might have got into trouble. So, what I'm saying is, go to the scum."

"Oh, well, okay, but I don't know. How do I find the scum?"

"Rises to the top. Just look around. Find the questionable people who are in charge of things."

"What things?

He didn't know that much about Pixie. He wasn't sure how far to get into it.

"Not good things," he finally said.

"Liquor?"

"Yes."

"What else is there that's bad?"

He gazed at her. She simply wanted to know.

"You worry me," he said.

# A Bill

*≻═┤═≺*

To provide for the termination of Federal supervision over the property of the Turtle Mountain Band of Chippewa Indians in the States of North Dakota, South Dakota, and Montana, and the individual members thereof; for assistance in the orderly relocation of such Indians in areas of greater economic opportunity; and for other purposes.

There it was, in the first line of the dry first sentence, the word termination, which instantly replaced in Thomas's mind that word emancipation with its powerful aura of expanse. In the newspapers, the author of the proposal had constructed a cloud of lofty words around this bill—emancipation, freedom, equality, success—that disguised its truth: termination. Termination. Missing only the prefix. The ex.

THE WIND rattled the metal blinds of the plant's industrial windows. Thomas pulled on his jacket. He had not finished eighth grade until age eighteen because he had worked with his father. They had harvested and planted, weeded and sweat. One summer he had dug that well. After he'd finished grade eight, Thomas had tried to educate himself, mainly by reading everything he could find. When he needed to calm his mind, he opened a book. Any book. He had never failed to feel refreshed, even if the book was no good. So it wasn't the words in the rest of the bill that stymied understanding, it was the way they were put together.

> Be it enacted by the Senate and the House of Representatives of the United States of America in Congress assembled, that the purpose of this Act is to provide for the termination of Federal supervision over the trust and restricted property of the Turtle Mountain Band of Chippewas in North Dakota, South Dakota, and Montana, for the disposition of Federally owned property acquired or withdrawn for the administration of the affairs of such Indians, for the intensification of an orderly program of facilitating the relocation and placement of such Indians in a self-supporting economy to the end that federal services and supervision with respect to such Indians may be discontinued as no longer necessary, and for the termination of Federal services furnished to such Indians because of their status as Indians.

He threw down the pages. Walked his round. But after he finished, he picked up the papers, put them back in order, and replaced them in his briefcase. He was empty of response. There was a hollow feeling, a thrumming, a sense that his body had become a drum. That anyone could knock on him and get a sound. That the sound, even if defiant, would be meaningless. And that whoever used the drumstick knew this and was pitiless. That person would strike and strike until the hide was worn out.

Who was that person? The person beating this drum? Who had put this bill together? Thomas wondered.

THAT SAME morning, Thomas made an expensive phone call to his old friend and boarding-school buddy Martin Cross. Martin was the tribal chairman of Fort Berthold, a reservation in western North Dakota, shared by the Mandan, Arikara, and Hidatsa, which was Martin's tribe. From a fellow boarding-school cutup, Martin had become a source of wisdom and a strategic fighter for Indian rights. Martin told him who was beating the drum: Arthur V. Watkins.

"He's the most powerful man in Congress," said Martin Cross.

"That's not good."

"No. And I don't know if it matters, but he's a Mormon."

Thomas paused. What Cross said sounded vaguely familiar.

"You know any Mormons?" asked Martin Cross.

"I don't think so."

"They haven't got to you. They'll come around yet. It's in their religion to change Indians into whites."

"I thought that was a government job."

"It's in their holy book. The more we pray, the lighter we get."

"I could stand to drop a few pounds."

"Not that kind of lighter," Martin laughed. "They think if you follow their ways your skin will bleach out. They call it lightsome and gladsome."

"They'll have some work to do on your tough old hide."

"Yours too."

Thomas cut the call short, remembering the tribe was broke. In fact, they were broker than he'd thought when he took the job, which supposed to pay thirty dollars a month. He hadn't yet actually paid himself. But the senator who'd pushed this bill from his side of Congress had a name, anyway. Arthur V. Watkins.

# Who?

AT WORK the next night, he laid out the pages again.

SO IT comes down to this, thought Thomas, staring at the neutral strings of sentences in the termination bill. We have survived smallpox, the Winchester repeating rifle, the Hotchkiss gun, and tuberculosis. We have survived the flu epidemic of 1918, and fought in four or five deadly United States wars. But at last we will be destroyed by a collection of tedious words. *For the disposition of, for the intensification of, for the termination of, to provide for, et cetera.*

He was back at his desk and had just punched 2 a.m. The last good sleep he'd had was how long ago? In the old house. He put down the paper and began to write to Archie. *As you know, Mama has taken over the care of a bright and beaming young fellow. Martin is a sort of altar boy to Wade. I don't mean to be sacrilegious, but when I see Martin standing by Wade with his shoes, or alongside him with a pitchfork or shovel, whatever he might need, I can't help but remember my old job at Holy Mass. Martin listens to Wade, too, and the other morning he said to me that Wade kept mentioning my clock and how I'm always punching it. With a sad look, Martin then observed, "With all that punching, it must be broke to a hundred pieces by now!"*

Thomas propped his head up in his hands, shielding his eyes.

The next thing he knew, he was jolted awake. Brain swimming, pulse scudding, he was sure that someone had tried to break into the plant. He turned off his lamp and lifted the steel flashlight, useful as a possible bludgeon. He didn't punch the clock because the click would echo. Soundlessly he stepped across the floor of the main room and into the acid washing room. He had always thought it entirely possible that someone, imagining that the jewels were typical gemstones, might break in hoping to find treasure. He had the flashlight and his keys. He could wallop them with his flashlight and rake with his keys. But he would probably be overpowered, tied up, slung into the bathroom. He hoped his head wouldn't hit a fixture. If he couldn't think and reason, he would not be able to oppose this bill.

Thomas crept along and at each new checkpoint found the jewel plant empty. Humming where it should hum. Silent where it was always silent. Booming and rattling in the usual places. Then he stepped into the dark workshop and saw the great silver arc of a white owl plastered against the window, stretching its wings. It was pecking at the glass, fighting its own reflection. The sky behind the owl was black, moonless, glinting with stars. Thrilled, he felt for his keys then tiptoed outside to see the owl more clearly.

Who?

He moved slowly around the outside of the building. The snowy swiveled its head to watch him, then stretched out its down-plumed leg and flexed its black talons. The bird seemed annoyed, blinked, eyed Thomas severely, and with a last suspicious peck at its glass rival, began to preen its feathers. Thomas watched it for a long time before it flowed soundlessly upward. He stood there a moment, waiting to see where it went. But it was gone, sucked into the black sky. Thomas had no jacket and no cigar so he went back inside and punched the time clock. Beside the time, which should have been entered on the hour, he wrote, *Went outside to answer Snowy Owl's question, Who? Owl not satisfied with answer.*

# Indian Joke

WALTER VOLD adjusted his reading glasses and peered more closely at the time card. Snowy Owl! He passed the card back across the desk to Doris Lauder.

"Typical Indian joke," said Vold.

He had noticed that she'd entirely stopped wearing perfume. That she edged away when he tried to get close. That when he had gotten close, she smelled oddly of mold.

"How so?" said Doris. "I don't get it."

She'd washed her hands with the mildewed rag from under the sink. She did this every day. She was willing to bear the smell so he didn't sniff her every time she passed.

"How shall I put it."

Vold tapped ostentatiously at his chin, hard as brass.

"The word is . . . the word is . . ."

To his relief, a word came into his head.

"Cryptic."

"Oh. I still don't get it."

Doris took back the time card with her moldy fingers, and studied the words again. LaBatte dawdled outside the door with a trash bin he was emptying into a larger trash bin. Vold took the card from Doris's hand.

"Mr. LaBatte," called Vold, nodding and gesturing as though he was signaling an airplane, "please come into my office and clear something up."

LaBatte came in, hard round belly leading, looking like an expert. Vold handed Thomas Wazhashk's time card to LaBatte.

"Miss Lauder is curious about what this means," said Vold.

LaBatte held out the card away from his face and scowled, mouthing the words. He looked up at the two of them and over-assumed an air of expertise.

"It means that Thomas the Muskrat went out to smoke a cigar. He sometimes will smoke a Snowy Owl brand. I'd say he got locked out, had to get back in through a window. Or he could have gone right through the wall, like a mist."

LaBatte walked off, laughing. Vold and Doris began laughing too.

"Very funny! Walked through the wall like a mist. Typical Indian joke right there!"

LABATTE STOPPED laughing as soon as he was out the door, rumbling down the hall. His eyes popped as he wheeled the cart ever faster. The mention of the owl was too disturbing. If Thomas had seen an owl, it meant a death. Soon. LaBatte was whisking through mental lists of people who might die. People he wouldn't mind if they died. People he would mind very much if they died. People he would be terrified and sick at heart if they died. And then himself, very close to Thomas, in a way, as they went to school together and sometimes overlapped at work. Yes, he was close enough to Thomas for the victim to be himself. Plus, he was guilty and in danger of being punished.

Very low, to the empty hallway, he muttered, "Help me, Roderick."

# Who?

✦━┃━✦

THOMAS WAS of the after-the-buffalo-who-are-we-now generation. He was born on the reservation, grew up on the reservation, assumed he would die there also. Thomas owned a watch.
He had no memory of time according only to the sun and
moon. He spoke the old language first, and also spoke English
with a soft grain and almost imperceptible accent. This accent
would only belong to those of his generation. This indefinably
soft but firm way of speaking would be lost. His generation
would have to define themselves. Who was an Indian? What?
Who, who, who? And how? How should being an Indian relate
to this country that had conquered and was trying in every
way possible to absorb them? Sometimes the country still ac-
tively hated Indians, true. But more often now, a powerfully
glorious sensation poured forth. Wars. Citizenship. Flags. This
termination bill. Arthur V. Watkins believed it was for the best.
To uplift them. Even open the gates of heaven. How could Indians hold themselves apart, when the vanquishers sometimes
held their arms out, to crush them to their hearts, with something like love?

# Flags

*⊱━━⊰*

THAT YEAR, his father was gaunt, his cheekbones jutting out. Thomas was always hungry. They were down to desperation food then—a bit of bannock smeared with deer fat. The day schools on the reservation gave out just one meal. The government boarding school would feed three meals. The government boarding school was a day's wagon ride if you started well before dawn. Thomas's mother, Julia, or Awan, wept and hid her face as he went away. She had been torn—whether to cut his hair herself. They would cut his hair off at the school. And to cut hair meant someone had died. It was a way of grieving. Just before they left, she took a knife to his braid. She would hang it in the woods so the government would not be able to keep him. So that he would come home. And he had come home.

THE FIRST thing Thomas noticed about the school was the repetition of striped cloth—red and white. Also blue parts. Flags. They were everywhere, dangling or hanging off poles, pinned onto collars, surrounding the blackboards, draped over doors. At first, he thought they were pleasing decorations. The teacher showed him that he must place his hand on his heart and repeat words the other children already knew. All while staring at the flag. Thomas copied the teacher's words though he did not know what she was saying. Gradually, the sounds took shape in his mind. And still later, bits and pieces were added to the design. He had been there a few months when he heard the phrase *a flag worth dying for,* and a slow chill prickled.

# Log Jam 26

＊┼＊

AS THE train pulled into Fargo, Wood Mountain wanted Patrice to write down the two addresses.

"Why?"

"Because you're a baby. I mean, not streetwise. This way I have a trail in case you get lost."

"I can find my way."

"In the bush, sure. You and your cramp bark."

"I have been in town."

"A city, Pixie."

"What do you know about it?"

"More than you. Once, I visited my sister. And I've had fights down there."

"Did you win any?"

"No."

"Well. You should have. Okay, here is where I'm going."

Pixie—Patrice—wrote the addresses on a scrap of newspaper. She didn't tell him about the emergency address. Bernadette was his half sister. Wood Mountain pocketed the bit of paper. As he rose, he looked down at her. Without thinking, like it was natural, he tried out the smile he practiced in the shaving mirror. Oh, and she responded, didn't she? Looked at him wonderingly. He felt her eyes on him as he turned around. Watching as he walked down the aisle of the train and out the door. . . .

And she was thinking, *What was that?* That smile? Like he saw it on some cheap movie poster. A smile like the dough in her lunch bucket—sad and raw. Not even half baked. Patrice settled back into her seat and took out the syrup bucket. She ate several pinches of the pemmican, looking out the window into downtown Fargo. The Empire Tavern. She saw Wood Mountain walking along. Swinging his duffel bag. If he walked into the bar she'd never speak to him again. He walked past.

Okay, maybe sometime, she thought as the train pulled out.

SHE SLEPT so hard the pattern on the seat's upholstery bit into her cheek. When she woke, and put her fingers to her face, she could feel the dimples from the harsh cloth. They had come a long way and were passing through St. Cloud. In no time at all now they would be in Minneapolis. The wiry lady had claimed the seat beside Patrice. Now she was using narrow silver needles to knit a white froth of yarn into a weblike blanket for a baby. The delicate folds streamed down and puddled in her lap. Patrice looked away from her, but the lady noticed that her seatmate was awake and introduced herself.

"Bitty."

"Patrice."

"What takes you to the Cities?"

"I'm looking for my sister, and her baby."

"Ohhh?" Bitty's face quivered as she talked. She was a flat emaciated woman. Her scalp showed through colorless wisps of hair. Her lips were pale and thin. "How is your sister? And her baby? I supposed you're going to visit the new baby."

The woman anxiously pursed her lips and squinted at her needles.

"Not exactly. She's lost. I mean, we haven't heard from her.

And I've never met the baby. I'm worried something has happened."

"Oh my goodness no, no, no! I hope nothing to the baby!"

The woman's needles continued to switch back and forth. The insectlike clicking intensified. Suddenly the woman turned to her, with an air of delivering a solution to the problem. "I'm going to pray for your sister."

"Thank you," said Patrice.

The woman closed her eyes but continued on without missing a stitch. Her clay-colored lips moved. A sweetness played across her features. Patrice turned away and shut her eyes to sop up the remnants of sleep. When she turned back, the woman was still praying and knitting. The blanket was even longer. Patrice nearly spoke, but the woman's lips were still moving, and her murmur was intense, nearly audible. Patrice turned away again and stared out the window. The flat lush fields were left behind and replaced by stands of oak and sandy pastures with milk cows grazing. In the distance, to one side, she could see a clump of tall brown structures. Abruptly, the back lots of tumbled houses and then brick warehouses lined the tracks. The pace slowed to a mild rocking and the size of the buildings increased. Soon taller buildings reared to either side of the tracks. Once, another train blurred past, inches away, like in a dream. At last, they slowed to a creeping pace and entered a structure of shadows and tall pillars where the train hissed to a stop.

"Here," said the woman, opening her eyes.

She rolled up the filmy blanket and handed it to Patrice.

"This is for your sister's baby."

The little woman slipped into the aisle.

"Thank you!" Patrice called, but the little woman did not turn around. Patrice held the blanket to her face for a moment.

It had a null scent—it didn't even smell of yarn. No, wait, there was something. A sort of powdery private sadness. The woman had lost a baby, Patrice thought. But the blanket felt like an insurance that she would find Vera and her baby. She pulled her makeshift suitcase from the rack over her seat and stuffed the good-omen baby blanket inside. Then she followed the other passengers along the aisle.

Patrice stepped down onto the platform and followed a sign to the main ticketing and waiting area. There were benches, like church pews but with intermittent armrests. The wood was solid, warmed and stained by so many people sitting. She sat down too. She remembered her lipstick, and applied a fresh coat with help from her compact mirror. People looked up, as they always do when a woman applies lipstick in public. Sometimes, Patrice did this as a test, or as a way of checking behind her, if she felt threatened. This time she looked into the mirror just to gather her determination. This was bound to happen. She was bound not to have foreseen something. What came next. How was she going to get from the train station to the address? She had supposed she could walk. Miles were nothing to her. But now she had seen enough of the size of the city to know it was more than miles. It was street after confusingly similar street. She needed advice. Maybe one of the women at the ticket window. She put away the lipstick and walked over to the window.

"Take a cab, dear. Just wait outside on one of those benches."

A taxicab, of course! Like in magazine stories. Patrice went through tall handsome doors, fitted with brass, and sat down on a bench near the curb. A car pulled up. She showed the address to the driver and asked how much it would cost to go there.

"Nothing," said the driver. "I'm going there anyway."

"No," she said. "I will pay you something."

"We'll see. Special price for a pretty lady."

She opened the door to get into the backseat.

"Sit up front, why don't you?" said the driver.

"No, thanks," she said. She was positive that she remembered the backseat from a magazine story. She would not be fooled. The man got out of the car and put her bag on the car's backseat. He opened the passenger door for her and ushered her into the car. All of this happened in a matter of seconds. He was a broad brown-haired freckled man with freckled hands. His suit was rumpled and baggy, and he seemed in a hurry. She sat in the front seat. He had that sharp smell, like Barnes, but also different, like he'd had a drink already. She wished that she'd taken a different cab. And it surprised her a little that he wore a suit and tie. He hadn't let up talking for a moment and was driving forcefully along, taking turns with great swings of his arms, sweating although the day was cool.

"You're from where? Never heard of it. What's your friend look like? What was she wearing last time you saw her? Say she has a baby, huh? And you're from where? Never heard of it. There's lots to do here. You'll like it here. You want a job? There's jobs. I can get you a job right now. You have to know the right people. I know the right people. A cabdriver? No, I'm not a cabdriver. I drive people around but I'm not a cabdriver. Here. I gotta stop here and see a fellow. You come in with me. Sit down, take a load off. No? Well I don't take no for an answer. Come on. I'll getcha going."

They had stopped in a zone that said No Parking at Any Time.

"I'm Earl. They call me Freckle Face. And that thing's for other people," he said when she pointed at the sign.

He got out, barged around to her side of the car, opened the door, and tried to coax her out. Letters of looping unlighted neon were fixed above a door. Log Jam 26. The place looked like a bar to Patrice.

"I'm sorry," she said, knowing she'd made a mistake. "I don't go into bars."

"Me neither! This place isn't a bar. No. It's a camera shop."

Patrice turned around, leaned into the backseat, and tugged her suitcase into her arms. She stood up beside the car holding the suitcase.

"I'm going now. How much do I owe you?"

"You don't owe me nothing."

His arm went around her and he tried to propel her forward. He would have had no luck except that another man, skinny with a black ducktail, was there suddenly. They held her elbows as she gripped the suitcase to her chest and together the two men swept her across the sidewalk. Through the doors. There was a grimy lobby, red carpeting. A dim space full of tables and chairs. A lazy muttering all around.

"Where's the cameras?" cried Patrice.

In the center of the club, a lighted tank of water. Huge and glowing, it cast a false greenish light on the surrounding tables. All of this passed by as in a panic she was whisked across the main floor, where she thought she'd better stay. There was a mirrored wall reflecting bottles of liquor. A dark corridor like a trap. How had she found the scum so fast?

Patrice crumpled to the floor in a stubborn heap. The men tried to pull her up, but she made herself extremely heavy. Wood Mountain hadn't told her how to deal with scum, just that she must find them. She forced the weight of her body to cling to the floor. "Let me go!" she yelled. With that yell, she triggered something in herself. An unguessed-of force. She reared up, swung her bag at the ducktail man. Connected. He bent over, grunting. A man drinking at the bar slid off his stool, walked crisply over to the scene. He was wearing a gray jacket and gray tie. His face was lean, yellowed, his eyes shadowed with sickness, glittering under the gray fedora he hadn't taken off even to drink his drink. His pants drooped around his skinny legs.

"What's wrong with her?"

"She's sick."

"I am not! They're trying to kidnap me!"

"That true, Earl? She seems like a nice girl. What is your motive here?"

"Trying to give her the job!"

"Well, let her sit down, have a drink, like in a regular place. Talk it over. Don't just drag her in. What's wrong with you?"

"It's how we got Babe the other time."

"You just dragged Hilda in here? You guys are apes."

Freckle Face let go of Patrice's arms, brushing them lightly as if in apology. Or to remove his behavior.

"It's unbecoming, how you just dragged her in here," said the drinking man. He nodded down to Patrice. "I'm sorry, miss."

"I don't suppose she would have come in here by herself," said Freckle Face. "It's not a clean place."

"It is a clean place," said the man in the gray suit.

"If you say so. But we need somebody tonight. And look at this girl. Don't she look like a waterjack?"

"Just Babe's size," said the dark skinny man. "For the outfit."

"That's what I thought."

"That's about enough," said Patrice. She stepped forward,

tried to gather her wits, disguise her shaking. Again, she found that her own actions built up her own boldness. She slammed away the men's hands, spoke loudly. "I'm here looking for my sister. I have to get back home in one week. He told me this was a camera store. I don't go to bars. I don't like men who go to bars. I want to go to a certain address. Find my sister. She's in trouble."

"She's an Indian too?" the skinny little man wondered.

"Jeezus. The average IQ intellect around here is about thirty," said the man in the beautiful hat. "Of course she's an Indian, Dinky, she's her sister."

"Well I didn't know," said Dinky.

"Camera store?" The jaundiced man raised the brim of his hat. Freckle Face shrugged.

"I'm Jack Malloy," said the man. He held his hand out. Patrice took it. The hand was cold and dry. Patrice was startled and looked more closely at him. He was definitely ill. Or maybe cold hands warm heart. Vera would have said that.

"Come. Sit down. Have a drink."

"I don't drink. I want to go to Bloomington Avenue."

"Why the hell you want to go over there?" asked Dinky. "It's all Indians."

"You just beat the dummy record," Jack said. "Get out of here. We have a lovely Indian princess we are trying to give a job to and you keep insulting her. Look, miss, you can have a soda pop. Billy in the back will make you a hamburger sandwich. On the house. All you have to do is listen to the job description.

"You *are* an Indian lady, right?" he said to Patrice. "Because you are a tad light, but . . ."

"From my father."

"Ah. The daughter of a chieftain?"

Chief Firewater, thought Patrice. She looked around the place. There were small windows, like portholes, and some tables underneath. She was hungry.

"If we can sit next to the door under one of those round windows, I will listen," she said. "And I want that hamburger sandwich."

"Absolutely. After you," said Jack, flourishing his arm. She walked to the table by the window and sat down on a little black chair. The table was painted deep purple and the surface was sticky. She put the suitcase on the chair beside her. Jack sat down across from her, a drink in his hand.

"Your traveling case is charming," he said. "Rustic." He gestured at the bartender.

"The refreshments are coming," he went on. "As well as my apologies. They know not what they do."

"I think they do know," said Patrice.

"Incompletely though," said Jack.

The bartender brought an orange Nehi soda, ice-cold, and set it down beside a glass of ice.

"So here's the thing." Jack hunched toward her. "This place changed owners last year, see. Before, it was an underwater theme. Mermaid Palace. Lots of shells and fish. The big tank. A trained mermaid worked shows in the tank."

"Trained mermaid?"

"Yeah. Wore a glitter tail. The guy who bought this place, W. W. Pank, made his money off timber so as a tribute to north-woods industry he decided on a lumbering theme. Thus, Log Jam. 26 is just a number. There is a Paul Bunyan type of theme to the drinks and such. The menu. We're still making changes with the décor. And of course the tank, which is what the place is known for. You heard of Babe?"

"No."

"Paul's blue ox. She hauls his logs. She's his sidekick. So that's the outfit. Babe."

"Outfit for what?"

"Instead of a mermaid outfit, a Babe outfit. Hilda used to wear the outfit, do the underwater tricks. Ox tricks. People love it, come from miles around, all through the city and beyond. They love the waterjack. I'm surprised she has such a following already, but there you have it. And shame on me. I have not even asked your name."

"Doris," said Patrice.

"Doris what?"

Patrice blanked out for a moment.

"Doris Barnes," she said.

"Do you have an Indian name? Is it respectful to ask? Or perhaps it is a secret?"

"A secret," said Patrice.

"As it should be. However, I could see you as . . . say . . . Princess Waterfall."

"No."

"Well, Doris. Have you any interest in the job?"

"Swimming around in an ox costume? No."

"You haven't even asked the salary."

"I don't care about the salary."

"Fifty dollars per night. Plus you keep all of your tips every other night."

Patrice was silent. Counting the tips, which she couldn't estimate, it was more than she made each week at the jewel bearing plant. For one night's work.

"I don't really want to," she said.

"Would you like to see the outfit anyway?"

"For a laugh," said Patrice.

"Then come with me."

A chubby florid man set a platter before her. Arranged upon it was a hamburger, with sides of lettuce, pickles, fried potatoes, and coleslaw.

"Mind if I eat first?"

Jack smiled—his teeth were long, brown, broken. She wished that she hadn't seen his teeth. But then she took a bite of the hamburger and forgot. Briskly, neatly, efficiently, she devoured everything on the platter. She wiped the tips of her fingers on a purple napkin.

"Impressive," said Jack. "Pretty soon everything will be lumberjack—the napkins black and red checks and so on."

He thought a moment, observed her meticulously cleaned plate, and said, "Of course, you would also be served dinner after the show."

"All right, let's see the outfit," said Patrice. "But I want the lights turned on in that hallway."

"Whatever you say," said Jack.

She picked up her suitcase and walked beside Jack, who greeted those he passed with a sardonic twitch of his mouth. He walked down the hall, up a narrow stairway. Opened a door.

"Your dressing room."

Patrice peered in from the doorway. An ordinary room with a maroon-gray-swirled linoleum floor. There was a built-in dressing table with a mirror with lights around it. Bottles of foundation makeup and a messy array of lipsticks.

"Waterproof," said Jack, flourishing his hand at the litter.

The dressing-table chair was flecked with old white paint and had a stained pink flowered seat cushion. Jack walked over to open a deep closet. Removed a cloth bag from a large box, and unzipped it to reveal the outfit. There was a blue rubber wet suit with white hooves painted at the ends of the hands and feet. Two large white disks with scarlet centers were where the breasts would be. Patrice flinched. Was that a dark shadow between the cow legs? She looked away. Jack held the outfit reverently in his arms. In a hushed voice he asked if she would try it on. She stayed in the doorway.

"Of course I won't."

"Would you just, please, hold it up to yourself?"

"All right."

Patrice pressed the rubber suit against her chest, the absurd hooves dangling.

Jack stared at her, sighed, shook his head.

"It looks like it would just fit. Perfectly."

Patrice thrust it back at him. With great care, Jack arranged the rubber so as not to put strain on any part of the suit. He put the outfit away and opened a large hatbox, which contained a close-fitting blue rubber cowl with small white horns. It fastened under the chin.

"This is okay," said Patrice, putting on the blue hat. "But I don't like those white circles on the cow's chest."

"Ox. Babe's an ox. And as things go, of course, the costume is really quite modest, you must admit," murmured Jack. "Not much skin showing. Not at all. Just a lot of blue rubber."

"No thanks," said Patrice. The fifty dollars plus was difficult.

"Well, so look here," said Jack. "Let's talk about finding your sister. How are you going to go about that?"

"I'll just . . . look. Go to the last known address first."

"And where are you going to stay?"

"I have a girlfriend."

"A friend from home?"

"Sort of."

"You could stay here. It would be a room-and-board sort of deal just to tide us over."

"Sleep under a table? No thank you."

"We could put a cot in the room."

She remembered about scum, but Wood Mountain had given no details. Frustrating. Would she be all right if she avoided the liquor?

"Sounds like a trap."

"And a strong lock on the door. Or, if you want, we have a hotel next door. Regular place. Clean. Just no ceilings on the rooms. Locks there too."

"I think that I'll find a cab to the place I was going. Right now."

"We could help you."

"Find a cab? One that won't kidnap me?"

"Again, profound apologies. So uncalled for. No. We could help you find your sister. I mean, this is a nexus."

"I don't know what that is."

"A central place. Like a train terminal. Where everyone meets everyone else. Look. It's about one p.m. right now. I will personally drive you to your address. I will personally accompany you to the door to ask about your sister. And take you anywhere else that you want to look. If during that time you find a place to stay and a good lead on your sister's whereabouts, then we say so long, goodbye, farewell. If no luck, you come back and do tonight's show. That's all."

"Why would you do all that?"

"You *are* the waterjack."

Jack spoke dramatically, looking into her eyes. The whites of his eyes were yellowed, like old paper.

"What's so great about this outfit? It's just a cow suit—"

"Ox. Made of blue rubber."

Patrice shrugged. She was still in the doorway. Jack gazed dreamily past her.

"To get this outfit made? We had to find a costumier down in Chicago. He had to create the molds for the rubber. Had to get the rubber, natural and not synthetic rubber. And the dye. It is difficult to find a dye that will take hold in the rubber and come out so blue—so brilliant! Dramatic. Hard to make it so the dye won't run, either, while Babe is doing the show. A rubber that positively won't bleach out or stretch out of shape. Hard to find. A rubber that won't start smelling gamey—you couldn't smell a thing, could you? That's why we use a special powder to dry it and preserve it from the depredations of insects, ensuring the integrity of the rubber. It is a very special suit, Miss Doris Barnes. And you are the first woman I have seen who might possibly do justice to the lady who last wore the suit."

"Who was that lady?" asked Patrice.

"Hilda Kranz."

"So why isn't she here anymore? What happened to her?"

"She fell ill."

"Oh. Well, so maybe she'll get better."

"Gravely ill," said Jack.

"I'm so sorry."

They walked back onto the main floor of the bar.

"All right," said Patrice. "I'll let you drive me to where I want to go. Then we part ways."

"Very good," said Jack Malloy. "We part ways if you find your sister. If not, you do the show. I will get the keys from Earl."

"He was driving your car?"

"He always drives my car."

"I don't like this," said Patrice.

Her brain was swelling. Her skull felt too tight. She wasn't tired, but disoriented. It felt like more new things had happened to her in the past hour than in her entire life before.

## The Wake-Up Shave

THOMAS CROSSED his eyes, blinked rapidly. Twisted his skin. Gave himself a snake burn. Spoke out loud. The hardest hour. And not even an owl to hear him.

"What else do you want? Us living on the edge of a handkerchief? Done. Dying out as quickly as possible. Done. Dying out with agreeable smiles. Check. Brave smiles. Check. Pledged to your flag. Check. Check. Check. Done."

Falon flashed into the room in his olive greatcoat. Then strode through the wall like a mist.

The wall looked spongy where Falon had walked through. Thomas went over, put his hands on the painted plasterboard. The dull green-gray was hard and cold.

"You got the best of us," said Thomas.

He turned from the wall and glanced at the band saw. Roderick was perched there, grinning in a mad way, like he would bite into the doctor's hand.

THOMAS STOOD. He'd brought his shaving kit from home. It was an experiment. Perhaps holding a straight razor to his own throat would keep him awake in the final hour before dawn. He gave himself the closest and most perfect shave a man could manage, contorting his tongue in his cheek, finding every whisker. It worked. That morning, and every morning after, he greeted the morning shift perfectly shaved and combed, alert and smelling of Old Spice.

## The Old Muskrat

❋—|—❋

"WHAT DID you all do in the beginning? To keep the land?"

"It was sign or die."

"How did you keep the last of it?"

"First they gave us this scrap, then they tried to push us off this scrap. Then they took away most of the scrap. Now, what you are saying is they want to push us off the edge of the scrap."

"How did you hold on?"

Biboon's breathy wheezing old man's laughter.

"I was young. But I was part of it. We did hold on. By our fingernails. And toenails. And teeth."

"How did you finally make them agree to it? The last of the land? What we have now?"

"We got together on it. Stuck together on it. Aisens, Misko-biness, Ka-ish-pa, all of them, Wazhashk too, kept clinging on and clinging on. We had to confront those settlers when they came on our boundaries. We almost went to war on that, but we kept our heads. We knew what would happen if we killed any of those settlers. We confronted them. We stuck together on that. Then we put up a delegation."

"How did you put up a delegation?"

"We petitioned for it. Don't forget, we had to go through the farmer in charge and that there Indian Agent out of Devils Lake. But we convinced them anyway. We wrote a letter. We got a school Indian to write the letter. And when we went there, we had, what you call them, signatures."

"A petition."

"Eyah."

"We could start there. Get everyone in the tribe to sign it."

"That would be something."

"Then we might have to put up a delegation."

Thomas blew across the tin cup of scalding tea he'd just made for the two of them. Biboon took a drink of his.

"I'll take the petition idea to the council. Emergency meeting tonight. Still, we're just an advisory committee. We have to answer to the Bureau."

"Look here," said Biboon. "This thing is different now. Survival is a changing game. How many people lose out if the government breaks with us?"

Thomas stared at his father. Sometimes he came out with things. As if he'd had his eyes on the workings of the reservation without setting foot in town. His implication . . . other people need us for their own reasons. Neighboring towns need us. That or want nothing to do with us. That or they could be afraid they would be saddled with a lot of poor people. Thomas would have to think this out.

"We're not nothing. People use our work. You got your teachers, nurses, doctors, horse-trading bureaucrats in the superintendent's office. You got your various superintendents. You got your land-office employees and records keepers."

All of these jobs and titles could be expressed in Chippewa. It was much better than English for invention, and irony could be added to any word with a simple twist. Biboon went on.

"Make the Washington D.C.s understand. We just started getting on our feet. Getting so we have some coins to jingle.

Making farms. Becoming famous in school like you. All that will suffer. It will be wiped out. And the sick people, where will they go? They sent us their tuberculosis. It is taking us down. We don't have money to go to their hospitals. It was their promise to exchange these things for our land. Long as the grass grows and the rivers flow."

"I still see grass. I hear the rivers are running."

"And they are still using the land," said Biboon.

"Still using the hell out of it," said Thomas. "But trying to pretend they didn't sign a contract to pay the rent."

The tea was cool enough to drink. The bitterness was comforting.

THE COMMUNITY building had a room set aside for gatherings, and that night Thomas convened the meeting of the advisory committee. They used Robert's Rules of Order, roughly translated into Chippewa. Thomas called the meeting to order and the secretary, Juggie Blue, read the minutes in both languages. Some members of the committee spoke Chippewa or Cree. Others spoke Michif—French and Cree. The languages had bits of English mixed in like salt. So they muddled along, passing the copy of the bill from hand to hand, reading bits of it out loud, arguing about the meaning. As they studied the language of the bill, anxiety seeped into the room.

"It looks to me like they want it all, finally."

"Relocate us. Haul us out of here."

"Want the ishkoniganan. Even the leftovers."

"We had an agreement. They broke it. No warning."

Louis Pipestone, whose son had barely survived the Korean War, and was still recovering in a military hospital, sat motionless. He stared down at the back of his hands, splayed on the table.

Joyce Asiginak said, "They want to 'relocate.' That's fancy for 'remove.' How many times were we removed? No counting. Now they want to send us to the Cities."

There was silence and the rustle of paper. Moses read the words out loud.

orderly relocation of such Indians

He set down the paper, unable to continue.

"Such Indians. Such Indians are we," said Louis Pipestone in a slow leaden voice. "Such Indians as can be the wasted in battle. The sergeant waved my son forward. He went alone. *Test the water.*"

Nobody spoke. Pipestone's boy had lost his mind, it was said, from being burned. Louis had gone to visit him. Come home and said no word for five days. Thomas broke the silence by suggesting a petition to protest the termination bill. Figure out how to get as many tribal members as possible to sign it.

"I will type out this petition," said Juggie. "Staple pages to the back for people to sign. We should also get hold of Millie."

Millie Cloud was Louis Pipestone's daughter. She was in college. Maybe she could do something, Juggie said.

"And me," said Louis, "I will bring these papers around to everyone and I will get it signed."

"Are you sure you want to take it on?" said Juggie to him, quietly.

Louis was a big man, like a buffalo, with a massive head and hunched shoulders. His legs were short and bowed, as if they'd bent under the strain of the top half of Louis. When Louis smiled, his cheeks bunched up like small round apples. His nickname was Cheeks. Now he smiled at Juggie. His big face sweetened.

"I got to do something. Can't just sit."

Thomas knew that Louis was not just sitting. He had an allotment on the edge of the reservation, on grazing land. He had help. His young daughter worked it with him, and Wood Mountain came over there to pitch in, but still. A small ranch was a difficult proposition. They kept a racing horse or two. Brought them up to Manitoba. Louis's son had sent a letter home from boot camp, Thomas remembered. Telling his father that army discipline was easy after Fort Totten. Louis was really saying that even the small amount of sitting he did was unbearable.

"Good," said Thomas. "It's important to get this going right now. It looks like this bill—we should call it by its name, House Concurrent Resolution 108, HCR 108—may it go down in infamy—"

"Hear, hear," said Moses Montrose.

"House Concurrent Resolution 108, we need another copy now. So bring along the one we have with the petition. Explain it, what we learned, how we view it. Would anyone like to move so?"

There was a motion, a second, a vote. The papers were turned over to Louis Pipestone.

"Also," said Thomas. "I would like to move we refer to House Concurrent Resolution 108 as the Termination Bill. Those words like emancipation and freedom are smoke."

"Hear, hear," said Moses, in a lordly way that made people laugh.

The next order of business was getting together a group of people to meet with the BIA in order to have the bill explained. That meeting was going to be held down in Fargo. A distant drive. They had a week to arrange to get down there and attend the meeting.

"It can hardly be done!" said Juggie. "To take off work. To get the people together. Nobody even knows what this thing is."

"They will start knowing tomorrow," said Louis.

# The Waterjack

※ ——— ※

2214 BLOOMINGTON Avenue was a battered brown three-story house, peeling white paint, broken windows blanked out with cardboard. An assembly of mailboxes hung by the front door. Next to the mailboxes, what looked like a list of inhabitants. Patrice paced questingly in the dead yard. Jack stood on the sidewalk, smoking.

"I'll stay here and watch for signs of life," he said.

The front steps had collapsed and there was no obvious way to get onto the porch. Patrice dragged a few things over from the littered yard, then assembled and climbed a makeshift pile of milk crates and boards. There was no name on the list that resembled her sister's. Patrice knocked on the front door. Abruptly, one of the rusted tin mailboxes gave up and clattered onto the porch, spilling a few envelopes. Even with the loud noise, nobody appeared. But the crash reverberated. Patrice had the sudden sense that the house had warned her. She shook off the feeling, knocked on the window next to the door. Thought she heard a scuffling sound inside. A dog started barking. Its bark was rough, high, desperate to live. She froze. Tears started into her eyes.

"Jack," she called. He didn't answer. The dog's voice weakened until it stopped. Patrice waited. Nothing. She picked up the scatter of envelopes to stuff back into the mailbox. Read the addresses first. One belonged to Vera Paranteau. The letter had come to her only, not to her husband, whom she had followed down to the Cities and who had apparently not married her, as she still had her own name. Patrice kept the envelope and stepped gingerly off the porch.

Standing on the sidewalk next to Jack, she tore open the envelope.

"Felony right there," he said.

She frowned at him.

"Tampering with the mail."

The letter was a personalized Last Notice (underlined in red) to inform Vera that her electricity would be turned off. It was dated July, two months ago.

"Next move," said Jack.

She looked at the house. Someone was in that house. The dog was being strangled or something.

"Jack," she said, "something's wrong with that dog."

"Maybe it doesn't like people on the porch."

"Wait." She walked around back. A strong garbage and piss smell came from the rear of the house. Two more cardboarded windows. But no sign of a person.

"Vera!" she called. "Vera!"

Nothing. Except the dog started up again, furious with hope.

She walked back to Jack.

"We have to go in there," she said.

"Breaking and entering," he said. "I will absolutely not flout the law."

The dog's rasping bark trailed off. She wavered, waited. Something so alien and wrong. Her skin prickled. Everything was trying to tell her something, but she couldn't decode the message. A cricket tuned up in the battered grass. At last she shook her head and handed over the second address, on Stevens

Avenue. Jack looked at the address and a wince of distaste flicked across his face. He flapped the paper.

"What?" said Patrice.

"I know the building. If you find her there, it won't be good."

THERE WERE several large square apartment buildings made of dark brown brick. The tiny patch of grass in front was mowed. The low bushes around the foundation clipped.

"This is not so bad," said Patrice.

"Don't be fooled by appearances," Jack said.

She stood on the front steps with Jack. No Paranteau on the list of inhabitants. They walked into the foyer. The small octagonal tiles, set in black-and-white rosettes, had been freshly mopped. Patrice was beginning to feel wobbly again. She might flood through the walls and doors. Still, they went to each apartment. Got no answer. Patrice put her hand to her face. Jack cupped her elbow in his hand.

"Are you . . . ?"

She tried to shake his hand away. Back at the bar it had been dry and cold. Now it was moist and hot.

"You should rest," said Jack, petting her wrist. "This must be mentally exhausting for you. We'll set up a cot in the dressing room."

She wrenched her arm from his humid grip. Then surprised herself by snapping her hand down on his wet wrist so hard that he flinched and stared at her. He grabbed at her with his other hand. She knocked that arm down with a quick vicious motion. A wood chop.

"There's one more place," said Patrice. "I'd like to go there. A friend. Bernadette Blue."

"Bernadette. As in Bernie? Bernie Blue? She's your pal?" Jack wrung his bruised hands and looked Patrice over in a harder, figuring way. He lighted a cigarette off the one he was smoking, and together they walked out of the building.

"So tell me again. Bernie Blue's your friend?"

He stared closely at her, his face glazed with an unhealthy sweat. Patrice gave up.

"No," she swung her head. The air pressed on her temples. "I can't say we're actually friends. A friend gave me this address so I could stay with Bernadette in a pinch."

"Listen." Jack seemed a little rattled, now, in earnest even. "You're better off in the dressing room at Log Jam 26. I swear."

ON THE way back downtown, in the car, Jack spoke to her. "Seems you're mixed up with certain places, certain people, and you just got here. At least you say you did." He shot a glance her way.

"I did just get here."

"But were you here before?"

"I wasn't."

"Because you don't belong here."

"Of course I don't. I wish I could go home right now."

"So what can happen to a girl in your situation, or your sister's situation, is this: with the unpaid bills and all, she runs out on the landlord. Makes it hard to get a new place. So maybe she changes her name, or maybe she moves in with somebody else. A friend, let's say. She pays the friend in money, or in services."

He eyed Patrice after the word services.

"My sister could do any number of jobs," said Patrice, oblivious. "But with a baby, that's harder."

"Oh, a baby."

"Yes, she has a baby."

"That's another story. Another complication. We should go, say, to where they go for help with babies. I wouldn't know about that."

"Can we do that now?"

"Jesus. No."

"We should go now. I want to go."

"They are almost closed. Besides."

"Besides what?"

"You might want to take a little rest before your show."

"Let me out. Let me out right now!"

"Doris Barnes, calm down. Please. This is not what we agreed to."

"No," said Patrice. "We had no agreement. Because I never said yes. However, I might consider. Not tips every other night. I want the tips every single night."

"Done," said Jack.

ON THE second floor of Log Jam 26, Jack set up the canvas cot. He found a pillow with a rumpled but clean pillowcase on it, batted it into shape. In the closet, there was a red wool blanket bound with a silky red ribbon. Hilda's. But what did it matter. The blanket and the pillow almost made Patrice cry. She could hardly stagger to the cot. Kick her shoes off. Lie down. A buzzing film of darkness came down over her and then she dissolved.

Patrice woke to *Doris Barnes, Doris Barnes*, someone shaking her arm, the smell of strong acidic coffee. She cried out and thrashed. No idea where she was. For a splitting moment, who she was. Then Jack's voice. "Settle down! You'll spill hot coffee all over yourself!" The awful shape of her reality.

"I can't do it."

"That's not what we agreed," said Jack. "Drink the coffee.

Eat the danish. Visit the bathroom down the hall. Then put on the suit."

He left her dressing room, leaving the lights on. The door creaked loudly. She ate the danish, which was cherry. Drank the coffee, black. She reached into her bag and took a handful of pemmican. Ate it slowly, pressing the tiny shreds up with a finger. At last she used the dirty bathroom down the hall. When she returned, the ox suit confronted her, unfolded in its open box.

"Fifty dollars," she said to the suit. "Plus tips. Every night."

She shoved a chair against the door, which creaked again. She took her clothing off carefully. There were nails in the walls, empty hangers. She hung up her blouse, skirt, light sweater. Her coat was already hanging and she could not remember having removed it. Her satchel sat on the extra chair. She was down to her brassiere and panties. Her money was in her brassiere. Unhappily, she removed her underwear. She looked around the room. Finally she folded her brassiere into a clump around her money, and wedged it into a space behind a drawer in the dressing table. She lifted the blue rubber suit out of its box and thought that she should start from the bottom.

Her feet fit comfortably into the painted hooves. She tugged the warm, pliant rubber. Smoothed it carefully along her ankles. The ox legs gripped her calves, knee, thighs, encasing her in a firm and resilient extra layer of flesh. She rolled the suit up her hips, across her belly, then moved her arms into the front legs. The suit fit ingeniously, and fastened in such a way that no water could enter. The hooves were cleverly split so she could use her thumbs and fingers. The hood, which fit below the horned cap, was snug and fastened easily below her chin, tightly over her ears, muffling sound. The dressing room contained a full-length mirror like the one in the Rolla store. She stepped before it and saw herself as alien and fascinating. The white targets over her breasts were different once the suit was on, and didn't bother her anymore. The shadow between her legs was just a trick of the light. A sinuous blue tail curled behind her, a droopy brush of hair at the end. She lowered the cap with the horns. Fastened the straps beneath her chin. The effect was not uncharming.

Jack knocked on the door. When she opened it, he pulled the cigarette he was about to light from his mouth, and held it pinched between his fingers for a frozen moment.

"Damn," he said softly, eyes wide. "Damn."

"I am ready."

"Yes you are you are you are. The first show's in half an hour. Does the suit feel okay?"

"It's comfortable."

"See? Quality."

He fiddled with the horned cap, adjusting the straps. She batted his hands away.

"The objects at the bottom of the tank are weights. Pick one up to keep you down. Drop it when you need to surface. Oh, I forgot, do you know how to swim?"

Patrice gave him a baffled look.

"Just asking."

"Late to be just asking."

"I'll assume yes. Now let me show you the standard water-jack moves."

Smoke eddied and wreathed around his head as he gripped his cigarette between his teeth and crooked his arms. Held both hands out as though cradling bowls of crystal goblets.

"Up right shoulder. Down right shoulder. Swivel hips. Over-the-shoulder peek. Tush wag. Bubbles. Kisses. Surface. Breathe.

Down again. Playful peekaboo. Tush wag with seesaw shoulder. Swivel hooves. Dukes up. Mock fight. Barrel roll. Ox writhe. Bubbles. Kisses. Surface. Breathe. Repeat and modify for twenty minutes. I'll signal. You have half an hour break. Then on again. Four shows."

"Right after I get my fifty dollars," said Patrice.

"Did I say that?"

"Plus tips."

"Really?"

"That's what we agreed to, Jack. And dinner afterward. Plus of course I sleep in this dressing room. Or I walk out of here, right now."

Jack laughed. "In the ox suit? I doubt it."

"Why don't you try me?"

"Such brinksmanship," said Jack. "I was kidding. Of course that's what we agreed to."

"Plus I want a bolt on my door. A key to the lock. If I don't get it, then I'll poke a hole in this suit."

"You're not very trusting. Are you sure you haven't been around here before?"

"My dad is a drunk."

"Oh, I get it," said Jack. "Mine was too."

He unhooked a key from his key ring, and gave it to her. She tested it in the door. He promised the bolt tomorrow. They walked out and she locked her door. She fit the key beneath the blue hood, behind her ear, and followed him to the end of the hall.

"Sit down," said Jack, touching a chair. Then he labored to pull open a trapdoor in the floor.

Noise surged up. And light. Wavering water light. Clinking of glass. Laughter. Bursts of talk. Jack left. Patrice sat in the chair

alone, waiting to be lowered into the tank. One day ago, overnight ago, she had laughed with her mother. They had enjoyed
the impudence of her disguise. What would her mother think
now? Mayagi. Strange. Maama kaajiig. Strange people. Gawiin
ingikendizo siin. I am a stranger to myself. Another person,
harder and bolder than the usual Patrice, had taken her over.
This Patrice was the one who forced Jack to bring her places, the
one who bargained for a key. This was again the sort of feeling
and thinking that could only be described in Chippewa, where
the strangeness was also humorous and the danger surrounding this entire situation was of the sort that you might laugh at,
even though you could also get hurt, and there were secrets involved, and desperation, for indeed she had nowhere, after her
unthinkable short immediate future rolling in the water tank,
nowhere to go but the dressing room down at the other end of
the second-floor hall of Log Jam 26.

# Left Hook

BARNES WAS waiting for Wood Mountain to enter the restaurant at the Powers Hotel in downtown Fargo. Jet-black glass. Mirrors. Plenteous breakfast. A snooty lady host with a small-town accent, who might not show an Indian boxer to his seat. He worried, but Wood Mountain saw Barnes's big haystack of hair immediately and walked over. The lady host didn't even follow him. Barnes had read over every item on the menu, twice. He loved a good breakfast. Wood Mountain sat down across from him in the low booth.

"Let's get the steak and eggs," said Barnes. "On me."

Wood Mountain was pretty sure that Barnes was buying him the fancy breakfast because the fight was off, and sure enough, it was. He crushed his fingers together, hiding his disappointment.

"All the way down here."

"Well, you nearly made it on the card. We'll introduce you to the guys. Now, at least, you can eat."

Wood Mountain poured half the cream in the little pitcher into his coffee. He'd trained like the devil, got his weight perfect, had his hair cut and styled, and no fight. But on the way down, he'd sat with Pixie.

"You know that girl Pixie?"

Barnes sharpened.

"What about her?"

"Sat beside her on the way down."

"So is she here, in town?" Barnes tried to ask casually, but Wood Mountain wasn't fooled. He took his time answering.

"Just passing through. She's on her way down to the Cities to look for her sister, Vera. Her husband's off the rails. Nobody's heard from her."

"Does Pixie have a place to stay down there?"

"Don't worry. She can take care of herself."

Barnes looked critically at his boxer. Wood Mountain was feinting. It was obvious to everyone, he supposed, that he, Barnes, was moony over Pixie. Well, who wouldn't be? Why pretend?

"You sure? Because my brother lives down there."

"Oh, I doubt she'd go stay with your brother!"

"Somebody to call if she got in trouble."

"Since I don't have a fight, I might just go down and be that guy."

Wood Mountain knew very well what he was saying, but he didn't care. He was getting tired of Barnes dancing around Pixie Paranteau. And he knew from Pokey that she was tired of it too. Barnes hadn't got him a fight, either, and Wood Mountain felt cheated. Yes, he'd work harder, he was no quitter, but seeing as he had some extra time on his hands now, and was carrying his field-work money, why not keep going on the train? Why not find Pixie and better, find her sister, be the hero he hadn't been in the ring against Joe Wobble. When she'd watched him.

"Yeah, I might just take that train," he said, sawing into his steak. He drenched it in soupy egg yolk, chewed. The hash browns were crisp on top, creamy underneath. He relented. Barnes was devoted, coached him for nothing. What was he doing? Barnes was miserable enough, seeking hopelessly after Pixie. Give him a break.

"Or maybe you should," said Wood Mountain. "I have the addresses she is supposed to look up. You could check in on her."

"I wish I could," said Barnes, slowly, meaning it. "I have to teach."

"Teaching. You can get out of teaching, can't you?"

"Of course not," said Barnes, putting down his fork. He was stern, affronted. "It's the beginning of the year. We review and lay down the proper foundation for the year's progress. It's essential. And by the way, have you applied yet?"

"Not yet."

"What? Boxing isn't a real job, not a lifetime job. We've talked about it. You were my best student. You could be a teacher."

Wood Mountain didn't want to be a teacher. He didn't want to apply to UND or to Moorhead or even to the State School of Science in Wahpeton. He wanted to keep doing field work, building up his muscles, keep boxing and keep training horses for Louis Pipestone. He loved racing those horses with Louie, trailering them to Assiniboine Downs in Winnipeg. Grace, Louis's kid, their rookie jockey. Wood Mountain also wanted to look after his mother, even though Juggie was doing fine on her own. He didn't say much about it, but he kept a clean house for her when she stayed in town at her cooking job. Or stayed with Louie. Wood Mountain, the boxer, son of Archille, grandson of a man who fought with Sitting Bull, wanted to stay home. Which, after all, was the same thing Sitting Bull had wanted to do.

"Oh well," he said. "I guess I could go down there, to the Cities. Help her out. But I don't want to."

"You said she could take care of herself. And she has a place to stay."

"She's not the kind of girl to get in trouble, is she."

"No," said Barnes, "she is not."

"Then I guess I'll go back home."

But when he returned to the station to buy his ticket back to Rugby, Wood Mountain found his words came out wrong.

"Ticket to Minneapolis."

"Which train?"

"The next one."

## Louis Pipestone

✻—│—✻

HIS FATHER had brought the good horse from Red Lake and bred it with a wild buckskin paint back in '38. That horse could run. Made some money, which was responsible for the presence of the 1947 Chevrolet pickup truck, green as the hills, that Louis drove slowly and deliberately down the main road. He'd mapped the reservation out in his head. He would start with the more remote places past the western boundary, where many tribal members lived, their land part of the original tribal agreement broken within only a few years of its making. He saw Awan, Moves Camp, Gardipee, and his friend Titus Giizis. Right across the line he parked his truck at the entrance to Zhaanat's place, hoping to catch her and her husband and daughter, all in one go. But old Paranteau was on another tear, and Zhaanat told him that Pixie had gone down to the Cities to look for their other daughter. Pokey was too young to sign, but he listened to what Louis said, in Chippewa, and added his mother's name in bold script with her hand lightly touching his wrist.

"Mii'iw," said Zhaanat. "A bite to eat?"

"Wouldn't go down bad," said Louis.

Zhaanat brought light bannock, a small dish of salt, fresh grease from a roasted duck, and a plate of shredded thigh meat. There was a bowl of dried berries, cold wild boiled turnips, pemmican, hot tea.

"Old-time food," said Louis, with pleasure.

"I am afraid to sleep," said Zhaanat.

Louis waited.

"Afraid to dream about my daughters."

"I heard your uncle saw Vera alive."

"With a baby."

Louis nodded, thinking.

"I am not in favor of this relocation. We lose our young people. The Cities keep them."

"I'm not going," Pokey said.

His mother nodded at him. "My boy."

"Pixie can fight anyone down," said Louis, shifting in the chair. "They won't mess around with Pixie. She's little, but she's tough."

"She chops wood," said Pokey. "Piles it up all fancy."

"If that Barnes trained her, she'd be a top featherweight," said Louis, sly.

"She don't have anything to do with him," said Pokey.

Louis raised his eyebrows, puffed his round cheeks, and winked at Zhaanat.

"I know someone else sweet on her. Wouldn't worry much," he said.

LOUIS GOT seven more signatures and then drove down the curved path to Thomas Wazhashk's house. A brisk wind was taking down the yellow leaves of birches where they stood in graceful ranks at the edge of a broad hayfield. Thomas was plucking the marigold seeds and filling a tin can. Sharlo was collecting the tiny dried heads of the moss roses, the seeds fine as dust. She was a quick, stormy girl with a sharp gaze. She favored her mother.

"Aaniin, Mr. Pipestone," she said. "Where is Grace?"

"On a horse somewhere."

"Did people sign?" asked Thomas.

Louis showed him the signatures on the back of the petition. Many of them were meticulous, boarding-school penmanship. Others were laborious, crafted by tribal members who only knew the shape of their own names. Some, written out by relatives, were accompanied as in the old days by the faint inked print of a person's thumb. It was an impressive number, to them both, and within the cardboard suitcase that served as Thomas's desk he found a large manila folder and an envelope, which would protect the document. Thomas pointed out Zhaanat's signature and asked after Pixie.

"She's down in the city looking for Vera."

"We've never lost somebody, in a bad way, from a relocation yet. Most of them come back after a few months."

"There's some staying out there now, too."

"Yes, the go-getters."

"Don't it ever bother you," said Louis, "that we're losing the go-getters from here at home?"

"That's why we worked on getting the jewel bearing plant."

"Her job is good. Pixie will come back."

"She would not leave Zhaanat. They're only hanging on because she's got that good job."

"Maybe I should give Grace the go-ahead to work there."

"She wants to?"

"No," laughed Louis. "She wants to race."

"Who's got the top horses now?"

"Big place west of Winnipeg, horse named Cash Out."

"Who's your top horse now?"

"That used to be Gringo. Now we have Picasso and our up-and-comer, Teacher's Pet."

"Can you drive down to Fargo for the information meetings?"

"Sure," said Louis. "I can pile eight in the back of my pickup."

"Oh, that's a good one. Say we bring up a heap big show of Indians whooping it up in back of a pickup truck?"

"I have a feeling those BIAs are maybe expecting that."

"We can take my car. I can squeeze in five. Counting me," said Thomas.

"Juggie can drive."

"She's got a good car now, I heard."

"Bernadette bought her a DeSoto," said Louis.

"What, a four door?"

"Sure enough. A four door. And two-tone."

"That girl must be making out good."

"You see what I mean, a go-getter."

"Juggie was always like that. Nobody could hold her back," said Thomas.

"And Wood Mountain. Him too. Someday he's gonna bust loose and beat Joe Wobble."

"I sure want to see that day," said Thomas. He paused. "You know, Louie, we should be thinking about putting up a delegation."

"It's that bad?"

"I think so."

"Washington?"

"Like the old-timers."

"Can't get it through my head," said Louis, lowering his gaze. "My boy put his life on the line."

"Like Falon," said Thomas.

"Falon," said Louis.

"This Senator Watkins is behind the bill."

"We should try to figure him out."

"That's what I'm trying to do. It's said he wants to teach us to stand on our own two feet."

Both men looked down at their feet.

"I count two," said Louis.

"Sometimes I wonder," said Thomas.

"Wonder what?"

"If one of them will ever say, Gee, those damn Indians might have had an idea or two. Shouldn't have got rid of them all. Maybe we missed out."

Louis laughed. Thomas laughed. They laughed together at the idea.

# Ajax

✦━━✦

THOMAS AND Rose lay side by side in the dim night.

"I went and had a drink," said Thomas.

All the stoppered emotions of the day came up under Rose's skin. A prickling, burning pressure.

"Don't take another one. I'll kill you."

He said nothing, but lay there knowing she wouldn't even strike at him. He wouldn't strike at her. They were not like that.

He turned to her, sinking. It was so much worse than anybody knew.

The drink had surprised him. He hadn't thought about it, hadn't even struggled. Just sat down with Eddyboy Mink and took it. Many years had passed before that drink.

"You'll kill me how? Poison?"

He watched her face. Her eyes glinted. Tears? No. Heat. Then her mouth twitched.

"You already got poisoned."

"You sure?"

"Remember those biscuits a few mornings ago?"

"No."

"That's because you were eating in your sleep. Wade made them. He was proud. Later on he tells me he couldn't find baking powder.

"'So I used this,' he says."

"What?" Thomas asked.

"He was holding up a can of my Ajax scrubbing powder."

"That *is* poison," said Thomas, impressed.

"He just used a pinch, or two." She put her fingers to her mouth. "I told him he could have poisoned you. He's been watching you close ever since. But looked like it didn't hurt you, so I didn't say nothing to you."

"I am too tired to die," Thomas said, but fumed. What? Were they just going to wait and see if he keeled over dead? He was feeling sorry for himself, he realized. And it was a relief to know. He could fight self-pity.

"Still," said Rose, lower, unwilling. "Please. No more."

To even use the word please seemed to gentle her. She raised her hand and grazed his cheek with her hard, warm palm. Thomas was sinking again, but now into the radiant comfort of which she was the center.

"I promise I won't."

"Let's put the seal on the promise," she whispered, and held his face between her hands. He put his hands on her hands and it was like they were both holding him together. Then he dropped his hands and went to her.

# Iron Tulip

***

FRECKLE FACE and Dinky lowered her on a rope with a twenty-pound lifting plate at the bottom. Patrice stood on the metal. Just before she went into the water, she took a deep breath and when the plate met the bottom of the tank she glanced at the creamy blobs of faces. They were meaningless. She swung around the rope with one hoof pointed cutely up behind her. She reached back for her tail, but it had floated up over her head and followed her like a blue snake with a head of false hair. She started bobbing up. Remembered there were other weights on the bottom. Props. She reached toward a pink one but at the last moment realized it was a shocking object. Next to it, an iron tulip, which she lifted and pretended to smell, coyly peeking over her shoulder. Suddenly, in joy, she kicked up her hooves and somersaulted backward in an arc. Then she dropped the tulip and surfaced. As she took a breath she heard applause, heard whistles. The noise of appreciation charged the water. She swirled down into a new substance. The moves were in her, easy. Poses out of magazines, but twisted loose from ads for refrigerators, canned peaches, cars, wringer washers. A finger to her lips, a hip switch, a rolling eye, the rope of tail to swing in a slow lasso toward a creamy blob. And by mistake, from the bottom, she plucked a naughty hatchet. Twenty minutes passed easily.

"You are a *sensation*," said Jack, as she dripped by a small electric coil of heat. "Don't get too close to that. You'll melt a hole."

She was sitting on a wooden stool. Jack had a little color. The sardonic parentheses around his smile had lifted. He said he'd noticed how she flinched from the "implements of pleasure" and that he would have them removed. "We don't need to be vulgar. And besides, the city could shut us down."

"I'd like to stay with using flowers, and maybe I could pretend to chop with that little hatchet, if you'd fix the end of the handle."

"An object of regrettable taste," said Jack.

"Oh, and I'd like to be paid the same night."

"How about in the morning? We could cut you a check."

"I'd like cash."

"Cash it is," said Jack, resigned.

He gave her a cup of hot coffee, but she only took a couple of sips, for warmth. Three more shows. But they passed in a blur of novelty. And then she was removing the suit and laying it out carefully on a sawhorse to dry. In the morning, she would dust the inside with the special powder that Jack said was mixed up to preserve it. Her dinner was brought to her on a tray.

A hot turkey and gravy sandwich. The thick white bread, soaked with peppered gravy, melted down her throat. There were butter beans and green beans. She could have had a mixed drink. But didn't want to turn out like her father. Instead, a scalding pot of sugared tea. Oh, that went down well. She used the bathroom again. Put her tray out in the hall. Locked the door. Then took her nightgown from her satchel and lowered it over her shoulders. She switched off the light and crept beneath the red blanket, pressing its satin edge against her cheek.

THE NEXT morning, she woke late and went downstairs. The bar was wilted and grim. A few heavy drinkers who had closed the place and slept in the street, in their cars, or not at all, were slumped over hair-of-the-dog specials. Their eggs came in whiskey shots. The toast came stacked five deep with butter on the side. Patrice ate her egg over easy, sopping the rich yolk up with buttered toast. She drank her coffee black and plotted her course.

"I'm going to the post office," she told the bartender.

"Heard you did good last night."

She smiled and put a fork in her purse. She had taken twenty dollars from her stash. Around the corner, she found a cabstand, took a taxi to Bloomington Avenue. As she got out and paid the driver, she had a sudden thought. She showed him the slip of paper with the Stevens Avenue address.

"Is there anything wrong with this place?" she asked.

"Not that I know of," said the driver.

"Are you sure? Someone said it was dangerous."

"Never had a problem there," the man said.

"Thank you."

So maybe Jack had been trying to steer her away. She walked up to the front door of the Bloomington Avenue place. The same windows were still cardboarded. The seeping sense of misery. As she slipped around back she realized the dog wasn't barking. She took the fork out of her purse and went up the broken back steps. She stuck the fork into the rotted wood next to the lock and pried it loose. Then she entered. All was too still. Death was in the house. She edged forward, gripping the fork. Her handbag dangled off her other arm.

The kitchen was empty, just a few vile cups on the counter, holding cigarette stubs. Stains and splatters everywhere, old grease fuzzy with dust. Leaves had blown into the dining room, the parlor. Everywhere a soft sinter blanketed the floor. Warily, she crept up the central staircase, the spindles broken out like teeth. There was a window, slightly cracked, grand, of stained glass. Another red tulip and green lances of leaves. A frame of gold and sea-blue diamonds. At the top of the stairs, a central hallway of chipped and dirty white paint with five shut doors. She would have to open them one by one. Holding her breath, she entered the first room, where she found the dog. It was at the end of a chain bolted into the wall.

A pallid thing, all bones, it tried to struggle to its feet, but it collapsed and lay there, too spent to pant. There was an overturned bowl and in one corner a glass jug half filled with water. Here and there, a few dried turds. An open window. She fetched the jug and crouched beside the creature, dribbled water beneath the flaps of its swollen muzzle. After a while, the dog's throat spasmed. Patrice got up and quickly opened the doors to the next rooms. In each one, a filthy mat, a gnarled blanket, sometimes shit, the smell of piss, a chain bolted into the wall and at the end of each chain an empty dog collar. She examined the chains, the collars. In one room, a line of beer bottles on the windowsill. Behind the last door was a stinking waterless bathroom. Strips of an old sheet. Dried blood. Two wadded-up diapers. She went back to the dog and this time she sat down, dribbled more water into its mouth, put a hand on its ribs. "You know where she is," said Patrice. "I know you do. Please. I need you to help me find her."

"She died on the end of a chain, like me," said the dog.

Four more breaths came and went, beneath Patrice's hand,

before dog gave a great rattling sigh. She sat with her fingers on its ribs until its body cooled and a flea hopped across her knuckles. Then she got up and walked down the stairs, out of the house.

Jack pulled up.

"I thought you might have gotten yourself over here."

Patrice opened the door and climbed into the car. She was not in her body.

"Let's go back to the Stevens address," she said.

"Oh no. No, no, no. We aren't going there."

"That's not what we agreed to," said Patrice.

JACK INSISTED on following Patrice as she knocked on every apartment door. A misty-haired blond woman with balled-up features appeared. She didn't know the Viviers, or Vera Vivier, or Vera Paranteau, or Vera. Had never met her. Had seen no forwarding address. The door shut. Patrice went to the next door. Jack rolled his eyes. At every apartment in the building she got the same answer. No Vera. Patrice walked slowly down the hall, then darted back to one of the apartments. Jack had already gone down the stairs. Nobody had opened the door the first time. She knocked on the door again, this time softly.

"Come on, let's go," called Jack from the stairs.

"Who is it?" said a voice, very low, on the other side of the door.

"It's the waterjack," said Patrice to the voice.

The door opened. The woman who opened was gaunt, and bald. Jack came running down the hall. Before the door slammed shut a voice from the next room cried, "Who's at the door, Hilda?"

"I said, let's go!" Jack grabbed Patrice's arm, pinching her. She pushed him so hard he staggered.

"Was that the Hilda? What's going on?"

"She's ticked at me," said Jack.

"Why?"

"Professional standards."

Patrice fought him away and banged on the door.

"She won't answer you now," said Jack. "We don't get along."

"Then take me to visit Bernadette."

"What a life," said Jack.

A SNEAK of flame, a slash of blue, a white tooth, a knife-edge glance at Jack. And then, when Bernadette recognized Patrice, a storm of sorrow and intensity. The outburst chilled her.

"Oh, honey! Oh, oh, oh!"

"What," said Patrice. "What? What? Where's my sister?"

"She ran off!"

Bernadette drew Patrice up the steps of a town house made of orange-pink brick. A curved stone entryway, a door of dark shiny wood with an oval frosted-glass window. Bernadette was not the shy, awkward tomboy she'd been in high school, hunching around in men's clothes. She was a stunner. Wearing a red silk kimono with pink blossoms. Hair hennaed to a glow and rolled in a certain movie-star way, lips carmine, eyebrows sharp black wings, eyes of an unsettling empty brightness.

"She stuck me with the baby," she said to Patrice. "You're here for the baby!"

"I'm here for Vera," said Patrice.

Bernadette shut her mouth, gave Jack a warning look.

"What's she doing here? She working for you?"

Jack ignored her questions.

"She just wants her sister."

"So sad how she left her baby," Bernadette sighed, in a different voice. "Wait down here. I'll get the baby for you."

"I'm not taking the baby until you give me Vera."

"You think I know where she is? I don't know. Never have. They don't tell me. She went off somewhere and got mixed up with some bad people, I suppose. Here, sit down. I'll get that baby."

The house was silent.

"Get Vera," said Patrice.

"Get her out of here," said Bernadette to Jack.

"Patrice, let's go," said Jack. "Bernie doesn't know."

"I think she does know."

"She's trying to help!" said Jack. He grabbed Patrice's arm and tried to pull her back through the door. She struck his hand off, tossed his arm down.

"I really don't know," said Bernadette, putting her face so close that Patrice could see the bruises through her makeup. "If you shut up and take the baby, I'll try to find out where she is. That baby is wearing me out."

"So find out. I'll come back for the baby," said Patrice. "And Vera better be here. I think you know where she is."

This time Jack gripped her arm so desperately that although Patrice could have shaken him off, she didn't. She let him pull her through the door.

# Woodland Beauty

*⇥═⇤*

WOOD MOUNTAIN got off the train and walked the mile to his sister's town house on 17th Avenue. Bernadette let him in. Threw out her arms and hugged him. The plush flowery steam of a recent bath rolled off her shoulders. From down the hall, a delicious thread of scent—roasting meat. She must be cooking for Cal. In the parlor, a carved wooden pushcart bearing cut-glass decanters filled with amber firewater. A couch to sink down in while his sister, or half sister, paced back and forth in a floaty red gown.

"She was here," said Bernadette. "I can't tell her much about Vera. She said she's coming back. Cal better not be here. But Jack was with her. Jack, of all people. Wouldn't tell me a thing."

"Jack. She sure took my advice," said Wood Mountain.

"Which was what?"

"Find the scum."

"Oh, she did that all right. Jack!"

Bernadette threw herself down beside him on the couch.

"He's still at the new concern. Log Jam 26."

"Is it a real place?"

"Real as any of his other concerns."

"What's he look like now?"

"Skinnier. Sicker. Junkier. Yellower."

"Junkie."

"They say he's been one for years. A controlled habit."

"Well, he will slip up."

"They always do. But as scum goes, he's not the worst, you know."

"Can you put me up?"

"I've already got that baby. Vera's. Cal's not happy about it. Suze is keeping care of the little sweetie. The dad's in Chicago."

"Where's Vera?"

Bernadette studied her nails.

"She got a job somewhere."

"Where?"

"Why you asking me for? How'd I know?"

Wood Mountain dropped it.

"The baby. Boy or girl?"

"Boy. Small. Worries me. Don't cry. But yeah, you can stay."

"Thanks."

"There's a little room, off the kitchen. Back-door key. Be real quiet."

"He knows I'm your brother, right?"

"Sure, I told him last time. But he don't believe me."

"So I'm liable to get what, shot?"

"He wouldn't shoot you. He doesn't like to make a noise."

"I see. Well. Guess I'll stay somewhere else."

Bernadette gave him three twenties. She reached out to hug him but he stepped back, holding up his arms.

"Okay, sis, thanks. Better go before I take a knife."

"In the kidneys. He likes the kidneys."

"Oh Jesus. Goodbye."

*≡*

WOOD MOUNTAIN walked west until he got to Hennepin Avenue. Then he walked north until he stood on the odd side of Hennepin, opposite Log Jam 26. He studied the windows, the people who came and went, mostly normal-looking men unaccompanied by women. In the window, a sign for the Lumberjack Special. A menu outside, fixed to a music stand. Jack was serious about his front, or maybe just liked the restaurant business, thought Wood Mountain, wondering if the food was any good. The twenties were warming his pocket. After watching for a while, he walked farther down the street. Went into the Decatur Hotel. The doorman caught him. "No Indians." So he walked back out, crossed the street, and took a room at the Josen House, next door to Log Jam 26. He paid for the night in advance, slipping a bill under a thick glass window, counting the change twice. Eat or sleep? He decided he would enjoy eating more if he was wide awake, so he went upstairs.

His room opened like a regular room, but when he went in he saw the ceiling was wire mesh. A cage hotel. It was probably too late to get his money back at the desk. But he ran back downstairs. Made a case that the clerk should have told him. The clerk looked pained and yawned. Wood Mountain trudged back upstairs. At least the place smelled reassuringly of flea powder. He checked the mattress, sniffed at the pillow, then pinched it up in his fingers and set it carefully on the floor across the room. He balled his jacket up under his head.

When he woke, it was late. Past dinnertime. His stomach was hollow and achingly empty. He spruced up in a bathroom so strongly disinfected it made his eyes water, and tried to hold his breath as he combed back his hair in the ravaged mirror. He went downstairs and out, entered Log Jam 26. Stared at the glowing water tank in the center of the restaurant. It was empty, except for a fake underwater pine tree. He sat down in a small booth. A wire clip on the table held a cardboard sign advertising

*Exotic Attraction! Woodland Beauty! Our Own World-Famous Wa-*
*terjack.* He studied the showtimes. He could order dessert and
coffee once he finished his food, stretch his dinner hour long
enough to see the waterjack. He'd find Jack and question him.
Get a lead on Pixie. Plus he would track down those addresses.
However. It was dark now, and showing up at a strange address
as a stranger in the dark might not be a good idea. Fresh start in
the morning. But also, he should not break training! He decided
to skip rope in his room after dinner. And decided that he'd
order a double meatloaf, no potatoes, drink one beer only. The
virtue of passing on the potatoes took the edge off his guilt. The
waitress, an older woman wearing a sequined hairnet, smiled
at him and filled his water glass. He pretended that he needed
more time to look over the menu. Finally, the second time she
came around, he ordered his meal. He told her that she could
take her time.

"You want to see the waterjack, huh?"

"It says she's a woodland beauty."

"Oh, she's a dear! But she's number three. They do use 'em
up fast."

Wood Mountain nodded, thinking of talent and good looks.

"I suppose they go on to higher things?"

The waitress looked startled.

"That's one way of saying it. One died. Number two's on her
last legs. Us who work in the restaurant think it's a scandal. But
management couldn't care less. Just hired this one straight off
the train."

"Weird," murmured Wood Mountain. He took a drink of the
iced water. She moved off. He listened to a young couple bicker
in the booth behind him. The woman wanted to go somewhere
else and her boyfriend wanted to stay. They didn't raise their

voices or twist their words. She said the waterjack attraction was stupid. He said it was educational. She called him a dimwit. He called her a killjoy. And it went on from there. While they were dully arguing, the waitress brought him a relish tray.

"Thanks," he said, happy. "Didn't know the special came with relish!"

"It doesn't, except for special people," said the waitress. She winked. Her sequins twinkled.

"I love a good relish plate," Wood Mountain said sincerely. The waitress beamed. It was true. Nothing said fine dining like a relish plate. Coming back down from Winnipeg, they would stop at a supper club if they had won. Wood Mountain regarded the arrangement. Ice-cold radishes carved into rosettes, carrot sticks, celery. Two kinds of olives, pimento loaf, sliced summer sausage. Miniature pickles, sweet and dill. Wood Mountain ate all of it and watched Jack, skinny and yellow, work the crowd. He wore a beautifully cut lightweight pin-striped suit in dark blue. Cut an elegant figure until he smiled. Wood Mountain could see his dark jagged grin all the way across the room. Wore his thin black hair swept straight back. Had an off-center wid-ow's peak. A golden ring sparked on Jack's right-hand middle finger. A watch glinted expensively at his cuff. As the crowd increased he tended more assiduously. Wood Mountain tried to catch his eye but Jack seemed in a kind of trance. Several times the featured performer was announced. Doris Barnes. It was a common name. Wood Mountain would have to tell Barnes about it, though, tease him maybe. Although the teacher was not much fun to tease. By now Wood Mountain's main course steamed on the table, a dense block of highly peppered meat draped with tomato sauce. The vegetables were wax beans topped with green beans topped with onion rings. An enormous heap. He speared each bean meditatively and planned, as he chewed, how to go about finding Pixie.

He didn't focus on the waterjack when at last her show started and she began swimming around in the tank. He ordered another beer instead of coffee. He glanced at the tank and dismissed the spectacle. What a letdown. A girl in a blue suit with little horns. So what. Shaking her stuff. Oh well. Then maybe. There was something about her. But oh well. Then he started to think maybe there was, really, something. Second or third dive, you couldn't stop watching her odd moves. Then. Then. He looked through the water-tank glass and locked eyes with Pixie. He jumped up. As he strode to the tank he realized that from her side the glass was probably distorted. But yes, the waterjack, bubbles streaming from her lips and nose, was without question Pixie. She swarmed to the hidden surface of the tank. Pixie Paranteau. Doris Barnes. He got it. Maybe. Maybe she had married Barnes. But that was impossible. Married to Barnes. Swimming in a water tank. Then she came down again and someone with a tank-side table tried to push Wood Mountain away, but he was gesturing at Pixie, jumping around and yelling her name. He raised his fist to pound on the glass and was seized. Yanked away by men who bore him backward, shouting Pixie! Twice, he escaped and punched like a hero, fought them off. But the freckly hulking fellow and his helper, a wiry determined little weasel, finally tied him up with their arms and dragged him out the door.

FROM INSIDE the tank, Patrice lassoed a creamy blob with her tail. She saw the shadow of dark fish behind her and pirouetted with hooves twirling for effect. There was stirring about and commotion in the blurred world beyond the glass, but nothing affected her. She finished out the necessary roster of shows, and was hauled into the ceiling. After she had peeled off the waterjack suit, the night waitress brought her tray up and said, "You've got an admirer, honey, and let me tell you, he's kind of passionate. I'd be careful."

"I like your hairnet, the sparkles," said Patrice.

The waitress looked down the hall both ways before she slipped a folded note from her pocket.

"And say?" The waitress bent down and whispered urgently. "Waterjacks don't last. You better quit while you still can."

"What happens?"

Freckle Face boomed up the stairs and the waitress yelled, "Put the tray outside your door when you're done. I'll pop back up here."

"What happens?" hissed Patrice. "And what admirer? Why be careful?"

Freckle Face blundered along the hall carrying a small chair from the restaurant.

"The waterjacks, they up and die," muttered the waitress, grabbing a napkin from her pocket and twisting it into Patrice's hand.

"Get going," said Freckle Face.

"We were just chatting," said the waitress.

"Jack wants the staff to respect the waterjack's privacy," said Freckle Face. "I am supposed to keep an eye out for intruders, fans, and such like that."

"Okay, I'm going," said the waitress. "You did real good to-night."

Her eyebrows went up and she stared spookily at Patrice.

Freckle Face set his chair down outside the door and parked himself, flipping open the *Minneapolis Star*. Patrice shut the door.

Her waterjack suit was off and she had dusted it with the necessary powder. It was nearly dry now, but she kept the big fan going. What now?

"I don't care if it's poisoned!" she said, uncovering her meal. As she gobbled meatloaf, she opened the note.

*It's me. Wood. Tried to get your attention but the goons ejected me. I am next door at the Grand Fleabag. Find me. 328.*

She thought back to the swirl of motion outside the tank. Her admirer? And Jack's greeting, shrill and angry, but relieved, when he found her in her dressing room getting ready for the show. It was like he was keeping her a prisoner. No. It was exactly that he was keeping her a prisoner. Freckle Face was outside her door. But the money? She had it. One hundred thirty-six dollars. If she worked two more nights, she'd have over two hundred. And she was packing them in. But maybe she should leave. Yes, she had already decided to leave, hadn't she? Because of what? Something. What the dog had said. What Bernadette had said. Almost said. No, the words were not out of her mouth, so it could be just that Patrice had thought she heard something that she definitely had not heard. And she wasn't going to hear it. Though she thought she should pay some attention to . . . what was it the waitress had said? Waterjacks tended to . . . but she was quitting anyway. She'd find out from Wood Mountain. She'd slip away in an hour or so, she decided, wearing all of her clothes and with her money stuffed in her underwear. "Now or never," she murmured, rolling an olive around in her mouth. Now or never. The olives dripped oil. Grease the hinges. Though it stung to leave behind good money. And she was so tired. So sleepy that it took the sudden pop of clarity, an image, to bring back her memory.

She was back in one of the rooms with the chains. The empty dog collar. It was not a regular dog collar. It didn't buckle. It had been sliced apart. The chain that the collar was locked onto—you'd need pliers to remove it. And the dried shit in the corner was human.

# The Average Woman and the Empty Tank

LOUIS PIPESTONE tended the petition like a garden. He kept it with him at all times. In town, his eyes sharpened when he noticed a tribal member who hadn't yet signed. Wherever they were—at the gas pump, mercantile, at Henry's, on the road, or outside the clinic and hospital—Louis cornered them. If they were waiting for a baby to be born, he'd have them sign. If they were laughing, if they were arguing. If they were taking a child home from school, they signed. If it looked like someone was bargaining with the bootlegger, he got both to sign. His smile would appear. He knew the power of it. "Cheeks." Arms hard as fence posts. A homely buffalo head on bandy legs.

MEANWHILE THEY had a problem. They had only one copy of the bill, and in spite of his great care, it was getting stained and tattered. Juggie was busy typing a copy onto mimeograph paper so that it could be printed. Others could type faster, but she was most accurate, proofreading as she went along. She was also putting together a tribal newsletter. This was a new idea that Thomas had thought up—a way of getting out the doings of the advisory committee so that people would start relying on something other than the moccasin telegraph for news.

Juggie was typing up the newsletter one night when Thomas stopped by. He had a key to the school's front office.

"How does it look?"

Juggie showed him the first page, each short announcement set off by a row of stars.

"We should have some jokes," she said.

"Jokes."

She held her fingers poised above the keys.

"I need a joke."

She was grinning at him. Her blunt face and her sharp eyes.

"You always have a joke."

But he didn't have a joke. He opened his mouth, shut his mouth, frowned at the floor. Stared at the edge of the desk as if he'd find a joke there.

"Just hold on," he said.

It was true. He always had a joke. People relied on him for jokes. After a moment or two of talking, Thomas always pulled out a joke, one he'd heard or one that just came to him. There would be a spurt of laughter. Then the conversation could proceed. But now he realized that he hadn't exchanged jokes or thought up jokes for . . . he couldn't remember how long.

"I'm out of jokes!"

"Very funny," said Juggie. "Give me one line."

He almost turned to go, then he thought about Wade, his little man, baking with Ajax, and he thought of himself, his first drink in years, and he thought of Rose.

"The average man is proof the average woman can take a joke," he said.

"Wait, say it again," said Juggie, already typing.

✳ ═ ✳

IT WAS one of those nights. Fee had put a piece of blackberry candy in the earflap. It got stuck to his head. Carefully he pulled it off, moved that she'd given him a piece of candy, which was rare at their house. He decided to save it to keep himself awake on the way home. Thomas was writing a desperate letter to Senator Milton R. Young, trying to disguise panic with cordiality. Around 2 a.m. Thomas's head hit the desk. He pulled himself up. Damned if he'd knock himself out falling asleep on the job. He slapped himself but he didn't slap himself awake. The slap sent him into a type of sleep he'd never experienced. He did his round, but most of his brain was closed away—he could feel it. Part of his brain had rebelled and was asleep. The tiny sliver of his waking self did the job. Locked and unlocked doors. Examined corners with the flashlight. Ate the night lunch. Folded half his sandwich in the clean bandanna Rose had wrapped it in. Made another round. Had a long talk with Roderick.

"How'd you do that, Roderick?"

"Change from a motor?"

"Yes."

"I had a talk with your brain. The part that's sleeping."

"Oh, that's funny. Why do you want to come around and bug me, Roderick?"

"I'm not here for you. It's LaBatte. I saved him before, remember?"

"Oh, I remember. You took on his jail time."

"First time they locked me up. Down in the cellar. They threw me in there. I owned up to what LaBatte did."

"Didn't I throw you down a coat?"

"You passed me a coat but it was so cold anyway."

"LaBatte thinks it got you then."

"No, it didn't get me the first time, not much. The second time maybe. I sure come out of there coughing like heck. Fever. But it wasn't nothing."

"They said you had to go to Sac and Fox."

"Who told you! The sanatorium. I went there."

"You were supposed to get better."

"I wasn't sick, dumbhead."

"Lots of boys had it."

"Let's face it."

"Let's face it."

"Fed me butter on everything, dumbhead. Butter on the oatmeal. Cream on the cream potatoes. Fattened me up. Six died but not me. I wasn't coming home in no coffin."

"Wait. No. Roderick."

Thomas spoke gently, breaking the news.

"You died. They did send you home in a coffin. On the train."

Roderick shook his head, puffed out his cheeks in exasperation.

"They put me in that coffin, sure! Put me on the train. But I was in there laughing. Told myself they'd sure be surprised when I jumped out on them."

"Your mom and dad go to meet you?"

"Nobody picked me up down there! No! Why? They knew I wasn't dead in that coffin. I was just kidding."

"I heard different, Roderick."

"Had to get outta the sanatorium."

"Why'd you want out if they fed you so good?"

"They sawed my lung out, dumbhead! Had to collapse it."

"You took LaBatte's punishment. He never wanted you to die for it. He felt bad all his life."

"What for? No skin off my nose. Wild Indian, me!"

"So you're visiting around?"

"Like I said. I'm here for LaBatte. He was my brother down

there. Fort Totten. You too. Couldn't break us apart. Cousins. I'm here to save him."

"What from?"

"His own dumbhead self."

"What's he doing?"

"Dumbhead things."

"For instance?"

Roderick nodded his head, sly. He looked from side to side.

"Wouldn't you like to know. You tell on us?"

"Never."

"LaBatte's stealing."

"Stealing what?"

"Anything can fit in his pockets. Whatever they don't count. Paper clips. Staples. Writing paper. Rolls of butt-wiping paper. Coffee. Sugar. Spoons it out of the bag. Little at a time. He's taking soap. He's taking crankcase oil. Just dribbling it into a jar. He's taking scraps of metal. He's working up to taking jewels."

"They're in a safe. He can't get in."

"Why you think not?"

"It's locked up, always. No key. A combination safe bolted into the wall."

"The combination's wrote down, dumbhead. He'll find it. Grasshopper knows it. But doesn't know it by heart."

"Anyway, LaBatte's no thief. You're making all of this up, Roderick. Saying these things."

"Sure I'm the dumbhead? Don't think so. You don't know everything, Thomas. Why else would I be here? Ask yourself that question."

"But you're not here," said Thomas, looking at the crust of a sandwich in his hand, a sandwich he did not remember eating.

✳═✳

HOW COULD it be that someone who was a fiction of his own brain told him something that was true? Because Thomas just knew Roderick was right. He had to confront LaBatte before he got himself in jail and ruined a good job for other Indians. He stuck around that morning, knowing that LaBatte was supposed to show up to solder some buckets. As his old school friend walked across the parking lot, Thomas stepped toward him. He was too annoyed to beat around the bush.

"Saw Roderick last night."

LaBatte's eyes popped. His crew-cut hair seemed to bristle with fear. He set his lunch box down next to Thomas, on the hood of his car.

"Roderick told me he was there to save you. Told me you were stealing from the plant. Working up to stealing the jewels."

LaBatte didn't even make a pretense of denying it. Who can argue with a ghost? He broke down, wiped at his face, told Thomas that he'd had a string of bad luck. And that was even before the owl.

"What owl?"

"Your owl."

"Owls are good luck for me. Especially the white ones."

"Nothing is going good for me, Thomas."

"What's wrong?"

"Broke again."

"But you have a job."

"Don't feed twenty. Or thirty."

LaBatte's family was a sprawling tangle of need and he was the only one with regular work. Thomas took out his soft old billfold, handed over what money he had to LaBatte, who took it and said, "Merci, cousin. I was going down a bad path, me. But I knew Roderick would help me. I saw what you wrote about the owl and thought I was a goner."

LaBatte began to sob like his heart was breaking through his chest. Thomas put his hand on his old friend's shoulder.

"Quit stealing. Ever seen the eyes on a grasshopper?"

LaBatte choked back a moan. "Grasshopper. Probably can see around corners. Don't know what made me such a dumbhead."

"That's what Roderick said."

Thomas shrugged off the chill LaBatte's word gave him.

"You better make a good confession and move forward."

"Yes," said LaBatte. "I been confessing my theft every week. Father's getting tuned up at me. 'Here,' I said last time, 'a little sack of sugar for you.' He roared out, 'Stolen?' Oh man alive, he kicked me out the confessional."

"I have to go," said Thomas. "I'm late for another one of those meetings." He picked up his lunch box.

He didn't want to hear the details of why LaBatte needed the money so badly. It would be the same as every story, including his own, though with the jewel bearing paycheck things had eased up considerably. There weren't enough jobs. There wasn't enough land. There wasn't enough farmable land. There weren't enough deer in the woods or ducks in the sloughs and a game warden caught you if you fished too many fish. There just wasn't enough of anything and if he didn't save what little there was from disappearing there was no imagining how anyone would get along. He couldn't have it. He wouldn't have it. Halfway back to town the car coughed and began to coast. He steered onto the shoulder. The gas tank was empty. He'd given LaBatte the money he was going to use to fill it.

For a long while, Thomas sat there with his empty tank, on

the empty road, looking over the empty field, at the empty sky. Not a cloud in it. Blue as heaven. Then of all things LaBatte tore right by him in his old clunker and didn't stop.

Thomas watched the disappearing mismatched back bumpers of LaBatte's car. It seemed to lift off the road and drift into the trees. He reached over to his lunch box. Maybe he'd left that crust. It was LaBatte's lunch box, full. A meat sandwich with real butter. More bread, this time with butter and sugar. A baked potato, still warm. Apples.

"Did it ever hit the spot," he said later to LaBatte. "Set me up for the walk to town, for gas."

LaBatte sighed. "And me, one dusty little candy."

# The Missionaries

＊—｜—＊

TWO YOUNG men wearing white shirts and black pants, with slicked-back brown hair, carrying two brown paper sacks, came walking down the dirt road to the Wazhashk house. It was a warm day for late September. Thomas saw them approach as he walked from the old house to the outhouse. He thought about putting off his visit, but they were proceeding slowly. They seemed to be having a disagreement. One stopped and turned around to walk away, then the other caught up with him and they started talking again. When Thomas came out of the toilet, the young men were closer. He walked into the house, washed his hands and face, dried off with a towel, and walked out to meet them in the yard. They looked as though they were from the government, though they were young.

"Good afternoon," he said.

He shook hands with each one.

"What can I do for you?"

"Have you ever wondered why you are here?" asked the taller of the two young men, eyeing him intensely.

"No," said Thomas. He was startled, but then, they were obviously from far away, from Bismarck, even farther. Maybe Washington. They, too, seemed taken aback by his reply. One recovered and said,

"Why not?"

"Because I know," said Thomas. "Don't you?"

The shorter of the two turned to the other and blurted out, "See?"

The taller hung his head and tried to sting the shorter fellow with his eyes.

"How about a cup of water?" said Thomas.

"Yes," said the shorter, who seemed to have control now of the situation.

"Follow me," said Thomas. He walked toward the house, up the three steps, through the door. The two young men hesitated.

"May we come in?" they both asked at once.

Thomas nodded and they followed him. A tiny child was creeping across the floor, and at the sight of them reared back, fell over, and started crying. Rose was taking care of a baby from down the road.

"Who are they?" shouted Noko, flattening herself against the wall.

Rose appeared from the next room, fists on her hips. She put her hand on her mother's shoulder.

"You scared her," she said ominously.

"We're sorry," said the young men, fumbling with their paper sacks.

Rose picked up the baby, jostled her in a comforting way, and flared her eyes at Thomas.

"They just want to know if we wonder why we are here," said Thomas.

"You took our land," said Noko. "Where else were we supposed to go?"

Rose looked down at the part in her mother's white hair, impressed by her answer and her vicious stare.

"Excuse me," said the shorter one. "Perhaps we can start over. I am Elder Elnath and this is Elder Vernon. How do you do?"

"Elder?"

"We were really asking if you ever wonder why you, as an ancient people, are here on this land?"

"I'm old, not ancient," fumed Noko, her hearing suddenly acute.

Rose patted her mother's bony shoulder.

"Wet your whistles, boys," said Thomas, dipping from the can. He handed each of them a cool cup of water. "Now, is there something I can help you fellows out with?"

"Elder Vernon didn't ask you the right question. We didn't have luck telling people who we are right off the bat, so he thought he'd ask a question with a bigger scope is the way he put it."

"Bigger scope?"

"Who put us on this land. What we are here to do. That sort of scope. Our job is really just to see if you want to read The Book of Mormon and pray with us."

"Mormon!" Thomas stepped back. "Do you young fellows know Arthur V. Watkins?"

"He's a writer," said Elnath, surprised. "He wrote *The Nephite Shepherd*."

"Is it a good book?" asked Thomas.

"Goodness, yes! In the Awakening of Zemnarihah the shepherd learns he is part of a secret society. But there are setbacks because of the Lamanites who still atone for the sins of Laman with their swarthy hides."

"Watkins wrote that?"

"I think he's our senator," said Vernon, the taller elder.

"You're from Utah."

"Yes."

"Why does he want to do away with us?"

"He doesn't want that!"

"He wants to terminate us."

"No, not at all!" Elnath became passionate. "We are charged with bringing you the gospel! You're all Lamanites."

"We're Chippewas here, Crees, and some French."

"It was revealed," said Vernon earnestly, "to Joseph Smith that you are people of the house of Jacob and children of Lehi."

"I've never heard of Joseph Smith, or those other people," said Thomas.

"Joseph Smith was a prophet."

"We get a lot of prophets coming around here," said Thomas in a friendly way. "And I have a religion. I'm more interested in politics. Why is this senator after us? Who is he? What's his message? Those are the things I want to know."

"Maybe you'd be interested in this."

Vernon reached into his paper sack and pulled out a small book with a black cover. He offered it to Thomas, who took it and thanked him. The young men finished drinking their water and Thomas walked them down the steps. He watched them as they disappeared down the road. They didn't look alike anymore, but they walked in exactly the same straight line, full of mystifying purpose.

# The Beginning

＊┼＊

AS HE did at the change of every season, Thomas gave his father a pinch of tobacco and asked for the story of his name. This story tied them together as Thomas was named after his grandfather, whose name had become the family surname. The original and real Wazhashk was a little muskrat.

"In the beginning," said Biboon, "the world was covered with water. The Creator lined up the animals who were the best divers. First the Creator sent down Fisher, the strongest. But Fisher came up gasping, couldn't find the bottom. Next Mang, the loon, ducked under the way they do."

Biboon curved his hand. "Loon tried. But failed." Thomas nodded in appreciation, loving the gestures he remembered from childhood.

"The Hell-diver flashed into the water, bragging it would succeed. That Hell-diver pulled itself deep down, and down. But no!"

Biboon waited, took in a deep breath.

"Last the humble water rat. The Creator called on that one. Wazhashk. The little fellow dived down. He took a long time, a very long time, and then finally Wazhashk floated to the top. He was drowned but his paw was clenched. The Creator unfolded Wazhashk's webbed hands. He saw that the muskrat had carried up just a little off the bottom. From that tiny paw's grip of dirt, the Creator made the whole earth."

"Mii'iw. That's it," said Biboon.

They were sitting outside. Biboon stared at the bright popple leaves, trembling and flashing as they swirled thickly off the branches. Once, the wild prairies had been littered with bones. Bones thick and white as far as he could see. He'd gathered and hauled the buffalo bones with his father. Eight dollars a ton down at the railroad yard in Devils Lake. His family had all dived to the bottom to scrape up dirt. But now his son was sitting with him. Their chairs tipped back against the whitewashed wall of old logs. The sun struck Biboon's face, no warmth to the light, a sign his own namesake was just over the horizon.

"I'm an old pinto pony, scrawny and always hungry. This winter might do me in," he said. His voice was light, amused.

"No," said Thomas. "You have to stick around here, Daddy."

"I'm a weight around your necks," said Biboon.

"Don't say that. We need you."

"I can't even dig a potato! Yesterday I fell over."

"I'm sending Wade down to stay with you. We need you, like I said. This thing that's coming at us from Washington. I need you to help me fight it."

"Oh, fine," said Biboon, putting up his fists.

# The Temple Beggar

AFTER SHE'D locked herself into her room, Patrice stripped and looked at herself in the mirror. She was not imagining it. A subtle but undeniable blueness was seeping into her. She touched her streaked belly. Her armpits ached and stung. A smell clung to her skin—the chemical perfume of the pest-killing powder that she'd dusted into the ox costume. She stared hard at herself. Was this really Patrice? Or was this itchy blue woman who'd just pretended to be a watery sexpot her other self? Pixie. Definitely Pixie. But she would leave that girl behind starting now.

Patrice put her bra back on, and packed it with money. She reached into her satchel. Her arm was weak. She was suddenly, alarmingly, so exhausted she could barely move. She managed to pack her bag and lay out the clothing she would wear. Then she shut off the light and rolled beneath the ribbon-trimmed red blanket. As she was falling asleep, she directed her body to exit sleep in a couple of hours. She told herself to remember exactly where she was when she woke up. There would be total darkness. She must escape without turning on a light that might bleed out under the door. She would have to rely on the fact that Freckle Face needed sleep, too.

She did wake. Fire was flowing down her legs. It shocked her, but she didn't cry out. By the feel of the air, she knew it was only a few hours into the deepest night. She rose, alert, found her bag, her shoes, her coat. The money was still wadded between her breasts in the little bra pocket. She sat on her bed, invisible, and went through the instructions she had given herself before sleep. When she was satisfied that she had followed each directive, she sneaked to the door.

She used the key, slipped the bolt, eased the door open. It was silent on its oiled hinges. She stepped forward and there was Jack, sitting on the floor directly across from her.

Jack's legs were stretched straight out, ankles elegantly crossed. His suit jacket was folded neatly beside him. Oiled strings of hair hung to his chin. The skin of his face was rippling like water. Expressions flowed across his features, a swift array shifting from surprise to joy to horror. He tried to lock his muddy yellow irises on her, but his eyes rolled back like the tiny windows in a slot machine. With his gilded skin and golden orbs, with his shirtsleeve rolled up and his hands open in supplication, he was a picture she'd seen somewhere, maybe in a magazine. A beggar at the door of some temple. She put her hand out and tucked the strings of hair behind his ears.

"Jack?"

He smiled at her like a child, face clear, then his eyes rolled back again. She slipped away, down the back stairs, out through the kitchen into the back alley. A man at the end of the passageway rummaged through garbage cans. He didn't notice as she walked by and turned down the street to find the Josen House. The wind was brisk, the temperature dropping. She went into the hotel, stepping over the bodies of men who had paid their dimes to sleep in the entry. There was nobody at the window, so she walked up three flights of stairs. 328 was at the hallway's far end. The hall was filled with the sounds of sleepers muttering, gasping, shifting, snoring, and the patter of rats across the metal mesh of the ceilings. The wind came through the cracked windows, cheeping and chattering. Occasionally, a rippling growl of thunder. At the end of the noisy hall, she tapped on the door. She heard him leave his bed and the door opened.

"Pixie."

He dragged her inside. She dropped her satchel on the floor. There was a window in the room. A low radiance from the lamps and signs below. She could see that his lip was swollen, his face cut. Her skin still burned, but her mind was icy clear. All that happened was now in focus and each incident stood out sharply in her thoughts. She sat down on his bed. He spread his jacket out and crouched on the floor. They began to whisper.

"I know, *know*, they took her," said Patrice. "Took Vera."

"She could be dead," said Wood Mountain, less gently than he meant to speak, but she shook her head.

"No, she's not. They took her someplace."

"I said I'd go back for the baby."

"Let's get her . . . him."

"Him."

"Then let's get out of here."

"We should sleep a couple hours. If we show up at Bernadette's now we could get ourselves killed. You take the bed. I'm good here on the floor."

She gave him the stiff-with-dirt blanket and covered herself with her coat. She breathed herself into a trance. As they slept, deeply, the wind rose and by morning a cold rain smashed against the window. Patrice woke lying on her side, and looked out at the gray field of sky. The hotel walls were made of cardboard, plywood, and pliable tin that shook stormily. She realized that what had registered earlier as thunder was the sound of men moving about in their rooms. Occasionally someone fell against a wall and a crashing boom reverberated down the hall.

Wood Mountain lay sprawled on the floor. She thought of Jack's eyes of ancient gold. An inch above Wood Mountain's head, copper-colored water bugs darted and shifted, sensitive beings that froze at the sounds of false thunder. As the vibrations fell away, they began again their earnest travels.

"Everett Blue," she said, and the insects scattered. He put his hands on his face before he opened his eyes, and mumbled, "They been after me all night."

"We have to go to Bernadette's now. And I have to use the . . ."

"Outhouse," he said. "You'll wish it was an outhouse. I'll go with you and guard the door."

A FEW minutes later, they left through the back entrance. Halfway down the alley, Wood Mountain stepped over what looked like a pile of clothes. Patrice recognized the pile as Jack. She bent over him, put her fingers to his throat.

"No," said Wood Mountain, "leave him be."

She waited for a pulse of life. It was faint, fainter. His spirit quickly puddled at her ankles.

"He's still here," she said.

"He's bad, Pixie."

She rose. Lifted her feet out of the gentle mud that was Jack's last trace of consciousness. There was a low gurgle as he seeped away.

Patrice went back into the hotel and stood before the window. The night attendant didn't move his head, but his eyes rolled toward her.

"There's a man dying in the alley," she said.

The eyes stayed fixed on her.

"It's Jack from next door."

The man nodded.

"We'll take care of him."

She left.

BERNADETTE PEERED through the beautiful oval window, opened the oak door. She was wearing a ruffled white pinafore and chopsticks in her hair. There was an air of sober exhaustion.

"Oh good," she said. "Cal's gone."

"Where's Vera?"

"I don't have her. Please," said Bernadette. "I could get in bad trouble."

She glanced behind Wood Mountain and Patrice before she nodded them into the entry. Bacon was frying and the same flowery steam wafted off Bernadette's shoulders.

"You hungry?" she asked.

"Always," said Wood Mountain.

A honey-brown woman came down the stairs into the foyer. Bernadette gestured to her and she unwrapped the bundle she held. The baby was frowning in its sleep. "Give her the baby," said Bernadette, and the woman handed him to Patrice. The baby was surprisingly dense, like a brick. Bernadette slipped into the kitchen. After a moment, Wood Mountain followed and leaned toward the closed door. Someone was talking to Bernie behind the door. He listened. Then the woman touched his shoulder and gave Wood Mountain a sack of baby things. Bernadette came out.

"Now get the hell out of here," she said, handing them a package wrapped in newspaper.

AFTER THEY were settled on the moving train, Wood Mountain unwrapped the newspaper package. A stack of pancakes and bacon. He folded one of the pancakes around some bacon, and handed the roll to Patrice. She held the pancake in one hand and kept the baby cradled on her arm. He'd just sucked down a bottle of milk. There was a tiny line between his brows, where his worry for the future resided. She stroked the line with her finger and tried to smooth it away. But the groove seemed permanent.

"Reach up in my bag," she told Wood Mountain. "Take out the baby blanket."

He wolfed the rest of the pancake, stood, pulled a cascade of white mesh from above. He handed it down to her. The blanket was large and stretchy. It fit around the baby twice. The fancy stitches made it look like she and Wood Mountain knew what they were doing with a baby. It made the baby look theirs, which made them look like a couple. Nobody tried to take their seats away. People settled themselves far from the potentially explosive bundle. Patrice wanted to say that she wasn't the mother and Wood Mountain wasn't the father and all of this wasn't what it looked like. But she only said, "Would you fold up that newspaper? Later, I want to read it."

You could hardly stand up and announce that she wasn't sure she even liked Wood Mountain, or would like him back if he happened to like her. She wanted to say that she was a working woman with a perfectly good job, that she was returning to that job because she was so good at it. There wasn't any reason to say these things. There wasn't a reason to think. She eased herself back, holding the baby, and tried not to take stock of what had happened in the Cities. But her mind kept churning. Were all of the things that happened real? The dog collar? The dog's words? Her poisoned ox suit? Jack's eyes of ancient gold? Bernadette with chopsticks in her hair? Who would believe?

"I'll take care of you until she comes home," said Patrice to the baby.

Wood Mountain was staring at her.

"What?" she said.

"Nothing." He looked away. It wasn't his place to argue, and he still couldn't figure out what those words meant, the ones from behind the kitchen door. Good or bad? He didn't want to tell Pixie until he knew.

THE BABY came with six diapers. A tiny pair of pale blue rubber pants elasticized at the waist and legs. Two glass bottles and four rubber nipples. Two cotton shirts with side ties. A warm gray suit that covered him head to toe. He'd been wrapped in table drape glassily embroidered with domes and turrets. There was another bottle of milk that was supposed to last the length of the train ride. The baby had sucked down the first bottle quickly and Patrice thought they'd have to run out for more in Fargo. But he slept and slept. He didn't seem to want to cause them trouble, said Wood Mountain, touching the whirlwind of hair at the baby's crown. Patrice propped up her arm, dropped the seat back a fraction, and held the baby across her chest. He clung to her like a warm cocklebur and put her straight to sleep. Later, he woke in a fit. His roaring squall unnerved her, and Wood Mountain stumbled into the aisle as she bore the baby to the train's bathroom. After he was changed and fed, she rocked the baby endlessly in the swaying corridor between the cars. When he fell quiet, at last, she realized her neck was damp with tears. Her own tears. Her mother would, of course, take care of the baby. Wouldn't she? Patrice couldn't do it all. She couldn't do any of it.

She walked quietly down the aisle and slid past Wood Mountain into her seat, transferring the baby into his arms. Was almost disappointed when he accepted eagerly and gathered the baby to his heart like a natural.

"What are you going to name him?" he asked Patrice.

"Name him? Why? He has a name. Vera named him."

Wood Mountain thought the baby was staring at him like he knew something.

"This baby likes me," he said.

"Oh, you think so?"

Patrice looked at him sharply, but it wasn't a way to get at her. Wood Mountain and the baby had locked eyes in fascination. They ignored her. She turned to the window although it was dark now and the glass held only a tired ghost.

# Wild Rooster

✦═══✦

THE SKY opened as they drove down to Fargo, passed through Larimore, heading for the meeting that would register their opposition to the Termination Bill. The road stayed wet. As night fell the tar froze slick. Thomas slowed and Louis roared past in the two-tone DeSoto. Four people were stuffed into the backseat. Juggie waved from the passenger window.

"Wish them two would get married up," said Moses. "Isn't regular."

"What do you mean?" asked Thomas, trying to hide his surprise.

"Ay, you. Altar Boy," laughed Moses.

From the backseat, his wife, Mary, said, "You, think you know so much!"

"Well, you're the one taught me everything I know," said Moses, in a fake meek voice.

"Let Juggie be Juggie," said Joyce Asiginak, who sat in the middle.

Eddy Mink sat behind the passenger seat. Yes, Eddy Mink. Sober, Eddy was brilliant and a shrewd talker, which was the reason Thomas drank with him in the old days. He'd be good on questions as Thomas had him studying up. The trick would be to keep him sober. Joyce and Mary were on that.

"I have nothing to say on the subject," said Eddy. "Getting married don't make no sense to me. It's priest-man talk."

"The renegade speaks," said Thomas.

"That's for damn sure right. I am a wild rooster back here with these two lovely hens. Don't you turn around, Moses. You'll see something will shock your mind, boy."

Joyce and Mary began to bat him around, laughing, but soon they were playacting with such violence that the back end of the car began to sway.

"Whoa!" Thomas shouted.

"Leave off!" Moses ordered.

"We're the last hope of the great Chippewa Nation," howled Eddy. "Don't wanna wreck us."

"Oh shut up, fool." Joyce laughed and laughed.

"Fool? I got some wisdom for you. Listen up. Government is more like sex than people think. When you are having good sex, you don't appreciate it enough. When you are having bad sex, it is all you can think about."

"You got a point there, Rooster," said Moses from the front.

They crawled along and then the road was dry and they made it all in one piece. There was no money to put them up, so Thomas delivered them to addresses near the heart of the city. He was staying with Moses's cousin Nancy and her husband, George. They lived in a small apartment with a convertible couch and a cot in the kitchenette. In the morning, Nancy, round and cute as a bear, surprised Thomas. He'd fallen asleep like he'd been dumped into a hole. Woke all fogged up. He didn't have his pants on so Nancy gave him coffee in bed. He drank it propped up on one elbow while she made oatmeal. Claimed he felt like a king.

"Rose never give you coffee in bed?"

"No!"

"Well, if you try it out on her first, you might get lucky."

"Oh, criminy."

"Not lucky that way. You have a bad mind!"

"I was called an altar boy last night."

Nancy laughed. "I known some wicked altar boys."

"Can I have a refill?"

"Get your pants on. Maybe then."

# Arthur V. Watkins

✦═✦

IF ARTHUR V. WATKINS had been a boxer, which he definitely wasn't, he would have been a brawler. You wouldn't think it of such an ideal-looking, respectable fellow. Classic preacher looks, semibald with a virtuous halo of whitish hair, spectacles. An aggressive air of cleanliness and godliness—that was Watkins. Dark tie. Pale suit. He was born in 1886, when Utah was still a territory, and he was baptized by Isaac Jacobs. In 1906, his father, also Arthur V. Watkins, wrote to Joseph F. Smith, "We have filed on land on the reservation for us a home." This happened during the allotment era, when the Ute people and the Uintah and Ouray Reservation, where the Watkins land was located, were relieved of 13.8 million acres of land that had been guaranteed by the executive orders of first President Abraham Lincoln and, later, Chester A. Arthur.

Arthur V. Watkins grew up on some of this land, which had been stolen by his father. In 1907 he was set apart. From Vernal, in Uintah County, Utah, he was called. He completed a mission in the eastern United States, and then returned to Utah. Eventually, he ran for office, working his way through state office to become a United States senator. During the hearings on termination he was said to "convey an air of rectitude that was almost terrifying." When expounding on termination he "howled in his reedy voice." Joseph Smith and the early

Mormons had tried their best to murder all Indians in their path across the country, but in the end did not quite succeed. Arthur V. Watkins decided to use the power of his office to finish what the prophet had started. He didn't even have to get his hands bloody.

## Cool Fine

✳︎══✳︎

AFTER THE train there was the bus and when the bus let them off on the highway near town it was a cool but fine autumn afternoon. Leaves were falling now in gusts. They began to walk. There were few people on the road and none going in their direction. Wood Mountain walked alongside Patrice, carrying her bag and his own. She lugged the baby. As she walked, she prayed, *Don't let him be home*. If her father was there, snarling and puking, she might run away. Back down to the Cities. She had the money! Wood Mountain's thoughts were very different. He had a name in mind for the baby. Archille, for his own father. That was that. He couldn't help it. He was being thrown around by these things—emotions—still sensations without name and only evidenced by his actions and sudden decisions.

"I thought of a name for him," said Wood Mountain after they had walked a couple of miles. He rubbed his face with his free hand to muffle his voice, doubting he should speak, unable not to speak. Sneaked a glance at her face. Said, "Temporary name, of course."

Still, no response.

"Archille." He could have kicked himself for saying it.

"Archille."

She kept walking. With every step, she lightly patted the baby's back. She'd tied the stretchy white blanket onto herself in an ingenious way so that the baby hung in a pouch, held fast against her breast. Her breast! He batted his head as if he were slapping at an insect.

"When my sister comes back," said Patrice, "we'll tell her you named the baby, nicknamed the baby, for your father. My uncle's told me how they rode the rails in their young days. Your dad was a good man."

She was not without compassion. But here he was, walking her home. Totally out of his way. She told him again that she could make it to her house just fine. But he said no, no, he would not leave her to walk alone with the baby. The satchel and the baby would be heavier by the mile, he said, and she was wearing her good shoes. They didn't look like the best for walking. He said, however, they were nice shoes.

"They hurt like the devil," she said. "I'm going to be lame at work tomorrow."

He took the baby and the luggage while she removed her shoes at a turnoff through the woods. There were paths everywhere and this was one of many paths to get to her main path home. You had to wade through a bit of slough on the way but that was all right. Her toes loved muck. She took the baby back.

"Gwiiwizens," she said, lifting him to her heart. It was what her people called a boy baby if they didn't want bad spirits to find him. If there was disease or danger around. Nothing fancy that could attract attention, just Little Boy. Although he knew and approved of that, Wood Mountain also knew that Patrice not using his name for the baby meant something. It meant . . . he stuck on this as he waded through sucking slough mud . . . rinsed his feet and returned his shoes to his feet. Walked up a hill knocking pukkons into his hat. For her. It meant . . .

It meant she wasn't having any of it.

Oh, but the colors were rich, the golds and yellows of the

woods, the ochres, flare of orange and crimson, green and green, all shades of green, setting off the flamboyant shafts and sprays of color that poured through onto their hair and shoulders and walking bodies. Their young bodies free of pain except an aching cheekbone for Wood Mountain and a blister on Patrice's right toe.

And why shouldn't she want someone to walk her to her house and become thereby a couple since he might love her and certainly loved the child? He was strong built, good-looking, had prospects in life, and she was attracted to him in spite of that witless smile. Which he hadn't tried on her again. To fall in love with him was the way of things. Wasn't it? Still, she did not take his hand, which hung next to her hand, twitched toward hers, but she used her hand to pat Gwiiwizens.

"Pixie," he said. "Oh, Pixie."

"Patrice. I keep telling you."

She gave him a look that would have shaved his face if he'd had whiskers.

He shut up.

She found herself doing the same things as with Barnes. Said things she knew would discourage him. Ignored the dangling hand, avoided the ready clutch, dispensed neutral glances when admiring smiles were expected. During the last mile, she admitted to herself that doing these things was easy with Barnes and far more difficult when it came to Wood Mountain.

⁕⊨⁕

ZHAANAT WAS not like the teachers and the nuns and the priests and the other adults who showed Patrice the world. Zhaanat had a different sort of intelligence. In her thinking there were no divisions, or maybe the divisions were not the same, or maybe they were invisible. White people looked at Indians like her and thought *dull stubborn*. But Zhaanat's intelligence was of frightening dimensions. Sometimes she knew things she should not have known. Where a vanished man had fallen through the ice. Where a disordered woman had buried the child who died of diphtheria. Why an animal gave itself to one hunter not another. Why disease struck a young man and skipped his frail grandfather. Why an odd stone might appear outside the door, one morning, out of nowhere.

"The stars sent a message to us," Zhaanat had said.

Patrice had stared at her mother, who had certainly never heard of a meteor. Because everything was alive, responsive in its own way, capable of being hurt in its own way, capable of punishment in its own way, Zhaanat's thinking was built on treating everything around her with great care.

ZHAANAT WAS walking down the hill with an apron full of cedar when Patrice and Wood Mountain came to the house. She dropped everything and ran to them, her face wild.

"We didn't find her yet," cried Patrice as her mother ran toward them, skirts flapping, braids unraveling, arms out. Zhaanat held her, the baby between them. Wood Mountain lowered his eyes. Pokey came around the corner of the house, carrying an armload of wood. He stood there, frozen.

"I only brought Little Boy home, Mama."

Patrice put Gwiiwizens into her arms and Zhaanat stared at the baby apprehensively, then critically, searching out Vera's features. She sat down with the baby suddenly, plopped on the ground as if her strength had given way. She was silent and Patrice knew her mother would be somewhere else, unreachable, until she decided to return.

"You should go now, Everett," she said to Wood Mountain. She looked around, carefully. No sign of her father.

Wood Mountain walked over to the door and placed her bag there. He nodded significantly at Pokey, then turned and walked away.

ZHAANAT EVENTUALLY gathered up the baby and herself. Walked into the house. The first thing she did was sit down and nurse him at her breast. Pokey didn't notice, but this made Patrice uneasy. She asked her mother why she was nursing the baby. Obviously it wasn't like she would have milk. However, Zhaanat said that sometimes in the old days, when the baby's mother couldn't nurse, the older women were sometimes able to take over.

"And I'm not that old," said Zhaanat. "My breasts aren't yet hard dried-up old leather pipe bags." In Chippewa, that was all just one word. They both started laughing in that desperate high-pitched way people laugh when their hearts are broken.

# The Torus

THE NEXT morning, Patrice waited on the road for Doris and Valentine, impatient to get away from the baby, who was desperately hungry. His bawl was like a tap turned on full blast. Zhaanat was still letting him nurse, but also trying to get him to accept the juice strained from boiled oatmeal. Pokey had walked to the school bus early. Nobody was on the road. Had they forgotten? Patrice paced in their direction. Her thoughts zipped around, landing here and there like flies. Skittering away. "I know," she said aloud. "I know I may be crazy. But I have to believe that my sister is still alive." She picked up a smooth piece of cloudy quartz and stared at it in her hand.

"I'm going nuts," she said and flung it into the brush.

She heard the growl of a motor, then gravel crunching underneath the tires of Doris's car, and closed her eyes in relief. The car pulled alongside her. For five days she had been another person, on another planet, in a different time.

"Gracious good morning!" she said, opening the car's back door.

"We stop for hoboes," cried Valentine. "Get in!"

"Did you find Vera?"

"No, she didn't turn up yet. I brought her baby boy home."

"A baby boy!"

They talked of nothing else the entire way. By the end of the day she had promises, so many promises. More bottles. Weeks worth of diapers. A diaper bucket with lid. Baby clothes and a blanket. Everything a baby needed, except a mother.

"I know somebody with leftover baby formula," said Betty Pye. "She wanted money but when she hears I'll bet she give it to you for free."

"I can pay," said Patrice, the waterjack. "I can pay her whatever she wants."

But that was for show because she was pretty sure Zhaanat's pipe bags would come through.

*—=—*

IF YOU revolve a circle around a pole, the surface of the revolution would be a torus. An inner tube. You can have a hollow torus or a solid torus, which is the torus plus the volume inside the torus—a doughnut, a jewel bearing. A metal spindle turns in a jewel-lined pivot hole. The hole is shaped like a torus, and the mechanism makes possible the ideal of frictionless eternal motion.

You cannot feel time grind against you. Time is nothing but everything, not the seconds, minutes, hours, days, years. Yet this substanceless substance, this bending and shaping, this warping, this is the way we understand our world.

Zhaanat was lying on her daughter's bed, in a slat of cool fall sunshine, the exhausted baby in her arms. They were drifting in frictionless eternal motion when Patrice entered, slipped out of her shoes. She took her hat off, lay down beside them, and opened her blue coat like a wing.

# Metal Blinds

THE BIG meeting in Fargo was held at the judicial building, an imposing pillared structure made of pale smooth limestone. The halls with their brass sconces and polished oak wainscoting opened into majestic paneled courtrooms, judges' chambers, deliberation rooms for juries, and many other small apertures and offices. The room that Thomas and his fellow tribal members entered also had the beautiful wooden wainscoting. The upper portion of the wall had recently been painted a dull chalky white. Through the north-facing windows a bland gray light seeped. A small woman in a black skirt and heels opened a set of flexible metal blinds.

The hushed light fell in bars on a polished table beneath the window. Four men sitting behind the table rose as Thomas and the other tribal members came into the room. Each was dressed in a suit and tie, all in various shades and patterns of brown and gray. They were from the BIA office in Aberdeen, South Dakota. Each man came forward to shake hands with Thomas, the other members of the committee, and the tribe's attorney, John Hail. Then each man retreated back behind the table.

Thomas put his briefcase down on a chair in the front row of chairs, between John Hail and Moses Montrose. The others filled seats to the right and left and in back, more than forty-five tribal members in all. Thomas passed his hand across his eyes, and looked down to hide that he was moved that so many had made the difficult trip.

"Welcome," said the area director, John Cooper. "Let it be noted that this meeting is taking place on October 19, 1953, and the time is one p.m."

The secretary's fingers began to rapidly tap the keys of her machine.

"Thank you," said Thomas. "We are here to discuss the purpose of the proposed legislation in connection with House Concurrent Resolution 108, which will terminate all federal recognition and support at the Turtle Mountain Agency."

He took a deep breath to try to loosen the grip of tension in his stomach. He hadn't eaten enough for breakfast, out of nerves. He asked if John Cooper would read the legislation for the benefit of his fellow tribal members, and then he sat down. Mr. Cooper passed a sheaf of papers to the lawyer for the BIA, Gary Holmes, who began to read each section.

After the first few pages, Thomas could feel the air leave the room. Brief phrases caught his attention and then the next packed sentence pulled it away. His voice was calm and scratchy. He paused often to clear his throat or utter a prolonged ummmmm.

> *disposition of federally owned property*
> *with to such Indians may be discontinued as no longer necessary*
> *cause such lands to be sold and deposit the proceeds of sale*
> *trust relationship to the affairs of the Band and its members has*
> *terminated*
> *termination*
> *terminating*

WORSE THAN listening to the reading of the bill himself was the silent consternation behind him. Thomas could not turn around without seeming rude to the speaker, yet he longed to exchange glances with Juggie and Louis, with Joyce and Mary, with the others who'd shown up from here in Fargo and from Grand Forks. They'd heard about the situation and trickled to this obscure office. Martin Cross had driven all the way across the state to support them. About twelve of the people there did not speak English, or understood it very poorly, and yet they had gone to great effort and expense to come to this meeting. As the words tapped like dry little hammers, Thomas thought about the places where his people lived. John Summer, old Giizis, Clothilde Fleury, Angus Watch, Buggy Morrissey, Anakwad, lived in pole-and-mud dwellings tucked into swales and hills, sheltered against the wind. They drew their water from sloughs or tiny springs, lighted their homes with kerosene. Yet here they were, each person, presenting themselves in worn immaculate clothing. As Indians had for generation after generation, they were attempting to understand a white man reading endlessly from a sheaf of papers.

Holmes paused to speak to Mr. Cooper, and Thomas turned around. His people wore a look of intense concentration, which, in the absence of the speaker, they turned upon him. He returned their gaze, sweeping his eyes to each person. Nobody looked away, as people would normally. All rested their unguarded expressions upon him and he accepted the gravity of their regard. When he turned back, he felt that something had been communicated to him. He felt it up behind his eyes as dry tears. Holmes picked up where he'd left off.

WHEN AT long last the reading of the bill was finished, Thomas rose and again turned to look at his friends and relatives. He asked for comments from the audience.

*Louis Pipestone:* Thank you. And now would it be possible to explain the bill so a hard-of-hearing old ranchman can get the gist of it?

*Mr. Holmes:* Simply, once and for all, it provides that there won't be any more Indian service for the Turtle Mountains. You will now be equal with whites as far as the government is concerned.

*Joyce Asiginak:* Well, equal is not the way we see it. Our rights go down. So this bill does not suit me in any way. The government is backing out of its agreement. You left us on land that is too small a size and most of it cannot be farmed. The government should give more land back, not kick us off the leftovers.

*Mr. Holmes:* Oh, good news! You will be relocated to areas of equal opportunity. It says so right in the bill.

There was utter silence in the room. Then an urgent rustling as people repeated, and interpreted, what he had said.

*Juggie Blue:* We don't want to leave our homes We are poor, but even poor people can love their land. You do not need money to love your home.

*Anakwad:* Gawiin ninisidotoosinoon.

*Louis Pipestone:* Anakwad here says that he does not understand, nor do many who have come to this place to learn their fate. He asks that this bill be translated into his language so that he may understand it.

Mr. Holmes, turning to his colleagues, raised his eyebrows and smiled. They, too, smiled indulgently, shook their heads with some exasperation.

*Clothilde Fleury:* I will sit beside the Indian speakers and translate.

The audience reshuffled their seats, Clothilde spoke quietly to Thomas, and then everyone waited, expectantly.

*Giizis (translated by Clothilde):* I would like to respectfully request that Mr. Holmes read the bill again. Half the people here did not understand it.

Holmes opened his mouth, closed his mouth. Coughed. He conferred with his colleagues. After ostentatiously pouring water into his glass, he took a long sip, and began to read. After a few minutes, he was stopped by Mr. Cooper.

*Mr. Cooper:* I propose that we take a short break.
*Thomas Wazhashk:* Sir, with all due respect, we have just this one day to understand a bill that is meant to take everything from us. Could those who need a break discreetly do so while the rest of us continue with this meeting? I further propose that Mr. Holmes repeat the simple version of the bill. He seemed to capture the meaning in a few sentences.

Thomas was surprised by his own boldness, but he stood firm. The meeting continued on in its flow with people leaving as needed, and returning so that the concentration in the room was not broken.

*Mary Montrose:* This relocation isn't my wish. How about you relocate some of our neighbors who aren't Indians? They are sitting on our best land.

*Mr. Cooper (abrupt laugh):* That is out of the question. We are here on your behalf, but we cannot do such a thing.

*Mr. Hail:* We know the Indian Department did not initiate this move that included the Turtle Mountain Chippewa Indians and the reservation. It was an act of Congress. Some members of Congress heard or seem to believe that the Turtle Mountain Chippewa are so far advanced that they should be relinquished by the government.

*Moses Montrose:* We are advanced in some ways. That is true. We have a lot of smart Indians in this room. But most of us are plain-out broke. We are working, but even if we did become rich, that would have no bearing on our agreement with the government. Nothing in the treaty says that if we better ourselves we lose our land.

*Thomas Wazhashk:* I am not sure what study the information about our advancement, financially speaking, was based on. But I will tell you it was faulty. Most of our people live on dirt floors, no electricity, no plumbing. I haul my own water like most Indians in this room. I consider myself advanced only because I read and write. Should I not be an Indian person because I read and write?

*Mr. Cooper:* There is no move to take away your identity as an Indian.

*Joyce Asignak:* That is exactly what is happening.

*John Summer:* We are still ourselves even if we advance. As for myself, I haven't advanced yet.

*Mr. Hail:* Congress is attempting to abandon its commitment to treaties that were made with Indians to last through time. You have heard the phrase "as long as the grass grows and the rivers flow." I represent a people who have survived quite a bit and need help getting on their feet.

*Mr. Holmes:* We didn't come up with this bill.

*Eddy Mink (standing steady, stroking his limp silk tie):* I would like to say a few words. May I be recognized? Thank you. The way I see it is the great state of North Dakota will have to take over services to our remote area, provide for education, and so on. The county will have to start caring for our bridges, maintaining the roads. They will also need to step up law enforcement and so on. I wonder if our wonderful county and state are eager to take on these rewarding opportunities?

*Mr. Cooper:* I am not sure that—

*Eddy Mink:* Of course, if the government carts us away and dumps us here and there—excuse me, relocates us—mostly we will end up down in the Cities. And if the BIA sells off our land, problem solved.

*Anakwad (translated):* Do you see any rich persons here? I don't know of anyone. I got a few cents in my pocket. That's all I got. Ever since the white man came in 1492, they started robbing the Indian of his riches.

*Juggie Blue:* They are just going to take our land away from us. In five years all the land on the reservation would be in white hands and we would be trudging up the road with our children, trying to find a place to light.

*Giizis (translated):* We don't want anything to do with this bill. We are going to fight it down. That is how it stands. We want things just as they are at the present and to go on as they are until something new comes out that is better than it is.

*Mr. Holmes:* Now can we take a break? This seat is getting pretty hot.

(Laughter)

*Buggy Morrissey:* I myself happened to be in Washington a few
  years ago. I talked with the secretary of the interior and
  the commissioner of Indian affairs. They said it would take
  several decades for the Indians to become independent. So
  I don't understand this bill. Maybe the future will show we
  can do it.

*Moses Montrose:* There was no provision like that in our
  original agreement. It was supposed to last in perpetuity.
  Even if we are to get independent, we should still be in the
  treaty.

*Eddy Mink:* The services that the government provides to
  Indians might be likened to rent. The rent for use of the
  entire country of the United States.

*✳═╪═✳*

THE OFFICIALS in the front of the room looked a little stunned
by Eddy's statement. And then the meeting went on for two
more hours, but no one said anything new.

As the meeting was about to be adjourned, Moses Montrose
suddenly spoke out.

*Moses Montrose:* Now I wonder and want to ask that in making
  a report after this assembly, just what manner are you going
  to put it to Congress?

*Mr. Holmes:* The various statements made here have been
  transcribed.

*Juggie Blue:* Then please transcribe this. We are all to every
  person against this bill.

Thomas took a vote.
For the bill—0.

Against the bill—47.

The meeting was adjourned. Everyone shook hands and left. As Thomas walked out the door, Louie stepped out next to him and said, "Remember my daughter Millie?" Thomas must have looked blank because Louie continued, "Checks, we call her?"

"Oh, Checks, yes."

"My daughter from my first girlfriend. She was a Cloud, but not from around here. And Millie turned into a university girl. Remember she came out here asking questions? Putting together her information to get some letters behind her name?"

"Oh, of course," said Thomas. "Our Chippewa scholar."

"Maybe she could help us with her findings."

"Yes," said Thomas. He was trying not to show despair. "Let's throw everything we can at them. They've got us on the ropes."

BEHIND THE cottony blanket of cloud, the sun's light was so diffuse that it was impossible to determine the time of day. Thomas thought it had to be quite late in the afternoon. He heard Eddy trying to persuade Joyce and Mary to stop with him for a drink.

"Eddy wants to wet his whistle," said Moses.

"So do I," said Thomas. "But I better stick to a root beer with my dinner."

"Then so will your tribal judge."

Moses might take a sip of whiskey now and then, but never did get drunk enough for anyone to notice. It was one reason he was the judge. He was being loyal to Thomas's vow by not drinking and Thomas knew it. And inside, he wanted a drink. It was like an ache in his brain. His thoughts swirled around the ache. A disquieted disgust gripped him, like the onset of an illness. As he walked along, it got worse. He was very large

or very small, could not decide which. The absence of shadows, the flat surfaces of Fargo's buildings and sidewalks, did
not help. He felt it coming. Wanted to duck. Winced. A sensation like when he was chastised at school gripped him. Like
when he went into a bank or bought something expensive in
an off-reservation town. Their looks pressing down on him.
Their words flattening him. Their eyes squeezing him. Isey,
for shame. As his mother used to say. But it was so much worse
in English, the word *shame*. It made him curdle inside. And the
curdling became something hard and sour. It became a black
sediment he carried around in his stomach. Or a thought that
stabbed so hard he might cast it out in a flare of anger. Or it
might stay in there hardening even further until it flew up to
his brain and killed him.

These official men with their satisfied soft faces.

He hated their approval just as much as he hated their con-
descension. And yet this truth was buried so deep inside him
that its expression only emerged, in their presence, as a friendly
smile.

LATER, THEY emerged from the restaurant they'd chosen, an
inexpensive Italian place where they'd filled up on spaghetti
and meatballs, which cheered them all up. Outside, Thomas
saw Paranteau. He was walking on the other side of the street,
warring with gravity, tipping from side to side. Every few feet
he stopped to steady himself, clutching a pillar, a windowsill, a
mailbox. His coat hung slack and billowed around his shanks.
Thomas sent the others on ahead and crossed the street.

"Hello, niiji," said Thomas.

Paranteau was staring ahead, fixing his squint at the end of
the street as if taking aim before starting to move. He did not

register Thomas's presence, but gathered himself and suddenly surged forward in an awkward gallop. He made it to an iron lamppost and held on to it like a man in a tornado. Thomas followed. Edged around Paranteau's rickety frame. He stood in front of Paranteau and gripped his shoulder. What a sight. Paranteau's hair was matted to his skull. His lip rolled out, thick as a wet cigar, and his mouth sagged. His wet red eyes bugged, all misery.

"Friend, cousin, it's me. Thomas."

Paranteau began to rock like a horse preparing to haul a too heavy load. His feet tried to abandon the lamppost but his hands would not unclench.

"No," he said. "Not yet."

"Yes," said Thomas. "You're blasted. We'll take you home."

"No no no. Not yet."

Thomas tried to pry Paranteau's fingers off the lamppost. They wouldn't budge. Paranteau began to fiercely pant and blow. He strained. His eyes bulged with such desperation that Thomas had to look away. Paranteau could not unlock his fingers. It seemed they were welded to the metal post.

"Oh my niiji," Paranteau wailed. "See how she loves me! My honey! She don't let me go!"

He began laughing in hoots and croaks.

"Oh my! Oh my! She got me, cousin!"

"You can get away," said Thomas. "Just take a deep breath now, let yourself relax, and she'll release you."

"Ah, yes," said Paranteau.

After a moment, Thomas realized that a stream of piss had emerged below Paranteau's left pants cuff. The stream trickled to the gutter and Paranteau began to weep.

"I was first on the team. Got the high score. Nobody outgunned me, cousin. Couldn't touch me once I made my break. And three pointers. In the clutch? I was your man. And jump? They called me Pogo. Remember?"

"Yes."

The basketball team had gone to state that year. Class B. And they had nearly made it to finals.

"You made the last shot. Almost took that game," Thomas said.

"That's right. Oh my cousin, I am sick now. I am dying off, me. End of trail."

Thomas worked away at Paranteau's fingers again, but it was useless. And they were hot, like all the life force in Paranteau was concentrating in his hands, burning with a contrary will. Finally, Thomas managed to pry up one pinkie. As if he'd raised a magic lever, all the fingers flew off at once and Paranteau sprang away. Leaping the way he used to. Pogo Paranteau. And then his legs gathered under him. He floated up like a buck deer and he was gone down the street, coat flying, tossed fiercely along by suffering.

Let him go, Thomas thought, walking back. Paranteau returning home would have been hell on the rest of the family. Better to let him skid out in Fargo and hope he survived.

$$X = ?$$

✸━┼━✸

BARNES FELT his fists blur with deadly speed! He was striking so fast that a breeze snapped his hair back and only his molten blue eyes, fixed on the speed bag, maintained an iron steadiness. He saw himself as from above. Then on a movie screen. Then through the wrong end of a telescope. How should he treat this betrayal? This flouting of trust? He'd found out from Pokey that Wood Mountain had helped Patrice bring the baby back to the reservation on the train and thence to their very home. To their yard. If it could be called a yard. The surrounding half-cleared woods.

He paused, sweat stinging his eyes, then punched again.

After all the time that Barnes had sacrificed to Wood Mountain! After all the training secrets that Barnes had lavished on Wood Mountain. After the rides and pickups, the loan of shirts, of robe, of equipment, and the bestowal of his coach's pride and hope! After all of that, not counting the many meals ferried from Juggie or bought at Henry's or that damn fateful breakfast with Wood Mountain at the Powers Hotel in Fargo, how had he the gall? And what should Barnes do when the horny boy dog showed up to train with his bighearted chumpish haystack of a coach?

"Oh, say there."

Barnes stood back and glowered at the quivering bag.

"Hello, coach! Hey, you're fast!"

Barnes turned. His hands itched. There wasn't any need at all to wonder what he'd do because he simply said, "Hear you took yourself down to the Cities to step in on Pixie Paranteau."

"She wants to be called Patrice."

Rage boiled up.

"Oh, oh does she?"

"Yes. But put your dukes down. She don't have no time for me, neither."

Barnes gave Wood Mountain the eye.

"Not like I made a move on her. I just, dunno. Just got the idea she could be getting in trouble. And I know how they pick up girls in the Cities because my half sister is mixed up with that bunch."

"What bunch?"

"Cal Strosky and them."

"What do they do?"

Wood Mountain looked at his feet.

"It's only because my sister had told me a few things that I went after her."

"Was Pixie in trouble?"

"She got herself out. She was dressed up like an ox."

"A what?"

"Nothing. She was looking for her sister but got the baby anyway, came home. I just rode along. It wasn't that important of an experience. But I just wanted to let you know I got the feeling that even if I did, which I don't, she wouldn't have any interest."

"Huh."

"Okay."

"So."

"So."

"So you think I have a chance?" Barnes dropped his voice. Then his voice stuck in his craw, a sobbing hiccup.

"What the hell's wrong with me," he croaked, punching at the bag.

Wood Mountain opened his hands, as if to help. His stomach gave a little. Finally, he spoke.

"Nothing wrong with you. She's—"

"I know," Barnes lashed out. "Pretty."

"No," said Wood Mountain, recovering himself. "Hell on wheels sharp. That's what she is."

*⸺‖⸺*

LATER, AS he tried to help his beginning algebra students track down the identity of the mysterious $x$, as in $x + 12 = 23$, his mind veered off into the construction of a whole other equation. Call it a love equation. He tried to regard himself dispassionately and assign numbers to his pros and cons. He thought out his chances in life, totaled up how good-looking and pleasant Wood Mountain was against his good-looking pleasantness and paying job and other attributes tangible and intangible. The thing that surprised him in constructing the equation was he couldn't decide whether his not being an Indian was a plus or a negative in her mind. Thus the equation kept shifting around, refusing to stay equal on both sides, popping up with more $x$'s and multiple unknowns to solve.

He squeaked out ahead when he posited being Indian as a negative, and gave his hair the same numerical advantage as Wood Mountain's hair. Then he woke the next morning and found quite a bit of hair on his pillow. Horrified, he pictured his father's horseshoe of remnant hair and restructured the equation to narrow his window of opportunity and widen Wood

Mountain's. How could he have forgotten age? Hair loss? Or did that matter? Did not being an Indian gain him, or lose him, say, half a decade and half a head of hair? He revised the problem again. And while trying to solve it wondered if the baby figured into it. He dropped his pencil and rested his chin on the top of one fist. He was also wondering whether he had actually heard Wood Mountain say that Pixie had been dressed as an ox.

"This way lies madness," said Jarvis, when he came into Barnes's classroom and found the straw-haired teacher staring into an invisible shifting plane of numbers that looked like space.

✳══✳

WOOD MOUNTAIN watched Picasso. A flashy brown and white with a map of North America spread across her back and withers. Although he planned on mentioning this clever observation to Pixie (he could not think of her as Patrice, sorry), it wasn't his but Grace's. Wiry, tough, unrelenting Grace. She was studying geography. She loved this horse even more than the new filly. Riding him was like riding the top of the world, she said. The paint's father was part Thoroughbred from down south in bluegrass country, maybe. How the paint markings had come through was a wonder, when the horse was so much else. Along with his boxing, along with the valuable pale horse Gringo, the paint had become Wood Mountain's stake in the future. Since riding the train alongside Pixie and watching the baby, Archille, sleep in her arms, he'd started thinking about his future. Grace riding the paint had given him an idea. He'd started training as a boxer twice as hard.

During the practice, he talked to Pokey. After the practice, Pokey jumped on Wood Mountain's back and the boxer took off like a racehorse. Barnes didn't like it, but he would not have liked it worse had he known that Wood Mountain had decided to run Pokey all the way home. In order to see Pixie, or the baby, or both. To be honest, he had woken up that morning anxious to see how the baby was doing.

He'd had to let Pokey off twice, and it was dark by the time he jogged into the yard with the boy on his back. He tried to keep Pokey there until Pixie came out the door. He'd wanted to see her face when she realized he'd run home with her brother on his back. But Pokey slid off, ran to the door, and only Zhaanat came out anyway. He tried not to ask after Pixie, but of course the words popped out.

"Fell asleep after work," said Zhaanat, jiggling the baby, who looked startled to see Wood Mountain. The baby's sudden light of recognition stopped his breath.

Wood Mountain went to the baby and spoke to him in Dakota, which made Zhaanat's eyes flash because in her traditions there were lingering scores to settle. He switched to Chippewa, and she relaxed. She even smiled at his infatuation with the baby. Wood became animated, popping his eyes, waving his hands, and the baby's eyes followed him until, startled, he gave a gurgling laugh. Wood Mountain did the same goofball move. The baby laughed again. The laugh made Wood Mountain so giddy that it bumped Pixie to one side of his heart. The baby held the center, and laughed again. By the time Pixie, rubbing her eyes, was up and around, Wood Mountain was inside the house sitting at the table. The baby in his arms was sucking away at the bottle of oatmeal juice. While he drew effortlly on the nipple, the baby swiped and snatched at Wood Mountain's face. When the baby got hold of his nose, Wood Mountain gave a soft honk, which made the baby shriek with happiness. This went on until the baby burbled and nodded off. Wood Mountain rose to leave, but Zhaanat made him sit down and eat potatoes fried in deer fat, soaked in gravy. He looked at the ancient rifle over the door.

"Did Pokey bring the deer down with that old gun?"

It looked like his grandfather's Sitting Bull–era rifle.

"Pokey?" Zhaanat smiled, pointed with her lips at Patrice. "It was her got that buck this summer. Fat. I dried that meat."

His thoughts switched from the baby to Pixie. Damn. Of course she had to be a good shot.

Wood Mountain remembered the fluffy pemmican and told Zhaanat that they had eaten it on the train, and it was good. While he complimented her mother, Patrice took the baby behind a blanket, into another room. He didn't stay much longer.

⋇╾╤╾⋇

BARNES HAD driven Wade home and spent a good hour talking to his father about the meeting down in Fargo. Thomas had taken off work to go, and he still had endless potatoes to get in. He'd put his intensity into pitchforking hill after hill. Wade and the girls would clean potatoes, bury them in the sand cellar. He left them to it, and asked Barnes in for tea.

"I don't understand why it's so bad," said Barnes. "It sounds like you get to be regular Americans."

They were sitting where Barnes always sat when he drove his boxers home and was asked, inevitably, in for a visit—the table central to eating, cooking, canning, drying, and processing foods, also playing pinochle and cribbage, bathing babies in dishpans, and visiting. The tea was nice and hot in the heavy old white mugs. Thomas was such a thoughtful, quiet fellow that Barnes sometimes saved questions for him because he knew that Thomas would ponder out the answers.

"Lots of people here thought the same as you," said Thomas. "But then we realized we have been holding out . . . how many years since Columbus landed?"

Barnes did his favorite thing. Mental subtraction.

"Four hundred and sixty-one," he said immediately.

"Well, closing in on five centuries," said Thomas. "Holding out through every kind of business your folks could throw our way. Holding out why? Because we can't just turn into regular Americans. We can look like it, sometimes. Act like it, sometimes. But inside we are not. We're Indians."

"But see here," said Barnes. "I'm German, Norwegian, Irish, English. But overall, I'm American. What's so different?"

Thomas gave him a calm and assessing look.

"All of those are countries out of Europe. My brother was there. World War Two."

"Yes, but all are different countries. I still don't understand it."

"We're from *here,*" said Thomas. He thought awhile, drank some tea. "Think about this. If we Indians had picked up and gone over there and killed most of you and took over your land, what about that? Say you had a big farm in England. We camp there and kick you off. What do you say?"

Barnes was struck by this scenario. He raised his eyebrows so fast his hair flopped up.

"I say we were here first!"

"Okay," said Thomas. "Then say we don't care. Since you made it through that mess we say you can keep a little scrap of your land. You can live there, we say, but you have to take our language and act just like us. And say we are the old-time

Indians. You have to turn into an old-time Indian and talk Chippewa."

Barnes grinned, thinking of Zhaanat.

"I couldn't do that," he said.

"That's natural," said Thomas. "Good thing you don't have to. I can't turn all the way into a white man, either. That's how it is. I can talk English, dig potatoes, take money into my hand, buy a car, but even if my skin was white it wouldn't make me white. And I don't want to give up our scrap of home. I love my home."

"I see," said Barnes. He thought about it. "But I heard you get to be citizens. Don't you want to be a U.S. citizen?"

"What?" said Thomas. "We are citizens."

"Vote? You already can vote?"

"Sure, back in 1924 we got the vote. After the black man, after the women. But we got the vote."

"Oh. Who did you vote for last year?"

"Not Eisenhower. Everything came out Republican anyhow. Both houses. That's why they passed this bill here. It's dishonorable to Indians."

Barnes blurted out, "Is it that you don't want to start paying taxes?"

"No," said Thomas, patient, "we pay taxes just like you. If we make enough a year, we pay taxes. Only difference, not on our land. You're not gonna charge us taxes to live on the ishkonigan land that is left over after your people stole the rest of it, are you?"

That didn't sound right to Barnes.

"This thing will break our land up, see," Thomas continued. "We keep it in common now. That's the way it works. We can sell to one another but it stays in the tribe that way. So this bill would break up our land and let the BIA sell it off. They'd

probably take a nickel on the dollar for it. Then we'd get relocated. Shipped off to the Cities. That's where we'd end up. Living
in those little rooming houses, what do you call them?"

"Apartment buildings."

"Those. Visiting around in little rooms. Streets with lights.
I've been there. Rose and yours truly wouldn't like it. We would
feel very gloomy about it."

"I can well understand," said Barnes. And as he sat in the little
house, with a gentle fire in the wood range throwing out just
the right amount of warmth, with the mug of cooling tea on the
richly scarred and polished wooden table, and a couple of doves
calling tenderly in the pine tree outside the window, he began
to feel gloomy too.

"If I married an Indian woman," said Barnes, "would that
make me an Indian? Could I join the tribe?"

He was awed at the possible sacrifice he could be making.

Thomas looked at the big childish man with his vigorous
corn-yellow cowlicks and watery blue eyes. Not for the first
time, he felt sorry for a white fellow. There was something
about some of them—their sudden thought that to become an
Indian might help. Help with what? Thomas wanted to be generous. But also, he resisted the idea that his endless work, the
warmth of his family, and this identity that got him followed
in stores and ejected from restaurants and movies, this way he
was, for good or bad, was just another thing for a white man to
acquire.

"No," he said gently, "you could not be an Indian. But we
could like you anyway."

Barnes's shoulders slumped, but what Thomas said was a
comfort to him. They could like him anyway. He'd be acknowledged, liked, and that was important because he didn't have his

heart set on any other woman in this world but Pixie. Oh, it was Pixie and Pixie alone. He had to fight every day to convince himself that she might, somehow, against the ever more perfect image of Wood Mountain, turn her sumptuous melting gaze upon him and reward him with the sort of smile he'd never seen turned his way, but had witnessed, once, when she'd laughed at and appreciated something Pokey had done.

"Appreciate me with your eyes," he thought as he drove home, her image bobbing up in the darkness. "Oh Pixie, only once, just appreciate me with your eyes."

The glowing lights and even the numbers on the dashboard cast a lonely glare. The equation of love balanced and rebalanced in his thoughts like a playground seesaw. Could he load his side with better attributes? Modest changes to his wardrobe? A subtle swirl in his hair to hide thin areas? And gifts. What woman doesn't like a gift? Well, maybe Patrice. A gift might prick her suspicions. But how about a gift to her younger brother, Pokey? Evidence of Barnes's generosity, but no strings attached. What would be wrong with that?

# Twin Dreams

WOMEN'S BODIES make such miracles. After a week of intense suckling by the baby, there was a trickle of milk. Patrice had believed her mother, but she was still surprised. Zhaanat told her with some assurance that in starving times a man had even been known to give milk, and insisted that by the change of the moon she would have a normal amount.

"Just until Vera's back," she said.

Every night now, as it grew colder, Patrice worked on the house. She remudded the spaces between the logs with clay dug up near the slough, and closed the tiny gaps between the window frames with dried grass. With her waterjack money she had bought boxes of plaster, whitewash, rolls of tar paper, nails, a hammer. She fixed the tar paper to the frame of the roof. She used a heavy mixture of mud and grass to close the eaves. After school and boxing, Pokey came home and helped her spread plaster on the inside of the walls. In the corner where he slept, they used rabbit glue to paste photographs and stories to the wall. Rocky Graziano, Tony Zale, Jersey Joe Walcott, Sugar Ray Robinson, and Archie Moore stared out, over their round gloves, in the soft dusk. These photos and stories were not from the magazines that Valentine passed on to Patrice, but from boxing magazines that Barnes gave Pokey, first a stack and then another and another. Although Barnes implied he'd read these magazines, the covers and pages were stiff and new. Also, he gave Pokey a winter jacket. Not an old hand-me-down coat either, but a brand-new red and black checked winter jacket that reminded Patrice, uncomfortably, of the lumberjack theme at Log Jam 26. The jacket had knitted cuffs, a thick snap-on pile collar. Barnes claimed that someone had given him this jacket and he was just finding the jacket a good home. It was obvious to Patrice that Barnes had bought it, which got her goat. As if she couldn't have bought her own brother a jacket? As if she wouldn't have done it if Pokey's old coat was worn out? Which it wasn't. Also she could have bought him the hat, brown wool with a bill and fold-down earflaps.

"Barnes give that to you?"

"Yes."

Pokey beamed and stroked the front of the coat. He brushed the pile collar with his fingers.

"Oh, it's real nice," said Patrice, but in a way that made Pokey look at her closely.

"Should I give it back?"

"No," said Patrice.

After all, how could she spoil her brother's pride? But also, once kids found out where his nice things came from, they would give him a hard time.

"Pokey, don't brag Barnes gave you presents, okay?"

"I wouldn't even!"

"And don't take anything else he gives you, okay?"

"Okay," said Pokey.

He looked over at his boots. They were brand-new handsome leather boots with black-and-white marled laces. He thought Patrice might say something, but she was slapping the glue on Zale, using a stick, giving the Man of Steel the beating of his life.

. . .

BEFORE SUNRISE, Vera always came back. As Patrice was float-ing out of her sleep, her sister would appear. Not as Vera had been when she left for the Cities, wearing high-heeled shoes, stockings, carrying a rose-pink cardboard suitcase. Not with her eyes all lighted up. Not grinning skeptically at something Pa-trice said, not pausing to gather her laugh. No, that was not the Vera who visited. One morning, Patrice was back in the alley where Jack had probably died. Again, Patrice stopped at the pile of clothing in the wet alley. Again, she pulled away the collar of a jacket. Only instead of Jack's skeleton smile it was Vera's twisted gaping face and blood-choked mouth. Another morn-ing she stood in the dust of a room empty but for a chair and a slashed leather collar, a stained and crumpled sheet. There were footsteps and Patrice whirled around. Somebody was in the room, there was scratching in the walls, and Vera said her name.

On more than one morning she was the waterjack, naked in the tank. Wavery customers drifted outside. One was Vera, curiously pressing her face to the glass. These weren't dreams, but vivid scenarios that flooded her mind. It was as though all that had happened to her in the city had to happen over and over, only with Vera always there, not found but somehow find-ing her.

"Mama, I have these dreams," said Patrice one morning, still jangled.

They were eating oatmeal, the baby sleeping in Zhaanat's lap. There were a few raisins sprinkled in the oatmeal, so they were taking their time, making sure that only one raisin came in every other spoonful, so they could last the entire bowl.

"Wiindamawish gaa-pawaadaman."

So Patrice told her mother about her dreams. Then she watched her mother's face grow stiff and still.

"It would be good if Gerald came down here, but he will be tied up with his ceremonies now," Zhaanat said. "We will have to handle this."

"Handle the dreams?"

Zhaanat stared at the table, smoothing the edge of the wood with her extraordinary hand, which fell, suddenly limp, into her lap. Before her eyes, her mother seemed to be draining of life.

"Are your dreams about Vera?" asked Patrice.

"They are the exact same dreams."

"The exact same dreams as my dreams?"

Zhaanat nodded heavily, frowning into her daughter's eyes. Patrice knew. The trembling started in a place behind her heart, but soon the shaking worked its way to just beneath her skin. Her body was quivering like an arrow that has just struck its mark. Her mother spoke.

"She is trying to reach us."

# The Star Powwow

❊⎯❙⎯❊

NOBODY SAW them coming, and instead of giving his usual warning bark Smoker went out on the road to meet them. Zhaanat carried the baby, not laced onto a cradle board, but folded into the web of silvery knitting, hanging in the folds of the baby blanket like a sack of sugar. Patrice walked alongside her, wearing cuffed jeans, saddle shoes, and a green sweater. Zhaanat wore green too, the dark calico dress with tiny golden flowers. They knocked on Thomas's door and Rose opened it.

"Oh, you!"

Rose's face relaxed in pleasure. She was fond of them both, especially close to Zhaanat, and she wanted to see the baby. She disengaged him from the froth of yarn and held him, examining his face minutely and coaxing him to smile at her. Thomas was sitting at the kitchen table while the children passed in and out and Noko railed at her daughter. He capped his pen. He had written to Milton Young again, and two other congressmen. He was setting up a meeting between Arnold Zeff, leader of the local chapter of the American Legion, and Louis Pipestone. Louis was going to set before Arnold Zeff the prospect of Indians who had faithfully served their country abandoned to beg in the streets of Zeff's off-reservation community. He was hoping the Legion would sign on against the bill. Thomas had a morning meeting with the superintendent of the school district. He would propose that they take on the funding of the reservation school once the federal government relinquished support. These ideas were the result of Biboon's and Eddy Mink's remarks about how the surrounding communities could be affected by termination.

Patrice and Zhaanat sat down at the kitchen table. Sharlo cleared away her arithmetic papers and Fee took her book into the other room. From her corner, Noko glared. She was wearing a gray wool shawl bristling with stiff white stray threads, and had her arms folded tightly against her chest, holding in her rage. The baby stirred hungrily. Without a trace of self-consciousness, Zhaanat took him back and began to nurse him. Rose made coffee. Noko's head reared back, a swatch of hair flipped up, her eyes bugged so she looked like a maddened egret. Thomas showed no surprise at all and Rose set down heavy scratched mugs full of scalding coffee, then sat down next to Thomas.

"We need your advice," said Patrice, giving Thomas a pinch of tobacco.

Then she told about the dog, what the dog said, the empty rooms with the chains fixed to the walls and the slashed leather collars on the floor. She told them only what pertained to Vera. Maybe she would never tell anybody at all about her brief employment as a waterjack. She ended with the train ride back, then fell silent. Finally, Thomas spoke. Tears of shock had swelled up behind his eyes, but he'd not allowed them to spill out. This thing was nowhere in his understanding.

"We have to go to the police," he said.

His voice was leaden with emotion but what he said was both unthinkable and disappointing to Patrice and Zhaanat. To seek police assistance for an Indian woman was almost sure to put her in the wrong. No matter what happened, she would be the one blamed and punished. It was for that reason unthinkable to approach the police, and it was disappointing because Thomas trusted their enemies.

"The policeman will never help us," Zhaanat said at last.

"We'll have to find another way," said Patrice.

"Let me sleep on this," said Thomas, although he knew he would never sleep. And they struggled to talk of other things, of work at the jewel bearing plant, of neutral things that could allow the mysterious horror to sink below their thoughts.

WHEN THOMAS went to work that night, he didn't take his briefcase along. He knew he would not be able to concentrate on the many letters of request and explanation that pressed upon him. Nor would he be able to plan the information meetings to be held in the community hall. He wanted to get the interpretation of the bill right for the meetings. But he knew he would not be able to find those words after what Patrice had told him. Driving to work had become ever more filled with dread. Dread that he would not be able to stay awake. Dread that on the other hand, he might never sleep again. Dread of the situation, ungraspable in its magnitude. Loneliness. The forces he was up against were implacable and distant. But from their distance they could reach out and sweep away an entire people.

And now this.

What Patrice had told him was so extreme an evil that it struck at his fundamental assumptions. He had always, even in the face of hatred or drunken violence, believed that people did bad things out of ignorance or weakness or liquor. He had never known or heard of the sort of evil that Patrice had spoken about—the chains in the walls, the collars, the dog speaking of her sister's fate. Moses Montrose was right. He was an altar boy.

Biboon, who was in his way an innocent, too, had raised him. Thomas couldn't make the leap of consciousness that would allow him to understand all that was implied by the existence of that room. His thoughts veered off whenever he tried to imagine what those rooms implied. He arrived at the jewel bearing plant, unlocked the door. He walked to his desk but did not sit down. He paced. Between rounds, he stared into the dim corners of the room.

THOMAS MUST have been asleep, or so tired he was in a trance. A faint drumming brought him to awareness. It was the owl again, he thought, confused. The owl had returned. It was banging on the back windows, fighting its own image in the glass. He jumped straight up, instinctively punched his time card, then bolted. He was out of the building, into the whipping cold, the door drifting shut behind him. He lunged back for the door. Too late. The door slammed and the noise resounded. He had no jacket, no flashlight, and no keys except, as always in his pants pocket, the car keys on a tab of beaded leather. The wind came down out of Alberta and swooped across Manitoba, honing itself to ice. Now, it stabbed. Although hardened by his years in that wind, he began to shiver. He slapped his arms, chest, thighs. There was no owl and the pounding continued. Why had he rushed out? He had to get back into the building as quickly as possible. But of course, he had done as he did every night, checked each lock, jiggled door handles, made everything secure. There was no way in except to break in and Thomas had never in his life broken into a building.

Except the time he opened the basement window for Roderick, but that didn't count. They had as good as killed Roderick down there. At least Thomas had managed to open a window by using a wire stolen from the Fort Totten machine shop. He'd formed the end into a hook and wiggled it through a crack to pull away a wooden latch—it wasn't much of a barrier and he'd done it easily. Then he'd thrown down the coat and apples and bread crusts and a handkerchief knotted around a lump of oatmeal. He called down to Roderick that he'd been seen, which wasn't true, but he had to get away. Roderick was sobbing so bad. Thomas hated that sound of sobbing in the dark.

If he had a wire now, he could poke it through a crack beneath the frosted window, about six feet up, in the women's bathroom. He would need a ladder or, no, he could drive his car over. He could stand on top of his car. He walked toward it, beating his arms across his body. Inside the car, he rubbed his hands together, started the engine. After a long few minutes the heater roared to life. He warmed his hands for a few moments. Put his head near the fan to warm up his brain. Unfortunately, he kept the interior obsessively clean. There wasn't a blanket. No extra jacket. But a wire? In the electrical system? No, he'd sooner spend the night in his car than yank a wire from it. The warmth was wonderful. He dreaded leaving it. He began to worry that if he were found dozing in his car outside the building he was paid to protect, Vold might think the job was too much for him. Might think that the stress of being a tribal chairman was too much to take on and still be an effective night watchman.

Outside, the drumming intensified. Thomas peered through the windshield. It seemed to be coming from somewhere far away. In a wind like this there would usually be clouds. But the sky was clear. The stars hung low and luminous. The drumming came from up there. It seemed to Thomas that the stars were drumming in the moonless deep. Having a fine old time. Wait.

He suddenly sprang out, walked around to the back, opened the trunk. In the trunk, there was an old rag rug he'd picked up at the mission bundles. He pulled it around his shoulders. Beneath the rug, there was a reel of wire. A cheap thin sort of wire that he'd bought for snares last time he was in town. It was floppy and droopy, but he thought it might do. He jumped back in the car and pulled it around, right up to the side of the building. Of course he would be all right. Everything would come out fine. He blasted the heater on himself, thinking about the source of the drumming. He could still hear it, a faint thrumming, from above. The drumming made him hopeful and soon he twisted off a piece of the wire. Thinking of the way the window catch worked, he made a loop at the end of the wire. He'd catch the little knob that held the window down, tighten the loop, and lift. He got out of the car to do this.

Twenty minutes later, hands nearly frozen, he climbed down. He'd warm himself up and try again, he thought, but this time when he turned the ignition, nothing. Over and over. Nothing. He waited. Tried again. Nothing. Nothing. Nothing. And he was becoming extremely cold. So cold his brain was slowing down. Even his armpits were numb and didn't warm his hands. He was so cold that he knew he must give up and walk toward the lights of town, not walk but run, if he wanted to live.

He stepped out of the car, into the open, off the gravel road into rough pasture gleaming with frost. He fell, went down hard, lay there stunned. It was as if he'd been dashed to earth like a toy. Without warning, they threw you down. That's how it was to live with them. Oh it was! Thomas had studied them. He had striven in every way to be like his teachers. And every boss. He had tried to make their ways his ways. Even if he didn't like their ways, he'd tried. He'd tried to make money, like them.

He'd thought that if he worked hard enough and followed their rules this would mean he could keep his family secure, his people from the worst harms, but none of that was true. Into his brain like a foul seep came the knowledge of what men had done to Vera.

He could not hold back the pictures. Knowing pierced his mind. Unbearable, what they did to her. And what they were still doing if she was alive and in their power. He cried out and felt that now he was welded by cold to the grass like poor Paranteau and his iron post.

The drumming grew louder and louder. Looking up, he saw the beings. They were filmy and brightly indistinct. How benign they were, floating downward from the heavens. They were formed like regular people, and were dressed in ordinary clothing, shirts, pants, dresses made of glowing cloth. Although he could see through them, they weren't exactly transparent. And they looked like they'd been hard at work. He had the sense the stars were always hard at work; shining away up there wasn't easy. One of the shining people was Jesus Christ, but he looked just like the others. They nodded to him in a comical way, understanding his surprise, and all of a sudden nothing hurt. Radiance filled him and he reared up, knowing that the drummers wished him to dance. Up in the clouds, down on earth, they were dancing counterclockwise, as the spirits do in the land of the dead, and they wanted him to join. So he danced with them. Every time he trod down on the stiff grass his feet pushed a watery brightness into the air. He was wearing an imaginary headdress that spilled light every time he bobbed his head. He looked down and saw that he was holding a dance stick made of wavering northern lights. Eyes glinting, heart roaring as the blood sprang to the tips of his fingers, he began to sing the song they gave him.

When the drumming stopped, Thomas climbed on top of his car, plucked the wire from his pocket, picked the lock to the bathroom window. He hoisted himself through that window and tapped down on the green linoleum floor. Then he walked out of the bathroom to his desk, scooped up his keys, punched the time clock, and raced out to the car. It started right up. He pulled it around to his parking place and he ran back into the building. Sat down. He was only two minutes off on his time punches. He poured himself a thermos cup of coffee and greeted the dawn.

## Agony Would Be Her Name

THE MEN smelled of hot oil, liquor sweat, spoiled meat, a million cigarettes, and they spoke in the language of the wolverine. Their beards ground against her face until her cheeks were raw. If she wanted to get away, she'd have to run through knives. If she got through the knives, she would have no skin left to protect her. She would be raw flesh. She would be a thing. She would be agony. Giant motors gnashed behind the wall. Occasionally, like a reverberating gong, she heard her mother call her name.

# Homecoming

THE LEAVES gold on green, bright in the soaking rain, padded the trails in the woods. All of the Wazhashks were hard at work. In the sloughs the little namesakes stockpiled green twigs. In the fields, the family pitchforked up the last of the carrots. Piles of squash, warty green, orange, mellow tan, solid little pumpkins, filled the cellar and were piled around the sides of the house. Braids of onions. Pale meek balls of cabbage. Crates of cream and purple turnips. Bushels of potatoes. Thomas hauled wagon loads. Wade and Martin argued themselves into the back, arranged themselves around the vegetables. Still arguing, they unloaded produce at the cafe, at the school, and at last the teachers' dining hall. Juggie Blue gave orders, telling them where to stack and pile. Tomorrow, there was going to be a parade, a community feed, a football game, and the crowning of royalty. Sharlo was in the Homecoming court.

"You in the parade?" Juggie asked Thomas.

"Not this time. The old man is going to sit in the car and watch. I'm going to sit right there with him."

"And Rose?"

"She's working on Sharlo's dress."

"Oh! What's the dress like?"

Juggie lighted up. She loved dresses, though overalls were her mainstay.

"Long, I think. Maybe . . . blue?"

Juggie narrowed her eyes.

"Long and maybe blue? That's all you can come up with?"

"There's a ruffle somewhere on it."

"You're useless!"

Thomas watched Juggie closely as they talked. As he walked away, he was reassured by her exasperation. She didn't seem to be treating him as if there were something wrong with him. He had also watched Rose closely. Was he changed after the visitation in the frosty field? Had he been acting strangely before it? How could a person tell whether he himself was acting strangely? Thomas hadn't told anyone about his experience, hadn't said a word about the shining people. He would tell Biboon, when the time was right, but dared tell no one else. What exactly would he say to someone who was not his own father? I was at a star powwow? I met Jesus Christ and he was a good fellow? They would laugh, think he'd fallen off the wagon, worry that his mind was giving out from the strain. And also, maybe most important, he didn't want anyone to interfere with the peace he had experienced since that visit. Although he was still tired and anxious, he wasn't filled with dread. His visitors had left something of their comforting presence.

Every night, checking twice that he had his keys, he went outside and looked up into the heavens. He sang, low, trying to remember the song they danced to. As for Jesus Christ, he thought he'd better go to Holy Mass.

THE RAIN let up and Saturday morning was clear and chilly. Everyone in the parade assembled just below the church, then set off in a straggling march to wind through town and end at the high school steps. Sharlo wore a bunch of yellow velvet flowers pinned to her coat, sat with her friends on the top of the backseat of the English teacher's convertible. Fee was in the parade as a trumpet player. Pokey was in the parade too. He hopped around in a pickup bed made to look like a boxing ring. He scowled, pretending to spar with the other boys. The junior boxers had wanted to go shirtless, but Barnes made them wear their jackets. He did allow them to wear the new Everlast boxing gloves, and they had a rounds bell to ding, borrowed from the post office window. Three old traditional dancers in beaded black velvet regalia rode in the bed of Louie's pickup. The young dancers followed. Wade had borrowed a dance outfit from his grandfather and he bobbed and hunted the ground with his eyes. A few of the women wore brown cotton dresses, imitating buckskin with cut cotton fringes. The women with the shorter bobs wore false braids made of nylon stockings stuffed with horsehair. They wore loom-beaded headbands and brilliant medallions. Two fancy dancers wore suits of red long underwear under their beaded breechcloths and feather bustles. They dipped and whirled, walked and laughed, waved and joked with the crowd. They were handing out pencils, one to every few children, drawing each yellow stick reverently from a cloth bag.

Grace Pipestone, in a cowboy hat, fringed circle skirt, and tooled leather cowboy boots, rode the new filly, Teacher's Pet. The horse was a dramatically pretty blue roan. Her eyes were outlined in midnight swoops and her dark socks made her quick trot look sharp and precise. There were others riding horses in the parade, but none were dressed as flashily as Superintendent Tosk, who wore a real fringed buckskin jacket and an eagle-feather headdress. This headdress always came out for special events and photos. Magnificently, it bristled off his head and trailed down his back. He rode one of Louie's most valuable horses, Gringo, who'd lost his formidable racing edge to love, and been set to stud. Gringo was a pale roan, almost a cremello, with gentle rabbity ears and a pinkish pie face. His mane, laboriously combed out, wetted, and braided the night before, had been unbraided and now rippled whitely along the curve of his neck. Grace had treated his tail the same way and its gleaming crinkles nearly brushed the gravel road. He was a glamorous horse who really deserved a better name. Wood Mountain had often said so. He was driving Juggie's green and white DeSoto, hauling a little trailer with bales of hay where Juggie and Deanna sat, dressed like hoboes. Juggie carried a sign that said *Busted by Termination*. Mr. Vold drove a large brown station wagon, draped with gold crepe paper, held at intervals by painted cardboard jewels. Fixed to the top of the car were a large watch and a rocket constructed by Betty Pye.

The other car representing the jewel plant was Doris Lauder's family car. Painted signs hung out the windows. Valentine rode in the front seat, of course. She chatted away with Doris about how to match plaids cut on the bias for a circle skirt. Patrice rode in the backseat with Betty Pye. The two held small sacks of homemade toffee, each square wrapped in waxed paper. Every so often they tossed a few toffees to the avid children who stood watching the parade. Two years before, Patrice had been in the parade with Valentine, both in the Homecoming court. They had made popcorn balls to throw, but too many had lost their waxed paper flying through the air, or shattered in the road.

Halfway along the route, Vernon and Elnath stood awkwardly beside the road. They had been strangers wearing black suits, now black overcoats as well, but now everybody knew they were the Mormons.

Patrice tossed a couple of pieces of candy toward them. Vernon bent over, picked them up, and popped one into his mouth. Elnath folded his arms and scowled, his eyes outraged and glittering.

"Did you see those two fellows?" Patrice asked Betty.

Betty turned. "Oh, they're the missionaries. But Grace Pipestone is converting one."

"What?"

"Louie let them sleep in his barn. And that one with his mouth full, he's sweet on Grace. But she said she won't look at him unless he turns Catholic. He's praying on it."

"I wouldn't bet on Grace," said Valentine, suddenly, from the front seat. "She's got bigger fish to fry. I happen to know Wood Mountain's got his eye on her."

"She's not even sixteen," said Patrice, indignant.

"Green eyes show, green eyes glow," said Valentine in a smug voice.

"What's that supposed to mean?"

Valentine turned to Doris Lauder and they both began to laugh.

THE PARADE moved slowly but then was over quickly. The vehicles, walkers, and dancers arrived in the high school parking lot. The Homecoming royalty climbed out of the cars and walked up the front steps to arrange themselves on the wide concrete landing before the double doors. Thomas had already parked his Nash close by, so Biboon could get out, sit on the hood, and watch the crowning of the king and queen. Now the frail old man sat expectantly in the weak sunlight, wrapped in an army blanket and enjoying the excitement. The crowd gradually fell silent.

To one side of the nervous royals, Mrs. Edges, the home economics teacher, stood with Mr. Jarvis. Each held a crown made of wire, tin, and silver sparkle paint. Other teachers held the red capes and scepters that would be presented to each monarch. First Mr. Jarvis paced forward and quickly crowned Calbert St. Pierre, one of Barnes's most tentative boxers. There was applause and a bit of cheering or good-hearted jeering when the cape was put on Calbert. Then the crowd quieted again. The horses cropping shoots of grass at the edge of the road nickered and huffed. Mrs. Edges walked forward, held the crown over each of the girls' heads, teasingly, before she finally lowered it onto Sharlo's brown pin curls, which were brushed into a fluffy halo all around her gleaming face. The crowd gasped. Sharlo's eyes widened in surprise, then her features twisted, raw with sudden emotion. Before she recovered and began to smile, some of the people in the audience were startled by memory.

THOMAS SAW his daughter at four years old, calling from a high haystack before she launched herself into the air. He whirled in the nick of time and lunged for her. The pitchfork he'd carelessly abandoned on the stack fell as she fell. It struck into the ground alongside her as they tumbled to one side. As he looked at it, quivering there, his chest expanded in a sob of horror. Sharlo patted his face. She was wearing the same mysterious expression of arrested flight that she wore, now, as she was crowned.

ROSE SAW her gleaming iron standing proudly on the dresser.

PATRICE WAS jolted back to the time she was crowned Homecoming queen on the very same steps. How, wearing the red cape and holding the fake scepter, she looked down into the crowd and they seemed so far away. Her heart swelled, a stone in her chest. And she remembered. How every single one of them had made fun of her when she was little, when she had been so poor she came to school in shoes cut so her toes could poke out, coatless until the teacher scrounged one up, underwear sewed from a flour sack, hair in long traditional braids. They had called her squaw. Even the other girls. They had called her dirty. But then once Vera was old enough to scavenge or make their clothing, and once Patrice had her breasts, and once her face changed from ravenous and elfin to enchanting, they saw her differently. Now she was queen. But she had not forgotten. She would never forget. And suddenly, yes, as she felt the weight of the crown, suddenly she wanted them, all of them, to bow to her. She wanted the boys who'd called her squaw, especially them, to go down on their knees as in church. As if before the statue of the perfect shining blessed smirking virgin. Yes, kneel! Oh, she wanted them to bow their heads in fear, as if her little tin scepter were a sword. She wanted to see the teachers bow, and then maybe glance up at her in awe. She wanted their heads to press down quickly, afraid she'd see that they dared to take a peek.

And the ladies who gossiped about her or made fun of her mother's hands, she wanted them to fear her. And the men, arrogant and looking her up and down, giving her a wink. Those men. They would turn their heads as though she'd slapped them. And Bucky. He could drop like he was shot.

Patrice had begun her walk down the front steps of the school in a trance. Nobody bowed. None of that happened. People yelled and clapped and everyone was nice. Except Valentine. Who from that day forward was unreliable as a friend. Yes,

Patrice thought, she should have made Valentine bow down, and stay down, and stop trying to embarrass her.

AS THE royalty made its way into the crowd and people turned toward one another to make plans, Gringo, the horse Superintendent Tosk sat upon looking splendid, gave a loud trumpet blare and lunged toward Teacher's Pet. Tosk grappled for the reins. The horse beneath Grace Pipestone nickered, enticingly. They were on the other side of the crowd, surrounded by people and cars.

Teacher's Pet craned backward, tried to stall, gave Gringo the come-hither. Grace kicked her filly, made a quick evasive maneuver, and trotted to the other side of Juggie's DeSoto. Juggie, still in hobo tatters, jumped over and snatched at Gringo's halter, but missed. Teacher's Pet wheeled around and Juggie saw that the mare was in heat, her vulva popped out, flaring and shutting.

Barnes, passing behind the horse, stopped and stood rooted in fear. He'd never seen anything like it. He waved his arms and ran for Wood Mountain. Juggie ran toward the horse, the rider, and yelled.

"Grace, get off! She's winking!"

Maybe Grace didn't hear, or maybe she did and wanted to get the horse away from people. Grace made a break out of the crowd, toward the schoolyard, or tried to. Teacher's Pet wouldn't go. She sashayed. Winked her vulva at Gringo. Wouldn't run until Grace used the decorative wheels of her spurs. Then Teacher's Pet charged away and Gringo's ears went up. Superintendent Tosk tugged Gringo's reins, eyes round with alarm, but the stallion tossed his head, gave an outraged squawk, and lighted out after Teacher's Pet, who was now running full on toward the schoolyard swings—thick wooden planks gently drifting on steel chains hung from a fifteen-foot-high iron crossbar. Grace steered her mare straight between the swings, but Tosk, sawing and shrieking, ran his stallion straight into a swing. It caught Gringo like a snare at the base of his noble throat. The horse reared, twisting the chain around him, folding Superintendent Tosk into the package, breaking the spines of eagle feathers, nearly hanging himself. Louis flung a blanket over Gringo's head and quickly untangled the superintendent. Grace slid off Teacher's Pet. As soon as the chains were gone, Gringo jumped up, cleared the teeter-totter in a bound, and galloped along the margin of the running track after Teacher's Pet, who ambled into the scruff of woods that divided the school grounds from a field of hay.

LATER, THAT night, there was a Homecoming promenade and dance. All of the couples, as dressed up as possible, stood in line to take a turn around the darkened gym. Each couple was plucked from the gloom by Mr. Jarvis's spotlight. Anybody could come to the dance, it wasn't just for high school students. People came to sit at the back tables and eat juneberry pies, table buns and jelly, squares of Juggie Blue's caramel sheet cake. They drank from bowls of punch set up alongside the desserts and watched the parade of couples.

Thomas and Rose stood against the wall, sipping on a mixture of juices sparked up with ginger ale. The Homecoming king and queen led off, two fiddlers playing a catchy Michif march. The spotlight cast a wavering patch where Sharlo appeared. Her crown, topped by a silver star, caught what light there was and she seemed to float along as she advanced. Perhaps she wasn't even touching the floor. That's what Thomas thought, disoriented, watching her move magically along through the gloom. She was one of the star beings, given, for her time on earth, human shape and form.

Then Angus and Eddy began to play in earnest and the couples broke off, swinging their arms and legs, shifting left and right, swapping hands and sometimes cuddling in a cha-cha, for a moment, right there on the floor. Between dances, Grace Pipestone took up the guitar, as did Wood Mountain. The old people sat watching at the back tables, nibbling from the pie table and drinking coffee. The music shifted between wild reels and bop. At last, to the shock of the old people, Mr. Jarvis announced that he would use a loudspeaker system to play some records loud enough to dance to, and for the first time a scratchy version of "Night Train," by Jimmy Forrest, was broadcast around the gym. It was wildly popular, played over and over, and Angus and Eddy soon took it up, live, with variations. Nobody wanted to dance to anything else for the rest of the night.

When the dance was over, Mr. Jarvis wiped his record off and stored it in its cardboard envelope. He reverently blew on his record needle, secured it, unplugged and latched his record player case gently shut. He picked it up and carried it out. He'd paid his own money for the spotlight and it went home with him.

Barnes was the last one out of the school. He lingered for no reason, still a bit crushed that Patrice hadn't come to the dance. Tears had burned behind his eyes earlier on, when he realized she wouldn't show up. Tears again! What was happening to him as a man? Barnes had quickly walked over to Patrice's friend Valentine and asked her to dance. She had a slim waist and agreed with everything he said.

Valentine was still there when he came through the front door.

"Why don't we give you a ride?" she cried out, taking his arm. She smelled a bit like whiskey. They walked jauntily down the steps. He glanced around, but there was no one to see. She got into the front seat of Doris Lauder's car.

"I only live across the road," he said. "Thanks. I can walk from here."

"No, you can't!" cried Valentine. "C'mon. We're on our way to a bush dance!"

He'd always wanted to go to one of those—fast music, wild dancing, homemade beer, wine, and maybe Pixie. So he got into the car's backseat and sat in the middle. After a moment, he stretched his arms across the backrest. He wasn't used to being driven somewhere by a woman, and it seemed that he should make himself as big as possible.

## The Bush Dance

*≯═┆═≮*

AFTER THE sex was over, they were bored and irritated. And
also there was nothing to eat. They didn't exactly break up, but
they did manage to ignore each other as they plodded around
looking for some juicy grass. There was the hayfield, but that
was cut and the stubble dry. So they turned back and walked
through the woods. Teacher's Pet heard the voice of her rider,
calling, but it didn't affect her the way it had an hour ago. She
just kept walking beside Gringo, who had entirely blocked out
human sounds and was still enjoying the perfection of his sensations. They passed through oak savanna, then birch woods,
then another unsatisfactory hayfield, then an abandoned yard
where they grazed in luxury and pooped out all the stress of
the parade.

They drank from a slough, rolled in the mud, and gradually
the world grew dark. They could have rested, but the wind was
cold and they began to wish themselves into the place of warmth
near the tiresome beings, who also sometimes offered a delight
or two. A gnarled apple, a block of carrot, a crust of bannock.
Oh, that! Gringo trotted toward the scent that came out on the
air before the crust, a carrot, an apple, might be brought to him.
They were near somebody's house.

From the house came the noises of others, maybe of their
own kind, or close to their own kind, or the other kind, too,
neighs and chuckles, gasps and whinnies, shrill toots and bursts

of air. They drew near, crossed gravel, crossed earth, then stood on a trampled tasteless scurf of weed waiting to be fed some real food. Grain would go down easy. But the stamping and squealing continued inside that familiar warmth and it didn't let up. Sometimes a human or two came out shouting or twinned up in the backseats of the stinking cars. Nobody with the right smell. Nobody with food. At last, heads hanging, they straggled over to the road and walked a few miles before joining the grass track that led to their own field. They felt too sorry for themselves to jump over their fence, and stood outside waiting to be let in. A gust of wind blew the gate wide. Gringo knocked rudely against Teacher's Pet as she went through the gate and suddenly she had the utmost repugnance for him. Out flashed her pretty little hoof and she opened a vicious gash in his pinky gold underbelly. It was his only imperfection.

# Hay Stack

✦━┃━✦

HE WAS sore, spiritually sore, so he went to the church and sat in a hard wooden pew. The bush dance had gone on all night. Barnes had blundered about, mostly doing a boxer's shuffle. He'd drunk whiskey. As always, it went straight to his head. His shuffle had turned into a lumbering jig and he'd stumbled out the door. In separate visits to the woods, first with Doris and then Valentine, he'd encountered a frightening degree of responsive kissing. Also, biting. Valentine had left her marks. The evidence was still upon him. He was pretty sure things could have gone further. But his feelings were with Pixie! Weren't they? Perhaps he was becoming promiscuous. How could he possibly go on teaching and boxing and training the other boxers, especially his protégé, when he was now attracted to three separate women at the same time and they all were, he imagined, the dearest of friends? It was a relief, but also upsetting, that he could think of anybody besides Pixie Paranteau.

The air in the church was soothing and faintly scented with spice. Perhaps incense. He was not a Catholic. He didn't know how to make the sign of the cross, but he waved his hand across his chest with a pleading gesture and looked up at the statue of the mother of god. She was fixed inside a painted oval with pointed ends. It reminded him of the mare at Homecoming. His mind careened from that thought. The oval was lined with red and decorated with golden points directed sharply inward. Within the center, she floated. Her gaze darted here and there as the light changed, an eerie effect. She was definitely keeping an eye on him. At no time did she seem to approve. And there were even times she hinted that he should adjourn the encounter. Just go his way and leave people here to live out their lives without interference from Mr. Barnes. Hay Stack Barnes. He didn't like it, but everybody up here had a nickname. And it could have been worse.

But here he was. He meant to face his problem head-on.

First, there was Pixie, of course. Oh, he'd been through all of that. There wasn't a known inch left unlonged for, undesired, uncataloged, although there was of course much unknown.

Second, there was Valentine. What a perfect heart-shaped name for a woman whose face wasn't heart-shaped at all, but thin, a narrow face, slippery eyes. Valentine was a bit sly, like a lady fox. Yes, a dainty lady fox trotting through the woods with a dead rabbit drooping in her jaws. Not exactly . . .

He pressed his jugular vein, his shoulder, a place on his chest where she'd actually drawn blood. Was it normal?

Third, surprisingly, Doris Lauder with her skin moist and white as a peeled apple. And that little hint of baby fat beneath her jaw and waist was just delectable. Her round arms and solid legs. The honey-brown red of her waves of hair. Clipped back, it wasn't much, but when she let it fly out! Oh, she was a russet peach. A toothsome tempter. And she was a known quantity at that, being not an Indian, which made her less exotic and fascinating. But maybe he'd had it with the fascination. Maybe he just wanted a nice girl he didn't have to work to impress. Maybe just a person whom he knew what was what with and who knew what was what with him.

. . .

"HERE YOU are," said Thomas Wazhashk. He slid into the pew beside Barnes and removed his mittens. He was dressed for winter in a heavy coat with a knitted muffler. "I've been cold," he said.

"I'm just praying a little," said Barnes.

"I came to do the same thing," said Thomas. "And I did. Had a little talk with Jesus way back in the corner. Sat there waiting for you to get up and walk back outside where I could bend your ear. But I need to leave now, so I decided to bother you. For which I don't mean to intrude."

"No, that's all right," said Barnes, flattered at having the sort of solitude someone could intrude upon. "What was it? I'm all done with my praying."

"It's about putting up a boxing card," said Thomas. "We are going to have to raise funds to send a delegation."

"It's about the bill, right?"

Thomas nodded. "It's not as if the government is going to give us money to go and testify against what they are aiming to do. So we are going to have to raise the money ourselves. They've set the time. We're on the March calendar. We have to be ready with everything by then."

"You mean"—Barnes was groping for the right set of words—"you provide testimony? That sort of thing?"

"Put up a lot of evidence against it. That's right. We are contacting a tribal scholar, too. She might be our secret weapon. And we need to pay for train tickets, a place to stay."

"So. A boxing card."

"With a cover charge. I figure if we put Wood Mountain up against Joe Wobble again we'll fill the house."

"I think you're right. But maybe Joe, or maybe Wood, aren't interested in a fight. It wasn't a good fight. I have questions."

"You're not alone. That's why a repeat of that fight would draw a crowd."

"Yes," said Barnes, "I can see that. We could use the community center. I can get Mr. Jarvis to put in a loudspeaker of some kind. We can get a real bell, not from the post office."

"And the right kind of ropes."

"Pretty girls. Scorecards," said Barnes, in hope.

"No," said Thomas.

"Well, a thought."

Thomas nodded. He didn't want to see Sharlo walk around with a number raised high overhead to be whistled at and leered at by rough men. It would be a clean fight and other boxers on the card, to lead up to the big event.

"If he's fighting Joe Wobble again," said Barnes, "I'd better get to work on him now."

This had set him free, he thought later, as he made his way out of the church. If he was working on Wood Mountain for the good of his people, then nothing—not his delicious but distressing feelings for all three of the girls, not even his secret rivalry with his star boxer—would mean more than getting Wood Mountain into fighting shape to beat Joe Wobleszynski.

＊━┃━＊

FUNNY HOW things happened, because that same week who should walk into the Four Bees restaurant looking forward to a farmer's breakfast but Joe Wobleszynski himself. And there was Barnes, hair combed down and held flat on his head with water so it resembled one of the golden pancakes he was forking off his stack. Barnes greeted Joe as he walked by, shook hands, invited him to sit down since he was alone. Joe declined to order food and said he was supposed to meet a friend, but he could sit with Barnes for a coffee at least. There were no hard feelings there. Or anywhere, really, with Joe Wobble. He was not out to demolish his opponent's coach, or even his opponent, outside the ring.

"Would you be up for it?" asked Barnes, when he'd described the venue, the reason for the card.

"Would I be getting a percentage here?"

"It's for that trip to Washington for them to testify, like I said. Nobody's benefiting. But it might help your standings if you definitively beat my guy."

"Yeah, I didn't like that whole timekeeper thing. It made me look like I was losing."

"You're a good man," said Barnes.

"Maybe. I don't know why I should care if they go to Washington."

"Don't you know any Indians?"

"What do you think? Hell yes, they work for us."

"On your farm, right?"

"Stone Boy family, couldn't do without them. They're good Indians. I started sparring with Revard, you know."

"He never said! He's improving. Now I know the reason," said Barnes, all strategic generosity.

"He's a strong kid," said Joe, smiling down into his coffee.

"You'd make a good coach," said Barnes, in earnest. "Look here. I found out some stuff. If this termination thing goes through, we all lose. I'll be out of a job. They'll be moving people off this reservation—won't be one anymore—the Stone Boys will end up in the Cities. This place is hollowing out already."

"I see that," said Joe. "My brother's off in Fargo and says he likes it."

"I'm not a big one for cities," said Barnes. "I wouldn't mind living out here."

Joe looked serious. "We'll have to find you a girlfriend."

Barnes waved his hand, not cheerfully. "Don't bother. I got that covered."

More than covered, thought Barnes, as Joe rose to meet his friend. Barnes watched. Square as a brick house Joe was, but leaning a fraction to the left, visible when he sat down in another booth with his friend. Barnes watched Joe's back for a few more minutes, noted that his left shoulder was definitely lower than the right. Good to know.

"WOBBLE'S LOPSIDED," Barnes said to Wood Mountain. "I don't know what it means, but it could be something to study."

Barnes had broken down and bought a speed bag with his own money. Wood Mountain was making it go.

"He walked kind of like this, sat kind of like that," said Barnes, replicating the left-leaning walk, the droop of shoulder. "Could be he got injured. Or maybe there's a weak spot in his training, something's off. We got to keep that in mind."

"Okay," said Wood Mountain. "Or maybe he was just a little off that day. Or maybe he's putting the fake on you."

"The fake? Could that be true?" Barnes was struck by the possibility.

"I dunno. But it makes sense somebody might try that."

"Like us," said Barnes. "Let me think."

"Nobody's stopping you," said Wood Mountain.

"I got it," said Barnes. "You're gonna wear a fake plaster cast on your right hand up your wrist. Just for a couple weeks. Take it off to train, but no other time. Nobody sees you without it. I'll get Jarvis to make it—he's good at theater props."

"Seems kind of underhanded," said Wood Mountain.

"Ha-ha!"

"Ha-ha what? Oh, underhanded! That's a good one!"

For the next half hour they came back to the joke again and again, finding more hilarity in it each time. They agreed it was a real shame they couldn't tell the joke around to people.

"It would become a classic," said Wood Mountain, a bit wistful. He hardly ever got off a good one.

"You winning will be a classic. So let's keep our mouths shut," said Barnes.

# *Thwack*

WOOD MOUNTAIN had begun to worry. The sound she made chopping wood last time had actually aroused him. Just a little. The clean split, the sureness of it, the certainty, the sound of her ax meeting the wood. Each of her strokes was accurate and powerful. There was just something to it he could not describe. Something it did to him. A shiver inside. A flipping fluttering. A warm drench of sensation that he'd hidden by suddenly sitting down in the chair and leaning up close to the table, with the baby, who regarded him with a gummy smile. Who the hell could resist? Zhaanat turned from her little stove and set a camp bowl on the table. She'd made him oatmeal, no raisins, no sugar, nothing. It had to be they were scraping bottom that week. It was Thursday.

Zhaanat saw him staring at the oatmeal.

"Don't worry," she said. "Our girl gets paid tomorrow."

She took the baby and began to feed him drops of oatmeal pablum on the edge of a spoon. The baby seemed to think it was a sumptuous treat, so Wood Mountain also ate the oatmeal, slowly, as the chopping went on. Thwack. Thwack. Goddamn. Cracks in his chest. Softness floating out. Thwack. Thwack. How could she do this to him? He flashed on her as the water-jack. He wanted to punch himself.

BARNES HAD got his uncle to come give Wood Mountain his wisdom. He was there the next day, a skinny fellow, excitable, with hair just like Barnes, sticking out over his ears on every side like a busted bale of hay. He also wasn't called the Music for nothing. There was actual music involved in his training regimen. He had brought an electric turntable and he played records, the latest ones, at the highest volume, fast and furious, to inspire jump-roping, cross-skipping, double-jumping. He worked the rhythm of Wood Mountain's combinations with speeded-up versions of "El Negro Zumbón" and of "Crazy Man, Crazy" by Bill Haley and His Comets. The songs he used stuck in Wood Mountain's brain and they were all he could hear. They colored his world. His fists began to move with their own life.

# The Tonsils

✳━┃━✳

SINCE THE Homecoming weekend and what Valentine and
Doris referred to as "the chirps," which had something to do
with a bush dance, riding in the backseat had become even
more annoying for Patrice. It was as if they were talking in a
secret language up there, referring to certain incidents with
nonsense words. But who cared. What did they know? The
two seemed so young that she envied them, and so ignorant
that she despised them. Scorn burned behind her tongue as she
sat there in the backseat gazing out the window, a serene look
pasted on her face. There was more than enough to occupy her
thoughts. At home Gwiiwizens was coming out of his new-baby
slumbers. Along with his charming, gurgly laugh, he was beginning to use his stare. He had an unnerving stare. Not soft,
like other babies, but hard. When his eyes fixed on Patrice they
drilled right into her soul. It was like he had something to tell
her. Had Vera left a message with him? A location? A demand?
Would he remember to tell her when he learned to speak? Her
heart beat faster. By then it would be too late. So far there was
no word from anyone Thomas contacted down in the Cities,
and no word from the one who might know. Bernadette had
to know. If Patrice went back down there, if she waited outside
Bernadette's house, if she cornered Bernadette, could she find
out what had become of her sister?

At work, she carefully sized up the others. Was there anyone who would possibly give up sick days, the way Valentine had given up her days? And not keep talking about it the way Valentine was now talking about her generous gesture? The one friend she might have approached, Betty Pye, had already used up her days getting her tonsils out. And she had perhaps gone a little too far with the tonsils. That day she brought them to lunch.

Betty took out her lunch box, which was an actual cardboard box covered with tinfoil. Then she put a jar beside her box. It contained some dark greenish-brown squiggles.

"Anybody besides me missing their tonsils?"

"I had mine out when I was at boarding school," said Curly Jay. She was down at the other end of the table. There was silence at the end of the table where Betty sat with her tonsils in a jar.

"I kept mine because they were supposed to be so unusual. Besides, they were mine!" said Betty to the group. She bit into her egg sandwich and chewed as she blandly reviewed her co-workers. They edged away from her. Doris said something and as usual Valentine laughed. Only Patrice did not look away from Betty Pye, but she also didn't look too directly at the tonsils, though you could hardly miss them. They looked like a couple of leeches. Patrice was hungry and had a baked potato for her lunch. She'd dressed out rabbits, deer, porcupines, all sorts of wild birds, muskrat, beaver, and pretty much could not be bothered by a pair of tonsils.

"Did you use up all the toffee in the parade?" she asked Betty.

"No," said Betty. She reached into her box and slid a wrapped piece across the table to Patrice.

Unexpected! Patrice put the toffee into her lunch pail. Zhaanat's face would light up when she brought it home. To make Zhaanat happy, just for a second or two, was one of her main efforts these days, and Pokey's too. Even the baby tried hard, she could tell. He made Zhaanat smile with his toothless little grin. But he never did smile when he looked at Patrice.

Mr. Vold came into the lunchroom with a self-important mug on. He informed them that higher-ups would be coming soon to inspect the premises. Everything must be perfect. Also, for the time being, there would be no more afternoon coffee breaks. He tried to make his weak eyes steely. Then he vanished. The women looked at one another, cleaned up every crumb, went back to work. After a while, they began to murmur. No coffee break in the afternoon? How would they manage? Just when you felt your body about to give, when your eyes crossed, when your neck was killing you, the thought of the coffee break was the only thing that kept you going. Without it? Collapse. Patrice still worked just beside Valentine, and when Doris wasn't around, sometimes Valentine still talked to her. They agreed about the coffee break. Then Valentine's tone shifted.

"You probably wonder what we have up our sleeves," she said in a coy whisper.

"Sleeves?"

"So to speak. Well, he kissed us. Kissed the two of us."

"At the same time?"

"Ooooh shaaaa. No."

"Aren't you going to ask who *he* was?" said Valentine after a while.

"Barnes?"

Valentine gasped. "Did he tell you?"

Something wicked in Patrice made her answer, "Yes."

And there was silence after that.

· · ·

BUT THEY talked to her on the way home, and didn't talk anymore about "chirps" or about Barnes. It was all so very strange.
Here she was, with no men on her mind, except the faceless
ones who had kidnapped, or maybe did something worse, to her
sister. No men but terrible men were on her mind. Patrice certainly did not think about Barnes, unless he was right in front of
her. And she didn't think about Wood Mountain either, though
that was harder because he stopped by regularly to see the baby.
Who smiled at him! Yes! Wood Mountain got the smiles that
should have belonged to Patrice. If she was jealous of somebody,
it wasn't Valentine or Doris, it was Wood Mountain.

WHEN SHE came down the grass road, she saw that he was
visiting again. The pale horse he liked to ride was tied to a
stump, chewing away on what Vera had always wanted to be a
lawn. Patrice stopped to pat his muzzle, scratch his ears. This
was better than having her father come home anyway. Miles
better. Inside the house, the baby was drinking from a bottle of
Zhaanat's fortifying rose hip tea. Wood Mountain was holding
the baby and the bottle. He was the only one in the house.

"That better not have sugar in it," said Patrice.

"Why not?"

"Sugar's not good for babies."

"It's just the baby tea. Don't worry. Your mom went out to
get some cedar to make a special bath, I guess.

"Cedar makes a baby stronger," continued Wood Mountain,
as if she didn't know.

Patrice stepped behind the curtain and changed into her
jeans. When she came out, she poked up the fire in the stove
and put on a kettle of water.

"You want to keep holding him? While I fill the woodbox?"

Wood Mountain nodded without taking his eyes off the baby.

Patrice went out and sharpened the ax, then split some wood to work out the aches in her back and shoulders. Wood Mountain felt each blow. When she came back in, Wood Mountain had the baby over his shoulder and he was walking around with a little pump in every step. The kind of jouncing walk that put babies to sleep. He patted lightly and sang an old tune, a lullaby, one of Juggie's. He was instantly an old hand with babies, the boxer. He could tame horses too. But that didn't mean she had to like him, though maybe, she thought, why not, a friend.

"Pixie? I mean, Patrice?"

Well, well. He was finally calling her Patrice.

"How about tea? Juggie sent some fresh-baked white rolls."

"Sure. Patrice?"

"All right, what?"

"Don't you think this baby might need a warm bag? And a cradle board?"

Patrice had discussed this with her mother. "He does need a warm bag. We were thinking of how to make it just yesterday."

"It needs to be two layers of blanket, with cattail down between the layers. That's how Juggie does it. And the cradle board, me, I can make that."

He said the last part offhand, but it was a big thing to make the cradle board. With their people, anyway, it was the father who made it.

"Okay, you do the board," said Patrice, as if it were just any old thing. "We're getting the blanket for the cradle board. Otherwise we have to cut one of ours in half."

"You each have one blanket?"

"Yes," said Patrice, "of course."

"Only one?"

She saw what he was getting at. How poor they must seem. But she was ready for that. As he must have noticed, she had taken some packages from her carrying sack. Some flour and bacon, some carrots and onions. Sugar in a twist of paper. Tea.

"As soon as I get my paycheck next week, we're going to have two blankets each and one for the baby. I have been saving."

"You can always get army blankets free at the mission."

"I know," said Patrice. "But Zhaanat doesn't like those. She says they have diseases in them."

"A lot of old people think that."

"She's not old."

"But she's from an older time."

"She is," said Patrice, pouring out the tea. That was as good a way as any to describe her mother. From an older time. The baby was asleep, but Wood Mountain kept holding him close to his body, inside his jacket, along his arm.

"Also," said Patrice, touching the baby's face, "Mama will bead the top blanket when she has the chance."

"Patrice. I gotta ask. Do you think Vera's coming back?"

Patrice turned and picked up the cup of tea. She gave it to Wood Mountain. Her hand began to shake. She'd had another dream, the same old dream. A small room. A dungeon.

"Yes, I know she will."

"How do you know?"

"I keep seeing her. I want to go back for her. But I don't know where to look for her. Do you know anything? Have you heard anything from Bernadette?"

"No, but something she said keeps bugging at me."

"What?"

"I heard her talk to somebody in the kitchen that time, and she said something that sounded like 'she's in the wood' or 'she's in the wall.' I couldn't remember after. I even thought for a while she was really in the wall. But that would be impossible."

Patrice remembered the voices. The stillness in the house. Her sense that Vera was very close. Her mouth went dry, she didn't think she could listen to another word. She put her hands to her ears.

"No, wait." Wood Mountain gently pushed her hands away from her ears. "Listen. Then I remembered 'hold.' 'She's in the hold.'"

"Hold?"

"Right. So that didn't make sense until Louie was talking with a buddy of his who was in the navy and he said something about the hold of the ship. So then I thought about what Bernadette said. 'She's in the hold.'"

"There's no ships around here, or ships down there."

"There's the Mississippi River, Patrice. And way up there, in our old tribal stomping grounds, the Gitchi Gumi, the Great Lakes. They have all kinds of ships."

Patrice sat down with her tea and stared evenly at Wood Mountain. It made no sense to her.

"Ships. They're filled with men."

Wood Mountain looked away, took sips of his tea. Kept patting the sleeping baby. Finally he put the cup down and said to her, quietly, as if he didn't want to wake the baby,

"Patrice. That's why."

But she shut her mind to what he said and walked back outside.

# A Letter to the University of Minnesota

Dear Millie Cloud,

You are perhaps surprised to hear from an old friend of your
father, but Louis suggested that I write. Knowing that you recently
conducted a study of economic conditions here on the reservation,
I am writing to enlist your assistance. As you may know, a piece
of serious news has reached us from Congress. According to House
Concurrent Resolution 108, our tribe has been scheduled for
termination. This is about the worst thing for Indians that has come
down the pike. I firmly believe that this bill means disaster for our
people.

I am writing to request your assistance in testifying before the
United States Senate Committee on Indian Affairs. We are told
that this testimony must be presented in March, but haven't the
exact dates as of yet. Your information at the earliest moment, and
assistance in presenting it, would be of the utmost value.

Yours very truly,
Thomas Wazhashk
Tribal Committee Member and Committee Chair

# The Chippewa Scholar

⁕═══⁕

MILLIE CLOUD had a favorite table in the reference room at the Walter Library at the University of Minnesota. She liked to sit with her back to the oxblood-bound collection of the *Diseases and Statistics Annuals of Minneapolis and Saint Paul*. She liked to keep on her left the great rectangular windows, shaded by massive trees in the summer, but bright now with only leafless branches twisting against the sky. To her right the card catalogs, librarian's desk, a blue globe of the watery earth. Before her, the door. She never sat in a room where she couldn't see the door, and she never chose a chair that wasn't against a bookcase or a wall. She did not like people to brush by her or touch her by accident.

It was readily apparent that Millie was fond of geometric patterns. Today she wore double diamond checks. Her blouse in black and white, her skirt in bright teal. Around her neck she wore a scarf printed with random blocks of gray and gold. Out of sight, hanging in the tiny wardrobe of her room, were five striped blouses, two sweaters knit in intricate cables of intersecting colors. Also three tartan plaid skirts and one pair of unusual trousers, blue and yellow. She wore brown-and-white saddle shoes, which she constantly thought of decorating with fine black lines. The day was cold, and she wished that she had worn her striped trousers. Her legs were tucked beneath the chair for warmth. She had draped her light woolen coat over her shoulders as she studied. Already the coat was inadequate. However, she loved it because the box pattern could be seen two ways and she was a walking optical illusion. Still, the wind went right through the fluffy fibers. She'd have to buy a new one and was also saving up for winter boots.

Millie had a job serving on the breakfast line in the dining hall, a job typing up titles and Dewey Decimal numbers for the card catalog, which she did afternoons from one to three in the basement of this very library, and a weekend job serving drinks in a bar called the Purple Parrot. She had a large square pleasant face, wore black glasses that pointed up slightly at the ends. As well as necessary, the eyeglasses were fashion aids, supposed to take attention away from, and hopefully diminish, her short, powerful neck and thick shoulders, resembling her father's. She was taller than Louis Pipestone, so the buffalo torso she'd inherited topped long gangly legs. She'd also inherited his hands, which were square and strong, but gripped a pen instead of reins. She didn't have Louie's good-natured attitude. She was irritable and forceful. Millie seemed to charge forward when she walked. Millie stated her opinions clearly. Millie spent most of her energy for fashion on combining patterns—she hated to purchase anything in a solid color and always found herself in a quandary. She kept her hair in a straight bob held to one side by a bobby pin. She didn't use any makeup but lipstick, a bright carmine red that emphasized everything she said.

Eventually, she thought she might try to be a lawyer. She might be good at it because she never backed down on anything.

Also, she might be bad at it for the same reason.

People didn't like her. Men were put off. She didn't care, much. She was her mother's only child. She had seen her father from time to time, and had even stayed with him when she conducted her economic and physical survey of the reservation, traveling from house to house.

Millie had noted the construction of each house, the condition of the roof and windows, if there were windows. She had noted how the house was heated, and how many people inhabited the house. Often she was asked inside, for, although she was brusque, she knew how to be friendly with strangers. There was, too, her very well-liked father. If she was invited in, Millie asked a number of questions about money and made a number of additional observations. On these trips she also met a number of relatives she hadn't known about at all. The survey and her findings became her master's thesis, and her long visit to the reservation was important to her. Having grown up in Minneapolis, she had wondered. Now she knew what it was like on the reservation and thought that living there would be quite a challenge for her.

For one thing, there were the horses. Everybody in her family rode them the way, in the city, she used to hop on a bicycle and travel around on a sidewalk or a street. They swung up and cantered around, here and there, even to the store or out on visits, with complete nonchalance. She couldn't get over it. At last, she had tried to ride the calmest mare. But she hadn't known how to start the horse.

"Just give her a kick," Grace had said.

Millie had given the wrong kind of kick and the horse galloped off like a maniac, tried to scrape her off against a fence. When she kicked again, it whirled and tried to bite her with its long green teeth. So much better to be here, accumulating and comparing data in the library, a shaft of neutral sunlight falling across a long wide wooden table. And when the dark came

down early, she happily switched on the reading lamp with its
green glass shade. For a short while longer, she ignored hunger.
At last, thinking about a cold shepherd's pie she'd bought yesterday and left on her windowsill, she decided to go back to her
room. She bundled her coat around her thick torso and thin
hips, and she tied a heavy fringed scarf of plaid wool around
her head. She put on her orange mittens. She had asked her
mother to make mittens this specific color so that she could be
easily seen as she crossed streets. They were thick and warm.
She made her way out and squeezed her books to her chest.
The heavy mittens and the textbook tomes acted as a windshield. On the way to her room she stopped in at the campus
post office and unlocked her box. She had a couple of letters,
which she slipped into her statistics book. She waited a minute
behind the student union door, taking deep breaths, before
making her way out into the wind.

AS SOON as she was in her room, she plugged in her comforting Salisbury, the electric heater she'd bought with some of
her scholarship money. It was her favorite winter possession,
just as her electric fan was her favorite summer possession.
She was sensitive to fluctuating temperatures and on a cold
day like this, Millie looked down lovingly at the golden metal
facing that surrounded the coil. Without taking off her coat
and mittens, she put the kettle on for tea. She had a two-burner
stove, gas, but she was always careful to make certain the burn-
ers were entirely off before she went to bed. Plus she always
opened the window a tiny crack, even in the deepest cold. On
the worst nights she had been known to get in bed wearing her
coat over her sweater and long johns, and once, at minus 40,
even a pair of winter galoshes. Tonight, the electric heater took

the edge off the cold air immediately. She got the shepherd's pie off the windowsill and put it before the heater. She poured hot water into the teapot, over the crinkled leaves, and when her tea was ready she poured herself a cup and stirred in half a spoon of sugar. She sat on her one chair, an old wooden kitchen chair. She rested her stocking feet on a stub-legged stool, close to the heater. The shepherd's pie gently thawed on a saucer, next to her feet. When it was ready, she'd use her gas burner, her frying pan, a bit of butter to brown the crust. Outside, the wind kicked up. Snow scoured the window, but couldn't get her. For Millie Ann Cloud, things didn't get much better. Sitting in her warm room while snow filled the atmosphere, toasting her feet in front of the glowing Salisbury. Dinner thawing. And two letters to open.

The first one was completely normal. It was from her mother, who now lived in Brainerd. She always wrote copiously, mainly about the antics of the dog, the cat, and her gadabout friends, comforting tidings but never of much interest. The second letter was from Thomas Wazhashk, and this letter interested Millie very much. In fact, it was a truly startling letter. First, that she was remembered, or known to anyone in the tribe except her family. Second, that her findings might be considered useful. Third, this business of termination. Whatever it was, she didn't think it would affect her personally. But to be considered useful by her father's people warmed her even more than the Salisbury.

## What She Needed

✦—|—✦

VERA HAD been sick for as long as she could remember—it wasn't just the movement, the swaying, the stinking little aperture into which she was locked and where the men entered and used her body, day and night (though she could not distinguish day from night). The cook's assistant, who was supposed to take care of her, was using what she needed on himself, and because of that Vera's agony was continual. Her insides were being pulled out. Her brain was heaving in her skull. The cook's assistant tried to taper her off, giving her diminished doses. Then what they both needed was gone. Vera itched, shrieked, moaned like a demon, threw herself against the walls. It got worse. She foamed and shat and made herself so horrifying that, one night, they dressed her in a dead man's clothes and carried her out of the ship and up a dock. The man who'd used up what she needed knew how it was not to have what they needed. He advised the other men not to throw her in the lake, which was cold, anaerobic in its depths, and would preserve the body they had used. So two of them dropped her, unconscious in her own filthy blanket, at the end of a steep alley in Duluth.

## Old Man Winter

✶═✶

SOMETIMES HE thought that his spirit would fly from tree to tree like a curious bird. He imagined that he would watch the living, call and sing to them. But if he went too far with that idea, it made him lonely. The living wouldn't know him anymore. No, he would walk on his four-day journey to the town of the dead. There, a feast was going, always going, every dish he liked spread across a wide table of yellow stone. Everything in that town would be golden in color, except perhaps the food, which would have its usual tasty colors—blue and purple berries, roasted brown meats, red jellies and breads and bannocks. He would eat and eat. The food would be shared with all the people he had lost, the people he missed. When he saw his beloved niinimoshenh, what would she do? Whistle to him? They used to use the chickadee's spring song. Yes, he would head to her straight off. He wouldn't hang around the living. Let them do what they must.

It was hard to leave just yet.

The beauty of the leaves was gone again, another quarter off the great wheel of the year. The elegant branches were stark against the sky. He loved it when the true shapes of the trees were revealed. He slept and slept. He could sleep for an entire day and night. It seemed to him strange that with so little time left he would choose to so deliciously spend it unaware. He still craved to drink in the greatness of the world. When on warmer days he bundled up and sat outside in his little chair, he felt the roots of the trees humming below the earth. The trees were having a last bedtime drink of the great waters that flowed along down there. Like him, before they went to sleep. Beneath that layer of water he sensed beings. They moved so slowly that humans were usually not aware of their existence. But he did feel their movements down in those regions. And yet deeper, far deeper, below those beings, there was the fire of creation, which had been buried at the center of the earth by stars.

Biboon added more wood to the stove. He moved his cot a little closer to the warmth. Then he lay back and closed his eyes. He was warm under the blanket, even his feet. He watched a circle of silvery women dancing in an icy field. One of them turned to him, gestured with her little fan of spotted wood-pecker feathers. It was Julia.

"I'll see you soon," he thought. But woke the next morning, warm in his saggy bed, even though the fire had gone out in the stove. Laboriously, he coaxed it back. Wade would come soon and stoke it up for the day. Most nights, Wade also stayed to watch over him. But Biboon had so much to think about that he didn't mind being alone. He pissed in his piss bucket. Boiled water and made his tea and oatmeal. As he ate, and sipped, he sang and thought.

When they sat together and his uncle touched Biboon's knee, it was a sign that Biboon should remember what he said. The stars were impersonal. But they took human shapes and arranged themselves in orders that conveyed directions to the next life. There was no time where he was going. He'd always thought that inconceivable. For years now he'd understood that time was all at once, back and forth, upside down. As animals subject to the laws of earth, we think time is experience. But time is more a substance, like air, only of course not air. It is in fact a holy element. In time the golden bug, the manidoons, the little spirit being he'd cracked out of a shell not long ago, flew to him. It happened when he was a tiny boy standing at the edge of a prairie coteau. From that place, he saw the buffalo trudging out of the horizon on one side of the world. They crossed before his eyes and vanished on the other side of the world in one unbroken line of being. That was time. All things happened at once and the little golden spirit flew back and forth, up and down through the holy element.

# The Cradle Board

✳═╎═✳

WOOD MOUNTAIN trained alone with Barnes, in secret, because he could not be seen using his hand without the fake cast. He had promised to tell no one, but felt badly about the ruse when he held the baby. It was like he was lying to Archille, and so at one point he whispered, "Don't worry, the cast isn't real." Gringo had to be ridden, so he took him over the trail, staked at the edge of the yard, strapped on a blanket. Louie had been making good money putting Gringo to stud. People came down from Canada, over from Montana, to breed their mares to a horse with Gringo's unusual coloring. Gringo had become familiar with the edge of the Paranteau yard, the beginning of the woods, and the long frozen grasses that he could pull.

Inside, Pokey was worrying his head about the match. Everyone was selling tickets, and everyone knew about Wood Mountain's injury. Perhaps sustained while picking mud from Gringo's hoof. Had the horse bitten him, or stepped on his hand, or cruelly managed to jam his wrist, or maybe thrown him once he got on to ride? Wood Mountain wouldn't say—not because the supposed injury was difficult to describe, but because he knew he couldn't use actual words to lie. His face would give him away. So he nodded at the horse or mentioned the stallion's name and shook his head whenever someone asked. Which was always.

"How'd you hurt your hand?"

"Gringo," he said, wincing.

"That damn horse," said Pokey.

"Shaaah," said Wood Mountain. "Swearing in front of your baby brother."

LATER AT the barn, Wood Mountain gave Gringo a rubdown and some grain. Then he stoked up the little stove in the corner where he slept. He sat down on a milking stool and began working on the piece of wood he was going to use for the cradle board. He'd obtained a cedar board from a friend in Minnesota; he'd also split a piece of ash, and was soaking it now to use as a curved head guard. Maybe he'd fit a flat piece onto the bottom of the board. That way the laced-in baby could brace his little feet when he was older.

Grace came into the barn and saw Wood Mountain shaving down the cedar with a hand plane.

"Hey," she said, "is your hand okay now?"

Wood Mountain looked blank, then screwed up his face.

"Ow," he said, setting down the plane. "I shouldn't of been doing that."

"Looks like you didn't mind," said Grace, suspicious. "Is your hand really hurt? I won't tell."

"Are you really flirting with that Mormon? I won't tell."

"No," said Grace. "He's gone."

"For good?"

"I think so. He was getting kind of, I don't know."

"Moony-eyed," said Wood Mountain.

"Maybe."

"What happened?"

"I wasn't leading him on or nothing."

"Oh, sure."

"Really! We were just brushing the horses together, and all of a sudden he says that if his seed mingled with a Lamanite's he would be damned to the unrelenting fire, but he would be willing to suffer. I said rest easy, no chance your seed's mingling with nothing here. But then I get curious and ask what's a Lamanite? He says didn't I know and I say no. He tells me I'm a Lamanite and I say no I'm a Chippewa. He says same thing as a Lamanite. But if I would take up becoming a Mormon I will turn whiter and whiter until I am shining in the dark."

"Hard to sneak out on your dad if you're glowing in the dark."

"How do you know I sneak out?"

"Sometimes when I'm too tired to go home I take a nap out here. That's how I saw your boyfriend tiptoe out to meet you the other night. He had his shoes picked up in his hands. Lifted up his knees. Looked so foolish."

"That's the night he talked about his precious seed."

"He was outta line. Think I'll smash him for that."

"With your broken hand? That hand you're using right now to unscrew the wood oil?"

"Ow."

"You're faking!"

"You won't tell! Not one single soul. I am trying to fake out Joe Wobble."

Grace started laughing so hard she had to sit down.

"C'mon."

"Don't you know?" she finally said. "He's trying to fake you out too. Walking around all crooked. Sometimes he forgets which side he's crooked on. All the girls know."

Wood Mountain gaped. "How'd you? What?"

"I thought you knew it. Everybody knows it."

"Does he know I'm faking?"

"Not that I know of. You're pretty good. Even I believed it up until I saw you working on the wood."

"I'm making a cradle board."

Grace stepped back, frowning.

"Something your mom should know about?"

"No, not that. It's for Vera's baby."

"Well, you should be careful. People are saying things."

"Like what?"

"Like that baby isn't from the Cities. Like that baby belongs to you and Pixie. Like you're trying to hide it from the priest."

"What would I care? No, this baby's Vera's."

"Why you out there all the time then?"

"Can't a man like a baby?"

"Sure. But usually it's his own baby."

"I never see Pixie. Almost never," said Wood Mountain.

"Oh, sure," said Grace.

"She don't care for me."

"And your hand's really broken. Men are so dumb."

She walked off, swinging her hair, slapping at the cribs. She stopped to scratch Teacher's Pet.

"Now don't you tell!" he called.

"About your hand or about Pixie Paranteau?"

"Quit that," said Wood Mountain.

He threw down the cloth he was using to wipe oil into the wood. He began planing the cedar board again, too hard, scraping off the oiled surface in curled strips. Grace looked back and was about to start laughing again. But something about his violent concentration and the way he blinked his eyes and squinted down at the board made her feel sorry for him. Then even sorrier for herself. She leaned close to Teacher's Pet and rubbed her horse's soft ears, gazed into her black liquid eye, whispered, "He's got it bad but he don't know it."

Pixie will split his hide, thought Grace as she walked across the yard. She pictured Gringo's belly, his pinkish skin laid open, garish before her father stitched him shut. They knew it was Teacher's Pet because there was a strip of Gringo's hide stuck on her hoof. But who cared. Let Wood Mountain find out how it felt. The air was hard and cold. She smelled snow and looked up. The moon was lopsided, like Joe Wobble. There was no wind on the ground but over west she saw clouds tossing up, erasing stars, coming on like sixty. She thought of going back to tell Wood Mountain about the storm. No, let the horses tell him. Let him sleep in the barn. She'd always known he was too old for her. She was done with him. He could go straight to Pixie.

## Battle Royale

**⋇═╪═⋇**

WHAT WAS it to be? A Battle Royale, a Friday Night Fracas, a Slugfest Saturday? Thomas mulled the problem over as he prepared the boxing card for the printer. Excitement Galore. Did that sound ridiculous? He and Barnes had matched up the oldest boys in the area boxing clubs, plus of course Wood Mountain vs. Joe Wobleszynski, the main attraction. Thomas was putting his own money toward some flyers that could be tacked up everywhere—the tiny bush stores, the schools, the off-reservation bars, the cafes and gas stations. At the bottom, he'd set the cover charge at "suggested 2 dollars" but knew they'd take whatever the crowd—he hoped for a crowd—could give. He finally decided on Battle Royale Benefit. At the bottom, he wrote, "Come one come all. Enjoy a fun night. Excitement Galore! Do your best to bring your representatives to Washington." Sharlo had drawn a puffy pair of boxing gloves in front of an American flag. He'd had her draw them over again to look more menacing. He pasted everything together at his desk, finished around 3 a.m., and dropped the flyer off after work the next morning.

After another meeting with Moses Montrose, he went straight home and staggered into the sleeping room, took off his shoes, and as usual put his creased pants and carefully folded shirt on the small bed beside theirs. He slipped beneath the covers in his undershirt and boxer shorts, draped another undershirt over his eyes, and began taking deep slow breaths. But his heartbeat filled his ears. His thoughts jaggedly sped the moment he rested his head on the old flattened pillow he jealously guarded for himself. Pictures as clear as though they'd happened yesterday flashed on. The look of Roderick when he was brought up the stairs, blinking, terrified, shaking, coughing, haunted. Half dead already. A few weeks later, he'd come to wake Roderick in the dormitory. His friend was still and his skin gray; he was barely breathing in the bloody sheets. Oh, Roderick. Would these electric shocks of memory ever quit? Worst, he remembered teasing Roderick, daring him, even getting him in trouble, and LaBatte pointing his finger.

*Who did this?*

*Roderick, sir.*

He didn't get as much sleep as he'd have liked; in fact, he was still tired when he woke up four hours later. Smoker barked his head off when Noko wandered away from the house, and there was a visitor looking for Rose to ask if Rose could keep her loud and furious baby for the afternoon. He tried to get a few hours in when the rest of the family went to bed, but again, his heart raced and his body was so tense he could not relax. And that baby was a howler. He'd see Roderick behind his eyelids, then worry about whether the boxing match would raise enough money, then leap forward to Washington, D.C. He worried what going to Congress would be like, what he would say, how difficult they'd make it, whether he'd choke up on his words. And he knew thinking this far ahead was useless and ridiculous, but his mind had seized its own irrational path and would not be controlled by logic. He couldn't argue himself into sleep.

When he finally stopped tussling with his mind and got up to go to work, he dressed in the dark as usual and sneaked out into the kitchen. There at the table, in the low light of the kerosene lamp, Sharlo sat with a blanket over her shoulders. She was hunched over a book, concentrating so intensely that she barely acknowledged him. He went outside to the privy and when he came back washed his face, hands, forearms, neck with cold water, to wake himself. Sharlo barely looked up. He put on his jacket, hat, and picked up his briefcase, his lunch box, his thermos of coffee. As he turned at the door to say goodbye and tell Sharlo to turn in, she sighed, shook her pin-curled head, and closed her book. She stretched her arms, yawning.

"That was a good one."

"Kept you awake." Thomas touched her hair.

"Here, you should take it."

It was a mystery book. But Thomas had too many letters to write and he was determined to investigate the book that the missionaries had left with him.

AFTER HIS first rounds were finished, Thomas poured himself a cup of coffee and took out the small dark book. He thought he should read the book in order to understand Arthur V. Watkins. After all, when Biboon had sent him to boarding school, he'd said, "Study hard because we need to know the enemy." Over the years, he'd realized the wisdom of that. Knowing the sorts of people he was dealing with, he'd been able to persuade the powers that be to locate the jewel bearing plant near the reservation. He'd been able to use their logic to get improvements in the community school. He used the education they had given him to advance his people—he'd often forgotten that was the point of his study, as Biboon had said, but it had turned out to be so. Yet, along the way the word enemy became confusing. The BIA higher-ups in the room in Fargo could have been the enemy, but they seemed more dismayed by the bill than excited to carry out its directives. John Hail, the town lawyer, was a friend. And even Vold—not exactly the enemy, not even an adversary. But Arthur V. Watkins was clearly an enemy—of the most dangerous sort: a principled enemy who thought what he was doing was for the best. But let me not call him an enemy, Thomas thought. I will think of Watkins as my adversary. An enemy has to be defeated in battle, but an adversary's different. You must outwit an adversary. So you do have to know them very well. In Thomas's experience, anyone who took on and tried to sweepingly solve what was always called the "plight" or the Indian "problem" had a personal reason. He wondered what that could be for Arthur V. Watkins.

The first intriguing surprise in The Book of Mormon was that Joseph Smith, their prophet, had also been visited by an extremely bright being who was semitransparent. Thomas put the book down. At first, his feelings were confused and maybe even hurt, the description was so close to his own private experience on the night he almost froze. But once he got over the feeling, he was somewhat relieved. These beings apparently appeared to others. They had come to tell Joseph Smith about some historical plates that seemed to be buried in several places. The book had its elements of suspense. For instance, the interior argument of a man named Nephi, who was not eager to murder a drunk man with his own sword, but was persuaded to complete the murder by the voice of the Lord. Nephi next impersonated the man he murdered, deceived his servant, and stole all his treasure—brass plates with histories engraved on them. Thomas's eyes began to droop. There was wilderness, women, Jews. Mainly there was this Nephi. Would Nephi tell this whole book? Thomas paged ahead. Again, his eyes began to burn and then he felt his head tip, jerked himself awake. This was going to be a very difficult night.

He persevered for another hour and began to read about Gentiles coming to America, which surprised him because he didn't think that things would move so quickly. But then again the book, for all of its archaic returneths and blameths, had its origins in America, so he tried to adjust. There was lots of righteous anger in the book. There was some fury about a great and abominable church, which Thomas couldn't place. There was a lot about the filthiness of other people and the cleanliness of Nephi's people. When he got to the downfall of the daughters of Zion, Thomas felt a pang for the women. Apparently the daughters were proud and haughty. But their punishment was excessive, Thomas thought. He liked the idea that they made tinkling sounds as they walked, like jingle dancers. But on a certain day the Lord took away the bravery of the daughters tinkling ornaments and cauls, and round tires like the moon. The Lord took everything away. The chains and the bracelets and the mufflers. The bonnets, and the ornaments of the legs, and the headbands, and the tablets and the earrings. The rings and nose jewels. The changeable suits of apparel, and the mantles and the wimples, and the crisping pins. The glasses, and the fine linen, and hoods, and the veils. And instead of a sweet smell, they got a stink. Instead of a girdle, a torn girdle. Instead of well-set hair, baldness. Baldness! Instead of a stomacher, whatever that was, they got a girding of sackcloth, and worst of all, burning instead of beauty.

Thomas, who searched out nice clothes and loved it when Rose let her hair flow long, wore her flame-colored dress and the strapped black shoes with curved heels, closed the book, depressed.

· · ·

THE FIRST thing he wrote down about Arthur V. Watkins was he probably liked plain dress in a woman and probably dressed himself simply and inconspicuously. No ankle bells for him. No flashy tie or two-tone shoes or broad-brimmed fedora. He definitely was a righteous fellow. How do you fight one of those?

AFTER WRITING responses to several newspaper articles and filling out an order to request a mimeograph machine solely for the use of the tribal council, Thomas remembered something from his boarding-school days. There, he'd strategized. The only way to fight the righteous was to present an argument that would make giving him what he wanted seem the only righteous thing to do.

# Two-Day Journey

※=|=※

VERA FOUND that she was walking. She was wearing a warm overcoat, a hat, and boots on her feet. She was on a road. She knew, as everybody around her knew, that the soul after death sets off on a journey to the next life. Sets out walking on a road like the one she was on now, dark and lonely, but clearly marked in the moonlight. To be dead was perhaps a relief. As she walked, Vera tried to remember the way instructions for the road went— she would be tested several times. She would hear the voices of the living, calling her back, but she must not turn around. She must continue on west. There would be certain foods she should not eat, but certain foods she could eat. There might be, she could not fully recall, a bridge or a snake, maybe a bridge with a troll underneath, or had she heard that somewhere else back there during her life? If she got far enough, she would hear the dead calling to her, encouraging her because after three days she would be weary. She was afraid that she might hear the sound of her baby crying from the town of the dead. She didn't want him to die, but she would run to him, wherever he was. At least he wouldn't be alone. After a while the air turned pale gray and she saw a sign, Highway 2. Then another sign, painted in black strokes, Firewood for Sale. She began to doubt that she was on the right road. She began to wonder whether she was even dead. Although she had been dead way back when she'd been alive. Maybe for a long time. Of that she was sure.

# Boxing for Sovereignty

✳—|—✳

THE SNOW held off and the roads were clear. A secondhand popcorn machine purchased by the school for sports events was tuned up and hauled over to the community hall. The scent of hot oil and the stutter of popping kernels warmed the crowd. Sharlo bagged the popcorn and Fee took the coins. Juggie was selling tickets at the door. Moses was counting money. Thomas was giving out the event cards and glad-handing people at the doors to the big hall, where the ring was set up. Inside, the boxers were secluded near the bathrooms. Curtains had been hung so they could emerge to cheers. The ring, posts, and ropes, a platform built by Louis with donated lumber, looked good enough. The referee, Ben Fernance, who was also the county commissioner, wore armbands and carried a small white megaphone. He made announcements, welcomed the crowd, while Mr. Jarvis fiddled with the ailing loudspeaker.

PATRICE AND Valentine had come early and were standing close to the ring, behind the chairs, which were for elders only. The crowd increased quickly and Mr. Jarvis appeared with a microphone and a gong. When he struck the gong, there was an exotic reverberation. He'd wanted spotlights, but that had proved impossible. His inspiration had been to use sound to direct the crowd. It worked. The buzz died down in anticipation, and then the boxers filed out to bursting cheers. Each was introduced along with his opponent. Although the majority of the crowd was Indian, picking up Sioux from Fort Totten and Devils Lake, there were plenty of neighbors from farms and towns within a hundred miles. The location of the match had shifted the balance, however, and there was little palpable animosity. Even Joe Wobble's family and supporters were good-natured, clasping hands with the Stone Boys, cheering on Revard and also his opponent, Melvin Lauder.

Mr. Jarvis had always wanted to narrate a fight, and felt it was his duty to make the conflicts as exciting as possible. After all, the boys were in this sport to build character, not hammer each other to a pulp. It wouldn't hurt to exaggerate their war-rior spirits.

"Stone Boy takes the punch without flinching, just like his name. Lauder keeps pressing him, hot to trot. But Stone Boy slips around him like a ballroom dancer! Right to the bread box. Left to the jaw! Lauder has a steel chin. Lauder shrugs it off. Stone Boy circles, sizing him up. Stone Boy goes wild with a mad flurry of bouncing blows! But Lauder's doing the hot potato! Fending him off! Aaaand the bell!"

Still more people wedged in, packing the room tighter, as the matches between the younger fighters were won and lost. John Skinner, a fighter from St. Michael, made a good show-ing against Tek Tolverson. The jolly mood intensified, Jarvis making a sensation out of every match. The fights, all won on decisions or points, weren't after all that exciting. Only once was there even a bloody nose. Jarvis narrated that like a dam had burst. Even when the grand finale was announced, the one everyone had come to see, there was a sense of goodwill. The fact that it was a benefit helped. Jarvis kept announcing that and thanking the crowd.

"Here it is, folks! The Main Event!"

Everyone knew by that time that Wood Mountain and Joe Wobble had each been faking their injuries. So the two decided to play that for laughs. Joe limped out leaning so hard to the left he staggered. Wood Mountain actually came out wearing the plaster cast.

"Here they are, my friends! Let's give them a hand as they approach the ring! Willing to go the distance even though they're fighting through the terrible pain of their separate injuries. What? What's this? The Wobble is straightening up! Wood is throwing his cast to the crowd! He's dropping his handkerchief and Pixie Paranteau catches the memento! Oh, I tell you, folks, it's a miracle. A miracle is what you're seeing. Two battlers fighting for sovereignty restored to health before your eyes!"

For the first two rounds, they tested each other's range, striking and deflecting. Wood Mountain was still the more studied fighter, pressing Wobble to the inside, giving no opportunities. But Joe Wobleszynski was potentially more dangerous, with no decrease in his punching power and perhaps some realization that in the last fight he'd given away his lack of strategy. It was clear, by round three, as Wobble's strong blows met only air, that Wood Mountain intended to wear him down and to demoralize him if he could.

Joe Wobble was slightly leaner than in the last fight, while Wood Mountain had put on a couple of pounds without giving up a hint of speed. Barnes and his uncle had made sure of that. He had drilled on speed and more speed. He had a natural sense of cunning. Jarvis himself had coached him on a trick, which he employed in the fourth round. Wood Mountain used a fake sag, as if he'd misstepped, to draw Wobble's most fearsome hard right. With a lightning fade Wood Mountain countered the missed punch with a left to the place where Wobble's out-crop of chin met the smooth line of his jaw. He was able to strike precisely there, with force, and get out of the way when Joe retaliated, managing only by chasing Wood Mountain into the corner to land several surface blows that didn't resonate but looked brutal and drew gasps. Again, with Jarvis's coaching, Wood Mountain remembered to cringe under the onslaught and Wobble went to his corner feeling he was in a surge.

"Be patient. Play the music when the time is right," said Barnes, packing handfuls of snow along Wood Mountain's left cheekbone. The music was a speeded-up version of the cancan, to which Wood Mountain had rehearsed a blur of punches that he could switch up to fit the situation. The flurry at one speed then switched to a higher speed and changed him from a boxer to a swarmer. It was how Jake LaMotta had beaten the French fighter Laurent Dauthuille in the ultimate round of the world heavyweight championship back in '50. It looked to all observ-ers, except the Music, like the switch-up came out of nowhere, some reservoir of heart, but the brilliant shift in momentum had been coming all along and was choreographed, he was sure of it.

"They're circling like panthers! No cat's paws though, folks. Wobble swipes like a grizzly bear! The Mountain swipes back! It's all brute strength. And now they're sizing each other up again. Look at that fancy fadoodle footwork!"

So far, the boxers looked undamaged. In fact, they looked magnificent. Joe, a milk-skinned prize bull, Wood Mountain, ropey and gleaming, glancing out under a shining swoop of hair. That was to change. In the sixth round Joe Wobble got tired of chasing Wood Mountain around and landed a solid punch that shifted Wood's nose across his face.

"And the Mountain takes it on the beak!"

Patrice heard the crack and her knees gave. Valentine went gray as a ghost. They clutched each other as the match stopped. Barnes worked on Wood Mountain, who reentered the ring, nostrils askew and stuffed with cotton. No sooner had the bell rung than Wood Mountain proceeded, with startling cool, to borrow Wobble's right hook to knock Joe to his knees. He got up, but now it was clear that the fight had begun, not in anger, but in dutiful violence, and the next two rounds were blurs of punishment. Still, the two were nearly even. Wood Mountain slightly ahead on points, nothing definitive.

"Stop the fight!" yelled Patrice. But there was pandemonium because one elder had accidentally struck another with a diamond willow cane and their families were trying to sort this out. Plus Joe's family was not sure what to do so they just yelled. And Wood Mountain's supporters weren't sure whether to stop the fight, so they raised the roof. Jarvis had to strike the gong again.

"Folks, folks, calm down. The fighters say they refuse to quit. They want to give it their all. The referee has accepted this. They say they feel good, feel fine, want to go the distance."

So the round began, but the crowd was muted. Joe opened a deep gash on Wood Mountain's eyebrow. Wood Mountain dealt a body blow that made Joe stumble across the ring. By the final moments, they were merely clubbing each other, moving in an earnest fog, and Jarvis was silent. There was no strategy, no design.

"It's just ugly," said Patrice, looking away.

When the gong sounded, people cried out in relief. They clapped in distress and left in disordered clumps. Wood Mountain did win on points but winning was beside the point. Joe

Wobleszynski sat dumb in a chair. Their eyes were swollen shut, lips split, eyebrows taped, ears ringing, noses snapped, brains swelling in their skulls, and every bone and muscle ached. It was wonderful, it was terrible, it was the ultimate. It was the last time either of them fought.

# The Promotion

UNFAIR, IT was so unfair. Valentine promoted to the acid washing room, where she got to wear goggles, gloves, a white hair wrap, and a protective rubber apron. So unfair because Patrice was faster, more precise, more focused, and produced a clean card every time. She was that good. Not that Valentine was bad at her job, not at all, but she wasn't as good at her job as Patrice. That was just a known fact. But apparently to Mr. Vold not good enough for a promotion.

"Fine work, fine work," he said, behind Patrice now. Today, tuna wiggle was on his breath. Patrice longed to punch him, the way Wood Mountain had laid Joe Wobble right down in the ring. The left jab and then the right cross. Classic. Not that it mattered. She pictured Mr. Vold's eyes rolling as he staggered in confusion down the hall. But of course, that would get her fired. She tried to concentrate. Misery was good for that.

No, she would not be miserable. It was Valentine's first day in the acid washing room and yes, Patrice was jealous, but she also missed Valentine sitting right there by her elbow, missed the shorthand communication they had developed. It made the hours pass by more swiftly. Today, how they dragged. And no coffee break. Vold really had taken it away in preparation for visits from Bulova and General Omar Bradley, and he'd never reinstated coffee breaks. Her neck hurt, the strain. She focused. She entered the hum of concentration. Then it was lunchtime.

Patrice went to the ladies' room first, because she dreaded listening to Valentine talk about how great her job was. And her raise. Valentine would say she wouldn't tell, then give in to telling, the amount.

"Buck up," Patrice told herself. "It's not like she's queen."

She walked into the lunchroom and sat down next to Betty Pye, even though there was a space next to Valentine. Anyway, her friend was absorbed in telling everybody at the table how heavy the rubber apron was and how weird it felt to wear rubber gloves all morning.

"My hands are puckered! Just look!"

*I could tell her a few things about wearing rubber outfits, getting puckery, also about turning blue,* thought Patrice. She put away the thought. Her lunch was a cake of oatmeal fried in deer fat, and some raisins. She ate slowly, to make every morsel last. She was so hungry, and when she'd finished her stomach still felt painfully empty. Or maybe Valentine was giving her a stomachache by talking about her raise. Still, it turned out to be less than Patrice had imagined, 90 cents instead of 85 an hour, and far less than Patrice had made as a waterjack. A Main Attraction. Everybody's eyes had been on her as she swanned and dived in the tank. True, the people were smudges, but their eyes were fixed on her. She was being admired, wasn't she? Or maybe not. She put that thought away too. Kicked it to the back of her mind. Valentine was asking her something. Everybody had turned to her, waiting for an answer.

"I said, Pixie—"

"Patrice."

"I said, penny for your thoughts!"

"My thoughts are worth a lot more than a penny," she said.

"Ooooooh," said a couple of women.

"How much?" Valentine persisted. "Here."

She pushed a dollar bill across the table.

Patrice picked up the dollar bill, flapped it in the air, set it down, and pushed it back. "Still not enough."

"Oh well," said Doris. "Guess we'll never know who Pixie likes."

"It's Patrice. And I don't like either one of them. You can have them both."

"I might get one of them," said Doris. "I'm going out with Barnes to the movies."

"That's nice. When are you going?" asked Patrice.

"Sometime," said Doris.

"What does that mean?" Now Valentine was questioning her.

"It means that I said yes when he said we should go out to the movies sometime."

"He said or you said you should go out to the movies?" Valentine persisted.

"Okay," said Doris. "It was the other way around. But he did say yes."

"I'm happy for you. Tell me when it happens," said Patrice.

Valentine said, "Some nerve, Doris," and got up to don her special protective clothing.

"You three should stop squabbling," said Betty Pye comfortably. "It's so much nicer to be on good terms."

"I know," said Patrice. "And the stupid thing is, all of this is over men. Valentine and Doris won't be happy until I'm locked up in a tower with a ring on my finger."

"You're funny. Try and find a tower around here."

"Maybe a grain elevator?"

"I'm lucky I have good old Norbert," said Betty. "We just bumble along."

"Are you going to marry him?"

"Oh, we'll elope if I get pregnant," said Betty Pye.

Patrice couldn't speak, she so marveled at Betty's answer. They were walking back to the main room, putting on their smocks. Patrice wished that Betty was working next to her. She wanted to know more about "if I get pregnant" and hoped that Betty would tell her.

WHEN PATRICE stepped out of Doris's car, she saw Thomas Wazhashk was visiting her mother. His car was neatly parked along the main road. He was, as all men seemed destined to do, holding Gwiiwizens when she walked into the house.

"Have you found out something about Vera?" asked Patrice.

"Yes and no."

"And?"

"We don't know where she is, but she was seen. In Duluth. She was taken in for vagrancy and released."

"She gave her name and disappeared," said Zhaanat. "But she is living. I knew she was living. She has been trying to call us."

"Call you?" Thomas knew there wasn't a telephone for miles.

"In her dreams, remember? In our dreams."

"Of course. I'm just tired. What's she doing now?" asked Thomas.

"I don't know," said Zhaanat. "For a while she was wearing green high heels. Then she was wearing men's clothes. She was walking along a road. But my dreams have quit."

"Mine too," said Patrice. "Last night I dreamed . . ."

She mumbled something, looked away. Last night she had actually dreamed about being kissed by a man from a magazine ad. He had stepped off the page, put down his cigarette, leaned across, and . . .

"How much money did you raise?" she quickly asked.

"More than halfway. Almost there if we find a person who can put us up in Washington. The hotels there are heap big expensive."

"Heap big," said Patrice. She laughed.

Thomas had carefully explained the bill to Zhaanat, and she was worried because if it meant she would have to pay taxes on her land she would have to let it go. They would have nowhere to live. Just like Juggie said, they'd be walking the road looking for a place to light. Although of course, thought Patrice, with her job she could probably afford to rent a place for them to live, somewhere. They'd have a better place if Valentine hadn't stolen her promotion. She had jokingly accused her friend of just that on the way home and Valentine just said, "All purple with envy, you!" But now Thomas was trying to outline his strategy.

"I have an ace card now. Louie Pipestone's daughter with that girl he never married. Well, it was the other way around. Her parents weren't happy that she was engaged to Louie. Said he was too much of an Indian. They squashed things."

"That's sad!"

"Yes, Louie was so blue over it. Way back when. Now that girl's grown up and got herself to college. She's working on a higher degree, even. We're going to see if we can use all she found out. The Congress thinks we are so advanced, rolling in cash, but we know we aren't. We don't have a way to prove it. We can't just go complain. We need the hard facts. We need a study."

"A study!"

It sounded so professional to Patrice. A woman from her own tribe doing a study. It sounded like something that she herself would like to do. Go to college. Do a study. She was smart enough, good at math, and her writing was always best in class. But she thought of herself as that little hide tent, stretched so thin. Without her, the family would collapse. You could not send money home when you were off in school. The baby needed a rug to play on. The floor was freezing cold. But even this floor, this small patch of ground, would be gone if they had to sell their land. They wouldn't make it. They would be like before. You don't forget.

Patrice went behind the blanket, into her room. She didn't dare raid her stash under the linoleum, but she did open up the spice tin. There was five dollars inside, all in change. She counted four of the dollars out onto the bed and brought the money to her mother. Put the coins in her hands. Zhaanat put the money on the table.

"That's for Washington," she said.

Thomas, visibly moved, said, "Thank you, cousin."

THE NEXT day, it happened. Mr. Vold sent Betty Pye to the workstation next to Patrice. He gave the direction at lunch, and Betty brought her things there right after. Such a relief. For a while they worked quietly. Patrice had promised herself that she wouldn't talk unless Betty talked. She didn't want to risk getting Betty in trouble, in case Betty wanted to stay clear of Mr. Vold. But within the hour, Betty asked what she was doing that weekend and Patrice murmured that she didn't know. Then she asked Betty what Betty would be doing that weekend and Betty said that she would leave the place and time up to Norbert, but after that she had a pretty good idea of what would happen.

"Say, Betty," said Patrice in a tiny quiet voice, "I only know in a general way what happens. I wish somebody would tell me the details."

"You mean you've never done it?"

Betty's voice was too loud, but fortunately Curly Jay had a sneezing fit at the same time, covering her.

"Shhhhh."

"Sorry, I just couldn't believe it."

"I'm scared to because, you know. For the reason you said you might elope."

"Let's go out and have a cup of coffee somewhere and I'll explain it all."

"Would you?"

"My god, somebody has to."

ON SATURDAY, Patrice walked into town with Pokey. He went to the center to punch on the speed bag. She went to Henry's to meet Betty. There she was, already drinking her cup of coffee. Betty was wearing a beige felt hat like a plump cake, with a cute feather. It perched on her dark permed curls. Her coat was rose colored with white rabbit-fur trim. Eye-catching. Her wide, round, merry face was avid and her lips puckered over her cup. She blew daintily to cool the coffee. Patrice asked for tea. She didn't drink coffee on the weekends. If possible, she napped in the afternoons.

"So," said Betty. "Nobody's never told you?"

"No," said Patrice.

That wasn't exactly true. Actually she'd always known what happened. She lived around animals wild and tame. Once, she'd watched minks mate in the rushes by a slough. She'd seen all sorts of things. She'd been trapped in the car with Bucky and his friends and knew what they were trying to do. Her mother had talked to her about these matters, but all in Chippewa, so she had a good idea of what happened, in Chippewa. But she wanted to know how it happened in English, because she needed to know the words for what might happen in case it happened with somebody who didn't speak Indian. She understood there were several ways it could happen, but not how that would be negotiated. It seemed strange, her having been a waterjack, that she didn't know. But she understood the fact that she didn't know might have been obvious to Jack Malloy. It might have been the reason he hired her. Sometimes she suspected it might have been Jack's job to mess with her, but he'd flinched when she smashed his arm. She was too strong.

Betty looked around carefully. The cafe was full, but not crowded. They were in a corner. Nobody would hear what she said. She told Patrice what an erection was. Patrice already knew. She tried not to think of Bucky and his friends. Betty told her how to get away from men she didn't like, who had erections. Again, that was nothing new. She told Patrice how to pretend to drop something, how to accidentally brush against a man, if she did like him and wanted to see if he liked her.

"Pretend you have something in your eye, and you can't see where your hand goes. Or bend over to pick something up by his feet. Brush your hand against it as you stand up. Oops! Then you smile at him, if you like what you felt. He knows. But if you didn't like what you felt, you get the hell away from him."

"Right," said Patrice. She thought of Bucky, now with his one crossed eye.

"Once you touch it, even by accident, they might grab you. So you have to be ready. Then if you do like it, and you want to try it, you find a private spot. In fall or early spring, out in the woods. In summer, you might get ticks. It isn't very attractive to be pulling ticks off to have sex."

"No."

"So it's better if there's a barn or a bed or he has a car."

"No car," said Patrice, but Betty was oblivious, and spoke with a clinical practicality, describing positions that made Patrice drop her face into her hands, laughing.

"Don't laugh! That's the way to get your hoo-ha."

"What?"

"Hoo-ha."

"I've never heard of that."

"It makes you feel like you're floating off. You are a kid, my goodness."

Betty went into such detail about the hoo-ha that Patrice's face grew flushed and hot. Her mother hadn't said a word about this, even in Chippewa. And button. Which button? Must be the other one, below the belly button. See, she thought, this is why I needed to talk to Betty.

"Whatever happens, I don't want to get in a family way. How do you stop that?"

"The rubber, but they don't like them. Or maybe you don't have one handy and you still want to do it. You will be okay if you just have sex the week after your monthly ends. Just that week, you're safe. It's what me and Norbert do. And of course we have his old jalopy. We go parking on the weekends. Way out on the section roads. Who are you going to have sex with?"

"I just wanted the information in case, but I don't have a plan."

"That's not what your friends think."

"They're so irritating."

"All the same, sounds like you could try with either guy. The only thing is getting rid of them after, if you don't like it."

Patrice looked completely mystified.

"I know. It's supposed to be you only do the deed if you are planning on forever. Getting married. But my aunt told me that if you are serious try it out first. It's no good to have to do it with one person all your life if it isn't any good. This is what my aunt said. Why be stuck with a dud?"

"You're so right!"

Patrice was even more impressed with Betty. She asked if she'd like a pastry, and Betty took her up on it. They each had a maple long john. As Betty put her lips around the frosted roll to take a bite, she met Patrice's eyes and started laughing so hard she almost choked. She put her pastry down.

"Oh my gosh, that reminded me!"

"Of? Oh . . ."

Betty was lapping the frosting off the top and sides of the pastry. Her tongue was thick and pale pink.

Patrice looked around, disturbed. What Betty seemed to imply had never occurred to her.

"And men can do it to women, too. It's like licking jelly out of a bismarck bun, a straight shot to hoo-ha."

"How do you know all this? Your aunt?"

"No," said Betty modestly. "Experience."

Patrice was a bit repelled, then completely awed.

"Now, don't tell anyone I told you."

"I wouldn't tell for anything."

Betty looked up and smiled at someone behind Patrice.

"Hi there, Hay Stack. Or I mean, sorry, Mr. Barnes."

"Hi to you, Betty. And hello, Patrice."

Patrice turned in her chair. Just the way Barnes said hello made her feel uncomfortable, like the air was pressing down on her. And embarrassed. What if he'd heard their conversation? And how much worse would it be if she tried him out and he was a dud?

"Hello, Mr. Barnes," she said in a neutral voice.

He took a step backward, gave a weak smile, and turned away.

After he left, a welcome refill on coffee and tea.

"The thing is," said Betty, leaning close to Patrice, staring at her in a weird way, her mouth smeared with frosting, "men want it so bad they will pay for it. Know what I'm saying?"

"Not exactly. . . ."

"They come up here and tell women they'll get married down in the Cities, let's go. Then down in the Cities they ditch the woman, sell her to someone who puts them out for sex."

"Puts them out . . . ?"

"On the street, looking for trade, getting men to pay them for sex. But then giving the money to the pimp."

"What's that?"

"You don't know nothing! A pimp is someone who owns the lady. Takes the money she got paid for having sex, see?"

"No. I don't see," said Patrice flatly. But she did see. Jack would have tampered with her slightly, just enough so that when somebody else came along she'd have that shame, then more shame, until she got lost in shame and wasn't herself.

"Okay," said Betty, uncomfortable. "I was making that up."

"Of course," said Patrice. She leaned away from Betty. Not wanting to be disturbed. This had now gone too far. Wanting to get back to the beginning of the conversation. Where she could try out sex and get rid of men.

"Were you pulling my leg about the hoo-has, the you-know-whats?"

"No. I wasn't making those up."

"Good," said Patrice.

She pulled her maple long john into pieces and couldn't finish it. The cream filling oozed out onto her plate. She had to cover it up with her napkin just to drink her tea.

## Edith, Psychic Dog

HARRY ROY, retired army medic, World War II and Korea, saw a person sleeping by the highway about an hour after dawn, and pressed the brakes. His old Studebaker rumbled to a stop. The sleeper was on the edge of the shallow ditch, in frozen weeds. He walked back to the crumpled form, bent down, and adjusted the person's woolen seaman's cap. An Indian with chapped cheeks and a pointed feminine chin. As he took the hand he knew for sure that he was holding a woman's hand. Delicate bone structure, ragged nails, bits of red lacquer. The pulse was weak and rapid. He thought of bringing her to the hospital. But he knew the hospital all too well. They might treat her like a drunk and after she warmed up just throw her out onto the street. He cradled her head, put his arm underneath her knees, and picked her up. Just bones, much too light. She was breathing all right and didn't smell of liquor. He carried her to his car, managed to hold her steady with one arm as he opened the back door. He tried to fold her inside. He couldn't be completely gentle about it, had to pull and shove. She was limp now, and he was worried. But her pulse seemed steadier than before and she was still breathing properly. He decided to bring her home.

Harry lived with an ordinary-looking smart brown dog, named Edith. As happens when one person lives with one dog, the dog became psychic. By the time Harry stopped the car, Edith knew Harry had picked someone up on the road. She waited silently, alert, in the driveway. Came close when Harry stopped the car and stood by him as he leaned into the back of the car. He pulled out the other human, staggered a bit as he drew her into his arms, righted himself, and began to walk. Because of the way Harry held the woman, Edith was prepared to guard her. She put her nose to the woman's leg. The woman had slept in the clothing of a man who cooked with grease, she had slept in snow and wild mint, near the carcass of a skunk, had recently been in town and before that out on the water. There was no harm in her, but she was confused, in despair, and might choose to sleep forever. Edith accepted all that. When Harry brought the woman into the house, Edith followed. She stood at attention, her ears flared forward, as he laid her on the sofa that Edith herself often claimed after Harry slept. It was a long soft couch and the woman was short. Edith didn't mind sharing.

BEFORE OPENING her eyes, Vera detected a man. She kept her eyes closed, tried to keep her heart from breaking out of her chest. There was a food smell. Her head turned to follow the smell.

"Open your mouth."

A man's voice, which made her tremble, but the voice was kind.

"I'm a medic. Can you manage a little soup?"

She mustn't open her eyes, but couldn't help opening her mouth. She was fed a miraculous soup filled with bits of tender meat, carrots, onions, barley. The man tipped some water between her lips and put a piece of bread in her hands. She kept her eyes shut, but slowly ate the bread. Gradually, as the food made its way into her body, she felt the strangeness of being on the other side of things. As if she'd passed through the guts of a tornado. She was still shaken inside, down to the marrow. After the food, her body ached for sleep so she slept and slept. Every time she woke, she kept her eyes closed. She didn't want to know what was out there.

Harry drew a bath, led her to the bathroom, because she still wouldn't open her eyes.

"Here," he said when she entered. "This is the sink." He put her hand on the porcelain. "Right next to it's the throne. Then over here's the tub."

He lowered the tips of her fingers into the water.

"And here's the lock," he said, bringing her back to the door. He placed her hand on the small metal bolt.

He shut the door behind him. Vera slid the bolt shut and groped her way over to the toilet. She peed for a full minute, then took off her clothing, felt her way to the tub and slipped into the hot water. The beauty of the sensation was so intense that fear dropped away. It felt like a kind of birth. She opened her eyes. Sunlight through a foggy window. A green plant on a shelf. The dim delicious fall air. She was a new baby—skin frail as paper, arms weak as milk, brain forming shapes into thought.

The next morning, she heard the man laughing. "Edith, you must have played your cards right. She let you keep her feet warm."

EDITH PLAYED her cards perfectly. She followed the woman. Settled near the woman. Understood from her scent that unspeakable things had happened to her and might happen again. The level upon which the woman was afraid had nothing to do with Edith, but it did have to do with Harry. She trembled when he came into the room, tried to hide it, put her hands under the blanket.

It was bad, but nothing Harry hadn't seen before. The twitchiness, shaking, jumpy eyes, bad dreams, sudden welling of tears but no sobs, the attempt to hide her fear. He sat in the room with her, reading his detective novels from the library, playing records. She wouldn't say which songs she liked. He liked cowboy music but thought he should stick to music without words. Calm music. No Kitty Wells. No Hank. And none of his upbeat Andrews Sisters and other big-band music from the war. He had a few old records his mother had listened to, ripply music, soothing. Sometimes her eyes rolled back and she began to flail as though she was shoving someone away. Touching her made it worse. Even Edith couldn't help. He'd put on the Debussy and wait.

# The Hungry Man

THE SNOW had come down in the night, heavily, covering everything. Millie knew the moment she opened her eyes. The air inside was different, filled with a cold radiance. It was a struggle to leave her bed beside the radiator. And she would miss the comforting nearness of her teakettle. But she had to pack. She had to leave. She had to wear the felt-lined zipper galoshes with fur trim. So unattractive. The heavy coat, which her mother had arranged for her to buy at a price she could afford, was a disappointment. It was a tweed coat with a quilted brown lining. Warm, but the tweed was woven with disturbingly random speckles of red wool. She had to counter everything with her new outfit of strict black and white lines.

She remembered that they'd nicknamed her Checks the last time. Would they now call her Stripes?

Her mother had also bought Millie a set of woolen long johns. But she didn't think she'd wear them. Still, just before she left, she stuffed them into her bag.

Outside, she practically needed sunglasses against the glare. Sound was muffled. At first, it felt like she was under miles of clear water. Then the shuffling of wheels and footsteps on the snow became normal. The first snow, even though it meant more and more snow, always lifted Millie's spirits. The bus was warm, and nearly empty, which was a relief. As she walked from her stop, her eyes got used to the brilliant world. When she entered the train station it was like a green drape fell across her vision. Blinded, she had to stop right out of the revolving door and someone bumped into Millie before her eyes adjusted. She strongly disliked being jostled by strangers. After she recovered, she took care to walk with a special alertness, dodging people in advance, yet keeping an even pace, until she reached the ticket window. That exchange went smoothly, at least. It was one of those days where she didn't even like walking down the stairs to the platform because it was almost impossible to not touch someone in the process of boarding the train. She held on tightly to her suitcase and focused on what it held. Her suitcase contained an onionskin copy of the study. Her advisor had the other copy. Several years of hard work had gone into the study and she had not had time to have it copied in the administrative office. The very fragility of its existence made her tense. Her father would meet her in Rugby, same as before. She would feel better once there was someone who respected the importance of the study. Who would help to guard it. For that reason, she'd asked her father to bring Thomas Wazhashk.

MILLIE WAS unaware that as she traveled along the snow followed in her wake like a vast whirling cape. The wind came up as they neared the flat Red River Valley and continued on through Fargo. Its force increased, kicking up ground blizzards that the train struck through easily, but which brought most car travel to a halt so that, when she finally and at last reached her destination, Millie had to wait until the train station was nearly empty before Louie and Thomas showed up. Her father immediately hugged her, throwing her into confusion.

"Oh, Checks," he said. "So glad you come here to help!"

Thomas shook her hand, which was reassuring. The men

were exhausted, having shoveled themselves out several times along the way. As it was impossible to leave that night, the stationmaster allowed them to sleep on the benches with a few other stranded travelers. Millie tried to settle in, using her suitcase for a pillow.

"That don't look comfortable," said her father. "Take my jacket for a pillow."

"I don't want the report in my suitcase to get lost," said Millie. "Or stolen or anything. It contains my only copy."

"How about I get that rope from your car and tie the suitcase to me and Millie?" said Thomas.

Yes, he has the proper respect for the document, thought Millie, with relief.

Thomas and Millie fell asleep with the suitcase between them, the rope looping twice through the sturdy suitcase handle and then tied tightly to each of their wrists.

Louie thought that, if anything, the presence of the rope announced that the suitcase contained something valuable and might tempt a thief. But none of their fellow refuge seekers looked remotely larcenous.

IN THE morning, they ate breakfast in a restaurant that advertised its Hungry Man Special in the window. They each ordered the special and the joke was Millie ate hers and what was left of theirs and she wasn't a man, but hungrier than a man.

"Sometimes I dream I am a man," said Millie, which was the sort of statement neither of them could meet with a response.

"Good thing the snow stopped," said Louie, squinting out the window.

"Hope we don't have to use that tow chain," said Thomas.

"Anyway, it's clearing up."

"Still kicking myself because I didn't put the chains on the tires yet."

"Maybe we should order Millie here another breakfast," said Louie. "Wouldn't hurt to wait until the sun hits the road a little."

"I'll take more coffee," said Millie. "But you might have to stop for me on the way. I'll run off behind some trees."

Louie had forgotten that conversations with his daughter were almost always interrupted by just this sort of uncomfortable statement. Both men responded to the waitress when she came to take their plates away and weren't sure, really, what it was safe to speak to Millie about.

"One *M*, one *E*, two *L*s, two *I*s," said Millie, out of the blue. "That's me." She smiled at them and said, "As long as we're waiting here, let's talk about the findings of my study."

# Good News Bad News

THOMAS MULLED over the detailed report.

THE GOOD news is we're poor enough to require that the government keep, and even improve upon, the status quo.

The bad news is we're just plain poor.

The good news is that the county, the state, and our neighbors in off-reservation towns do not want us on their hands.

The bad news is this isn't just because we're poor. They don't like us.

The good news is we are sheltered by roofs.

The bad news is 97 percent are made of tar paper.

The good news is that we have schools.

The bad news is that so many of us are illiterate.

The good news is a cure was found for the latest scourge to hit us, tuberculosis.

The bad news is so many parents died and their children grew up in boarding schools.

The good news is we have this report.

The bad news is also this report.

# Flying over Snow

*❈━❙━❈*

PATRICE SLOWLY dusted her workstation with a small, soft brush. The snow was falling in heavy sheets. Now there would be no chance to test the possibilities of Betty Pye's information until spring. She had decided on Wood Mountain for the test because if it didn't go well he was less "sticky" than Barnes. She had in mind the tiny dots of burrs that slapped all the way down pants or a coat, folding the fabric into a new seam. Sticky. It seemed that Wood Mountain had many admirers. He might even have his eye on someone, which would make him less liable to stick to her. Also, if something went wrong, which she didn't expect, she could give him the baby to raise. Yes, it was an outrageous thought! She'd never heard of a woman doing that. But look how good he was with babies. The only place she could think of to try out sex was outdoors in the woods, but now that snow was falling thickly that wouldn't work. Unless she somehow made it work. She adjusted her equipment and began her meticulous task. Yesterday, Betty Pye had sneezed all over her magnifying glass, necessitating Mr. Vold's application of a special spritz of glass cleaner and some polishing with a soft cloth. Today Betty was out with a terrible head cold, so there were no distractions. How she missed Valentine. And coffee breaks. Also light. Darkness fell so early this time of year.

. . .

DORIS AND Valentine were already in the car when she walked out.

"Sorry," she said, getting into the backseat.

"We almost left you," said Valentine. "Doris is itching to get on the road."

"No, we didn't," said Doris. "I had to warm up the car anyway. Valentine, you always exaggerate."

"I don't!"

Patrice leaned back. She could feel the heat inching toward her feet, which were already going numb in her thin boots. She needed heavier socks. A sweater beneath her coat. Her lucky-find blue coat had been good only through October. She thought of how Pokey was dressed so warmly thanks to Barnes, and felt guilty again for choosing Wood Mountain over him, even though it was a meaningless choice given the snow. At least the road was clear enough, the driving not impossible. Up front the argument was turning to teasing and laughing, so Patrice let her own thoughts float free. What if she visited Wood Mountain's house when Juggie was gone? Or what if they happened to borrow Juggie's car? What if . . . oh what if . . . what if they made their way to that old abandoned cabin up the hill, the one Vera used to work on, thinking it might be the start of her own house someday? No, how ridiculous. It was just as cold as outdoors in that cabin, and maybe branches had even grown through the walls. But there was still a rusty little tin stove up there, she thought, and she could bring blankets. However, that would mean she planned this whole thing out, which made her head whirl. She closed her eyes. Wood Mountain's strong chest, bare and glistening with sweat and heat. The look on his face the first time he adored the baby, but that adoring look directed at her—wait, she didn't want that. Wood Mountain was a personal experiment. She was only planning to try him out, not be adored or loved or anything that would make him sticky, like Barnes. But wasn't he a little sticky anyway? Coming over to see the baby?

No, he was not sticky. He never even looked at her anymore. And now that snow had fallen he wouldn't be riding Gringo up there. That horse was too valuable to stake out in the cold. She wouldn't see him, in fact, at all. A flicker of disappointment. And again the thought of that old cabin, or Juggie's car. That fancy car that Bernie Blue got for her. With the money that Bernie made, somehow. Patrice's thoughts shifted.

How had Bernie made the money? Bad ways, for sure. Bernie was living with a shady, violent man who perhaps gave her money. For some reason. Maybe love. But did a shady, violent man give a woman that much money out of love? Patrice had no idea. She'd made a pile there as a waterjack, so maybe there were other things Bernie did to make a pile. Sex things Patrice hadn't known were even jobs, the way she hadn't known swimming in a tank dressed as a blue ox was a job. Or maybe, she thought, the sort of drugs that Jack had obviously taken. They had to be worth money, like liquor was worth money. Her thoughts veered. Maybe Bernie had something to do with the collars and the chains and the menace of that boarded-up house. Maybe Bernie had something to do with where Vera went, and maybe the money that bought the car had something to do with where Vera went. The things that Betty had tried to tell her about were true, and maybe had to do with where Vera went. Also the things that Wood Mountain had tried to tell her on the train and later about the boats so big she couldn't imagine them were also the things Betty Pye had talked about, and had to do with where Vera went.

These were possibilities that she knew other people knew, and had always known. They were things that she, Patrice, tried to keep from thinking about. But now with full weight they crashed upon her and she gave a sharp cry, there in the backseat. She thought Valentine would turn around, but no, she was engrossed in a passionate conversation about doily making and embroidering pillowcases for a hope chest being so boring and irritating that she couldn't do it anymore. The nuns had taught her. But no more! She wouldn't do it! Not for anything. No to the hope chest. She'd get married without a hope chest. Doris agreed with vehemence. Valentine tossed her head and looked angrily out the window. She was silent. Her face was reflected in the glass and from the backseat Patrice could see how Valentine's eyes shifted from side to side, glittering with sadness. Valentine had never embroidered for a hope chest. She had embroidered for nuns during the years she spent as a little girl in boarding school, poking her fingers and trying to get the designs right. Her mother had nearly died of tuberculosis and Valentine had nearly died of loneliness during those years.

<hr />

PATRICE PUT on her long underwear, padded overalls, two layers of wool socks, her father's overboots, and took a coil of wire from its nail beside the door. It was her day off, but she wasn't going to walk or hitch a ride to town. More snow had fallen during the windless night and now it lay suspended in the trees, outlining each branch and twig. There was a magical hush. It was the sort of day Patrice liked for snaring rabbits.

Zhaanat had made her daughter a pair of snowshoes out of bent ash and sinew. Wearing them, Patrice could go anywhere, suspended like the snow in white cold. Down along the frozen slough she tied reeds together over rabbit trails, securing her snares. She was carrying a large cloth bag looped around her waist, and as she crossed the slough she pulled fluffed-out cattails off their woody stems and filled the bag. She set snares in the underbrush leading up to Vera's cabin. The cedar trees that Zhaanat had planted in damp spots were almost black in the cold, asleep. Their medicine was gentle this time of year. At last she climbed through a tangle of raspberry and birch to the clearing where the cabin stood. There it was, a tiny pole-and-mud box hung with snow. It still had its doors and narrow windows, the glass miraculously still intact. She could see, it was true, a few popple trees growing out of the roof. These were laden with snow and added to the air of enchantment. It was so quiet there. So dear. Oh, Vera. How could she have imagined taking Wood Mountain up here for crude love, no matter how curious she was?

Am I just curious, or am I like Betty? Is there something wrong with being like Betty? I'm no better, she thought. A swooning, dripping, hungry sensation came over her. No, I'm no better than any other woman. But the thought didn't help her longing, so confused with shame. Instead she thought of how cold, how dark it would be inside the cabin, even if you made a fire. Probably a skunk was living there. Patrice turned and traced her way back, not along the same trail. She wanted the slow drifting-down remains of snow to cover her scent around the snares. She took a more difficult way home, traveling beside a ravine where the snow was heaped up and the footing uncertain. Halfway home, she stepped out upon a patch of snow that collapsed into a depression lined with leaves.

It happened so suddenly that after she fell she sat in the leaves for a while, bewildered, but comfortable, and with no wish to move. She took her snowshoes off. Above, on top of the ravine, she heard small birds murmuring—the plump gray ones who scratched up the snow for food and traveled in flocks. Her snowy plunge had only briefly disturbed them. She turned her head. Behind her, a narrow aperture through leaf-clogged roots, and behind that, a profound and friendly darkness. It looked cozy, the bed of leaves, the curves of dry bare roots. This could be my love nest, she thought; if a man liked it here, I might like him.

But yes. The place looked alive, the bank of the ravine, the leaf cave. Felt alive. From its mouth she caught the unmistakable fug of bear, but it was a quiet kind of odor, seeping up from under the dense oak leaves. She thought she should be afraid, but she wasn't. She knew the bear was sleeping hard. Now she was sorry she hadn't carried the rifle along. This was the best way, the only way, really, to kill a bear with the old contrary gun her family owned. Still, she'd have fallen with the rifle slung over her shoulder. She was lucky enough to have landed unhurt in her snowshoes. She shifted around to make herself comfortable. Outside, the snow drifted down the layers of air, flake by flake. Watching the snow glide down put Patrice into a trance, and now she could sense the slow inflation and release of the bear's lungs, which made her even sleepier. Perhaps the leaves were warmed by the bear's bulk and slow heave of breath. Patrice rolled herself into a ball and closed her eyes. It was time for her weekend nap, anyway, and how often did a modern working woman get to sleep with a live bear?

SHE WOKE in the cave of leaves with a tingling sense that something good had happened and might happen. Then she remembered that she'd been sleeping only feet away from a bear. She put her snowshoes back on and left quietly, walking at first, then loping lightly, knees high so her snowshoes would clear the snow, all along the bottom of the ravine. The cold air flooding her throat was a source of power. Sleep was a fuel, too, making her springy and buoyant. She was so much stronger than she'd thought. And fearless. As she went downhill she was nearly flying across the snow.

"THE OLD man, he's close," said Zhaanat when Patrice came in the door.

"How do you know?"

"I found a track this morning. I smelled him out there. Signs."

"And his luck's due to run out."

There was a certain timing. After two or three months of wandering around, Paranteau would generally stagger and steam into the yard, raving.

"I'll be the night watchman," said Patrice, and went out to get the ax.

The night was clear but the wind had changed.

Patrice brought the ax inside and put it on the table. She had bought kerosene, and she could keep the lamp on all night. She got her book, some paper, and a pencil. Pokey curled up on his mattress. Zhaanat went to bed with the baby.

HALFWAY THROUGH the night, Patrice realized she hadn't thought of Wood Mountain even once since she'd awakened in the leaf cave. Maybe she had even lost interest. The intense focus of those thoughts and plans seemed remote. Why would she waste her time figuring out men when she was a person who had slept with a bear? She was wide awake now because she'd napped that afternoon. She kept the strength she'd gained in the minutes she'd slept. Bigger ideas were called for. Why should anything be impossible?

In the deepest hour of the night, Patrice loaded the stove and put on her boots and her coat against the cold jabbing into the house. The wood crackled, burning hot. Then the split logs fell into coals. Everything ceased. She listened hard. Nothing, nothing, nothing. But she could feel the calm breathing of the night. She put on her mother's mitts, took the ax, stepped out the door. Outside, there was resounding silence. The black sky was a poem beyond meaning. *This World is not Conclusion. / A Species stands beyond—/ Invisible, as Music—/ But positive, as Sound.*

# Snares

✦─┼─✦

"WOULDN'T DORIS and Valentine like to see me out here setting snares?" said Patrice to her little brother the next day. "There, see the place where the rabbit jumped? Set it right above."

"I know! Quit bossing me!"

Pokey looped the wire and fixed it to a branch that hung low over the spot.

"All my friends catch rabbits and hunt," he said. "Your friends are useless."

"They do have jobs. And they belong to the Homemakers Club. They sew and make gardens and raise chickens."

"I wish we had chickens," said Pokey. "I could put them in the little shed."

"They'd freeze solid."

"Maybe you should get it over with, Pixie."

Pokey was the only one she let call her Pixie.

"Get what over with?"

"You know."

Patrice was the person she'd been before her thoughts had turned all muddy. She felt superior to the person she was before she slept with the bear. She indulged Pokey with a smile.

"I suppose you mean Hay Stack?"

"He's nice to me. But I know why. So not him."

"Wood Mountain?"

"Wouldn't be half bad."

"So less than 50 percent awful." Patrice shoved his shoulder lightly. "I'm aiming for something more like in the 90 percent good range."

Pokey batted at her. "He does say you're a smart one."

"He does?"

"He says you're probably too smart for him."

"He's probably right."

Pokey looked skeptical, then dejected.

"Gego babaamendangen, nishimenh, don't worry. Let's check the snares I set yesterday up by the old place."

Patrice had told her mother about the bear, but in Chippewa, which Pokey didn't understand very well. She'd used the most complex words she could think of too, so that he wouldn't figure out what she was talking about and get some idea about trying to shoot the bear himself. Zhaanat had listened to her with her eyes shining, the baby sleeping on her heart.

As they approached Vera's cabin, they walked across the frozen slough, searching carefully along Patrice's trapline. They found one large white snowshoe hare, frozen solid, and another smaller cottontail. They walked uphill, beating through brush, and then stepped into the presence of the cabin. The undisturbed calm of it made Patrice so lonely that she said no when Pokey wanted to look around inside.

"It's Vera's," she said.

"I'll just look in the window then."

"No," she said, but he walked up to the cabin anyway.

He stood at the window with his hands cupped around his eyes.

"Someone's sleeping in there," he said. "Curled up by the stove."

"Come back," said Patrice.

She knew whoever was in there wasn't sleeping. There had been no tracks yesterday. Pokey's were the only tracks up to the place today. From the way Pokey's face looked when he returned, she knew that he knew also.

"Let's go home. And don't tell Mama."

"I guess not," said Pokey. "What you gonna do?"

"I'll go into town. Get Moses Montrose. Or Uncle Thomas. But don't tell Mama yet."

"I won't. I'm scared who it might be."

"Me too. Could you tell if it was a man or a woman?"

"It was wrapped in a blanket."

"I think maybe I'll get Uncle Thomas," said Patrice.

THE COLD squeezed and burned as Thomas, Patrice, and Wood Mountain made their way up to the cabin. Wood Mountain pulled the toboggan that Zhaanat and Patrice used for dragging game over snow and which Pokey used for rushing down hills. Pokey wanted to go, but they made him stay with his mother, who sat absently by the stove, rocking the baby. Zhaanat had now been told what was in the house on the hill. She had lost her balance and fallen back onto the table, as if struck by a great blow.

They kicked away enough snow to open the cabin door, and entered. Patrice knew before Thomas pulled aside the blanket. Even before he briefly uncovered the face, she knew the shoes. Thin shoes with holes showing the pasteboard he wore inside. Her father's shoes. And the liquor bottles. Empty pints, six or more. His death had probably been painless.

Both men stepped back and put their hands up to the heavy woolen hats with earflaps that tied underneath their chins.

"Don't worry about your hats," Patrice said, furious. "Let's just get him down the hill."

So the men loaded him up and she walked ahead. The fact that he'd chosen to come back and die in Vera's house made her so angry that she became overheated as she tramped along. Now Vera's place was stained by the death in its walls. Patrice's eyes kept watering. Not tears. She wasn't crying. It was the cold. And the terror that it might have been Vera. All she could think of when she thought of Paranteau were the times he'd arrived home drunk and dragged all of them into his ugliness. When he'd made Pokey fly into the wall. She knew there were other times, but she could not remember them. Good riddance, she thought. Nobody spoke. They were all on snowshoes and made it down before dark. Pokey came out of the house. His face didn't change when he found out who it was. He helped put his father in the lean-to. The men stayed outside while Patrice went inside. Her mother looked away when she told her who it was. Patrice knew she didn't want her daughter to see the relief on her face.

NOW POKEY was the one throwing his emotions into wood chopping. Maybe he'd loved his father. Or maybe he thought he should love his father. Before the men left, they hauled a fallen tree out of the woods and sawed it into stove lengths. Pokey and the others would keep a fire going for Paranteau. They couldn't tell how long ago he had died. But his spirit would still be wandering, said Zhaanat. They needed to send him on the path. She wanted him buried in a cleared spot behind the house. Where I can keep an eye on him, she said. Wood Mountain drew up that same night with a wagonload of wood. He made several fires on the burial ground. They would have to soften up the earth to dig the grave. Wood Mountain brought an ice pick, a shovel, and a big pot of Juggie's boulette soup, generous balls of meat and soft potatoes and carrots in a peppered broth thickened with flour.

THAT NIGHT, Patrice was awakened by a sound that started low and gathered force until it became a high-pitched shriek. It came from inside the cabin, from where her mother was sleeping. Or was it from behind the wall, where her father lay frozen? Patrice dived blankly into sleep. At one point she realized that Pokey had crawled into her bed and was curled against her back.

IT WAS hard to leave for work the next morning. As she walked out of the house, Patrice glanced into the lean-to. Her father's corpse was still there, wrapped in a blanket, on the cot where he used to sleep off his binges. Which should make her sad, Patrice thought, but she wasn't sad. She was just glad he hadn't come back to life, which did make her sad. How sad it was not to be sad.

When the car pulled up, Patrice saw that Valentine was glowering out the backseat window. She opened the back door.

"Why are you sitting back there?"

"Doris told me to."

Valentine folded her arms and glared straight ahead.

"Get in the front seat," said Patrice.

"No," said Valentine. "I'm just doing what Doris told me to do."

Doris was pretending that nothing had happened. She wouldn't speak. Whatever they'd argued about was stupid, thought Patrice, but she remembered the sorrow in Valentine's eyes as she looked out the front window of the car, and she said, "Please then. Please get in the front seat. Whatever you argued about isn't worth it. You two are best friends."

"You are my best friend," said Valentine, in a voice that was low but still loud enough for Doris to hear.

"Us three are best friends," said Patrice. "And maybe while we're at it we should add in Betty. Come on, get in the front seat. We'll be late."

"Yes," said Doris, "we'll be late. Come on."

"Say you're sorry!" cried Valentine.

"I'll lose my temper," said Patrice, surprising herself. Such authority in her voice. "Valentine. Get in the front seat."

Valentine got out of the car and sat in the front seat, holding herself like an injured bird. She wore a slim brown coat with a plush collar. It looked very nice on her. In the backseat, Patrice closed her eyes. One fine day, she would have a car of her own. And a coat like Valentine's. Anything could happen now. She remembered when she woke in the leaves—the tingling sense that something good would soon take place. Was that about her father? Was finding him dead the good thing that had happened?

*Patrice, you are hard.* So pitiful, he was so pitiful. Why didn't she feel it more? He'd probably died while she slept in the leaf cave. The odd sense of that day's buoyancy came back to her. She saw herself bounding along the bottom of the ravine. She hadn't known that she'd been carrying a weight. Then it was off. Her father's violent descent had hung over most of her life. Dread was gone. It had left when he died. She hadn't realized it was so heavy.

She worked at the jewel bearing plant all day. Unable to fake sorrow, she told nobody about her father.

# Cradle to Grave

THOMAS WORKED on the grave house while Wood Mountain finished up the cradle board. They were working in Louie's barn because he had all of the tools—the saws, planes, rasps, the splitter, vise, hammer, and the sanding rocks. Neither of them spoke. Thomas was using a sharp chisel to dovetail the ends of the boards. He didn't like using nails in a grave house. He made a few small rafters for the roof and then planed out the necessary shingles. He'd seen them made with tar paper or bought shingles, but he felt close to Zhaanat as he worked—she had asked him to make the grave house because she knew he did it the old way. Except, Thomas wondered, was this the really old way? Biboon said that his father remembered a time when the dead person was carefully wrapped in birchbark and then fixed high in a tree. It seemed better. You were eaten by crows and vultures instead of worms. Your body went flying over the earth instead of being distributed to the tiny creatures living under the earth. This grave house probably came about after they had been forced to live in one place, on reservations. Mostly, they had Catholic burials. He wanted to ask Wood Mountain which he thought was better, tree or dirt. However, Wood Mountain was finishing the cradle board.

"I suppose we shouldn't tell Zhaanat we were making the grave house and cradle board at the same time," he said to Wood Mountain.

"You think it could be bad for the baby?"

"I'm not superstitious," said Thomas, although he certainly was. Just not as bad as LaBatte with his fear of owls and his reading of random omens in everything. Wood Mountain said that he'd light some sage and bathe the cradle board in the smoke to take the whammy off.

"That'll work," said Thomas.

From the top of the cradle board, Wood Mountain was using Zhaanat's finest sanding tool—horsetail plant split and glued onto a piece of wood. It was bringing out the narrow lines in the white cedar. He had a jar of tea and a jar of vinegar in which he'd left some pennies for a week. After he'd sanded the wood smooth, he painted the bottom of the cradle board with the tea, which gave it a soft brown color. He painted the top of the wood with the penny vinegar, which tinged the wood with pale blue, including the head guard. He tied several pieces of sinew to the head guard. Sometimes he found small ocean shells while working in the fields. Some were whorled; others were tiny grooved scallops. He drilled holes in them and hung them from the lengths of sinew.

"Barnes was saying there used to be an ocean here," he said to Thomas.

"From the endless way-back times."

"Think of it. Vera's baby will be playing with these little things from the bottom of the sea that was here. Who could have known?"

"We are connected to the way-back people, here, in so many ways. Maybe a way-back person touched these shells. Maybe the little creatures in them disintegrated into the dirt. Maybe some tiny piece from that creature is inside us now. We can't know these things."

"Us being connected here so far back gives me a peaceful feeling," said Wood Mountain.

"That's what it's all about," said Thomas. "And now we're putting another man in the earth. Maybe a drunk, but he wasn't always a drunk."

"Sometimes when I'm out and around," said Wood Mountain, "I feel like they're with me, those way-back people. I never talk about it. But they're all around us. I could never leave this place."

# The Night Watch

※—‖—※

THEY HAD left a tree with strong branches standing near their house. You could hang a deer from that tree and dress it out. Or a bear. That's what Zhaanat was doing when Patrice came back from work. Of course she'd gone after it. A bear was a walking medicine cabinet. When a bear was killed during hibernation, its meat was milder, sweeter. Patrice had been compelled to tell her mother, but she had hoped her mother would not kill the bear. Now Zhaanat and Thomas were working carefully on the hide. Skinned-out bears looked too human for Patrice and she hurried to the house. She could hear them singing to the bear in low voices as she stepped inside. It was warm and close. People were sitting around the stove, at the table. The baby was tucked away in Juggie's arms and Rose was making bannock bread. People sat on Pokey's bed and on her mother's low mattress. Some had brought their blankets, thrown over a shoulder, so they could sleep on the floor. Patrice knew everyone, or almost. Her curtain was pulled aside and the one person she didn't know was sitting on Patrice's bed, alone, clinging to a cup of tea. She was perhaps a few years older than Patrice, with flat dark hair and cat glasses. She was wearing a confusing sweater with black and white lines. Patrice's quilt was also mostly black and white. Who was she?

Someone had put up a blanket in a corner, for privacy, a

place where Patrice could change her clothes. She put on long johns, overalls, and an old mission sweater. She took her fur mitts down off a shelf. She put on a knitted hat and when she came around the blanket the woman she didn't know took in her transformation with surprise.

"Hello," said the woman. "I'm Millie Cloud."

She didn't put her hand out, so Patrice put her hand out. Millie examined Patrice's hand as if it were unusual, like Zhaanat's hand, but then she grasped it almost with desperation. Millie's grip was hard, like a white-person grip.

"Your hand has calluses," Millie said.

"I like chopping wood," said Patrice. "I'm going out there to chop wood right now."

"I have never chopped wood," said Millie. "When was your house built?"

"I don't know."

"And I see you've used tar paper to good advantage. Did your father work on that?"

"Him? That would be the day. He was a drunk," said Patrice.

"You're very forthcoming," said Millie.

"Well, that's my bed you're sitting on," said Patrice.

"I thought so. I noticed your stack of magazines. Do you mind if I'm sitting here?"

"What can I do about it?" said Patrice.

She amended her comment to say something pleasant, mumbled that Millie was welcome to read her magazines, and walked away. She would much rather have buried her father with just a few people around. Not this crowd and someone she didn't know, but had heard of, for this was the Chippewa scholar. She should have been nicer. She remembered that she would have to get information on how to go to college. Patrice spoke to a few more people, accepted a few hugs, ate bannock and Juggie's soup. Then she went outside. Pokey was still chopping wood.

"You can quit for a while," said Patrice. "It looks like you've been chopping for a whole day."

"Not really. I have to stop and warm my hands up all the time."

Patrice shed her mittens and took up the ax. She ran warm. It took a long time when chopping wood for her hands to get cold. Pokey took a load of stove lengths into the house. Patrice got into her rhythm and everything else fell away. She forgot the strange woman on her bed, blending in with the pattern on her quilt. She forgot her complicated feelings, or got them out, down the ax and into the wood. She forgot the kindness of the bear and how she had betrayed it, although maybe, as Zhaanat always believed, the bear had intentionally given itself to her. It still seemed to Patrice that her fall had been an accident and that the bear had just accepted her presence in its sleep, or not noticed her, or maybe the bear dreamed of her because surely the bear smelled her in its sleep and knew she was there. What was it, to be dreamed of by a bear?

Not something that happened to most Homecoming queens, thought Patrice, or to most waterjacks. Surely it didn't happen to many jewel bearing plant employees.

Wood Mountain was at the grave place using his pickax on the frozen ground. As she worked on the wood, they began to chop in alternating blows. Which was comforting. It gave her strength. It meant the work was getting done. Her father would soon be safe and she would be safe from him. They would all live easier. Never again would her mother have to go to sleep with a knife beneath her pillow and a hatchet at her feet. Never again would Pokey have to cringe. Never again would Patrice have to wipe her father's piss and shit out of the corner. Or hear him weeping in the lean-to, calling for them like a lost soul. Although she did hear him one more time.

## The First Night Watch

After she had worked for a while, Patrice went into the house and ate another bowl of Juggie's soup. The sacred fire had been burning ever since her father had been found. She walked out to the fire holding a tin mug of her mother's tea. She offered a few drops to the fire. The tea was made from aromatic cedar fronds and melted snow. It was her favorite kind of tea. There was something about the water that was swirled through the heavens, frozen, scooped up, and boiled with cedar. You couldn't name it. But the hot tea, made of ingredients that joined earth and heaven, radiated its penetrating force through her body. The tips of her fingers stung and her stomach warmed. She could feel her blood awaken. She sat down with the men by the fire. They treated her differently when she wore her father's boots and the big coat and overalls. She listened to them talking about her father's basketball exploits. Pogo Paranteau. She had heard it all hundreds of times. Sometimes when, with a gesture, one of his old teammates imitated his distinctive jump shot, she even laughed.

## The Second Night Watch

Thomas left to work on the grave house, hoping to finish it before morning. The other men took turns with the pickax and shovel, chipping the grave out of closely bound roots and glassine dirt. In the background there was always the sound of their effort. The blows were thin, strange, ringing out in the woods and bouncing off the trees. Gradually, as the diggers entered the earth, the sound was muffled. Finally the men left the fire and went in for food. Patrice was alone. Once, her back prickled. She looked around, but nothing. She turned back and fell into a fire-trance, staring at the way the wood whitened at the edges as the fire glowed from the center. Just at the corner of her vision, something moved again. She looked around. At the edge of the woods, at the bottom of the trail, something or somebody was slipping through the trees. She watched it flickering in and out of the branches.

## The Third Night Watch

Again, in the deepest part of the night, Patrice was alone at the fire again. The men had finished the grave. A more profound stillness had fallen. She positioned a log at the hottest point. Then, watching as the coals sucked in air and arched flames seized at the new wood greedily, she fell into a state of exhaustion so profound that her body vibrated. Her mind unclasped. Again, something moved. She looked. Saw the slipping of the seen and the emergence of the unseen. A being stooped low and carefully peered out of the brush. It was her father, eyes gleaming from black hollows, wearing the same colorless raggedy clothes they'd found him in. He saw her. It seemed he wanted something from her. He opened his red weepy mouth as if to plead. Maybe he was thirsty. Or hungry. Yet there was something so pitiful and longing in the way he looked at her, dead now, called by the other dead people, violating the laws of being dead the way he always violated the laws of being a living man.

Yes, he wanted to take her with him, just as he'd always wanted her before.

Patrice stood up, thinking he might move away if she moved, and sure enough, he began to lunge along through the woods again, through crowded black trees, toward the place where his grave was waiting. She could see the black slit in the earth. He stopped there, stood at the lip of darkness, looking down. That was when his voice began, low at first, then sharpening to a high whistle. His voice flew at her, whining and bending the air. She stood as it whipped the fire into tall flames. It thrashed the bare branches and drove clouds to scud like gray smoke across black space. His voice was trying to pull the life out of her. She shook, heart pounding in her throat. As the wind whirled around her, gripping her body, tearing at her face, she could feel herself beginning to hover. She threw her weight into her feet and began to laugh.

"You can't get us! You can't get us now!" she shrieked.

Someone had come up behind her and her throat shut. But she slowly dared to look. It was her mother, staring at the place where her father was climbing down into his grave. For a moment, Zhaanat's face was exalted by ferocity, but then she slowly shifted her gaze to her daughter, and Patrice thought she was seeing her own face, lighted from below by a reflecting mirror of clouds and water. Yet it was only a bowl of soup that her mother was holding out to her, strong with bear meat and steaming hot.

## Daylight

Wood Mountain brought the grave house. Thomas would sleep and then they would conduct the burial. Zhaanat and Pokey

had tied Paranteau into a blanket and covered him with bark
thawed and rolled back around his shape. Gerald had arrived in
the night and his people were arranged on the floor of the house
in a puzzle of blanketed forms. Three women slept on Patrice's
bed with their children, so she folded herself into a corner, underneath her heavy coat. Millie was already sleeping there, head
covered with a scarf, feet sticking out in fur-trimmed galoshes,
odd and touching, like a child's.

OTHER PEOPLE began to arrive. Whole families. Some brought
food, some came because they needed to eat. The LaBattes
showed up, everyone with their own bowls to carry home leftover food. LaBatte wept. He'd been drinking with Paranteau
and Eddy a few nights before, but he said nothing, though he'd
reported, for Patrice, to Mr. Vold so that she could take off work
for the funeral. It was still deeply cold. Bucky came, wearing a
coat and a blanket over the coat. Patrice saw him from where
she stood. His hair was matted around his head, caked like the
pelt of a dead animal. When he entered Zhaanat's house, dragging his leg, everyone fell silent. Bucky walked effortfully up to
Zhaanat and pointed at his face, the cheek and flesh drooping
down on one side. His mouth was disarranged, unable to fully
close, drool frozen down his neck, one eye crossed.

Bucky bent over, took from his pockets the pair of shoes he'd
stolen from Patrice. He went on his knees and pushed them
along the floor. He gave a moaning mumble that sounded like
"Take this off me."

Zhaanat looked at the shoes, observed him closely, not un-
kindly.

"Your actions put that on you. I had nothing to do with it,"
she said.

Bucky collapsed on the floor.

"Then doctor me, please doctor me."

In the incoherent jumble of his words there was none of the old Bucky left.

He is helpless, thought Patrice. As helpless as I was. But if he gets his strength back, he will hurt us.

LATER, AS Gerald talked to Paranteau's body and told him what to look for and what to do when he arrived on the other side, Millie came up to stand with Patrice. When Gerald paused, Millie asked what he had said, nodding when Patrice told her in a low voice. There was a dazed, rapt look on Millie's face. At last the men used ropes to lower Paranteau into the ground.

## Two Months

### Thomas

THE DATE was set. The hearings were scheduled for the first week in March. That gave the Turtle Mountain Advisory Committee about two months to save the tribe from ceasing to exist.

### Millie

Millie Cloud sat on the floor wearing her winter coat. She was hunched over a notebook held tight against her thighs, and she was writing rapid notes on her visit to the Paranteau funeral. She had never been to an event like the funeral, had never heard the strangely agreeable off-key and repetitive songs, nor had she heard more than a few words of the Chippewa language uttered in the Pipestone house. When she had conducted her survey, she was nearly always addressed in English. Now she understood that the English was for her benefit and that most of the people around her, including Louis and Grace, spoke the traditional language. All of this was fascinating to Millie, and while she could hardly take notes during the ceremony, she had closely observed the proceedings. She had taken up her notebook as soon as possible and was sitting in the corner of the bedroom she shared with Grace Pipestone. She was freezing cold, while Grace slept on the bed beneath two heavy blankets. As soon as every detail that she could remember was written out, Millie took off her coat.

Wearing her warmest socks and the long johns that, incredibly, she had almost decided not to bring, she tiptoed across the room and slid under the blankets, next to Grace.

## Barnes

There was a square wooden table in what he'd taken to thinking of as his monk's cell. Upon this table, Barnes placed the early Christmas gift from his uncle. It looked like a small suitcase made of bleached alligator skin. But the skin was plastic and he opened the case to reveal a turntable, arm, needle, dials. He plugged the electric cord into the one outlet in the room. He took a record from its sleeve and set it going, then lay on his saggy bed and closed his eyes. The immortal voice of Slim Whitman filled the air. Three women were his fortune. How would his life unfold? Barnes turned over, cradled his head in the pillow. Each woman whirled through his head, trailing scent and smile. Barnes flipped back and hugged his other pillow. He needed two for comfort. One for his head, one to hug all night. *Which one was made for me? Oh gee, my heart is broken in three.*

## Juggie

Couldn't the boy see? His face was all banged up and would never be the same. Nobody else seemed to notice. It was for a mother to compare before and after. Her heart pinched. The perfect human she'd created had been tampered with by those stupid fights. What was the point? For a moment in life, anyway, he'd been handsome like his father. And smart. Now he seemed to have lost even the small amount of common sense most young men possess. He had brought her the cradle board to admire! Made her touch the wood.

Smooth as silk, he said.

Oh, was it.

What the hell was she supposed to say?

## Betty Pye

Norbert, Norb, oh, Norbie! The door handle dug into her back
and her neck was sore from holding her head steady. Otherwise
banging the back of her head against the backseat window—that
would hurt. The beginning had been, as always, like flying right
out of her body. But this part she could take or leave. When, oh,
oh, oh, Norbert, Norb, when, Norbie, oh, was he going to quit?
Over his shoulder she could see the opposite window. A face appeared in the heavy glass, blurred and hungry. Betty opened her
mouth. Her scream was trapped by a gobbling kiss. Norbert put
his head back down, and she decided not to scream. The door was
locked. If she interrupted Norb, he would have to start all over.
Anyway, the face had disappeared. Who could it be, these miles
from anywhere, so far out on the section road that she could see
only one dim and lonesome light? Who would be walking alone
out here at night? Oh, oh, oh. Norbie! Finally. Cold was knifing up
her back. She knew the face. She smoothed down her clothes, fixed
her hair, used a dainty tissue to pluck up the biinda'oojigan and
another couple of tissues to roll it up and place it in the side pocket
of her purse. Somehow, yes, she knew the face. She used a few
more dainty tissues and climbed into the front seat. Aww honey,
aww honey, Norbert was saying. Niinimoshenh. Aww honey, aww
niinimoshenh, she said back to him. She put her plush hands to
his cheeks and cradled his face. A soft kiss. Let's go home now.
Get the car back to your uncle. It's all cleaned up? It's all cleaned
up. Mii'iw. She had to think. Who was it? She knew that face.

## Louis

It became a sacred mission—to obtain the signature of every person who lived on the reservation. There were others, who lived elsewhere, but it was beyond his power to track them down. His green pickup truck was up on blocks. Juggie needed the DeSoto to ride in to work. What? Should he saddle up one of his horses and ride the back roads? The sun was out and he could walk. Snowshoe along the paths. Millie walked out of the little room where she slept next to Grace. Of course Grace was with the horses. Millie had certainly not dressed for the cold in those little ankle boots. He had given her a pair of his socks. Astonishingly, she asked if she could ride a horse. Millie wanted to get over to Zhaanat's place. And here she was scared of horses ever since her bad ride. He said that he would go with her and then continue on to get some signatures. He put his mind to which horse was placid enough for Millie. None of them was placid at all. They were touchy from being cooped up or anxious to get out of the wind and back into their barn. Even old Daisy Chain was skittish, and besides, she was retired. But Millie asked again, determined, and he had learned that when she was determined he'd best give in immediately and save butting heads with a version of himself.

## Thomas

Two months and a few days to save themselves as a homeland and a people. So why, when he had no time, did Thomas find himself staring blindly into space at work or writing long discursive letters not to individuals important to their case, but to friends and family? Why did he doodle and why did he now read

Sharlo's mystery books, which easily kept him awake? Why couldn't he bear down and concentrate? Because he was scared, that's why. What on earth would a person do in Washington? How would they get there? Where would they stay? What if Arthur V. Watkins took him apart? The word was out on Watkins. He raked Indians to pieces with his words and his ways. What if Thomas failed? If he couldn't speak up? If he couldn't argue the case? If they got terminated and everyone lost their land and had to move to the Cities and he had to leave his home behind? What of his family? What of Biboon?

## Patrice

Just before Christmas her eyes began to smart. Maybe she'd snow-burned them checking her trapline on a too sunny day. Maybe the close work was beginning to tell. It wasn't bad at first, as long as she resisted the need to rub them. She could still—blinking, squinting—focus on the card. She could pluck up the jewel bearings, glue them correctly, and complete her work. But too slowly. The Grasshopper rasped his legs. The pain began to sharpen. Pus glued her eyes shut when she slept. When she got home from work, exhausted, she lay on her bed covered in quilts, while Zhaanat bathed her eyes in balsam tea.

That helped, and she was always able to go back to work, but the burning kept coming back. Zhaanat boiled down the tea and Patrice carried a small medicine bottle of it. Every day, during lunch, she bathed her eyes in the medicine. She did it in a women's bathroom stall, so that nobody could see and tell on her. She was afraid that she might lose her job.

## Words

The word used for ejaculation—baashkizige—is also used for shooting off a gun. The word used for condom—biinda'oojigan—means gun case. Millie entered these words into her notebook. Fascinating.

## Vera

One afternoon, with Edith looking on, good old Harry knelt beside the couch with a ring. He asked her to marry him. She closed her eyes. She had just awakened but she was still tired. Before she could answer him she fell asleep again. Later, in the evening, he was on his knees again. This time, she let her eyes open. He looked like a way out of her mess. She took the ring and put it on her finger. Then she hid her face. He said he wouldn't even kiss her. He said that there would be no hanky-panky for a long time. Never, she thought. A few nights later he stood in the doorway making with himself. The vibrations woke her up. The slickering sound.

"Holy Jesus," she shouted, sitting up. "What the damn hell do you think you're doing?"

Harry flipped the lights on. He was holding a bottle of milk. He'd been shaking the milk because the top was frozen. He couldn't sleep and was going to heat it up. Did she want some?

## LaBatte

No sooner had he stopped than it began to get around. Francis Boyd asked him on the hush-hush to get him a little coffee. Just a cup from the can. He'd use those grounds four times, he said. Lilia Snow asked for toilet paper. She was tired of the Sears catalog. It was scratching up her little peach. Junior Bizhiki wanted a glass beaker like she'd seen in her friend's kitchen. "I don't do that no more," he said to her, alarmed. "I never did that anyway. I mean, what are you talking about?" Gordon Fleury said he would appreciate it if LaBatte could get him tools. Any kind of tools. LaBatte this time was outraged. He was insulted. He slammed the door of his ramshackle house, nearly busting it off. Well, you didn't slam doors on this reservation. You didn't slam doors in a person's face. That got around. He got the nickname Slammer. Which wasn't such a bad nickname. He took it with good grace. It was a better nickname than several others he had lived down. And a better nickname than Fingers or Pockets or Father Christmas or the other name he was afraid of getting, Jinx. He was in danger of getting that name because he used the word so much. But he used it because he knew what he knew. For instance, he knew that Pixie had a jinx on her. He could tell from her eyes.

# New Year's Soup

OH, IT was good. Filled your belly. Made you smile. Cured your hangover. Kept you moving in the cold. It was made with onions, balls of meat the Michifs called boulettes, potatoes peeled and boiled just right. You stirred in flour and got the broth. Pepper and salt. That's all it was. Sometimes you just cut the meat up. That was good too. There wasn't a way to go wrong, as long as it was hot. And you made bread if you had the flour, fried if you had the grease, in bannocks the Michifs called gullet, in little raised squares or beignets that people called bangs. It was food you could stretch way out. Zhaanat made it with bear meat. Cured the common cold. Cured the uncommon. Didn't cure trachoma. You couldn't put soup in your eye.

"You should go to the nurse," Wood Mountain said. "Hey, I'll take you into town. You can ride Daisy Chain and I'll run beside you. I am still in training but my mother told me not to fight no more."

"Do it," said Zhaanat. "My medicine doesn't fix this, just holds it off."

Patrice rode into town on the tough old horse. It was a plodder and Wood Mountain ran half a mile out, ran back, walked beside her for a while, ran out front again. The hospital was made of brick. The waiting room was stark, the chairs hard. Patrice had been vaccinated against smallpox at school. Even Zhaanat had been vaccinated. "White-man diseases need white-man cures," she said. But for all else, Patrice turned to Zhaanat's medicines. This was the first time her mother's cures hadn't worked. She'd never seen the doctor or the nurse. Or waited in this ominous little room.

The nurse was thin and gray, hair pulled into a bun. She wore a long gray dress with a starched white collar, and had the bearing of a no-nonsense nun.

"What are you here for, young miss?" she said. Her voice was thin and dry. Patrice blinked at her.

The nurse asked Patrice to stand close to a bright lamp, told her to open her mouth and used a thin wooden stick to clamp down her tongue.

"You have good teeth," she said.

She peeked into Patrice's ears, took her pulse. At last she stared into Patrice's eyes, focusing on one, then the other. Then she put her clean cool fingers below and above Patrice's watering eyes. Up close the skin of the nurse's face was fine as paper, creased in tiny lines, almost transparent. Even through her tears Patrice could see this. The nurse pulled down on the lower lids and up on the upper lids.

"Good we caught this in time. You might have gone blind," she said.

She left Patrice sitting in the tiny room painted a peculiar green, the shelves holding glass jars full of cotton balls and thin wooden sticks. Blind! Blind! Patrice kept hearing what the nurse had said. When she returned, the nurse gave Patrice a small jar of medicinal ointment.

"You wipe a bit onto your eyes."

Afterward, Patrice must wash her hands scrupulously, said the nurse. She must watch her family for signs. Her voice was stern. "Blindness results from lack of hygiene. Where do you live?"

"Minneapolis," said Patrice.

Lack of hygiene, thought Patrice. The nurse might come into our house. She could make an official assessment and report all the ways our ways aren't up to her standards. The health officials might even attempt to take the baby. This had happened to other children. Still, thank god, thank god, I will not be blind! Her neck was itching, a sign she'd better get right out of there. She thanked the nurse.

Before Patrice left, the nurse asked her to come back when the eye doctor would be in and gave her the date of the eye clinic.

"Why?" asked Patrice.

The nurse made her promise.

Outside, Wood Mountain was still waiting with Daisy Chain.

"You don't have to walk me home," said Patrice. "I can go down to the store and find a ride."

"We go back the way we came," insisted Wood Mountain. "She fixed your eyes?"

"I won't go blind," said Patrice.

"Blind!" said Wood Mountain. "My grandmother went blind."

"What a terrible thing. I would lose my job. I couldn't chop wood. I don't know what else. I would miss all of everything."

She couldn't come close to saying what she meant.

"All the beauty."

"I guess you don't mean me," said Wood Mountain. "All the beauty." But it sounded like he hoped she meant him too.

"Of course I meant you too," said Patrice, still in shock at the thought. To lose all of this. She hadn't truly considered it before, and then to know it could have happened.

"My grandmother got around real good," said Wood Mountain. "She said that her other senses opened up. She could hear everything, everywhere, and smell? She could smell you even if you didn't make a sound."

He spoke quickly to cover up the jolt of pleasure that her words had given him.

"I never knew that," said Patrice.

Already, her eyes were less scratchy and the light was more benign. The cold fresh air stirred her. I won't go blind, she thought. The sun was low in the sky, casting slant regal light. As they plodded along, the golden radiance intensified until it seemed to emanate from every feature of the land. Trees, brush, snow, hills. She couldn't stop looking. The road led past frozen sloughs that bristled with scorched reeds. Clutches of red willow burned. The fans and whips of branches glowed, alive. Winter clouds formed patterns against the fierce gray sky. Scales, looped ropes, the bones of fish. The world was tender with significance.

"Onizhishin, so beautiful," Patrice murmured. She had dismounted and was walking beside the horse. Wood Mountain leaned over and kissed her. He hadn't meant to and was completely demoralized when she hoisted herself onto the horse, slapped its rump, and rode away. He watched the horse clomp down the road. Daisy Chain wouldn't trot for long. Soon they were walking again, slow enough for him to catch up with little effort. He actually tried *not* to catch up with them, but inevitably they matched pace. For a while, neither spoke.

"Wish I could take it back," Wood Mountain said at last.

"It's okay," said Patrice. "I was surprised."

"How could you be surprised? I'm out at your place all the time. People say we're together."

"They even say the baby's our baby," said Patrice.

Disturbingly, she laughed.

"I wish he was," said Wood Mountain in a sudden fit. "I wish you were with me."

As soon as he said this, he felt he'd blurted out the very truth of his soul. He needed her. Wanted her. It was all over for him. She was his one and only. In a mad surge of certainty he grasped Daisy Chain's halter, stopping them, and in a near frenzy cried out, "You're the one for me. The one and only! I need you, oh Pixie! I mean Patrice! Please for god's sake marry me."

He looked crazily up. Her face floated against the clouds. She gazed down, her soft wounded eyes sending the most delicious sensations through him, although she said nothing. They resumed their slow walk home, thinking their separate thoughts, she relieved because she hadn't promised anything, he relieved because she hadn't said no.

TRUE, IN the moment, Patrice had wanted to say I want you too, my man! I need you too, my man! Yes! She hadn't wanted to say I love you. He hadn't said that. But even in the moment of crisis, when he spoke so wonderfully, from his full heart, a part of Patrice had observed. A part of her mind was thinking, even talking about herself, "She's feeling this, her heart is going so fast she's dizzy, look, she's so happy, she's so wildly happy, she's falling, she's falling for it, falling." Once Patrice was home, she went straight to work on the woodpile and that voice kept talking to her. Some of the girls she'd started school with had been married for years. Some of the girls had three, four, five children. Some of the girls looked like middle-aged women. Washing clothes with snowmelt. Washing clothes for an entire family. Freezing the clothes dry. Clothes whipping in the sun. And her mother had never even made the slightest suggestion that she marry Wood Mountain. So why should Patrice marry? A disappointing thought struck. Now that he'd told her his secret feelings, Wood Mountain was sticky. She couldn't try him out. She would be going against one of the few things her mother had said in regard to love, "Never play with a man's heart. You never know who he is." Zhaanat had meant he might have some sort of spiritual power that could harm her if he loved her and was rejected. And Patrice thought another thing her mother said was definitely true—you never really knew a man until you told him you didn't love him. That's when his true ugliness, submerged to charm you, might surface. After all, it had happened with Bucky.

# The Names

THINGS STARTED going wrong, as far as Zhaanat was concerned, when places everywhere were named for people—political figures, priests, explorers—and not for the real things that happened in these places—the dreaming, the eating, the death, the appearance of animals. This confusion of the chimookomaanag between the timelessness of the earth and the short span here of mortals was typical of their arrogance. But it seemed to Zhaanat that this behavior had caused a rift in the life of places. The animals didn't come around to these locations stained by the names of humans. Plants, also, had begun to grow fitfully. The most delicate of her plant medicines were even dying out altogether, or perhaps they had torn themselves up by the roots to drag their fruits and leaves to secret spots where even Zhaanat couldn't find them. And now even these half-ruined places that bore the names of saints and homestead people and priests, these places were going to be taken. In her experience, once these people talked of taking land it was as good as gone.

# Elnath and Vernon

THEY WERE sick of each other's company. So when Milda
Hanson offered each of them a room in her farmhouse, yes,
separate rooms, tears of longing boiled up behind Elnath's eyes.
His throat clenched so hard he couldn't even speak. Vernon had
to muster his voice to turn down the offer. Missionary rules
and their president had insisted on a shared room, always. They
could not leave each other's company for more than bathroom
breaks. For if one of them fell into the grip of temptation, the
other would be there to witness, and then to write to their area
president, or even call, in an emergency.

Nevertheless, one of the rooms had two beds and the house
was perfect—off the reservation and only a mile from town.
The Lord had provided beds that weren't side by side but across
the room from each other. Which was something. Mrs. Hanson
was a widow who had leased out her fields and lived alone now.
She said that she would feed them. They bowed their heads at
her words. Besides thankful, they were dizzy with hunger. Pancakes landed on their plates that night and bacon beside. Mrs.
Hanson, neckless, burnished to a rare glow, prideful, watched
them eat. They hardly breathed. They were so hungry they
nearly choked in eagerness. Her look turned to pity and she
slowly shook her head. Her wispy nest of hair was pinned up in
the shape of a question mark. What were they anyway? What
kind of religion? She'd get an earful of that.

That night Elnath lay across the small room, at least ten feet away from Vernon. It was wonderful. Milda had allowed them two quilts each and on top of the quilts they had draped their winter topcoats. They were warm, almost too warm, but they knew by morning Milda's well-fed woodstove would be down to ashes and embers and the cold would knife in.

In spite of his exhaustion, and even more, his tiring resentment, Elnath was awake. He was wrestling with whether or not to make that fateful call to Bishop Dean Pave. He didn't want to tell on his brother in the Lord, but he couldn't let the lapses continue. During a mission call to the Pipestone ranch, and there had been several, Vernon had excused himself as if to visit the privy.

Inside the house, Elnath had continued to share with Louis Pipestone the many wonderful proofs of his knowledge of scripture and the interesting benefits of his religion. He'd only quit after declaring that his was the sole religion to have originated in America. Usually, when he said this, he received an approving smile no matter whether or not they were heading toward baptism. But the bull-built man had shut his lips firmly and leaned forward, glowering from under his brow, for all the world like he was going to charge. Elnath had stuttered to a halt. After a long moment Louis had rearranged his features and given a surprising cherub's smile.

"We got our own religion here," he'd said. "Our own scriptures even. Only thing, they come out like stories."

"Of course," said Elnath. "We are aware of the grip of the Pope."

"Everybody around here's Catholic, but I don't mean that," said Louis.

"Well then . . ."

Confusion. Elnath had to wonder if some Holy Roller had got here first.

"Like I say, our own religion of our tribe," Louis went on. "We are thankful for our place in the world, but we don't worship nobody higher than . . ." Louis gestured out the window at the dimming sky, arrested clouds, the sun dissolving as it sank through layers of clouds. The barn was also in view and that was when Elnath saw Vernon coming out of the barn instead of the outhouse.

VERNON'S ABSENCE had been short. Hardly enough time to get up to the worst kind of sin, though Elnath was pretty sure that Vernon's aim was the girl they'd seen riding the horse in the parade. He'd started laughing, partly out of surprise at Vernon, partly because he thought that Louis was making a joke about his own religion. Whatever it was that Indians believed, Elnath was pretty sure it could not be called a religion. He'd thought that Louis would start laughing too and be impressed that for once Elnath had caught on to his deadpan humor. But instead, Louis had taken on a somber fire and given him such a look. And the silence. Even now, Elnath got a cold feeling in his stomach. And here he'd been thinking that people on this reservation were those Lamanites of yore who had been raised into civilized Nephites, as Vernon had asserted. The silence lasted until Vernon came back.

"We'd best be going, Elder Vernon," said Elnath.

His voice still squeaked when he was under duress.

Now, as if to torment him, he heard the scrabble of mice and a whirl, squeaking, more scrabbling. The sounds felt like a manifestation of the thoughts trapped in his brain. They rushed from side to side behind the walls of his skull. He was struggling. On the one hand he was pretty sure that if the situation were reversed, which would never happen, Vernon would turn him in. He wouldn't think twice. He hated Elnath even worse than Elnath hated him. Though not hate—a word he was taught should not exist—not hate. It was just that he didn't have love. An insufficiency of love. But that was the very reason he could not make up his mind. Was he, Elnath, really worried about Vernon's soul? Or did he just want to get rid of Vernon, to receive a new companion? And would telling on Vernon benefit Vernon? His companion would be disgraced. The money Vernon's parents had saved, and the money Vernon had saved, all to go on this mission, would be wasted. You couldn't get over a failed mission just like that. Being sent home could seriously damage Vernon's standing in the community, maybe for life. But if Vernon's soul was really at risk, his standing could be damaged for eternity. Elnath's thoughts swayed, circled, then stuck between his options. A thought, in the form of a feeling, came creeping toward him.

Elnath wanted to turn away from the crawly sensation of this thought. He didn't want to be touched by the notion, but the touch kept coming back. This thing seemed beyond words. But finally, as he drifted toward unconsciousness, words did form. Sentences, written on a blackboard, were constantly erased. One sentence lingered.

*Talk to Vernon about it.*

Elnath started awake. Going to your bishop was a clear rule. No rule said "Talk to your companion." On the other hand no rule forbade it. Yet the possibilities of what Vernon was doing were so private, so impossible to clearly address. What words would Elnath even use to approach him? To speak so directly? Nobody had ever taught him that speaking to another person about private matters was a sin, but it felt like a sin. These sensations he was having felt like symptoms of a disease called emotion. He and Vernon would have to acknowledge this humiliating condition. Elnath had given testimony but this was different. Not done, in his family life or his church life, with his few friends. You talked to the Lord in a locked room inside your soul, a deep buried light surrounded by the moat of your heart. It was a place you didn't go with other human beings, especially one in the shape of Vernon.

# Night Bird

*⋇—‖—⋇*

SHE HAD been to school with Bucky since first grade, and the way he had invited her to take a ride was so nice. Summer. The backseat window rolled down. Please get in. Come on. The smile. He was always nice, nicer to her than usual, sometimes, which might have rung alarm bells. But she hadn't been a suspicious person up until that day. Three boys were sitting on the front bench seat and only Bucky in the back. She got into the back and one of the boys, Myron Pelt, slipped into the backseat beside her. That didn't feel good and later, she wished that she'd kicked up a ruckus right then. As soon as they pulled out, speeding up too fast, Bucky made his move. Patrice pushed him off and Bucky threw himself back on her. Myron held her arms. She twisted, tried to kick. Bucky's hands went under her shirt and his fingernails dug into her. Then he tried to press her knees apart with his knees and fumbled with his pants. His stale breath on her. The slime from his lips. "This isn't much fun," she said. All the boys in the car laughed. She froze to ice. Then she said, louder this time, "This isn't much fun for *you boys.*" She felt the edge of their attention. "Let's go to the lake. We'll go out in the bush. I know where. Then I'll show you all a good time." Where *that* came from, she never knew. But it was all they would remember. Myron let her sit back up. Someday, when she got around to it, she would kill him, too. They drove down the bumpy road to the lake. She showed them where to stop, right in front of the lake. Bucky took her shoes. "She can't run now." Fool. For she could run. Hell for leather she could run. And she did. And she dived in the lake. And they ran after her but maybe they had to take their shoes off or maybe they couldn't swim but she knew how to swim because that was how they got clean in the summer. She'd loved swimming with Vera. And she thrashed her arms forward and swam hard until she was really out there. Her dress was lightweight. She didn't take it off. Nothing could weigh her down. They were tiny on the shore and still she kept swimming. When she saw her uncle's boat she swerved toward him.

That night she took a lamp behind the blanket and looked at the scratches, the bruises. There was even a bite mark on her shoulder. She'd felt none of it. But she could still feel where his hands went. She was shaking, squeezed her eyes shut, crawled under the blanket. The next day, more bruises had surfaced from under her skin. There was that phrase "they got under my skin." She'd showed these marks to her mother and told Zhaanat everything that the boys had done. And they had her only pair of shoes. Her mother had let her breath out, sharply, two times. Then she put her hand on her daughter's hand. Neither one of them said a word; it was the same thing with both of them and they knew it. Later, when Patrice heard about Bucky's twisted mouth and how it was spreading down his side, she looked at her mother's face, serene and severe, for a clue. But Patrice knew that she herself had done it. Her hatred was so malignant it had lifted out of her like a night bird. It had flown straight to Bucky and sank its beak into the side of his face.

# U.S.I.S.

✳═╪═✳

"WHAT KIND you got?"

"Lucky Strikes."

"Oh, good. I mean, damn."

Juggie handed a cigarette to Barnes and they sat in the kitchen, at the white enamel-topped table she used to knead bread dough right after dinner. Early in the evening, she'd popped the yeast-risen dough through the round of her thumb and first finger, all the while humming along to the radio. Now the pans of rolls were all nicely baked, resting under clean dish towels on her baking rack. The air was fragrant with new bread and crispy tobacco smoke. She'd turned down the radio but could still hear Johnnie Ray.

"This is the life," she said, contented.

"This is the life," said Barnes, sad.

"What's wrong with you?"

"It's no secret."

The corners of his mouth drooped.

Goddamn everything about this man was probably drooping, thought Juggie. Glad my fellow doesn't have this problem. Then she felt bad for thinking such a thing. And she wished how he wished her to feel: she felt sorry for him.

"Just give up," she said.

"Easy for you to say. It's your son who took Pixie from me."

"Hay Stack, you have to listen now. Nobody steals the heart of a lady, especially one like Pixie. She decided on the man she wanted to give her heart to, and that's that. Just give up."

"You're no help."

"Look around you. Turtle Mountains is famous for beautiful women."

"So I have been told."

"Oh, don't give me that crap, so I been told! It's true and you know it. Just let your eye wander. You're starting to look like a damn fool."

"I don't care."

"Did you go out with Valentine?"

"I'm scared of her. She bites. Plus she's laughed at me a couple times since the bush dance."

"She's my half niece."

"What?"

"Never mind. Just go out with her."

"She's too sharp for me. She'd turn me down."

"I'll ask her for you."

"Tell her not to bite me."

"Big man like you? What a chicken."

"I'll get rabies." He smiled. Maybe the biting was not so bad. Barnes put his cigarette out in the government-issue ashtray. Juggie picked up a heavy steel spoon labeled U.S.I.S. United States Indian Service. She stirred her tea with the giant spoon, waiting for his answer. He said nothing more, so she took that as a yes.

VALENTINE LIVED out on the main road. Her family had a little business fixing cars so the cars were scattered all around, available for parts. Juggie drove up and parked by a gallant old

Model T that was sitting on a couple of logs. Her half brother, Lemon, came out the door of the pleasant paint-peeled house.

"Nice herd of cars you got," said Juggie.

"At least they stay put," said Lemon. "Not like Gringo last fall."

Juggie laughed. "Old Gringo's never been the same. Where's Valentine?"

"How come you want Valentine? She's due home."

"I got something to ask her. I'll wait."

As they were walking across the beaten-down gray snow of the yard, there was the sound of an engine and Doris Lauder turned into the driveway. Valentine got out of the car, laughing, and waved her friend away.

"Is it woman business?" asked Lemon.

"Yep. Bye," said Juggie, walking over to Valentine.

"Hi, auntie."

"Hi, girlie. Hay Stack wants to ask you out."

"Well," said Valentine, pouting at her mittens, which she only wore when Doris or Pixie weren't around, "I am tired of taking Pixie's used men."

"Pixie never used him," said Juggie. "He's brand-new, at least around here."

"Never used him, but still. Secondhand."

"For cripe sakes. You're the only one who used him. Gnawed on him. He's scared of you. And even," lied Juggie, "he's tired of that Pixie."

"Is he?"

"Very tired of her."

"Well then, he may ask me himself." Valentine's tone of voice was insulting.

"I don't know why he would, Miss High Tone Jack," Juggie said. "In fact, I don't think he should get mixed up with you now. I changed my mind."

Juggie stomped off to her car, muttering.

"Wait!" cried Valentine.

But Juggie punched the gas and roared off.

THAT EVENING, well after dinner, Barnes came around and offered Juggie another cigarette.

"Quitting," she said.

"Just trying to say thank you."

Barnes looked suspiciously cheerful. Juggie just looked suspicious.

"Valentine came over by herself and asked me out."

"Well well well," said Juggie, taking the cigarette. "My little half niece comes to her senses. That's a first."

"Don't you go talking down my girlfriend," said Barnes.

"Girlfriend! My my my." She blew out a ring of smoke, then another right through it, and grinned with satisfaction. "You want my advice?"

"Yes and no."

"I'll give it anyway. For another Lucky. My last before I really quit. Don't chase her. Not too much. She's the type who likes a man to hold off a little bit."

"Do you think I chased Pixie too much?"

"For the last time."

"Okay, forget her. I know. I'll be suave and debonair."

Like hell you will, thought Juggie. That's just the thing a man who's neither of those things would say.

"Be like Cary Grant," she said, finally. "Don't let your feelings play out all over your face. Just use your eyes. And the corner of your mouth."

Mouth?

A look of distress passed over Barnes's face. He was thinking of Valentine's pretty bow-shaped mouth and the glint of her sharp teeth between her lips. How could a man willing to take a punch be so unnerved by a woman's pearly whites?

# The Runner

ON THE way home from work, Thomas saw something disturbing out of the corner of his eye. A boy was running alongside the car, keeping right up with him. Thomas was going twenty, thirty, sped up to forty, then fifty, and still the boy kept running. He could feel the boy's eyes on him. Thomas knew that if he glanced over he would not be able to turn his attention back to the road. Because of course the boy would be Roderick. He knew that the running boy was a hallucination and that the two or three hours a night he'd been getting this week were not enough. The boy veered away once Thomas reached town and Thomas drove carefully the rest of the way home. By then, the fright had awakened him so thoroughly that he was afraid he'd have trouble falling asleep.

"I saw Roderick again," he told Rose over his breakfast, a bit of venison, potatoes, oatmeal. "He was running beside me on the road."

"I'm coming with you tonight," said Rose.

THAT NIGHT she rode with him to work. The cold was deep and the wind was up. The snow was drifting along the surface of the road in shapes that twined and twisted in the headlights.

"Sometimes I get hypnotized by the snow snakes," said Thomas.

"I'll pinch you if you look glassy," said Rose.

"Well, pinch me nice then, in a good place."

"You're bad. Anyway, I'm not singing to you."

The only songs Rose ever sang were wordless and repetitive lullabies that put her babies straight to sleep.

"Also, I brought you a few surprises for lunch," she said. "And the biggest surprise of all is that I am going to make you put your head down on your desk. I'll keep watch while you take a good nap."

"I believe that would be against the rules."

"Who's going to know?"

They rolled along quietly.

"Except Roderick," she said. "But he won't tell."

"Now don't you go joking about my ghost," said Thomas. "We've gotten reacquainted pretty good since the old days."

"The two of you talk?"

"It's mostly a one-sided conversation. But then again sometimes I hear words in my head. Things he said long time ago."

"You're going bats, old man."

"That's what I'm afraid of, wife."

"How long is this business going to last?"

"After we go to Washington, I am taking a break."

"You don't notice, but it's hard on us."

"I do notice."

Thomas took her hand, her strong knobby hand, which had never been a girlish hand. Ever since she was a little girl, she'd been known as a worker. She could outwork anyone. Her own mother had said so. The base of their marriage was work, each pitching in when the other flagged, like tonight. He squeezed her hand. She squeezed his hand back. That's how they sometimes talked. They got to the door just as LaBatte was leaving. He saluted. Went out and coaxed his car to life. They could hear it sputter and pop a few times before LaBatte roared off with a backfire down the road that stalled him out, then another backfire, and a slow roll toward home.

"He works on his own car," said Thomas. "He should take it to Lemon."

Rose put her things near the desk, pulling up a bench. She trailed along when he made his first round, then spent a long time in the ladies' room. She couldn't help but like the plumbing. When she came out she was smiling. Her hair was combed and she was wearing lipstick.

"Hot running water."

"Someday," said Thomas. He looked at her again and suddenly felt shy. "You're dolled up."

"Just trying to keep you awake."

"It's working, real good."

They drank a cup of coffee together. He was moved that she'd come with him, Rose with her household burdens, her make-do challenges, her care for their parents and the endless children of people in trouble. She took care of everyone around him and now she was taking care of him, and wearing lipstick. She looked demurely down into her cup of coffee and then raised her eyes to his. He looked back at her and everything else fell away. It was only Rose and always Rose. They held each other's eyes for so long the tension made them laugh. And then there was a noise from the darkest corner.

They waited. A shadow shifted. There was a small creak. Maybe a slight settling of the building. Then the shadow crept away, distinctly crept away, and the back of Rose's neck prickled.

"It's him," she whispered.

Thomas said nothing. If it was Roderick, he wanted her to see him. But nothing else happened and eventually they relaxed.

Rose told him to put his head down on the desk. He refused. They made the next round and Rose led with the flashlight. When they sat back down she gave him a sandwich out of the lunch box. It was a boiled chicken sandwich dressed with a little gravy. She had canned six chickens that fall. This was the last of them.

"Put your head down and sleep," she ordered when he had finished.

Her voice was so strict that he relented. The moment he put his head down on his folded arms he was filled with a crushing sense of relief and comfort. In an instant, he was gone.

RODERICK WAS sitting behind the motor, not on it, not where Rose could see him. He had his hands out in front of his face and was pretending to eat that chicken sandwich. Homemade bun. He used to work in the school bakery. Working in the bakery was how a kid could have a full belly at night. You stole whatever dough you could get and put it in your pocket. It was called fringing. You fringed the dough. Then you ate it in bed at night and it swelled up and filled your belly enough so you didn't wake up hollow and sick. To get a job in the bakery, you had to be good and keeping that job was the only thing Roderick cared about, so for a long time he was good. Then a kid got caught and Mrs. Burton Bell checked all their pockets. He was fired. So he no longer cared and all the bad he had resisted came right out. He ran away. Again and again. He became a runner. That's how he ended up in the cellar and got so cold. All because of bread dough. And he couldn't taste it anymore even if he could have had some of that sandwich. He'd started coming here, to the jewel bearing plant, because it was a new place and he was tired of all the old places on the reservation. Plus, of course, he liked to be around his old pal Thomas. Sometimes Roderick found a place to sleep for a year or two. But when he woke up he was always a ghost, still a ghost, and it was getting old.

WHEN THOMAS woke up he didn't know where he was, that's how deeply he'd slept. He raised his head off his arms and opened his eyes and there was Rose, keeled over on the bench. Her head was pillowed on her coat and she had draped a sweater over her breast and arms. She looked so peaceful there. He made the next round but didn't go outside to smoke his cigar; instead, he sat down at his desk and fiddled with his pen. He was so close to getting the county commissioner from the next county over to write a letter that would strenuously object to taking over federal responsibilities for his people. There was not a sufficient tax base on the reservation to care for roads, not to mention schools. Oh yes, in this case they needed all the minor officials of white townships and counties that they could scare from behind their office desks. Thomas began to write.

## Missionary Feet

✦━✦

ALTHOUGH THIS seemingly eternal mission was enough walking for a lifetime, and although Vernon looked forward to the end of the day (especially now that there would be Mrs. Hanson's blessed food), at night, every night, he woke to find his feet moving. They ached, they needed rest, and yet his pale narrow bony long-toed feet would not be still. It was as though they had ideas of their own. He could not control them. He was grateful that the Lord had called the two of them, Elnath and Vernon, to be transferred soon, but he was also afraid that they would have to walk down to Fargo.

Although the feet, he thought resentfully, wouldn't mind even if they froze. It was as though they did not belong to him at all.

The only thing worse than trying to fall back asleep as they twitched and shuddered was when he found that his feet had decided to travel farther from the bed. Sometimes the feet decided to take Vernon for a stroll. A couple of times he woke to find himself in Milda Hanson's yard. Then the driveway, as though he'd gone to fetch the mail.

He missed the family he'd been thrilled to leave behind. He missed his one-toothed grandmother and his fetching aunts and ugly uncles. Mostly he missed the fantasy that someone might love him. A someone sweet as pie who used to descend from the rafters of his childhood home and cuddle around him in his dreams. He had to be very careful not to let his mind go to meet that someone even in his sleep. And he must not, ever, ever, think of Grace. Most of his body complied, but not the feet. The sore and rebellious feet wouldn't listen.

One night he found himself out on a lonely road in moonlight. He was wearing his overcoat but the burning cold feet were shoeless and the stones of the gravel cut into the naked soles. On the way back to Milda's, he saw an old jalopy parked beside the road. He stopped and peered in the windows. In the backseat there was a flailing sense of motion and the noises of animals fighting in the dirt. He drifted onward and only later, his damaged feet finally stilled beneath the covers, did it occur to him what he had witnessed. He froze in keen disappointment. He was disappointed with himself for not having intervened to stop two souls from sinning. Now they were lost.

## The Spirit Duplicator

❊─┃─❊

"DAMP OFF the press," said Juggie, delivering the droopy final page of the economic survey into Millie's hands.

Millie put the page straight to her nose. Like a child, thought Juggie.

The page was indeed still damp and the scent of fresh aniline dye flooded Millie with euphoria. It was perhaps her favorite smell. She also liked newly pumped gasoline, fried celery drenched in buttermilk, and rubber cement. She had come along to the office to help Juggie. There were thirty-five copies in increasingly fuzzy purple type. But also, there were four special copies made by a ghostly hand with access to the more sophisticated photocopier located in the office of Superintendent Tosk.

Those copies were for the file that Thomas was building. Juggie's access to the superintendent's office, however, was limited. The mimeograph machine that Thomas had requested had not arrived, might never arrive, and so they had to make do with dittos. After thirty copies, the master degraded and Millie was there to type a new one. The copies would be sent to all of the local and state officials, the newspapers and radio announcers, anyone who might be interested in the economic state of affairs that prevailed here.

Millie removed the slip sheet and inserted the master sheet with the carbon into the typewriter. She was finicky about getting it straight from the get-go.

"They're always getting it wrong out there," said Juggie. She'd brought her cinnamon rolls. A treat for Millie. Cinnamon rolls and coffee would take them far into the night.

"Long time ago," Juggie went on, "they sent a fool from Wahpeton named McCumber to count Indians. Of course he wasn't a fool. He knew very well what he was doing. Most of us were off hunting and he counts only full-bloods so in consequence our reservation, which was already down to twenty townships, gets mashed down to only two townships. That's what I mean by getting it wrong."

"Indeed," said Millie, now cleaning the typewriter keys with a special brush, "indeed."

It was a word she had resolved to use instead of yeah.

"Getting it wrong meant people starved dead. We don't have enough land or all our people in one place ever since."

"The government was operating on a set of assumptions tantamount to wishful thinking," said Millie. "I suspect as always they simply want our land."

"Wait," said Juggie. "Let me write that down."

Millie was so pleased that she struck a wrong key and made an error. Bit her lip in vexation. She turned up the platen and used a razor blade to gently scrape the carbon off the back of the paper. Then she covered the mistake with correction pencil. She blotted with correction putty and inserted a small piece of carbon paper. She retyped the letter and removed the extra carbon paper and kept typing. What Juggie said was true. A mistaken census survey had been used to convince Congress that the Turtle Mountain people were prosperous. But it was much bigger than that. Millie couldn't set out in sequence or exactly form the why of it into a paragraph. It was something about being an Indian. And the government. The government acted like Indians owed them something, but wasn't it the other way around? She hadn't been educated in a boarding school or educated in any way about Indians. From her Catholic schooling, she would never have known about Indians at all except as a bunch of heathens who were vanquished or conveniently died off. She'd hardly known her family and was as assimilated as an Indian could be. And people hardly ever recognized her as an Indian. So why did she firmly see herself as an Indian? Why did she value this? Why did she not long for the anonymity of whiteness, the ease of it, the pleasures of fitting in? When people found out why she looked a little different, they would often say, "I never thought of you as an Indian." And it would be said as a compliment. But it felt more like an insult. And why was that? She thought about Pixie. Or Patrice. She wasn't sure which name. The two of them were in the same league, not in prettiness, more in coloring, and maybe Pixie had thought these things out. Millie thought about Pixie's mother, so forceful, so elegant, so knowledgeable. And Pixie knew everything that Zhaanat knew. Did she know how extraordinary she was, Pixie, in being so much like her mother?

"Oof." Millie had made it through a couple of pages. Perfect. She was, of course, an excellent typist. But, thinking of Zhaanat and Pixie, she'd grown inattentive and misplaced her fingers on the keys, wrecking an entire line. And she'd almost reached the end of the page. So this time she had to entirely remove the paper, use a razor to excise the mistyped line, retype the line on other paper, razor that out and fix it into the master with transparent tape. Then the business with the scrap of carbon paper. And the exacting problem of precisely placing that repaired line below the previous line. Of course, she was very good at this. She had typed her entire master's thesis, of which this was only part. All the men with her in the program had hired women to type theirs. She looked down on them for it.

By the time she finished, the night was half over. And Juggie had fallen asleep on a blanket in the corner. Millie drank a cup of coffee, still hot, from the thermos, and ate an entire magnificently coiled roll, licking the icing and freckles of cinnamon off the fork that she meticulously used. Other people ate with their fingers. Indeed. Not Millie. Knowing that, Juggie had even brought cutlery and plates. So let her sleep, Millie thought, and fixed the first master sheet onto the drum of the spirit duplicator. She turned over the fluid tank, made the necessary adjustments in the pressure, the wick, the guide rail. Then she started turning the hand crank, lovingly, growing happier and happier as the intoxicating smell of duplicating fluid filled the office air.

# Prayer for 1954

✦━┃━✦

ON THIS night who is awake in the hills?

AN INCREASINGLY delighted young woman operates the ro-
tating drum of a spirit duplicator. A lanky missionary stumbles
in his sleep along a frozen road. A traditional Chippewa-Cree
woman rubs bear grease into the skin of a wakeful baby. A very
old man is talking to the small lights that came to visit him and a
very old woman is dreaming fiercely of having crossed the roiling Red River to escape her enemies. A big thatch-haired blond
man tries to get to second base with a slender woman who sits
up suddenly and says, "You're sure clumsy." An extremely drunk
fellow is bawling in the snow, pleading that his curse be lifted.
Another man, only half drunk, plays an endless card game with
his brothers, who tell him that his conversion to Mormonism is
ridiculous and will tarnish the good Catholic name of LaBatte.
Yet another man, damaged, powerful, and bearing the name of
the place where he was born, has fallen asleep in the horse
stall by his small woodstove. In the next stall a horse named
Gringo is the only horse covered with a blanket and still not
satisfied. He presses his head to the thick boards and thoughtfully gnaws the rich wood. Gringo would certainly prefer oats
or barley and throws his head back and forth, stomps, hoping
that his servant will appear. But nothing happens and the night
goes on and on.

. . .

A SOLID and much fatigued woman sleeping on the floor of the tribal office begins to talk in her sleep. *Too much salt*, she says.

A YOUNG woman with soft, bright eyes, often referred to by her teachers as "elfin," is filling out an order from the Montgomery Ward catalog and purchasing a wristwatch.

THE CURSED man is crawling toward his parents' house, where every single person is sleeping hard. He feels like he has been punished enough for something he did just because he wanted to. If his brain worked he could name grown men right and left who had done the same and were walking around in good shape, smiling with their whole mouth, opening and shutting both their eyes. Yes, he'd cuffed her around. Yes, he'd almost nailed her. But nothing happened! It's not that he shouldn't have tried. Just that he picked the wrong girl.

SEVERAL MILES away, a worried man with a flowing pen is doing Palmer exercises at the jewel bearing plant. He revolves his wrists, flexes his fingers, turns from side to side in his chair. Once he is finished, he faces forward and writes yet another letter to Senator Milton R. Young, a letter laying out strategy and signing off with polite desperation. Next, with no hope, he writes a courteous missive, full of jokes, to the other North Dakota senator, William "Wild Bill" Langer, who is in favor of termination. There is nothing to lose and Thomas can't help liking Wild Bill, who once barricaded himself in the governor's mansion and refused to be removed from office. If the isolationist Langer had had his way, maybe Falon would not have died in a distant war. The world would almost certainly be much worse off, but Thomas would have his brother, Falon, in reality, not just walking through the wall now and then. And speaking of lonesome spirits . . .

RODERICK DIDN'T seem to be around tonight but there was such a strange feeling. As if the pen held everything balanced on the reservation as Thomas wrote. And wrote.

## You Can't Assimilate Indian Ghosts

EVEN AS a ghost, Roderick was never going to be assimilated. You can't assimilate Indian ghosts. It's too late! He didn't go to their white hell and didn't go to their white heaven. But he died in Sac and Fox country, too far away to meet the deadline for Chippewa heaven. So he followed his coffin home and just hung around. He listened in on things. It was after his death that he found out the term. What they were up to. Assimilation. Their ways become your ways. He took stock. When they shaved his head and it grew out all fuzzy and spiky, Roderick sort of liked it. Like fur, he ran his hand over it. There were certain things he really went for. Canned peaches. But not the hard shoes. The trumpet. But not before sunrise. A warm woolen jacket. Wool socks. But then again, if they hadn't killed them off he could have had a curly buffalo jacket. And curly buffalo socks. Tuberculosis. For sure, he didn't like that. Did they have illness in the old days? He hadn't heard of any and he had to wonder. What did Indians use to die of? Animals, accidents, cold, other Indians. He had heard back then there were so many animals, animals everywhere, so nobody starved. You could be kicked by a horse or gored by a raging buffalo. He was obsessed by how he might have died. Anything would be better. Battle, for instance, staked to a spear and fending off his enemies. No, the horror and agony he had been through, he'd not forgotten all these many years. Of course, the years were like an instant to him as a ghost. He had gone to old Paranteau's funeral thinking maybe he could sneak along or follow him on the journey to the afterlife. He was ready for somewhere new. But old Paranteau had died drunk and veered off the holy road. And Roderick had turned back because he smelled the boiling-hot bear meat that Zhaanat had cooked in three changes of water, like his mother. He could smell anyway. And he also liked to hear Zhaanat talking. No to assimilation! There were no swear words in Chippewa but lots of words for sex and Roderick liked to hear about sex. He regretted that he hadn't had it, but of course he knew all about it now. He knew too much. Long ago, he'd stopped haunting people when they started acting sexy. But when Zhaanat and the old people talked about sex it was funny. He laughed a ghost laugh. Which sounded like water off an icicle, or like twigs in the woods rubbing together, way up high. But sex in general? It was a farce. Which was what it was to act assimilated. So he didn't. Except it was very hard to not be assimilated all alone, and he wished he could go home.

## Clark Kent

✶═╪═✶

THE EYE clinic was set up in a corner of the hospital, with a line outside the small room where the visiting eye doctor conducted his tests. Patrice stood in line for an hour. The eye test consisted of charts and lights and cards with black lines. After the doctor wrote down all of the results, he lowered a large set of lenses before her face and switched magnifications on each eye until the shapes in front of her resolved. When she was finished, he took a few more notations and then informed her that her prescription was not uncommon and that he could fit her with eyeglasses that very day.

"Eyeglasses? But I don't need eyeglasses."

It hadn't occurred to her that the tests led to eyeglasses because she had no trouble seeing things.

"Your reading-distance vision is better than 20/20," he said. "You need glasses to see things far away."

"I do see things far away."

"You will see them more clearly."

He left the room and came back with a cardboard box. From the box, he removed a set of eyeglasses. They were the same kind of Indian Health eyeglasses everybody wore. The frames were black and square. He put them on Patrice's face and made sure the bows fit behind her ears.

"There," he said. "Perfect fit. You may take them off to read."

The eyeglasses felt heavy on her nose and she didn't think

she would get used to seeing everything framed by black plastic. She was very conscious of the way the bows sat behind her ears. Patrice walked down the hospital steps and it didn't seem there was a big difference. Everything seemed absolutely normal. Except that when she looked at Wood Mountain waiting at the bottom of the steps, she could see every detail of his battle-marred face. She could see the expectant hope, the love she didn't want him to utter again. As she walked down the steps toward him, she realized that she'd never been able to read people's faces at a distance; she had never seen their expressions. She hadn't even realized that, from a distance, he looked different now. You wouldn't call him handsome now that his nose was so smashed. She stopped on the stairs and looked past Wood Mountain, toward the cars and houses, the trees and the water tower. The precision of the world took her breath away. The crisp lines of brick. The legibility of signs on doors. The needles of pines standing out sharp against more needles and the darkly figured back of the trunk.

When she looked in amazement at Wood Mountain, she could tell he was going to laugh.

"What's so funny?"

But she felt there was something very funny too. Here she was in another disguise.

"You look like Superman's girlfriend."

"No I don't. I look like Clark Kent."

"Oh, waa, you do!"

Wood Mountain held his arm out for her and she took it, like in the movies, but she needed him for balance. The glasses made her feel like her feet were very far away.

"Which way home, Clark Kent? The long way or the short way?"

A chinook wind had blown through the night before. The world was dazzling with snow and dripping with light. The road was sparkling with water and the air was warm and soft. And the birds, the birds were out, singing their spring songs in the middle of the winter.

"It's all the same way," said Patrice.

Halfway home, on the road, Wood Mountain stopped her. He cradled her face in his hands. He didn't kiss her. He kissed the corners of her eyeglasses, then held her hand as they resumed walking.

"What was that?"

"I couldn't help it. Those eyeglasses."

"I look like a boy," Patrice laughed.

"No you don't," said Wood Mountain. "But you do look brainy. I pity a guy who bothers you."

As they continued on, the brilliant snowdrifts threw so much radiance their eyes could not drink it in. Their eyes had to shut some of it out. They could feel the darkness around the edges. Someone had taken a stoneboat through the woods and a trail was packed, so they went down that trail. The blue light enveloped them, a gentler light.

"Bother me," said Patrice.

"Bother you. I never thought I'd put the moves on Clark Kent."

"Well, do it anyway," said Patrice.

Wood Mountain held her with her back against his chest. His hands clasped around her padded waist. They were dressed very warmly but they'd both have snow down their neck and pants if they did it the old-fashioned way. She turned and kissed him until his head swam. She had a skirt on, but wool stockings underneath it.

"Let's find a log to sit on," he said. "I'll sit on the bottom. You can sit on top of me."

She didn't know what he was saying until they found a place to sit. He put his hands on her breasts, under her coat, and she blanked out a little. Oh, so good. He adjusted their clothing when she lowered herself on top of him and soon she remembered what Betty had said and asked him. He took a packet from his inside jacket pocket.

"I been keeping this handy every time I see you," he shyly said, and put it on. Then he was inside of her, too eagerly. Tears started into her eyes, blurred her eyeglasses, and he edged away. She adjusted her eyeglasses, and gasped to start again. So they did, and it got better. Although it wasn't the best thing of all, like Betty had said, Patrice wondered if she would become obsessed, as Betty had also said. If so, she would think of nothing else. As it was happening she really didn't care. However, once Wood Mountain became helpless and deranged, and once he called out and then was still, she did care. She cared very much. She held his head against her heart, still wearing the orange mittens that Millie had given her. From the branches, all through the woods, snow dropped in clumps. Beneath the snow, melting runnels of water murmured. A woodpecker drummed into a tree so hard the wood rang like a bell. Their breathing slowed until they were breathing in perfect time. It seemed like maybe they were thinking one thought, too, but she didn't want to test that out, and so she didn't speak. They restored their clothing to its old arrangement and stayed on the path. They were purified. That's how they felt. Their desire was gone for now and they felt like children. She laughed at nothing and threatened to wash his face with snow for him, and he said to do it, so she took a handful but only touched his cheeks and fed him snow when he opened his mouth. The taste of the snow was eternal to Wood Mountain. He fed the snow to Pixie and it melted on her tongue. Her eyeglasses fogged. She was beginning to come down. She was beginning to touch the earth. But it was only when they got within sight of the cabin that she felt her chest squeeze shut. She could hardly catch her breath. She said goodbye to him and wouldn't let him in the door.

# Checks

***—|—***

THERE WAS a problem. Millie was running out of patterns. She went to the mission bundles with Grace, but found only florals. Millie detested flowers on fabric.

"Picky," said Grace.

"I know what I like to wear."

"How about this?"

Grace held up a circle skirt with broken lines, but they were broken in a random sort of way that made Millie faintly ill when Grace whirled it around with an inviting smile.

"It's got your name on it, Checks."

"I don't like it."

"Picky!"

Millie was having that feeling that came over her when she was around too many old things—a kind of panic. She'd diagnosed herself with several forms of claustrophobia. Also, she was pretty sure she could not testify in Washington, not in any clothing she possessed.

"Let's get out of here."

"Wait!"

Grace held up a black and yellow checked shirt, the perfect size for her. It had a pointed collar, three-quarter sleeves, and darts. Then, while Millie was admiring the shirt, Grace reached deep into a pile and teased out a remarkable garment. It was a long heavy dress made of six different fabrics, and each of the fabrics was a different geometric pattern. The colors were the same—blue, green, gold—but each combination differed in an intricate way. It was made of twill and the patterns were woven into, not stamped onto, the fabric. Millie held her arms out. Her heart swelled. She paid the nun for the blouse and the dress, then walked out to the entryway, where she sat looking at each panel of the print. Each was intricate and mysterious as the manifold signs on Persian rugs. When she stared at the patterns they took her inward and down, beyond the store and the town, into the foundations of meaning, and then beyond meaning, into a place where the structure of the world had nothing to do with the human mind and nothing to do with the patterns on a dress. A place simple, savage, ineffable, and exquisite. It was the place she went to every night.

# The Lamanites

＊—|—＊

"THEIR HATRED was fixed, and they were led by their evil nature that they became wild and ferocious, and a blood-thirsty people, full of idolatry and filthiness, feeding upon beasts of prey, dwelling in tents, and wandering about in the wilderness with a short skin girdle about their loins."

"What do you think, Rosey?" said Thomas. "It's us."

He read the description again.

"No," said Rose, "that's more like Eddy Mink."

Thomas closed The Book of Mormon and went back to studying the text of the bill. He had also written to Joe Garry, president of the National Congress of American Indians, for more information about Watkins.

"The fact of it is," Garry had replied, "Watkins has no sense of humor."

That was even more frightening than the Mormon bible.

Watkins had also refused to appropriate sufficient money to relieve the Navajo, who were in a desperate situation down there in the desert. Watkins said that the Navajo "were used to poverty." But his remark was widely circulated and perhaps he felt the sting. Thomas decided to hit the economic plight hard. It seemed that Watkins wanted Indians both to disappear and to love him for making them disappear. And now that Thomas had read as much of The Book of Mormon as he could stay awake for, he understood why this man was completely dismissive of treaty law. In Watkins's religion, the Mormon people had been divinely gifted all of the land they wanted. Indians weren't white and delightsome, but cursed with dark skin, so they had no right to live on the land. That they had signed legal treaties with the highest governmental bodies in the United States was also nothing to Watkins. Legality was second to personal revelation. Everything was second to personal revelation. And Joseph Smith's personal revelation, all written down in The Book of Mormon, was that his people alone were the best and should possess the earth.

"Who would ever believe that cockeyed story about the peep stone, the vision in the bottom of the hat, the golden tablets? This whole book was an excuse to get rid of Indians," said Thomas.

Rose heard him and started to laugh.

"All the stories are crazy, if you think about it," she said.

Which got Thomas thinking. What religious book was any better? The Holy Bible, full of power and poetry, was also filled with tall tales. Thomas had found them enthralling, but in the end they were all just stories, less important than the Sky Woman story, the manidoog at creation, the Nanabozho stories. To them all, especially the humorless book Elnath and Vernon had left, Thomas preferred their supernatural figure Nanabozho, who fooled ducks, got angry at his own butt and burnt it off, created a shit mountain to climb down when stuck high in a tree, had a wolf for his nephew, and no conscience at any time, who painted the kingfisher lovely colors and by trickery fed his children when they starved, who threw his penis over his shoulder and his balls to the west, who changed himself to a stump and made his penis look like a branch where the kingfisher perched, who killed a god by shooting its shadow, and created everything useful and much that was essential, like laughter.

# The Lord's Plan

✳═╬═✳

IT WAS getting so Norbert stopped pretending that they were going to do anything else. He didn't warm her up. No candy for Betty. No love talk, no pretense. They didn't go to the soda fountain or for a scenic drive or to a movie on the days it changed and they didn't even listen to the radio once he stopped the car. He just got down to business. And this was not all right with Betty, although she was fine about jumping into the backseat with him. One night, she managed to slow him down, it was going well, and in fact she was becoming very hot and happy, when the car door opened and Norbert shot right out. He had been squeezed up against the door, his head pressed to the window as he labored away above. The door had unfortunately opened as he withdrew from her and thrust himself up between her breasts. He skidded off her body and flailed his way belly down onto the slick road. Betty thought the latch had popped by itself until someone outside said, "Could I have a minute of your time to tell you about the Lord's plan for your soul?"

# The Committee

LOUIS DIDN'T want to leave his horses. Moses was laid up with a bum leg. They needed coaxing. Otherwise, the committee for Washington would consist of Juggie Blue, Millie Cloud, and Thomas Wazhashk. They had received an offer to stay at Ruth Muskrat Bronson's house. She was the executive secretary of the National Congress of American Indians and ran the whole shebang out of her house because they didn't have funds for a Washington office yet. Shortly after they accepted, she said she couldn't take them in after all. Consternation. They found a cheap hotel.

"I don't think I can do this," said Millie to Juggie. "I can't sit in front of a bunch of senators. I don't trust my voice."

"Have you ever before lost your voice?"

"No. But I say things."

"Everybody says things."

"My things come out wrong."

Juggie went silent. Millie did say things that offended people or set them off. What if she did this to a senator and wrecked the testimony?

"Can't you testify about the study?" asked Millie.

"Hell no," said Juggie. "I'm already there to read Thomas's statement if he croaks. I'd be a mess if I had to think about yours too."

"Let's get Patrice to take my place."

"Are you crazy?"

"You seen her new glasses? She looks serious. Patrice is the only one who will study my study until she knows it backward and forward. And she's good at talking."

JUGGIE AND Millie drove to the jewel bearing plant and waited for Patrice to get off work. When she walked into the parking lot they waylaid her.

"Can I give you a lift home? Millie and me have something to ask you," asked Juggie.

"No thanks," said Patrice, but they insisted until she waved Doris and Valentine off.

"So?" she said as she got into the backseat of the DeSoto. Millie turned around and stared through her disconcerting eyeglasses. Patrice stared back at her through her equally disconcerting eyeglasses.

"See what I mean about the eyeglasses?" said Millie as they pulled out onto the main road. "They hide Pixie's eyes. She's much less cute, but that would be a good thing."

"For what?"

Patrice felt disconcerted in general, as if this had happened before. Oh yes, she remembered. There had been Bucky, and then the last time she'd been coerced into an automobile she'd ended up wearing a poisonous waterjack suit and swimming in a glass tank.

"Good thing for what?" she said again.

"Good thing for giving testimony in Washington, D.C.," said Millie. "I can't do it. I have to write things out before I know what I should say. You can think on your feet."

"Why would you have to think on your feet? Don't you just read the study?"

"They want to question me."

"Oh no. I can't answer questions. I don't know everything about your study. I can't do it."

"Yes, you can," said Millie. "You're not that stupid."

Patrice was used to Millie's way of talking.

"I'm not stupid at all, Millie. But I have to stay home and work."

"The tribal council will talk to your boss. I'll help out with your family."

"You're there a lot anyway," said Patrice.

"Taking notes," said Millie. "I might change from economics to anthropology."

"Whatever that is," said Juggie.

"I won't do it," said Patrice. "But I'll practice with you, Millie, so you won't go off the rails."

"You should come with us," said Millie. "In case I do go off the rails."

"I wouldn't mind that at all," said Patrice.

"THE MEETING will come to order."

Thomas commenced with the formalities and since Millie was there, and said she knew personal shorthand, she was the one who took notes, including notes on the notes Juggie had taken at the last meeting. The real business of the council was to decide who would go to Washington, D.C.

"Moses?"

"My leg has been acting up. I believe that I will pass."

"Louis?"

"A bad time of year for the horses."

Louis had got county and state officials to sign a letter of support. He was still working on the local chapters of the American

Legion. He could go up to anyone and get their signature with his bull body and cute smile. He could even get people to donate cash money. But he didn't want to go to Washington.

"You just need to be there, so they see we have a delegation."

"I wouldn't be no good. All I'd think of is they wrecked my son," said Louis.

Thomas looked down at his sheaf of papers and passed his hand over his forehead. He was extra tired that day and fighting dizziness.

"We know that Millie doesn't want to go," said Thomas. "But Patrice can back her up if we raise a little more money. Plus, she can testify on the jewel bearing plant. What about you, Juggie? Don't let me down."

"I'm not missing this. Doesn't come by every day."

"It won't be a tourist trip."

"That's plain. But I am ready to read your statement if you get sick on the city water."

"That won't happen," said Thomas, waving his hand. "I'm on the wagon."

"You better all be on the wagon when you're there," said Moses.

"You best come and ride herd on us," said Juggie. "There's no telling what a bunch of crazy Chippewas might get up to."

"Quit trying to trick me into it. I'm an old man."

"This here's your one chance at the big time before you die, akiwenzi."

AFTER THE meeting was over, with everyone still rattled, Thomas gave Patrice and Millie a ride. As often happened now, Millie came home with Patrice. When she got there, she sat down at the table by Zhaanat's stove and took out her pencil and notebook. She was drawing one of the plants that Zhaanat regularly collected. She was trying to puzzle out the desiccated leaves.

"I have to come back in the summer," said Millie. "I can't identify these plants when they're all dried out like this."

"That's miskomin," said Patrice. "Mama uses it for everything. It's a woman plant. Helps with cramps, strengthens the womb, makes the milk flow. But she uses it for general things too. That's why she's got so much of it. And this here, gaagige-bag, is a woman plant too."

"Indeed," said Millie.

Patrice had taken advantage of a canning lesson at the farm agent's and brought home a crate of jars for her mother. Pokey had made a sturdy rack of sapling sticks and fixed it to the wall. The rows of jars filled with crushed leaves and stripped roots had intrigued Millie. Other medicines were strung up in the corner or braided with long tails, like the wild onions Zhaanat cherished.

Millie sharpened her pencil with a pocketknife and kept writing in her notebook. It looked familiar.

"That's a school notebook," said Patrice.

"Government issue. I met the math teacher and let him know that I needed a few of these."

"You met Hay Stack? I mean, Barnes?"

"I did. Grace and me went over to pick up Wood Mountain where he was training. Barnes told me to come over and see his classroom."

"So did you go?"

"Sure. He said he liked my checked blouse. Said it gave him ideas."

"Well, that's fresh," said Patrice.

"Fresh," said Millie. "Fresh ideas, yes."

"No, I mean . . . oh, you know."

"Oh! Not those kinds of ideas. How to teach math by blacking out certain squares on a grid. I saw what he meant."

"Getting back to the survey, they might ask how you got the information."

Millie told how the idea for the survey came about after she'd visited her father, and then told her adventures in getting the interviews, all in great detail. She told about the academic program that she was in and how she obtained the scholarship money. She listed her other papers, her slim credentials, her references, her grades. Now it was Patrice taking notes with a sharp pencil. Millie would have to tell all of this in case one of the senators tried to discredit her information.

# Scrawny

✴═┃═✴

SOMETIMES WHEN Valentine looked at Barnes sideways, through half-lidded eyes, he felt like the soft rabbit he had imagined in her jaws. Of course, he'd hoped she would be sweet underneath it all, like a Valentine's Day candy. Be Mine. He'd gotten to second base, almost. She was an expert in swatting off his hands or even slashing at his privates. Fear increasingly left him boneless. Limp! Hay Stack! It was clear to him that if she were to become more welcoming to him, there must first be a proposal of marriage. Talk about strict Catholic. Of course, Barnes respected this. On the other hand, a man was a man. As a result he was getting so fast on the speed bag and blurring the jump rope so regularly that he'd lost pounds, actual pounds. He'd trimmed down on Valentine's watch.

"You're getting scrawny," she'd observed.

Now plus clumsy, he was scrawny. He'd certainly never been called that before. He was a bulky man, he knew it, and oh could he prove it, if only she'd be a bit more like her soft heart-shaped name.

# The Journey

THEY SLEPT in their coach seats. Caught the next train in Minneapolis. Slept in their seats another night. Thomas read his testimony obsessively, trying not to make too many marks on the papers he had to read out loud. Patrice checked her watch, then checked it again. She couldn't wait to wind it every night. She had also bought the expensive mercantile suitcase. Plaid. Two shades of green with red lines. A latch that sprang open with a loud businesslike click. Juggie had hauled onboard a beat-up overnight bag stuffed with sandwiches, cookies, dried apples, whole carrots, raisins. They didn't want to spend their money in the dining car. They slept in their seats a third night and woke in Washington. Hauling their suitcases down the platform, they tried not to stumble with fatigue. They took deep breaths and lugged themselves and their baggage up a broad flight of stairs. Then, hearts pounding, eyes burning, they found themselves standing in a vast series of soaring vaults.

The size of the place stunned them. There was a low ceiling of cigarette smoke, and over that sheer light. The air was hushed near the floor, but the space encompassed and was surrounded by a roar so loud it seemed a single physical presence, although it was composed of revving and moving motors, horns, honks, bells, sirens, whistles, blares, beeps, growling brakes, and howling tires, and below those sounds even smaller ones, the whispers of footsteps, the rustling of papers, the murmuring of conversation, the clinking of spoons and forks and the settling of cups, the eating sounds, the rustle of coats put on and taken off, the beating of tin gongs, and the ticks of clocks and squeaks of motion or rubber overboots or pleasure. They stood inside their own quiet like a pocket.

For Thomas and Moses, the city noise was so disorienting that they couldn't move. Juggie treated the noise like weather. She didn't sort sound from sound or mind the details. Millie had lived near the university campus on University Avenue, so she was more accustomed to noise. Patrice had prepared herself. They finally organized themselves, squeezed into a cab, and were taken to the Moroccan Hotel. It was a small place, clean but shabby. Their rooms were on the street side of the building and only on the second floor. Even with the windows closed, the noise pounded in. Thomas and Moses shared one room, and the three women shared the other room. Juggie had asked for one of the beds to be a double bed, but the two beds were each single.

"We're not even going to flip a coin," said Juggie. "My bones hurt and I kick. You two can share."

They'd eaten at a diner in a state of mad exhaustion, and now they took turns slipping into tepid baths. Then it was time to sleep. Millie was wearing a pair of pajamas covered with eye-numbing diamonds and dots. Juggie wore one of Louie's soft old ragged shirts. Patrice was wearing a nightgown made of limp blue cotton, from the free pile at the mission. She rolled in next to Millie, back-to-back. They pulled the covers up around their necks, though the room was warm. Juggie and Millie fell directly asleep. Patrice alone was left awake, buzzing. People seemed to be talking only inches from her head, although they were a story below. At first she listened to each intriguing fragment, and then with no transition into sleep she began to feel conscious again, though she kept her eyes closed. She could feel Juggie and Millie moving around the room and thought that it must be morning. But when she opened her eyes, the light was long. It was still only very late in the afternoon. Her eyes fell shut.

SOMETHING STOLE into her then. In a new place, with different sounds and different air, that which she had been resisting found purchase. There was a tearing sensation. As if she were being split through the center. And there was a wracking wild beating of her heart. She couldn't breathe. Her arms lifted—if only he were there, to hold her. Her face softened. If only his face would brush her, to kiss her. The snow melted on her tongue.

"Wake up," said Juggie, nudging her. "We're hungry."

"Let's go," said Millie. "There's a diner down the street."

"It looked decent," said Juggie, and she pulled on Patrice's foot. "Get a move on."

# Falcon Eyes

✶═┃═✶

PATRICE WALKED into the gallery overlooking the floor of the House of Representatives. Her scarf and jacket were still damp with rain. It was the day before their testimony was to take place and they were trying to get oriented in the Capitol. She sat down. Glanced warily at the people around her. Noticed an extraordinary-looking woman in bold lipstick. This woman was so striking that it was hard for Patrice not to stare at her. She glanced briefly at Patrice, then focused downward on the view of the House floor. Her dark hair was pulled back in waves that curled handsomely at the nape of her neck. She had strong queenly features and wore a pale brown suit with a short slim-fitting jacket and a midcalf skirt. Motionless, eyes fixed, clutching the black purse in her lap, she stared with raptor intensity at the semicircle of seated and standing representatives. Talk on the House floor began regarding the economy of Mexico, and although Patrice had difficulty following the speakers, the gravity of being in the halls of governmental power seemed to cast a spell over the observers.

"Viva Puerto Rico libre!"

Patrice didn't recognize the sounds as shots until she turned her head and saw the pistol in the woman's hand. She was on her feet, a tall woman. Again, she cried out, "Viva Puerto Rico!" The pistol looked like a war trophy that Patrice had once seen in Louis Pipestone's house, a Luger. That's what she had. The

woman aimed high, over the crowd, but someone else was
shooting downward. Too shocked to duck or even move, Patrice saw men fall on the floor below, others scrambling behind
desks and podium. Then it was over. The guards crashed into
the gallery and seized the woman's gun, then her. They dragged
a small man out of the aisle, another man, how many? And then
everyone in the visitors' gallery stumbled around in horror and
confusion, before they were told that they would be questioned
before they were allowed to leave.

Patrice stood in line for an hour. The guard who finally questioned her frowned suspiciously and motioned her to the side.
It occurred to Patrice then that the woman with the dark hair
could have been her sister.

"Where are you from?"

"North Dakota," said Patrice.

"Are you a tourist?"

"Yes," said Patrice, fearing she would be detained over any
complication she might name.

"Do you have identification?"

Patrice handed over her pass from Senator Young and a small
cardboard card that she'd been given when she started her job at
the jewel bearing plant. There was a Defense Department seal
on the card. The guard handed them back and gave her a tight,
grim smile.

"Did you see anything?" he asked.

"I was sitting by her, the woman."

"Let me take your information down."

"She shot her gun into the air. She didn't shoot any member
of Congress."

"Oh really? Good for her." His voice was sarcastic.

Patrice walked outside, down the longest steps she'd ever

seen, and looked around for her tribal members. There were squad cars, whooping sirens, swarms of police officers. Tourists and reporters were clustered along the streets. Patrice was directed away from the Capitol, and easily found Thomas and Juggie, waiting for her. Moses had gone back to the hotel. She hadn't been frightened of the woman. In fact, although it was terrible, she knew, Patrice had been thrilled when the woman stood up and yelled. What made her do such a thing? What was Puerto Rico?

"Did you see it happen?" asked Juggie.

When Patrice couldn't answer, she realized that here in Washington she'd seen people shot, a thing she'd never seen before, even on the reservation, a place considered savage by the rest of the country. She had no emotion. The men below her had crumpled, fallen, maybe cried out, and she hadn't even reacted. It was the woman in the pale brown suit she'd watched, her falcon eyes, her fearless cries, how she held the gun with both hands, how she had tried to unfurl a piece of cloth, red, white and blue, to snap it out. And how awkward while holding the gun. How Patrice's impulse had been to say "Here, let me help you." To shake out the cloth for her. A flag, certainly a flag of her country. And why?

Everything was suddenly overwhelmingly massive: the Capitol, the monuments, the insides of the buildings, the stairs down, the blood—there had certainly been blood on the polished wood and cushions of the chairs. Patrice staggered a little and said she needed to go back to her room and curl up in the bed. She was trembling. Juggie held her elbow.

"I saw it all. Yes, I did," said Patrice. "There was a woman."

# Termination of Federal Contracts and Promises Made with Certain Tribes of Indians

*⟩≡|⟨*

JOINT HEARING
BEFORE THE
SUBCOMMITTEES OF THE
COMMITTEES ON
INTERIOR AND INSULAR AFFAIRS
CONGRESS OF THE UNITED STATES
EIGHTY-THIRD CONGRESS
SECOND SESSION

PART 12
TURTLE MOUNTAIN INDIANS, NORTH DAKOTA
MARCH 2 AND 3, 1954

STATEMENT OF THOMAS WAZHASHK,
CHAIRMAN OF THE ADVISORY COMMITTEE,
TURTLE MOUNTAIN BAND OF CHIPPEWA INDIANS,
NORTH DAKOTA,
AS WELL AS STATEMENTS BY
OTHER COMMITTEE MEMBERS,
JEWEL BEARING PLANT EMPLOYEES,
A GHOST, A PhD CANDIDATE,
AND A STENOGRAPHER.
REMARKS BY SENATOR ARTHUR V. WATKINS
ARE DIRECT QUOTES FROM
THE CONGRESSIONAL RECORD.

. . .

THEY WALKED into a large room lined with honey-colored panels. An imposing semicircular bank of ornamented wood, divided into desklike seating, took up one end of the room. Muted light poured upon the structure through a vast window. A long rectangular table was placed in the forward center of the room, facing the great desk. They all shook hands with Senator Milton R. Young, mild and thoughtful, with a boxer's granite chin. All the way from Fort Berthold, Martin Cross, friendly, craggy, astute, chatted with the senator. Thomas stayed by the table talking with them while the rest of the party sat down in the chairs directly behind the table. Moses and Juggie muttered to each other. Patrice tucked her hands in her lap. Beside her, Millie sat gazing straight ahead, in a trance of terror.

Millie was looking at a recessed panel behind the places where the senators would be seated. Perhaps it was a doorway. It was decorated with sharp vertical angles. Congruence is lucky, she thought. Lucky, lucky, lucky. And I'm not superstitious. As she did when in distress, she was also assessing the way objects lined up in the room. The doorway, if it was a doorway, was perfectly centered, which was reassuring. But the heavy drapes, pushing aside the flood of radiance coming through the window, hung slightly crooked. This made Millie want to cry. And she did not ever cry. She steeled herself and took comfort from the great bronze sconces to either side—they defied geometry. The fixtures looked like outsize flashlights. Each admitted a glow that seemed feeble in the already light-flooded room. The flashlights diverted Millie, but now her blood fizzed in alarm as she rose. She took her oath with the others and seated herself at the desk to the left of Thomas. With rustles and low talk, the senators conferred. Millie calmed herself by checking and rechecking the page order of her statement. Senator Watkins began to speak. Millie panicked until she looked up at him and saw that he was yet another man who didn't know how to type.

To one side, below the giant desk, sat a woman in a severe suit. She posed her fingers over the keys of her stenotype, and began. Aha. There was no excuse for this sort of thing. It occurred to Millie, then, that the woman, the stenographer with the handsome machine, would also be taking down and typing up her words. Millie allowed this idea to slowly fill her with a secret confidence.

SENATOR YOUNG spoke well and said exactly what the tribal committee members had hoped he would say. He insisted that the state could not step in and take over the responsibilities of the federal government. That, if anything, the government should fund an expensive job-training program on the reservation.

THOMAS BEGAN.

FIRST, THE introductions, the courtesies, the insistence that the record show that this trip by tribal people to Washington had been paid for by the generosity of local people, not the government. Nothing was said about the boxing match.

SITTING BEHIND Thomas in the row of supporters and interested parties, Patrice blinked and remembered Wood Mountain's broken eyebrow. For a moment that snowy day, her glasses had slipped and she saw how the scar had formed across the bone, a living and still healing interruption. What would she do about him?

. . .

INSTEAD OF arguing the premise of termination itself, the tribal committee had decided to buy time. The government's five-year plan was insufficient because the reservation was currently unable to sustain itself without support. Hammer that. Then as a point of outrage demand more money from the government.

A DESCRIPTION of the Turtle Mountain Reservation.

A STATEMENT of strong opposition. Then a ladle of corn syrup— appreciation for the efforts and time of the government, extra dollops for Senator Watkins and Associate Commissioner of Indian Affairs H. Rex Lee, the authors of the two measures that would strip the people of everything.

WATKINS INTERRUPTED. Watkins started talking.

THOMAS THOUGHT: Oh hell, stick with it, stick with it, don't let him give you the teacher-eye, don't let him throw his eight-dollar words at you, don't let him . . .

. . . AND suddenly Roderick was in the room.

## Roderick

The instant that Roderick saw Senator Arthur V. Watkins, he knew exactly who he was. Watkins was the teacher who'd taught the Palmer Method, the little man who'd whacked his hands with the ruler's edge, who'd pulled his ears, who'd screeched at him, who'd called him hopeless, who'd punished him for talking Indian. Watkins was the man who'd dragged Roderick to the cellar stairs and said to Thomas, "Would you care to join your friend?"

*Senator Watkins:* In my area, whites got the poor land on the reservation. Within a year, however, the Indians leased their allotments. They just didn't want to farm. That is true today. I think most of the Indian allotments are under lease to white people. That is why I seriously doubt that Indians like to farm.

## Patrice, Thinking

He's another white farmer like Doris Lauder's family who picked up cheap Indian land after the taxes came due on allotments. I know damn well he didn't get the poor land because no white person would buy it. He got the only farmable land.

*Senator Watkins:* If I may ask, do you work, Mr. Wazhashk?

*Thomas Wazhashk:* Yes. I farm.

*Senator Watkins:* It is too bad we haven't more like you in these tribes.

*Thomas Wazhashk:* What farmable land there is on the reservation is mostly farmed by Indians.

*Senator Watkins:* I have noticed Indians, wherever I have seen them, in mechanical jobs, jobs requiring skill with their hands. They seem to like that.

## Patrice

They seem to like that? I guess they do. I guess we do.

## Millie

I won't look down at my dress. I won't get lost in my sleeves. But I'll be fine because I'm dressed in the elements of geometry. Beyond which I must not go in my thoughts until I have delivered my study.

*Thomas Wazhashk:* In view of the fact that employment has shown a considerable downward trend throughout the United States as a whole, we believe the relocation program is ill timed and would be fraught with insurmountable difficulties. We want to point out that the relocation program has limitations. It doesn't cover our problems.

*Senator Watkins:* I wouldn't say it covered them all. No. Because, after all, the government can't solve your problems for you. Most of them have to be solved by yourselves.

## Thomas

Is that you, Roderick?

## Roderick

Yes, it's me. Hold out. Don't get mad. They don't like an Indian to have brains. Ignore old Mr. Pantywaist and put your sentences together.

*Senator Watkins:* Oh, surely. There would be nothing permanently cured that you don't cure yourself. No government, no matter how benevolent, can put ambition into people. That has to be developed by themselves. You can't legislate morality, character, or any of those fine virtues into people.

You learn to walk by walking.

## Thomas, Thinking

We didn't get to the Turtle Mountains by riding in a covered wagon.

## Roderick and Thomas

For the rest of his life, when Thomas thought of the moment his teacher asked whether he wanted to join Roderick in the cellar, Thomas imagined saying, "Yes, yes, sling me down there, you scabby rat." But he hadn't said that. No, Thomas had gone silent and let Roderick take the blame. But it hadn't been entirely out of cowardice. No, because after all, it was just a cellar and Roderick had been in worse. No, because behind the teacher's back, Roderick shook his head at him to stay. He knew that kids had been forgotten down there a week at a time. No, it was strategy. From up above, Thomas could bust Roderick out.

*Senator Watkins:* Let me ask you a few questions about you personally. You don't have to answer if you don't want to. I am not requiring this of you, but it may help to illustrate the situation. What do you do for a living?

*Thomas Wazhashk:* As I mentioned, farming. Also I am one of the guards at the Turtle Mountain ordnance plant, the jewel plant, where they make jewel bearings.

*Senator Watkins:* What are jewel bearings?

*Thomas Wazhashk:* We have brought an example of a jewel
   bearing, as well as a magnifying glass, which you will need
   to see that jewel bearing. We also have an expert on this
   work. Miss Patrice Paranteau. May I call upon her to give
   expert witness?

*Senator Watkins:* She must be sworn in, but yes.

*Patrice Paranteau (after being sworn in; head buzzing with fear,*
   *holding the card, the example, and magnifying glass):* This little
   wire that you see here is a wire made out of tongue steel,
   and that is set in the machine and worked back and forth
   until you finally drill a hole in the jewel. Through the
   magnifying glass you will see there is a tiny hole through
   this jewel and everything is polished, inside and outside.
   It has to be to the certain dimensions stated on the card,
   which you see here, and it is also cupped, so that it will hold
   oil for lubrication purposes.

*Senator Watkins (ignoring Patrice and addressing Thomas*
   *Wazhashk):* What can these people do with the training for
   this work?

*Thomas Wazhashk:* I believe the average pay is 75 to 90 cents an
   hour. As for me, I take home $38.25 a week.

*Senator Watkins:* Some of the Indian women who have families
   labor there, too, don't they?

*Thomas Wazhashk:* Yes; most of the Indian women employed
   there have families.

*Senator Watkins:* Why do they take women, rather than men?
   You have plenty of men, haven't you?

*Thomas Wazhashk:* They give tests. They give you manual
   dexterity tests, and I believe the women are better in that
   than the men are. And now, if I may take the opportunity,
   Miss Millie Cloud is here to introduce her field research

study conducted on the social and economic conditions on the Turtle Mountain Reservation.

## Millie

"If this might be introduced into the record . . . ," said Millie.
Then she began.
Reading her study out went like a blur.
The questions were many.
So passed one hour, and the next. At last, a recess.

## Roderick

Remember how you buttered that white teacher up to the teeth? Called him sir, sir this, sir that, thanked him constantly, asked his advice. Then stole the keys from his suit pocket? Then you let me out and slipped back the keys.

## Thomas

"Should I try it?" Thomas whispered.
Thomas watched as Senator Watkins walked down the hall. With his small entourage, he walked down the stairs. Thomas followed Senator Watkins down the stairs. He found the senator's office and entered. He was about to explain who he was to a secretary, when Senator Watkins emerged from the inner office.

"HELLO THERE," said Senator Watkins. "What can I do for you?"
"I'm here to thank you," said Thomas.
"Well, well," said the senator.

"I wanted to thank you for your concern for our people. You have obviously taken our situation to heart, and I was struck by the kindness showed to us in your carefully listening and thoughtfully weighing our testimony on the termination bill."

"In all of my days as a senator, nobody has ever thanked me for listening to their testimony."

"I call that an omission," said Thomas.

As he left the senator's office, he was thinking, I am and we are absolutely destitute and desperate. This is a sign of how bad things are. I am willing to forgo my dignity to try to butter you up to the teeth. I hope it helps our cause.

## Goodbye

After the next day's testimony, the little delegation was anxious to leave the Capitol. Yet they lingered, as if their presence might still have some effect.

# The Way Home

＊＝｜＝＊

## Thomas

On the way home on the train, as the gray snow, the blinding snow, the dark fields flew by, as the birds raved and twisted in vast flocks above, moving in eerie specks and spirals, as Thomas glimpsed, silenced, untold numbers of boarded-up or curtained-back windows and rickety fire escapes, scruffy trash yards, blackened brick walls and dumps, he reviewed every moment, every word. Had he said such and such? What had it meant when the senator adjusted his eyeglasses? How would things go? Thomas was convinced that he'd destroyed their chances. He couldn't point out exactly how he'd done it, but he knew. And the other thing. The senator had also asked every single Indian person who testified about their degree of Indian blood. The funny thing was, nobody knew exactly. No one had answered with a numeral. It wasn't something that they kept close track of and in fact Thomas hadn't parsed out his own ancestors—determined who was a quarter or half or three-quarters or full blood. Nor had anyone he knew. As the miles rolled on, this began to bother him. Everyone knew they were Indian or not Indian regardless of what the rolls said or what the government said, it was a given or not a given. Long ago, a guy in a bar had made a family tree for him. When Thomas looked at the tree, he pointed out the Indians and came out a full-blood, though he knew there was French somewhere. Then the person made the tree again and made him more white, more Indian, more white. It turned into a game. And it was still a game, but a game that interested Senator Watkins, which meant it was a game that could erase them.

EACH OF them bought newspapers to keep as souvenirs. They read about what had happened in the House of Representatives. None of the representatives were killed but one was in serious condition. It was surprising, now, to think that the hearings had not been canceled. And that they had only been lightly searched on the way in the next day, though there were plenty of extra guards looking fierce and vigilant.

## Patrice

Now I know. I know how Wood Mountain felt after that fight, she thought. Not on the outside, of course, but on the inside. All of the adrenaline gone, all the fight out of her, but each moment clear and emphatic, the faces of the senators in every detail. Especially Senator Watkins. The word supercilious. That was the word for every detail. Watkins's coin-purse mouth. His self-righteous ease. The way he held himself, giving off that vibration. Filling the air with sanctimony. Another word that flung itself into her mind.

IN THE newspapers, there was quite a bit about Puerto Rico so Patrice had her answer. And there was a large picture of the woman who had jumped to her feet and shot the pistol. Her luminous hot eyes, her slash of lipsticked mouth, blurred in the newsprint. Patrice ran her hand over the grainy photographs and carefully stashed the newspapers in her bag. She leaned back and saw the woman's eyes. Lolita Lebrón. Viva Puerto Rico. She wanted her country to live so badly she'd been willing to kill. Was there something wrong with her? Or was there something wrong with Patrice? If this opposing testimony didn't work, if they lost their scrap of universe, if her mother was forced to live in a city, which would kill her, if Vera was never found, if, if, if she had Senator Arthur V. Watkins on his knees before her and his life in her hands. What if that. What if that? Mr. Smug Mouth. Mr. Sanctimony.

He'd be in danger, she thought. I do things perfectly when enraged.

PATRICE HAD trouble sleeping on the train that ride. Every time she was about to drift off, an image intervened. She saw her hands as her mother's hands. She saw her mother's fingers, strong and supernatural, clenched around Freckle Face's neck, Bernie's neck, the senator's neck. Patrice tried to stop the pictures but they returned. She was inhabited by a vengeful, roiling, even murderous spirit. That same spirit had hatched the bird that pecked Bucky's face. When she got home, she'd clean up the sweat lodge and ask her mother to help her get rid of these thoughts.

## Moses

He missed his wife. She was a small, orderly, kind woman with an impertinent smile. They'd been together since they were children. There wasn't a time without her. This was the longest. He had taken one of her knitted scarves with him, a red one, and at night he'd slept with it next to his face, even on the train. Their children called them "the old-timers" because their love was like that—old-time. They held hands. They kissed. Called each other niinimoshehn. Good morning, my little sweetheart, he said to her every morning. He was in a terror that something might happen to her while he was gone. Maybe he could call her cousin, who lived in town, from a phone? Maybe it was less expensive now? If something had happened, they would have sent a telegram, said Juggie, several times. He was worrying for nothing. But the feeling that something was going to happen wouldn't let him go and he got out with Thomas hoping to distract himself. During their layover in the Minneapolis train station, they planned to find a tobacco shop and buy themselves, and Louis, a few cigars.

## Thomas

As Thomas walked among the tall ornate iron pillars with Moses, he realized that for some time he hadn't felt right. Feeling odd had sneaked up on him. Oh, he knew that he wasn't mentally right. Who could be, after all of this? But physically, now, too. He leaned against a pillar, catching his breath. Strength was draining from his legs. A sharp pain was sneaking up the right side of his face. Moses turned, beckoning him along. Thomas kept going, hoping he could walk it off.

## Juggie

"Oh, let them go find their stinking cigars," she laughed. "We've got a good hour here, girls. Let's find coffee and test the city doughnuts. Ambe!"

## Thomas

The patterned tiles of the stone floor rose. He was on all fours, then diving down, swimming through blackest blackness. He had a sense of how tiny he was. And the world, monstrous space, it swelled, greater, greater, all space and water. He knew back there, somewhere up there and all around, swirls of motion. Shouts and calls. He must ignore everything and keep swimming down, and down, even though this blackness was becoming thick and resistant. And he could barely keep moving. He must find a mote of strength, then another even smaller mote, to keep pulling toward the bottom of this blackness. He had to reach the bottom before he could come up. That was the muskrat's task.

"AANDI?" HE said, waking. "Where am I?"

"You are in the hospital. You had a stroke."

Confronting him with yellow wolf eyes was a tall white nurse, hair a tufted mane of gray. He would not have been surprised to see pointed ears on either side of her starched and blazing white cap.

He asked, "Have you finished measuring the earth?"

He was a fleck of dust that she might shake off her tail. Her teeth were long and stained. He saw that indeed the wolf had finished measuring and his heart tightened in his chest.

# *If*

✦═✦

THE FIRST layer of blanket was washed every day. The next layer every week. The top layer was ornately beaded indigo trade wool. The beaded white vine was the trail of life. Maple leaves, multicolored roses, and Zhaanat's favorite shapes branched off the vine. Wood Mountain laid Archille on the cradle board and packed cattail fluff all around the baby's bottom and skinny thighs. Once Archille was all trussed up in his cradle board, he grew calm and sleepy. Wood Mountain carried him over to Pokey's bed and put him down. Frustrating because he and the baby were alone in the house. This was the perfect time. The stove was throwing heat. Zhaanat had gone out to pick cedar. If Patrice were only here, he would ask her the same thing, again. Marry me. He couldn't live this way. She'd say yes this time, she would, yes? There was even a pot of boiled tea. He heard steps outside, couldn't see who it was. Someone was talking. Running. His heart thumped like he was going into the ring.

A woman was at the door. Wood Mountain was breathing fast, a little dizzy, and his mouth dropped open. He didn't know what to say at all. This was not Patrice. She was a stranger, or at least he thought so at first. Her eyes were lost in deep hollows and her face was so thin that her teeth looked huge. She was wearing a brown canvas jacket, overalls, and a brown knitted hat. He gaped at her when she said, "What are you doing here, Wood Mountain?"

He shook his head.

"Don't you remember me? It's Vera."

A gray-bearded man walked in behind her, ducking his head, a shy stunned look on his face. It was dark inside and he blinked as his eyes adjusted.

"I won't be staying for long," he said. "My dog's in the car."

Vera gave him a long look. Then she reached up, on tiptoe, and brought down the family's rifle. She tried to give it to him, but he wouldn't take it.

"Please," she said. Her face was strained. There were tears in her eyes. The man smiled, his teeth faintly glinting through his beard, his eyes unhappy. He put his hands up and said the family would need the rifle. Then he turned and went out the door.

Archille made a tiny sound and Vera's eyes went wide, staring into Wood Mountain's eyes, and he knew that she was putting together him, the baby, her sister, her mother, all possibilities. He knew that she didn't think that this was her baby. The crazy thought that he could walk out with Archille and disappear jolted through his brain. He picked up Archille in the cradle board, proud of its beauty and in love with the tender little sleeping face. Archille was wearing a small fur hood.

"He's yours," he said to Vera, but he didn't look at her, just at Archille.

She collapsed like snow. By the time he got her back up and put the baby in her arms, Zhaanat was home and the two were clutching each other with the baby between them. Wood Mountain walked outside and went over to Daisy Chain. His legs were shaking and his arms so weak he couldn't pull himself onto her back, so he took her halter and led her down the road. Somehow he hadn't imagined what would happen . . . if. *If.* Now *if* had happened and he couldn't imagine not belonging to Archille.

# Tosca

IT WAS a case of mutual exasperation, thank god. During an episode of agonized light petting she sat up and said, "Take me home." Which Barnes gladly did. As she got out of the car she said, "Goodbye, and I mean that." Barnes leaned out of the car as she walked past the snowy hulks of cars in her father's yard.

"Do you mean goodbye as in goodbye for good?" he called.

The cutting breeze stung his cheeks and forehead. It was March, goddammit! He'd never known the sort of cold they had way up here.

She turned around and by the look on her face she did mean that. He sank back into the car, behind the wheel, relieved as all hell.

HE DROVE straight past the gym. Was he going to work out on a Saturday night? No. He was going back to his room in a state of mysterious elation. Plus dejection. A guy could have feelings, and contradictory ones. Why not? He'd just received another present from his uncle. It was an opera recording. Although Barnes did not suppose opera was considered a manly taste, he secretly thought the recording was pretty good. In fact, it made him weep. Luxuriantly weep. He played it only when he was alone. After weeping, he often fell into the sweetest dreams.

# The Salisbury

‹—|—›

MILLIE HAD been the one to call an ambulance and to insist that Thomas be taken to the University of Minnesota Hospital. He'd been admitted right away, and now he was bundled up in a hospital bed, high on a quiet floor. As a relative, Patrice was the only one allowed into the room. She sat beside the bed on a metal chair and rested her eyes on his face. He was not fully unconscious, but he was more than just asleep. Although his expression was calm, gentle, untroubled, Patrice was flooded by fear. She could feel him hovering around outside his body.

A nurse came in and took his vital signs. Patrice was afraid that the brusque woman had shooed away his spirit, but when quiet fell once more, she could feel the soul of Thomas swaying above the bed. Thomas was the closest thing she had to a father. She put her hand out, near his hand, and closed her eyes. After a time, she began to speak in her mother's language and the words came that her mother used in the beginning of every ceremony. These words invoked the spirits of the winds that sat in the four directions and the spirits of the animals that came from the four directions. She invited all of these representatives and spirits to enter the room. Time fell away. The window glass vibrated as the wind rose. People passed in the hallway, talking.

LATER ON, when the nurse assured Patrice that her uncle's signs were stable, she left with Millie and walked to her rented room. It was cold inside the little studio, and Millie told Patrice to keep her coat on and sit in the chair. She drew up a stool, next to Patrice, and turned on a small heater. The Salisbury's coil bloomed red and a comfortable heat flowed toward their legs.

"This is a nice place," said Patrice, nodding at the table. "What's that?"

"It's a plug-in teakettle. There's no kitchen sink, but I have a full bathroom and that hot plate. I bought some meat pies. My mom calls them shepherd's pies and over by Michigan they call them meat pasties. There's this little grocery where they make them fresh or you can buy them frozen. Also, I did buy two apples."

"We've got a meal," Patrice said.

Millie got up and made the tea, stirring the sugar in with a ceremonial flourish. She had dusted and straightened up her little room. Her pleasure in having Patrice here was so extreme that she found it hard to breathe. Something kept catching in her chest. She handed the teacup to Patrice and also gave her a saucer, matching.

"This hits the spot," said Patrice.

Millie sat back down on the stool and blew across the surface of the tea.

"You're the first person who ever visited me."

"You probably haven't been here long," said Patrice.

"Oh yes I have. I just never invited anybody. Not that anybody asked, but that's how it worked out. You are the first."

"Well, I like it here," said Patrice. "I like the bare walls."

"You like the bare walls?"

It was hard for Millie to contain her elation. "I keep thinking I should put something up," she said. "Pictures. But then I wonder, of what?"

"People put too much stuff on their walls."

Millie took a sip of hot, sweet, tea. It was delicious. Soon she would fry up the pies and they would eat the apples. Then they would go back to the hospital and visit Thomas. And after that they would return and go to bed.

"I'm sorry I have only the one bed."

"We can double up again. You're a nice calm sleeper. Sometimes when it's cold I get Pokey and Mom and the baby all of us under the blankets. Pokey kicks, but it's the only way to stay alive."

"I leave the window open a crack because of the gas burner. Sometimes when I wake up in here I can see my breath."

"Sometimes our blanket is covered by frost from our breathing. We have to crack it off in the morning."

"Sometimes I wonder why I like it so much here alone. Why I'm so happy."

"You don't have a boyfriend?"

"Nobody appeals."

"Same for me. I'm thinking of Wood Mountain, though."

"He's handsome, so I hear. I can never tell."

"Handsome even busted up."

"Well, you, you're beautiful," said Millie. Her voice thickened, clogging her throat. She opened her mouth to blurt out words of love. She hadn't really known these words were in her, but all of a sudden they were forcing themselves out of a hidden aperture in her heart. She made a sound, but Patrice spoke first.

"You know, I was thinking, Millie, after Vera comes home I was thinking I want to adopt you. I was thinking that you could be my sister."

"Sisters. Oh."

"Could you be my sister?"

"Well, sure."

Millie knew enough from her interviews to understand that being adopted by a Chippewa was a special mark of friendship and honor. But for some reason what Patrice said didn't make her feel all one way. She was both happy and for some reason disappointed. And her feelings ran on this way in the silence. Companionable though it was, she felt unsettled and was left wanting by what Patrice had offered. It was as if a marvelous design had flashed before her, and disintegrated, before she could grasp the figures it conveyed.

# The Lake, the Well,
## the Crickets Singing in the Grass

❋═❋

THOMAS WAS ranging far and skimming back and forth in time. He was out fishing on the lake when Pixie got the jump on him. She surprised him by swimming up to his boat. He helped her flop over the side into the bottom. She lay there, gasping. No, he was gasping. He was in a hospital, and he was surprised about still being in the boat. She'd never said why she swam out to him, but he saw the boys back on shore and even from a distance they looked ripping mad. Not long after, Bucky was hit by a twisted mouth. People said that only the most powerful medicine people could fling that twisted mouth. What happened to Bucky scared the other boys, who let out the truth of what happened in the car. So Thomas knew. If that young fool's face had not sagged, Thomas would have taken him out and thrashed him like a field.

Thomas drifted in the white bed for a while, then found himself back in the boat. Yet again. Pixie wasn't with him this time. Over to the west, the sky was rolling up a storm. So far no lightning. He started up the little 75 putt putt and sped toward the place he'd parked his car. Too late—in a rush the storm was on him, whirling him from the boat and tossing him high. When he splashed down, shock drove the air from his lungs. Infinitely heavy, he sank. This time, like in the train station. He went down all the way to the bottom, but it wasn't the bottom of the lake.

No, he was back in the bottom of the well.

The WPA had given out money for well-digging equipment on the reservation, and he and Biboon had set to work using a windlass and a pile of stones that they had been picking from their fields for years. They started in dry September, so they would be sure to dig the well deep enough to always have water. The government had also issued an iron well ring. They dug out the interior of the ring and mortared the stones together on top. As the ring sank deeper, they kept setting stones into the sides of the earth. Thomas took turns with Biboon, until together they had dug below the surface. Whoever was digging filled the bucket tied onto the windlass with dirt, and the top man cranked it up to the surface. The top man, who was now almost always Biboon, sent rocks down in the bucket to shore up the sides.

Thomas was down past the heavy black topsoil and well into the clay. It was fine, thick stuff, extraordinarily dense. Biboon kept trying to get Julia to bring a wheelbarrow and make pots out of it. She wasn't interested. By day four Thomas was sick of clay. He hated clay. Overnight it would sour in the well hole and when he dug, the taste coated his tongue. His nose was lined with fine clay slime. His lungs ached and his chest tightened. He began to wonder if some sort of gas was filling up the hole, which smelled increasingly of sulphur. However, here in the hospital bed, at night especially, he began to find a certain comfort in the well. The smell was intense, but maybe it was rubbing alcohol. And the earth was exuding warmth. It was almost cozy. He was not afraid, which surprised him, because he had been afraid while digging.

In fact, to his shame, sometimes he panicked. Sometimes he could feel his throat closing, in fear. He'd had to stop himself from imagining the earth could give way beneath him and swallow him up.

Sometimes he'd almost wanted to die rather than go down that hole again.

Now, it didn't matter. Nothing could harm him. In the boat, in the well, in the bed, he was safe because there was nothing he could do now and he didn't have to go back to Washington. In spite of the dreadful possibility of losing his life or mind, this was a vacation. Or would have been if Rose was with him. If only they were lying on the fold-down backseats that made into a bed, together in the Nash, on their second honeymoon, and the crickets singing in the grass.

# The Ceiling

THE TWO women lay in bed talking up into the fuzzy gray air. After visiting Thomas, and finding him much better, they'd bought oatmeal. Each had eaten a bowl with butter, sugar, and cinnamon. Their stomachs were warm and full. The cold had diminished. How contented they were. Millie was talking about the classes she would take next semester. Patrice was listening to the titles of the classes.

"What do I have to do to become a lawyer?" asked Patrice.

Millie told her.

LULLS FELL between their words as they drifted. Sometimes it seemed like they were talking in their sleep. Finally, Patrice was sure of it, Millie was out, breathing slow and deep. She could drop off now too. As she was floating away, the darkness of sleep resolved into the face of Wood Mountain. Patrice came to consciousness with a jolt. After that half-awake moment in Washington, she'd managed not to think about him, and yet they had made love, and looked into each other's eyes. They'd played at being children and washed each other's faces with snow. She loved him. Didn't she? How was she supposed to know?

If Betty Pye had been beside her, she could have asked. But not Millie. She couldn't ask Millie. So Patrice continued to ponder her feelings. She wasn't, as she'd heard in a movie, *swept away*. But she didn't want to live her life by movie examples. She wanted to know for certain who she was supposed to marry. Shouldn't it be obvious? Perhaps, she thought, when Vera came home it would be obvious. She couldn't leave until that happened. She was depending on it to happen. Yes, Vera would resolve everything.

She drifted off again, then startled awake again. Her eyes flew open and she looked into the gray. Patrice had never allowed herself to imagine a situation where Vera did not return. She knew, as Zhaanat knew, that Vera was alive and that she would make it back to them. Somewhere below, a car passed, and the reflections of its headlights revolved across the ceiling, which Patrice saw now was not smooth and pale like the walls of Millie's room, but cracked, peeling, and ominous with gloom. Oh, why did it have to look like that? It made her think she might be wrong. That Vera might not come home. Grief crept up.

Damn ceiling, thought Patrice, all I need is for a big ugly spider to walk across you. I need to look at something twinkling with lights.

She slipped out of bed and walked over to the window, half covered with surging ferns of frost. Another car turned a corner and the patterns leapt out with green and golden fire. Alive, they seemed to say to her, alive!

# Greater Joy

✣ ══ ✣

"YOU FORGOT to lock your heart," said Elnath.

"No, I didn't forget," said Vernon.

"Then what happened?"

"Her eyes picked the lock."

They were standing side by side in the light, holding their elbows. There was no way they could go out into this cold, and so they had each feigned illness and after breakfast climbed the stairs back to their room. Now they stared, blinking, out the one small rectangle of window, across miles of fresh snow. The white glare jolted them even in the dim room.

"She put her temptations before you," said Elnath.

"It wasn't that, no. I can't say she meant to."

"But she did," said Elnath.

Vernon did not speak.

"What I want to know is whether you are quitting the sin."

"Quit. Oh, I'm quit."

"All right then."

"So we call and they come get us?" said Vernon, after a few moments, stinging with shame, struggling with hope. "We are quits, you and me, also?"

"I think we should tough this out," said Elnath.

His voice was hateful, thought Vernon.

"It's too damn cold. I don't see where it's wrote that we should have to die."

"I don't see where it isn't."

Vernon opened and shut his mouth. They stood at attention, their shoulders stiff, arms locked across their chests. What they wanted to do was haul off and fight.

LATER, THEY hitched a ride into town with Milda. She went to the grocery store. They found a way to visit LaBatte. Vernon recalled the reasons they were sent. How the Indians were teachable, meek, open in their hearts, how they were so gentle. Willing to please, like submissive children. But not LaBatte. He'd already backslid, wasn't willing to get baptized, or even let them in the door, and as he was their only possibility and the cold was flaying them alive, they decided to start walking back to Milda's car. Without warning Elnath changed direction. He said that he was going to the next town. Vernon knew it was death to follow him, but had no choice about it. The wind went through his overcoat like it was paper. His hands went numb. His face burned. He stumbled because his feet were blocks of wood. When Louis Pipestone stopped on the road and picked them up, when he told them he could drop them in Grand Forks, the tears of cold in their eyes turned to heat. There was a church member in Grand Forks who would take them in. They could ask Milda to send their few possessions. As they thawed out, blood returning in surges, they prayed to bear the intolerable fire of life, and knew they had been called to a greater joy.

# The Owls

✳══╪══✳

AS BARNES dampened his pillow, Louis Pipestone was driving Juggie's car down to the Cities in order to pick up the stragglers. That's what he called them because he couldn't rid himself of the guilt. Mile after mile, he fought it. Through Grand Forks, through Fargo, through Fergus Falls, and onward. He came through Royalton, St. Cloud, and still it was there. Louis knew that if he'd been with the crew in Washington, things would have been different. Thomas would not have collapsed like that. On the stopover in the Cities, Louis would have gone out to fetch the cigars. He was sure that somehow he would have saved Thomas. Only when he reached the city, and with great difficulty found the hospital, only when he'd been allowed into Thomas's presence during visiting hours, did Louis feel some relief.

Thomas was still in the hospital bed. But he was sitting up and when he saw Louis, his face came to life with that big Thomas grin, the glint of tooth gold.

"Your horses must have got out again!"

"I'm down here to corral you," said Louis.

"Patrice said you're bringing me back in high style."

"Rolling the red carpet all the way to Juggie's automobile. Then you ride up front, in the seat of honor."

"You could have brought my car."

"Then Wade couldn't hot-rod it all around the back roads, like he's been doing."

"More like Sharlo, she's the driver."

"Okay then, Sharlo. Picking up her girlfriends along with the big bag of flour I saw her wrestling into the trunk the other day."

"That's my girl."

Millie and Patrice came into the room with the nurse who was filling out the discharge papers. Louis went back down to guard the car.

ON THE way home, as they were driving through snowed-over fields, incandescent in full sun, Thomas tried to tell Louis about what had happened in the train station when he and Moses went to buy cigars.

"I didn't feel it when I hit the floor, but then I looked up and saw the owls. There was a flock of them, snowy owls, flying over me in a wave. I know LaBatte would say they wanted to kill me, but I know they had come to keep me safe."

"That's a pretty good story," said Louis. "We should call you Owl Man now."

"I wouldn't mind it," said Thomas. "But I'm just a lowly muskrat."

"Speaking of LaBatte and owls, he was taking your night shifts?"

"He still is, far as I know."

"What I heard is he quit because an owl kept trying to get in."

"That's my owl. He must live around there, keeps attacking himself in the window. Must think this other window owl is poaching in his territory."

"Well, he sent LaBatte flying. Says he wouldn't go back for anything."

"Maybe it was Roderick, too."

"Old Roderick? From school?"

"He comes around. Not in a bad way. But he puts the fear of god in LaBatte."

"So that's why he's all holy. Juggie says LaBatte's at Mass every single day now, always taking communion. He's trying to get a job in maintenance, working on the church road and shoveling snow up there."

"Gee, I'll miss LaBatte coming around with his dire predictions."

"Don't worry," said Louis, "you'll see him around, and he'll always have a dire prediction for you."

"I miss my little owl," said Thomas. "The one I had as a pet. He nested in the barn bones of the roof."

Louis glanced sharply over at him.

"The barn poles," said Thomas. For a while he was silent. "Rafters," he said in a low voice.

## The Bear Skull in the Tree
## Was Painted Red and Faced East

WOOD MOUNTAIN walked past the bear skull and knew it was Zhaanat's way of saying thank you. Patrice wasn't home yet, and he wanted to visit Archille. As he neared the house, he heard them crying inside, or was it laughing, or was it both? He called out and then entered. Vera and Zhaanat were watching Archille stand, fall, pull himself up, sway, and balance for a moment again on the bearskin rug. Every time he tried to take a step, he plopped down and a laugh gurgled out. When he saw Wood Mountain, he threw out his arms and gave a baby roar of love. Vera, blurred and muted, stared at Wood Mountain when she saw the baby's reaction.

"Archille," said Wood Mountain, scooping him up, eyes only for him. "Archille, my boy."

Zhaanat said to Vera, "See, what I told you."

Vera got up and put water on the stove to boil.

"His name is Thomas," she said in Wood Mountain's direction.

Wood Mountain did not acknowledge her, kept playing his little games with the baby. Vera brought tea over to Wood Mountain and scooped up the baby to play with her on the bed in the corner. The baby fought his way past her arms to try to get back to Wood Mountain. As the baby barreled across the rug, Vera's mouth twitched. The baby's intense determination was comical, but it was not that simple.

"I told you," said Zhaanat again.

"I see now," said Vera. "He loves the man more than he loves me."

"Or me," said Zhaanat. She didn't mind.

"It will change," said Wood Mountain, holding him. "Pretty soon he won't remember you were gone at all."

In his heart, he did not believe what he was saying.

He brought out a piece of bacon for Archille to exercise his first teeth on. The baby gnawed the fat with the relish of a wolf pup. Again, Vera laughed. It was not a normal laugh. There was a sob in the laugh, and it trailed into a dark rasp. Wood Mountain looked over at her and noticed that a newly whitening scar divided one eyebrow. Another ran across her chin. Her hair was chopped short, like a woman in fresh mourning. Her fingers had trembled when she handed him the cup. When he accepted the cup, he felt a spark of lightning. In spite of this damage, he found her compelling. They used to say "those Paranteau beauties," meaning Vera and Pixie.

"You named him Thomas, for your uncle," he said.

She nodded and warmed her palms at the stove.

"You named him Archille, for your father," she answered after a while.

WOOD MOUNTAIN came to visit day after day. Once Patrice returned and went back to her job, he usually came during the times she was at work. Each time he visited, he noticed something about Vera. One earlobe was ragged, as though it had been bitten. One finger was crooked, as though it had been broken. One eye sometimes looked sideways, as though it had been knocked that way. One tooth was missing, but you couldn't see it unless she laughed with her whole body. And she did laugh. That finally happened. The same tooth was missing from Wood Mountain's jaw. All of the places that she was hurt, he was also hurt. As the days passed her features healed and she went outside more and more, tramped along the traplines, gathered reeds for mats, made baskets to sell like her mother did, sewed small garments for Thomas Archille. Or was it the other way around? Sometimes even Vera called him Archille now.

PATRICE CAME home one day, saw them together, and recognized it. She saw Wood Mountain bend over her sister, who was holding Archille. The baby sneezed and they marveled together. It was just a sneeze. She couldn't understand it, but as they doted over Archille together, her sensations of confusion and desire and possible love sank away. Her feelings became muddy and heavy. At last, she didn't recognize the feelings at all. One day she happened to come home while Wood Mountain was leaving the house. He came down the road just as Doris was dropping her off. He didn't have a horse so he was always walking now. He stopped when he saw her coming toward him.

"Patrice," he said, not meeting her eyes. "I gotta talk to you."

"I know all about it," she said.

He lifted his gaze to hers and she did not look away.

"I'm in love with both of you." He tried that out.

"No you're not," she said. But she wasn't angry. Or if she was, it was just an instinct that she had no time for. The feelings were like icy muck. She had to drop them.

"You don't sound mad." He was relieved. He rubbed his eyebrow. "I just don't want you to think . . ."

"It was good," she said. "It was good out there." She pursed her lips and glanced toward the tangle of trees where they had made love. An arrow thin as a reed shot through her. "But when I was walking back to the house it didn't seem right."

"It didn't?" His voice was eager.

"When I looked at the house, I just knew she'd be back. I thought of how you love Archille. Maybe I knew that when you saw Vera, her ways would be your ways with the baby."

"Yes. Her ways are my ways."

He seemed satisfied and she felt lighter, like maybe she had dropped the heavy strangeness and could go on. They walked back into the house together and Vera looked up at them when they entered. She was finishing off a basket. Wood Mountain made the split ash frames and Vera wove red whips of fresh-cut willow in and out. The scent of the willow was sharp and secret. To move past her own feelings was the only way, thought Patrice. She would embrace anyone and anything that could help put together Vera's demolished heart.

# The Duplicator Spirits

*※═┃═※*

MILLIE WORKED late, preparing a master of the chairman's report, which would be distributed to the tribe. She was going against her principles by typing for a man. But in this instance, she'd interviewed Thomas and added her own details about the trip to Washington, so she felt it was reportorial. It was a cold spring night and in an hour Juggie would come and fetch her. When the master was finished, she immediately fixed the first page onto the drum of the spirit duplicator and began turning the crank.

THIS TIME, along with each duplicate, a spirit came off the press. In 1892, these people had signed the first Turtle Mountain census. Mikwan, Kasinicut, Wazhashk, Awanikwe, Kakigido-asin, Kananatowakachin, Anakwadok, Omakakiins, Mashki-igokwe, Swampy Woman, Kissna, Cold, Ice, Dressed in Stone, Foggy Day Woman, Speaking Stone, Mirage, Cloud, Little Frog, Yellow Day, Thunder. For some reason, tonight they traveled down the star road to wander around their old homeland, before flooding back into the other existence. They kept flying off the duplicator. Coming Voice, Stops the Day, Cross Lightning, Skinner, Hole in the Sky, Between the Sky, Lying Down Grass, Center of the Sky, Rabbit, Prairie Chicken, Day Light, and Master of the White Man. They were the original people who mingled with the Michifs who came down from Canada and over from Pembina, French-Cree-Chippewas who swirled across the earth, first hunting buffalo. All were cast together onto allotments, to break apart the earth, to learn the value of a dollar, and then how to make one dollar into many dollars and cultivate the dollars into a way of life.

MILLIE DIDN'T know about it because to tell the truth she was a little tipsy on the smell of duplicating fluid. She thought there might be something strange going on, because she kept hearing voices as she turned the crank. Surprised whees and awkward thumps, as if children were jumping on the floor. And the room filled with whispers. Perhaps the wind was up outside. When Juggie appeared, Millie quickly shut down the duplicator and collected the pages without collating them. Outside, the fresh cold air made her head pound so badly she squeezed her temples with her bare icy hands. Once she was in the warm car, her headache went away. But over the growl of the motor she thought she heard singing and drumming. It was even louder at the Pipestone ranch as they walked toward the house.

"Do you hear it too?" she asked Juggie.

They stopped and drew their coats tight around them. Juggie pointed at the sky. Millie looked up into the moving atmosphere. The lights were green and pink, bleeding radiance and dancing flames. She could hear a faint crackling, though no more singing and drumming.

"They're looking after us," said Juggie. "Those dancing spirits. I'm frozen. Going in."

Millie stayed outside watching until cold pinched her feet and she got a crick in her neck. She'd had that funny feeling about the duplicator, but thought that if the northern lights had anything to do with it they would have chosen an electrostatic copier, as the lights were themselves electrical impulses born of powerful conflicting charges between the sun and the magnetic poles of the earth. What Juggie said, "They're looking after us," echoed what Zhaanat had said about these lights being the spirits of the dead, joyous, free, benevolent. Even cold to the bone, Millie watched them for a while longer, deciding one explanation did not rule out the other, that charged electrons could be spirits, that nothing ruled out anything else, that mathematics was a rigorous form of madness, that she would go out on a regular date with Barnes, that she had to because he'd asked her with an equation, and who could say no to that?

# À Ta Santé

✦━┼━✦

PATRICE STILL had perfect reading-distance vision, and her speed and precision with setting the jewels for drilling had returned. She could feel herself working with the utmost efficiency, the way she did when she was in a rage. But she wasn't angry. She was out to make money. Her shoulders began to ache and her fingers were going stiff by the time lunch rolled around. She flexed and rubbed her hands. She still had her dented syrup pail.

Betty Pye strolled into the lunchroom.

"Now you've been to Washington, D.C., are you too good to talk to me?"

"Yes," said Patrice. "Have a chair."

Betty plumped down next to her and pulled a boiled egg out of her pocket. She shelled it in a greedy motion and ate it in two bites. Out came a boogid. Across from her, Valentine rolled her eyes. Out came another fart from Betty, just for emphasis.

"Excuse me please," she said in a fake prissy voice. "Eggs always make me flatulate."

She patted the shining lumps of hair perched over her ears. Smoothed the rickrack bodice of her flowery green dress.

"You fart instantly," said Valentine, "after eating eggs. I don't believe it."

Betty snapped her fingers. "Like that."

Patrice looked into her lunch pail like it would tell her fortune. She sighed. A carrot and a boiled potato. Maybe a little salt would help. She asked Betty, who handed some over in a twist of paper as she bolted down another egg.

"How come you eat them if they make you boogid so bad?" asked Curly Jay.

"What's a little boogid?" said Betty. "I like eggs. Did you sign the petition?"

"I signed it."

"I think Patrice should present it."

"Valentine would be better," said Patrice. "Or Doris Lauder."

"Doris won't do it," said Valentine. "She doesn't want . . . you know what she doesn't want."

"Grasshopper juice," said Betty.

Patrice choked. How many times had grasshoppers squirted their brown juice into her hands? The thought of Vold. She put the lid back on her lunch pail.

"I'll do it," said Valentine. "I want my coffee break. By the time I get off work I can hardly move my hands."

"It was supposed to be temporary and we were supposed to get it back," said Betty. She farted again and raised her finger. "You may quote that."

AFTER WORK, as she rode in the backseat through the drizzly spring rain, Patrice thought about the money. More was called for. She was working extra hard because she planned on asking for a raise. The idea that Vera would take her job now seemed absurd—Vera was not in any shape to work in the outside world, and she wouldn't leave her baby. Patrice was now supporting four at home instead of two. But, a surprise. Wood Mountain had taken a job driving school buses. It was a good job, a federal job. And along with the understanding that he and Patrice had reached, the job cleared the way for him to marry Vera. Not only that, but they planned to work on the cabin behind the house. They were constantly talking about how they would fix it up during the summer. Once they moved into the cabin, Patrice would only be responsible for Pokey and her mother—but there again something unexpected had developed. Millie had returned to the university and had written that she'd changed her program. She had decided to become an anthropologist, and wanted to study with Zhaanat. Millie was applying for money to pay her informant.

"It isn't a lot of money," she said in her letter, "but between that and what Patrice saves maybe she can go back to school."

Doris and Valentine let Patrice off and the big car pulled away down the road. Patrice started down the path, the ground spongy. The snow was sagging into the earth. The air was wet and rich. Sap was coming up in the trees and Zhaanat would be out tapping the birches. During the winter she'd carved spiles to hammer into the veins of the trees and saved tin cans to collect the sap. The cold sap was a spring tonic. When you drank it, you shared the genius of the woods. As Patrice drew near the house, she saw that her mother was sitting on a stump near the fire, tending the kettle of sap. Patrice went inside and changed her clothes. When she came out her mother held out a jar she'd dipped from the bucket. Patrice sat beside her on another friendly stump. Zhaanat poked a stick to adjust the steadily burning logs, then lifted her jar.

"Millie's going to make you famous," said Patrice, lifting up her jar of sap. "Someday there will be a book."

"I don't care about that," said Zhaanat, "but we can use the zhooniyaa."

Grinning, she lifted her jar, like the Michifs lifted wine, "À ta santé."

Patrice tapped her jar to her mother's. "À ta santé."

Together they drank the icy birch water, which entered them the way life entered the trees, causing buds to swell along the branches. Patrice leaned to one side and put her ear to the trunk of a birch tree. She could hear the humming rush of the tree drinking from the earth. She closed her eyes, went through the bark like water, and was sucked up off the bud tips into a cloud. She looked down at herself and her mother, sitting by a small fire in the spring woods. Zhaanat tipped her head back and smiled. She gestured at her daughter to come back, the way she had when as a child Patrice strayed.

"Ambe bi-izhaan omaa akiing miinawa," she said, and Patrice returned.

# Roderick

AGAIN, HE missed the train. But there were so many Indian ghosts in Washington that he decided to stay. For a while, Roderick eddied around the station. When he'd moped enough, he went back to see the sights, which, after all, he'd missed out on, being so attentive to the living. He saw the monuments, he saw the statues, he saw the buildings. In one of the buildings there were so many voices that he could hear them laughing and bickering from the outside. He flowed in, poked around, blustered into the storage areas. Oh my! Drawers and cabinets of his own kind of people! Indian ghosts stuck to their bones or scalp locks or pieces of skin. Some of the holy pipes were singing monotonously. Other ghosts were uproariously gambling with their own bones. There were ghostly ghost-dance shirts, buzzing war shields, gurgling baby makizinan, and sacred scrolls choked with spirits. Indians brought from the top or bottom of the world as living exhibits, then immediately turned to ghosts. For centuries, Indians had gone to Washington for the same reasons as the little party from the Turtle Mountains. They had gone in order to protect their families and their land. It was a hazard of travel for Indians to be lynched from streetlamps as a drunken joke. Ghosts with rope necklaces. It turned out the city was packed with ghosts, lively with ghosts. Roderick had never had so much company. And they were glad for somebody new. Glad he stayed behind. They argued with him. Why go back there? Who's waiting for you?

# *Thomas*

HE REMOVED his thermos from his armpit and set it on the steel desk alongside his scuffed but no longer bulging briefcase. His light work jacket and battered old fedora went on the chair, his lunch box on the cool windowsill. He punched his time card. Midnight. He picked up the key ring, a company flashlight, and walked the perimeter of the main floor.

He checked the drilling room and tested every lock, flipped the lights on and off. He stepped through the reinforced doors of the acid washing room, shone his flashlight on the dials and hoses. He checked the offices, the bathrooms, and ended up back at his desk. A new lamp had been issued to him. Now a stronger power of light charged the surface of the desk. He sat down. He had missed a number of birthdays, which he kept track of in a tiny yellow spiral-bound notebook. He'd picked out a stack of flower embossed cards at Rexall for each grandchild, son and daughter, friend and relative.

At the bottom of each card, he signed himself "the muskrat" and drew a small supple little fellow writhing through the water, or curved over, cleaning its paws, or just sunning himself on a log. Thomas had taken to doodling now and then. It had started when he'd encountered some trouble finding his words. He'd been cleared, good to go, after the stroke he'd suffered at the train station. But sometimes his brain skipped. Sometimes his brain hid a tantalizing word from him in its folds. He had to relax his mind and sneak up on the word. The doodles were a way to win the hide-and-seek game he had now begun to play with his memory. Pictures occasionally dislodged a word. Also, sometimes now, a word failed to come to him when he was speaking, and in those times he substituted a descriptive phrase for the word, comically, and got a laugh. Just the other day he'd forgotten the word for car trunk, and said, "automobile cave with a hinge," which was taken for wit. As with the time he'd asked Rose to wear her "namesake dress" because he couldn't find the word for the color red in his mind. Rouge, scarlet, carmine. Rose. So many words came later. And from Sharlo he'd requested "a book of twisting ways," when he'd meant a mystery. She liked his description. Nobody seemed to have caught on to the trouble he was having, and he certainly wasn't about to make it known. But he knew, and he knew when he was beginning to think first in Chippewa, the language of his childhood. Was he going back? Sometimes, as when he sat in the circle of light drawing little muskrats, he felt the raw dread of further robbery. His mind was everything to him, but he hadn't the slightest notion how to save it. He just kept diving down, grabbing for the word, coming back up. The battle with termination and with Arthur V. Watkins had been, he feared, a battle that would cost him everything.

LATER, DOZING in the lamplight, he saw muskrats everywhere. Their small supple forms slipped busily along the floor at dusk, continually perfecting their burrows. He saw them pulling soft weeds and holding juicy roots in their tiny paws to eat. "What is my name?" he asked one of the little creatures. "Wazhashk gidizhinikaaz," it said.

His name. Would there be a time he wouldn't know himself?

Was this bit of paper given to him so that in an extremity he could retrieve his name at least? He put the scrap of paper into his mouth. All of a sudden he and his father were sitting outside the old man's cabin. Thomas stared at the bright popple leaves, trembling and flashing as they swirled thickly off the branches. Frantic yellows and golden red and orange leaves filled his eyes. But it's spring, he thought. I shouldn't be here. Something's happening to me again. He looked around and saw that the wild prairies were littered with bones thick and white as far as he could see.

The bones tipped and staggered, assembling into forms, and took on shaggy flesh. The grass rippled and billowed like a green robe and the animals crossed vast and vaster numbers. The earth trembled in a serpentine rush, blew away, and vanished into the sky.

Thomas remembered the jelly bun in his lunch box. Rose had made his coffee hot and strong. He shook his head, wiped his eyes, settled back into his task, underlining words in the birthday wishes and adding his own greetings, forming his letters with precision, until it was time again to punch his card and make the last round of the night.

THE TURTLE MOUNTAIN BAND of Chippewa was not terminated.

MY GRANDFATHER recovered from his initial stroke and went on to work on improving the reservation school system, writing a Turtle Mountain Constitution, and writing and publishing the first history of the Turtle Mountains. He was tribal chairman until 1959. He was promoted to supervisor of maintenance and worked at the jewel bearing plant until his mandatory retirement in 1970.

IN 1955 the women of the Turtle Mountain jewel bearing plant attempted to unionize. According to my grandfather, this raised a ruckus all the way to New York. "Accusations, allegations, fabrications of the imagination, rumors, prophecies, threats, and counterthreats flew thick and fast. Bribe in the form of dinners were offered from both sides—and accepted." In the end, unionization was voted down. However, pay increases were immediately authorized. A cafeteria was completed. And the workers regained their coffee break.

## My Grandfather's Letters

Aunishenaubay, Patrick Gourneau, was the chairman of the Turtle Mountain Band of Chippewa Advisory Committee during the mid-1950s, supposedly the golden age for America, but in reality a time when Jim Crow reigned and American Indians were at the nadir of power—our traditional religions outlawed, our land base continually and illegally seized (even as now) by resource extraction companies, our languages weakened by government boarding schools. Our leaders were also answerable to assimilationist government officials: as an example, just look at the "advisory committee" in my grandfather's designation. He and his fellow tribal members had almost no authority. Their purpose was to advise the BIA, but they seized any opportunity to represent their people. The 1950s were a time when the scraps of land and the rights guaranteed by treaty were easy pickings. With the postwar housing boom, the fabulous Klamath and Menominee forests were especially coveted. It is no coincidence that those tribes were among the first five slated for termination.

My grandfather wrote a series of extraordinary letters during 1953 and 1954. They were addressed to my parents. My mother gave them to me to look after because I was born in 1954. Patrick Gourneau had attended government boarding schools at Fort Totten, Haskell, and Wahpeton. The letters are written in graceful "boarding-school handwriting" familiar to those who were schooled in the Palmer Method, and they are packed with remarkable, funny, stereotype-breaking episodes of reservation life. Altogether, they compose a portrait of a deeply humane intelligence as well as a profoundly religious patriot and family man.

A first speaker of Ojibwemowin, my grandfather was the son of Keeshkemunishiw, the Kingfisher, and the grandson of Joseph Gourneau, Kasigiwit, head warrior of the Pembina Band of Ojibwe. They had lived by hunting buffalo across the plains into Montana. My grandfather was of the first generation born on the reservation. His family made the desperate, difficult transition to farming. Eventually they were successful. Patrick wrote about his magnificent truck garden, delighted in details like the moss roses he grew for beauty, and told stories about how he planted oats but somehow harvested flax. He recounted funny things his children said and avowed love for his wife, Mary Cecelia LeFavor. He confided in my parents and spoke of new anxieties that had complicated his job as chairman of the advisory committee. At the time he wrote, the job paid thirty dollars per month, but the tribe was dead broke so he didn't collect those wages. He'd received word of the Termination Bill and immediately understood that this was, as it has been called, a new front in the Indian Wars.

"Most of the pending legislation, if passed, would result in the end of our last holdings on this continent and destroy our dignity and distinction as the first inhabitants of this rich land," said Joe Garry, then president of the National Congress of American Indians.

"This new bill is about the worst thing for Indians to come down the pike," said my grandfather.

Although I had many times read his letters for solace or inspiration, eventually I thought to read his letters in conjunction with a stack of the termination-era research I'd put aside. Once I did, setting his carefully dated letters against the time line of the bill, which gave tribes only a few months to mount a response to Congress, I realized that my grandfather—along with others in the tribe, astute friends like Martin Old Dog Cross, and non-Indian allies—had accomplished something that altered the trajectory of termination and challenged the juggernaut of the federal push to sever legal, sacred, and immutable promises made in nation-to-nation treaties. Of the initial tribes slated for termination, the Turtle Mountain delegation was the first to mount a fierce defense and prevail. Now I could see the desperation and exhaustion behind my grandfather's jokes. He was a whirlwind, writing all night long and attending meetings all day long. Sometimes he slept only twelve hours per week. I had as well the knowledge of what his pursuit of a seemingly impossible task, reversing termination, cost him, our family, and Indian Country.

In all, 113 tribal nations suffered the disaster of termination; 1.4 million acres of tribal land was lost. Wealth flowed to private corporations, while many people in terminated tribes died early, in poverty. Not one tribe profited. By the end, 78 tribal nations, including the Menominee, led by Ada Deer, regained federal recognition; 10 gained state but not federal recognition; 31 tribes are landless; 24 are considered extinct. Ada Deer's recent memoir, *Making a Difference: My Fight for Native Rights and Social Justice*, is great reading on this subject.

Much of this book was written in a state of heavy emotion as I remembered the grief my grandmother and my mother's siblings endured as the continued political fights took their toll and my grandfather's health began to fail. Eventually, he suffered a long decline. Yet Patrick Gourneau never stopped being funny, optimistic, and kind. I hope this book reflects his gracious spirit. Also, I like to think that the efforts of the Turtle Mountain people helped other tribal nations negotiate the long messy nightmare of termination. In 1970, Richard Nixon addressed Congress and called for an end to this policy. Five years later, a new era of self-determination for Native people began.

There are many people to thank. First of all, Patrick and Mary Gourneau and the remarkable family they raised, including my mother, Rita Gourneau Erdrich, an artist who meticulously saved my grandfather's letters and the mimeographed chairman's reports that included his articles and jokes. Thank you to my dear aunt and friend Dolores Gourneau Manson, my aunt Madonna Owen, and my uncle Dwight Gourneau, who has served Native people all of his life, notably as the chairman of the boards of the American Indian Science and Engineering Society (AISES) and the Smithsonian's National Museum of the American Indian (NMAI). Thank you to my uncle Howard Gourneau, our family's Pipe Keeper, and to Roberta Morin. My sister Liselotte Erdrich, writer, poet, and our family historian, gave me invaluable advice and support. I'd like to thank Judy Azure for dancing for us all. Our tribal historian, Professor Les LaFountain, gave this manuscript an invaluable early read that was full of brilliant suggestions. Denise Lajimodiere also made important changes. I am very grateful for the response and reminiscences of Zelma Peltier, whose mother worked at the jewel bearing plant. Gail Caldwell bucked me up when I had doubts. Brenda Child, Northrop Professor at the University of Minnesota, listened at length to the evolution of this book, and gave me fireside pep talks, generous advice, and introduced me to the joys of research at the National Archives. My mother talked at length about her life on the reservation in the 1950s. It was a joy to share her memories.

The Turtle Mountain delegation really was partially funded by a benefit boxing match. The work of Chippewa scholar Millie Cloud was based on a combination of people, including Marie Louise Bottineau Baldwin and Sister Inez Hilger. Dr. David P. Delorme authored the actual economic study that surprised and impressed the congressional committee. The meeting with the BIA in Fargo relies on the transcript of the actual meeting, as does the testimony in Congress. Leo Jeanotte, Edward Jollie, Eli Marion, and Theresa "Resa" Monette Davis Revard were some of the members of the original advisory committees. It is moving to me that Martin Cross came to lend his expertise, considering the devastation his tribe was suffering at that time with the inundation and destruction of their beloved homelands by the Army Corps of Engineers. For his support of the Turtle Mountain people, Cross was threatened several times with termination during testimony. He was a strong and principled advocate. On the other hand, Senator Arthur V. Watkins was indeed a pompous racist. But to give Watkins his due, he also was instrumental in bringing down Senator Joe McCarthy and ending an ugly era in national politics.

*Garden of Truth: The Prostitution and Trafficking of Native Women in Minnesota*, authored by Melissa Farley, Nicole Matthews, Sarah Deer, Guadalupe Lopez, Christine Stark, and Eileen Hudon, was the source for Vera's story. Divena, a mermaid working in a large fish tank at the Persian Palms in Minneapolis during the 1970s, was the inspiration for Pixie's waterjack.

Disturbingly, the memory of termination has faded even among American Indian people, and it was my sister the poet and artist Heid Erdrich who encouraged me to write this book to keep the knowledge alive. (Indeed, the Trump administration and Assistant Secretary of the Interior Tara Sweeney have recently brought back the termination era by seeking to terminate the Wampanoag, the tribe who first welcomed Pilgrims to these shores and invented Thanksgiving.) My sister Angela Erdrich, M.D., helped greatly by passing on to me the research materials on termination that she collected long ago through Baker Library at Dartmouth. I'd like to express my deep appreciation to Joyce Burner, a librarian at the National Archives at Kansas City, who told me she loved a treasure hunt and proceeded to find my grandfather's boarding-school files, letters in which he argued his way *into* boarding school, as well as the actual ballots cast during one of his elections. I would also like to thank National Archives librarian Elizabeth Burnes for her devoted work. As always, I am most grateful to Terry Karten, an editor who offers inspiration as well as critical reports, and Trent Duffy, a copy editor of unequaled skills. Thank you also to Jin Auh and Andrew Wylie for steady work on behalf of all my books. My daughter Pallas provided technical support and is our family's guardian angel. Kiizh lights our way. Netaa-niimid Amookwe, Persia, Ojibwe immersion teacher at Waadookodaading School in Lac Courte Oreilles, Wisconsin, is my consultant in Ojibwemowin, but all mistakes are mine. This book included a difficult editing transition handled with patience by Amber Oliver, John Jusino, and Lydia Weaver. Thank you! As always, thanks to Milan Bozic for cover design, Fritz Metsch for interior design, and Aza Abe for her creation of this book's cover art, which is based on the spectrum of the northern lights.

Lastly, if you should ever doubt that a series of dry words in a government document can shatter spirits and demolish lives, let this book erase that doubt. Conversely, if you should be of the conviction that we are powerless to change those dry words, let this book give you heart.

## ABOUT THE AUTHOR

LOUISE ERDRICH is the author of sixteen novels, volumes of poetry, children's books, and a memoir of early motherhood. Her fiction has won the National Book Award, the National Book Critics Circle Award (twice), and has been a finalist for the Pulitzer Prize. She has received the Library of Congress Prize in American Fiction, the prestigious PEN/Saul Bellow Award for Achievement in American Fiction, and the Dayton Literary Peace Prize. Louise Erdrich, a member of the Turtle Mountain band of Chippewa, lives in Minnesota with her daughters and is the owner of Birchbark Books, a small independent bookstore.